**Altogether, a score or so of the Free,
and three hundred awaiting them
in the valley below.**

It would be brutal, Yulan knew. But they should win. If his people were better than Callotec's – and they were – they would win. If Kerig was strong – and he was – they would win.

He reached down and freed his knife from its sheath on his calf. He held the tip of the blade poised above the ball of his thumb and watched Hamdan. He felt his heartbeat, marking off the moments. Pacing out this last little stretch of quiet. It paced, and paced. Slowly.

Hamdan, without looking round, raised one hand and gave a casual, almost dainty, beckoning flutter of his fingers. Yulan sank the point of his knife into his thumb. Blood swelled out, a delicate red orb. He returned the knife to its place; sucked away the blood. Then kicked his heels into his horse's flank.

Yulan and the riders crested the skyline in the same moment that the archers' first arrows took to the air. The fifteen horsemen plunged down the slope, loosing screams to sharpen the pounding of hoofs. It was like falling, Yulan thought; plummeting like a stooping hawk.

They came so fast, so sudden, that heads were still turning, weapons still being drawn, alarms still being cried, as the fifteen crashed into the side of the long three hundred.

Praise for
WINTERBIRTH

"Putting the epic back in epic fantasy." —scifi.com

"Heroic fantasy splashed with *300*-style gore...Ruckley's real-istic characters and sparing use of magic breathe new life into well-trod epic territory." —*Entertainment Weekly*

"The author's unapologetically stark yet darkly poetic narrative displays a refreshing lack of stereotypical genre conventions, ensuring a fervent audience of epic fantasy fans looking for something innovative in a genre that can be anything but." —*Publishers Weekly* (starred review)

"Ruckley is an imaginative, dramatic storyteller. He's created a world that seems real, with characters who are well-drawn out and far more than one dimensional. It's an engrossing read, one that leaves you looking forward to the next book." —Associated Press

"An epic tale of revenge, betrayal, and greed...an intriguing and imaginative story." —*Dreamwatch*

"*Winterbirth* by Brian Ruckley is an amazing novel and one that I would highly recommend. Ruckley shows his prowess at world-building by creating a breathtaking world where surprises are reg-ular and no one is safe from death." —thefantasyreview.com

"A gripping story that builds to a grim climax. No one who enjoys heroic fantasy should miss this." —*Times* (London)

"Readers who like their fantasy dark, multithreaded and politi-cal will sink their teeth into this one." —*Kirkus Reviews*

ALSO BY BRIAN RUCKLEY

The Godless World
Winterbirth
Bloodheir
Fall of Thanes

The Edinburgh Dead

The Free

THE
FREE

BRIAN RUCKLEY

www.orbitbooks.net

Copyright © 2014 by Brian Ruckley
Excerpt from *Winterbirth* copyright © 2006 by Brian Ruckley
Excerpt from *Promise of Blood* copyright © 2013 by Brian McClellan

Orbit
Hachette Book Group
1290 Avenue of the Americas, New York, NY 10019
HachetteBookGroup.com

Printed in the United States of America

RRD-C

First US Edition: October 2014

10 9 8 7 6 5 4 3 2 1

Orbit is an imprint of Hachette Book Group, Inc. The Orbit name and logo are trademarks of Little, Brown Book Group Limited.

The Hachette Speakers Bureau provides a wide range of authors for speaking events. To find out more, go to www.hachettespeakersbureau.com or call (866) 376-6591.

The publisher is not responsible for websites (or their content) that are not owned by the publisher.

Library of Congress Cataloging-in-Publication Data/Control Number: 2014936882

ISBN: 9780316233491

For
Chieftain, Dave, Dougie and Alan

Partners in pretending, many years ago.
Maybe this is one result of all that pretending.

Contents

PART THREE

Every man is condemned to freedom.

Jean-Paul Sartre

PART ONE

When Drann Was Seven

When Drann was seven, his grandmother Emmin – they called her, out of her earshot, Old Emmin to distinguish her from Drann's similarly named sister – sat him down and told him a story. He liked it when she did that. She had more learning, and better words, than the rest of them. The family had come upon thinner times since Old Emmin's youth, and none of them had matched her schooling. She often whispered to him that he was smarter than the rest of them, which naturally pleased the young him no end.

The story she told him was, more or less, this:

When I was young (Old Emmin said) the Empire, those makers and keepers and lovers of orphans, thought they might have for themselves the Tormond Valley, that's just three hills over from here. It was as green a stretch of land as you could imagine, back then. Full of fat cattle and fat folk. And gold to be panned from some of the hillside streams, too, which made it a place any lord'd like to call his own.

So the Emperor thought he'd have it, since our Regent Queen, Amyllis, was young and this Hommetic Kingdom she ruled even younger. Perhaps a bit soft, a bit weak. That's the way emperors and their like think. They'd have come sooner, if they'd not been busy with a thirty-year war a thousand miles away. A lucky thirty years for us.

Anyhap, the Emperor sent two hundred Orphanidons – all feathers and plate and lances, those fierce boys – and an army, and called the valley a part of his landright. Done, and done, you might think. But not.

The Regent Queen came to the top of Haut Law, to a place where a stream sprang and ran on down into the Tormond. She brought with her a thing that nobody knew then, but which we call the Bereaved now. A Permanence. A terrible thing. It sat in the grass, at the very spot where the brook was born from the ground. The Queen bade a Schoolman whisper into its ear, and he did.

The Bereaved wept. Black tears. Stinking tears. They trickled down its face and fell, one by one, into the water. That done, Amyllis took the Bereaved back to the palace by the lake and had the School hide it away in their keep, where it hides still.

And the Bereaved's tears flowed down from the Haut Law into the valley, and plague took all the lands of the Tormond. The grass withered, the trees broke, the soil sickened. The people died, with their guts bleeding and their skin boiling and the nails rotting out of their fingers. When they tried to flee into our lands, they found the Queen's men barring their way with arrow and sword.

So they ran, instead, alongside the Emperor's proud army back whence it had come, and carried the plague with them into the lands of the Orphans. Thousands upon thousands died. More folk than you've ever seen, or ever will see. They went down like scythed grain. You could smell their dying and their burning even here, for weeks. Made me ill, like I'd not been before.

When the dying was done, the Regent Queen sent word to the Emperor, and said: "I have done this thing that you might know, and remember: set but one finger upon us, or that which is now ours, and we shall have away your entire arm, unto the very gristle of your shoulder joint."

And that's why, little Drann, even now it's those thieving, shit-hearted Hommetic bastards who rule over the Tormond – wasteland that it is – and over us, and not the mad Empire of Orphans.

Drann always enjoyed the stories Old Emmin told him. They were much more interesting than anything his parents let him hear. They fed his dreams and his fancies.

2

Late To The War

Seventeen-year-old Drann blinked. At first his vision was messy, as if water was running over his open eyes. He blinked again and it cleared. He found he was looking at an ant, clambering on the stem of a drooping flower, only a finger or two from his face. It was brandishing its hair-thin front legs in search of something else to climb. To hold on to. A tiny black ant. Drann watched it, and wondered why he was lying here with his face resting on grass, down with the ants and the flowers. It felt a good place to be – comfortable – but also strange.

There were indistinct sounds coming to him, he could not tell whether through the air or from the soft ground beneath his ear. Thumps and bumps; voices that though oddly dulled and muffled carried alarm and anger. He frowned at that, still watching the ant. And the frown set loose heavy pulses of pain in his head, and cleared his hearing.

"Get up, you dung-bred shirker!' someone was shouting at him.

Drann rolled on to his shoulder, struggling to lift his lead-heavy head. He was in a wood. There was a man standing over him, shouting at him. A man flushed with fury, spittle at his lips. Stocky, pepper-haired, pepper-bearded. Older than Drann's father.

"Take up your spear and fight or I'll gut you myself."

The man had a sword in hand, a shield on his arm. He flourished the blade in the direction of Drann's stomach. This was Creel of Mondoon, Drann thought dreamily as he stared at the dancing point of the sword. Why would a lord – a famed, fierce lord at that – be talking to him? That was a thing that had no place in the world.

"Wipe the blood from your brow and get on your feet, farm boy," Creel snarled and swept away, stamping amongst the trees, shouting over his shoulder. "They'll be on us again, and if I'm dying today it'll not be because you're too bone-frit to stand up."

Blood? Drann thought numbly. He touched a fingertip to his forehead. It came away wet. Sticky. Blood, right enough. And the sight of it snapped him back to his senses, to his memories. To the awareness that he, and Creel, and all of them, were indeed well set to die today.

"I'm not afraid," Drann muttered as he staggered up, though the lord of Mondoon was already gone. "I hit my head, that's all. I'm not afraid."

Drann had come late to the war, and thought he would have no great part in it because of that. He found himself upon the winning side, yet he had killed no one, fought in no battles. He could not decide whether he should regret that or not. It felt a cowardly kind of vengeance to have exacted upon the tyrant and his legions of taxers, usurers, confiscators. By the time Drann finally took up his father's spear, and walked away from the village in search of an army to join, others had – it turned out – already bought his revenge for him with their lives, and all but won his freedom from the Hommetic yoke. He had paid no price save bruises and blisters.

Creel of Mondoon was not Drann's lord, but his motley army had been the closest to hand when Drann finally went in search of the war, and amidst the chaos few people cared about such niceties as fealties and duties. Certainly Drann did not. He cared only that someone – anyone – gave him the chance to let loose some part of the angers that had gathered themselves in him. If they were not given some channel to flow down, he felt they might burst him.

So he had marched south, one more insignificant pair of feet amongst the many following Creel, and realised that the war was melting away even as he thought himself walking into it. The armies of the King crumbled, their vigour spent in battles fought before Drann had even left his home. The rebels – Creel's great column and all the others – roamed freely, widely, and found nothing to oppose them save a few stubborn towns with desperate garrisons, a hundred little bands of warriors-turned-bandits. And not once had Drann needed his father's spear for anything other than leaning on, or rapping against his feet to knock mud or manure from his boots.

Until today. Until he had the misfortune to be one of the two dozen levymen sent out from the camp with Creel and his guards to climb a hill a quarter-day's march away. At the time, it had seemed like a piece of good luck, not ill. He had spent the previous half a day and half a night pounding stakes around Creel of Mondoon's camp – to guard against an attack that no one actually believed would come – and had nothing to look forward to but more of the same hand-blistering work. Anything was more appealing than that prospect.

Why that particular hill needed climbing, Drann had no idea, of course, though one of the other levies said that on a clear day you might see Armadell-on-Lake from there. Perhaps Creel just wanted to see the King's city, and know there was no longer any King within its walls. All Drann cared about was that, as far as he knew, no one in his village had ever set eyes upon Armadell-on-Lake. It would give him a small tale to tell upon his return, though not quite of the glorious sort he had imagined himself recounting.

Not to be, it seemed. Not even that small tale, of climbing a hill.

Back on his feet, Drann found his legs soft and loose. He had to press one hand against a tree trunk to avoid a prompt return to the grass and the company of ants. He had been running, he remembered. They all had. Even Creel and those of his household warriors still alive, since their horses had been watering along the stream when the attack began and were all dead or taken or scattered. Running up through the sparse, dry woodlands fringing the valley.

There had been a scream, back down the slope, and Drann had turned his head to look. Seen nothing but the silent trees, and turned back just in time to run into a low branch. A thick, solid branch gnarled with knots and burrs. He remembered the blow, and then the ant climbing the flower right there in front of his blinking eyes.

Drann did not know who the attackers were. One of those thousand little bands of bandits, most likely, except that there was nothing little about this band. They had come flooding down the hillside, churning and splashing their way across the stream, howling like dogs. Some of Creel's stern warriors had stood and fought, cutting down the first ten, dozen, of the raiders as they breasted the near bank of the watercourse, but there were too many.

It had been the lord of Mondoon himself who roared: "Into the woods, into the woods!"

And in the woods, it had been worse. Creel and his trained men – those still alive – stayed close together, climbing up and away from the killing ground by the stream. Drann's fellow levymen scattered. He saw some of them casting aside their weapons to unburden their flight. He saw others, not far behind him, overrun by their ragged pursuers, pulled down and speared or beaten. His heart punched hard and fast against his ribs. He heard the scream, turned to look, and ran into the branch.

Now, he staggered after Creel's disappearing form. With legs enfeebled, and a dizzying throb in his head, the slope seemed steeper than ever. There was, at least, not much undergrowth. Just thin open woodland stretching up towards the higher ground. He had lied to Creel, Drann realised: he was afraid. He must be, for there was nothing in his mind but the anticipation of a hard, sharp blow to his back. He did not know quite what it would feel like, to be speared, but he knew he would fall, and that was what he expected, and imagined, as he laboured up towards the end of the woods. The vision of that fall, with a spear point in his back, crowded everything else out from his thoughts. That must be fear.

When the trees at last gave way and Drann came blundering out into brighter light and open ground, he dared for a moment to pause and to look around him. Creel and his guards were pounding on and up over the thin grass, making for a rocky knoll at the summit. Over to Drann's left another couple of levymen – not much older than him – spilled out of the trees. One of them fell; the second stopped and made to help him to his feet but then thought better of it and turned away again. Too late, for their pursuers came rushing up, yelping and hollering, and hacked them both down.

Drann felt sick, from exhaustion, from horror or terror; he did not know which. There was shouting close behind him, in the woods. He fled from it, making for the lord of Mondoon and that jagged, ragged hump of bare rock upon which he was arraying his last ten or so defenders. It was the only place that looked even remotely like sanctuary, for a farm boy who knew he could not run much further.

"Set your feet to these rocks and yield not a pace," Creel was growling as Drann fell amongst the grim-faced warriors of the lord's household. "Running'll not save you now. Only thing that might is finding some iron in your heart."

The last remnants of Creel's former escort company were emerging from the trees, scattered in ones and twos all along the edge. Dying in those ones and twos, many of them, as they were shot down with arrows or impaled on hungry spears. The bandits, or king's loyalists or whatever they were, streamed out on to the high ground. They came without order or rank, a chaotic flock of carrion birds jostling and calling in their haste. More and more of them, until Drann realised that it was not sanctuary he had found but the place where he would die.

He scrambled to get to his feet once more, but one of Creel's men pushed past him and knocked him on to his backside. He was the only one of the levies to have reached the lord's side, and the warriors seemed entirely uninterested in his presence. Contemptuous of it, he thought.

"I'm not running," he heard himself shouting as he stood up.

He had no idea why he would say such a thing, or think it wise. But then wisdom had never been his greatest attribute, to hear his mother talk.

"I can see that," Creel muttered at his side, startling him. "You want some sort of reward, boy?"

"No," Drann stammered. "No, sire."

"Good. There's none coming here today. Fight and perhaps you get to live. That'll have to be enough for you."

Drann tightened his hands about his spear. He realised with surprise that his heartbeat was slowing. His mouth was dry, but he did not feel sick any more. He looked out between Creel's warriors and saw a great crowd of men rushing up the hillside, meaning to kill him and strip his corpse, and he was not afraid. It seemed too late for fear.

He glanced up. The sky was blue, flecked with delicate white strands of high cloud that drifted slowly westward. It looked peaceful up there.

Arrows came first, clattering and pattering down on rocks and into the grass all around. They were poorly aimed. Creel's warriors hunched behind their shields in any case. Drann heard the dull thunk of arrow striking wood once or twice. He had no shield himself, so folded down into the shadow of one of those big men as best he could.

The knoll was too rugged and too boulder-strewn to allow for the sort of shield line Drann had seen Creel's well-trained men practising since he joined the army. All they could do was to each find a piece of ground that gave them a sure footing and fight upon it. Their attackers were too impatient, or too short of arrows, to hold back. They surged on, and Drann and the rest rose to meet them.

It was not as he had imagined fighting to be. It was faster, and more confused. More desperate. A mass of flailing, lurching figures. Gasps and grunts and the rattle of spears, of swords. It was hard to tell who was friend and who foe, and his body acted before he had time to sort one from another. He lunged with his spear, felt it hit something – perhaps flesh – once or twice, the impacts shivering up the shaft and jarring his hands.

His feet slipped over slick rock; he stumbled. A wild-eyed man with a thick black beard loomed over him, an axe raised above his head. Drann's spear was tangled in his legs. He started to close his eyes, but a dark blur of movement swept across in front of him and his assailant was down, knocked from his feet by two men reeling around, locked together in violent embrace. Drann hauled his spear free and thrust it at the axeman's face. It was only a glancing blow, carving open the man's cheek, but it was enough. The man rolled away, bloodied, and first crawled then staggered back down the slope.

They all did. Drann watched them go in disbelief, his chest

heaving, that feeling of sickness back in his throat. It all seemed too easy, too fast, and so it was. The retreat did not last. As Creel himself dragged a wounded man back over the rocks, and propped him up against a boulder, Drann watched their enemies gathering, bickering, and then spreading themselves out, thinning and reaching to encompass half the knoll with their ragged line. He could have wept then, at the brief flowering and instant withering of hope. It would have been better never to have caught its scent. All the weakness, that he had thought gone, was back in his legs.

It began again, the surge up towards the few men atop the rocks, the reaching for their blood and lives. This time, to Drann's puzzlement, it seemed that in amongst the footfalls and the cries of fury, there was the pounding of hoofs too. That could not be right, he thought. For a moment, it seemed it must be his heart, thudding inside him, but then as blade met shield once more and the struggle was renewed, a horse came bursting across the shoulder of the knoll, and atop it a great and terrible rider.

He was tall and his skin brown-tinted, this newcomer, with a scalp clean-shaven and smooth as polished stone, save for a single thick length of black hair folded and pinned into a knot atop his head. A heavy leather waistcoat, with plates of metal, encased his chest. A long sword was in his hand, and it moved as fast and free as swirling water. The horse cast men aside as it ploughed through the throng. The blade carved them away from its flanks.

So sudden and so fierce was the charge, like an eagle plunging through a flock of lambs, that horse and rider burst through and out on to open ground, and there they wheeled, the horse rearing up and gouging the air with its forelegs. Already, their arrival had spread enough alarm to scatter some of the bandits, who were tumbling and bounding back down towards the edge of the woods. And there amongst them Drann saw another horseman. Another southerner, to judge by the hue of his skin, whose horse danced and jinked around as he flicked arrow after arrow, absurdly fast, in amongst the fleeing men. The reins hung loose and limp across the animal's shoulders, yet the archer barely swayed and it seemed that almost every arrow found its intended home.

Only then did Drann realise that there were those amongst their attackers who did not know, or did not care, what was happening behind them, and had not yet had their fill of slaughter. They pressed in against the last of Creel's guardians, and clambered over the rocks that kept them from the lord. Creel himself fought like a wounded boar, crying out in incoherent rage as he slashed at those who tried to reach him. Drann pushed away a corpse that had fallen across his legs, pinning him against a boulder. It was far heavier than he ever would have imagined. He took a few steps closer to Creel, trying to keep his spear up, not knowing what else to do. He was near when Creel went down, thrown backwards by a man who rushed him with only a shield, punching the metal boss into the lord's chest.

Drann acted without thought. He thrust his spear at a flash of exposed skin, and it drove into the man's neck, knocking him sideways. In the urgent moment, it seemed a small, unremarkable thing. Then the blood came, as Drann was dragged

forward, falling across Creel himself, and his spear tore free of
flesh. He kept hold of it somehow, but could not easily rise as
Creel struggled beneath him. He managed to twist on to his
side, in time to see a lean, hard-featured man clad in tattered
hides rushing towards him and the lord of Mondoon, vaulting
over a hump of rock, a knife almost as long as Drann's forearm
ready for the fatal blow. Leaping at them, to put all the weight
and force the world could offer into the blade.

And there was a flash, and a strange sound unlike anything
Drann had heard before, and the man's head was apart from his
body, springing away as if on a string. Making a dull noise as it
landed and rolled. The decapitated corpse crumpled and curled
and fell at Drann's feet, spitting blood out across his boots. He
looked up, into the face of a woman, who stood between him
and the sun so that he had to narrow his eyes to make out her
features. They might have been cut from stone, so impassive
were they. She stared at him with cold eyes, much as if she was
regarding some entirely unremarkable hummock in the ground.
Her fair hair was tied back. Her sword, clad in the dead man's
blood, came slowly down. Drann suddenly realised that she
might, in those moments, have been deciding whether or not
she should kill him. He probably did not look much like the
defender of a landed lord.

Apparently satisfied, though nothing in her expression gave
so much as a whisper of her thoughts, that blade descended to
her side. She shook the notched shield on her other arm and
resettled her hold upon it. She looked away.

Drann rolled off Creel of Mondoon, and found that the
fighting was done. Dead and wounded littered the ground

around the rocky knoll, and stretched back towards the silent, still trees below. Here and there, a few survivors were limping, or running, or staggering back towards the safety of those woods. The two southerners, swordsman and archer, had dismounted and came striding up to stand beside the woman, all three of them staring down at Creel, who was grunting and muttering but did not seem injured. They paid no heed to Drann, sitting there in a state of amazement at the way his heart kept beating, the air kept easing in and out of his chest, and he kept living.

The tallest of these three, the first to have come, leaned and extended a big hand to Creel.

"Can I help you to your feet, lord of Mondoon?" he asked, with just the faintest hint of mirth in his voice.

Creel glowered at him, but reached to clasp hands. Drann glimpsed a fleck of movement in the sky, over the southerner's shoulder. A dark scratch against the blue, skimming down towards them.

"Arrow . . ." he started to say, hoarsely, but he need not have spoken.

The woman was already glancing up and casually lifting her shield arm. No other part of her moved. She simply caught the arrow upon the wooden circle. The loud, sharp crack of it smacking in made Drann blink. No one else gave the smallest sign of surprise or alarm.

The archer sniffed, and took an arrow from his own quiver.

"You want me to do something about that?" he asked, staring back along the path of the offending shaft, at some target Drann could not see from where he sat.

"Is he going to try again?" the swordsman asked, still bent over and holding Creel's hand in his.

"Not likely," the archer reported. "Running like a hare now."

"Let him go, then," the swordsman said, and hauled Creel, one-handed, to his feet.

"You're a sight-boon," Creel grunted as he wiped the flat of his sword across his breeches.

"I imagine so."

"Where're the rest of you?"

"Coming along. We three thought it best to hurry when we caught the sound of the hunt."

"Well and good," Creel muttered. "You can follow us back. Make your own camp. Outside, mind. Keep a little ground between us, yes?" He shot a sharp, meaningful glance at the southerner, who said nothing. "Come and find me in my tent tomorrow morning."

"I will."

The lord of Mondoon sheathed his sword, flexed his wrist and rolled his hand around.

"I'm not dying today, then," he mused. "That's something of a surprise."

"Of course you're not dying," the bald-headed warrior smiled. "You've not paid us yet."

And with those words Drann belatedly understood what, and who, these people were. And realised that he would, after all, have a story worth the telling if he ever got back to his village.

3

Desert Lions, More Likely

In the early morning Drann stood watch, perhaps two hundred paces from the Free's camp. He should have been asleep, but he had traded the duty with one of the other levies. The man had looked at him as if he was an idiot of the most ridiculous kind when he proposed it, and wandered off to find his bedroll shaking his head and murmuring about the rank stupidity of youth. Drann did not mind. His bloody adventure in the company of Creel of Mondoon had rendered him too agitated, too distracted, to easily sleep on the lump-rucked ground, and he had not yet had his fill of the Free.

From his perch atop a rock he could see them well enough, camped there a little further, and a little lower, along a ridge overlooking Creel's army. It felt almost unreal. He was watching the inheritors of a name out of old tales, a fragment of Old Emmin's histories come to life. He had fought alongside them yesterday – if you could call his efforts fighting – and that was a thing he doubted anyone back in his home village would

believe, when he reported it. The Free: last and greatest by far
of the mercenary companies. Makers and breakers of lords and
kings and legends.

As he sat there on his hard seat he had counted them over
and again, marked every detail of their manner and appearance.
The three who had proved saviours at Creel's knoll yesterday
were there, archer, swordsman and ice-faced woman. Drann
knew who the swordsman was now. Yulan, Captain of the Free.
With them in their makeshift camp were another six archers,
not southerners these, but drawn from every part of the land
to judge from their faces and hair. They were dressed alike,
though, in hides and tanned leathers.

And then two more, who did not fit the mould of warrior
quite as the rest did. A man and a woman of early middle age,
who wore no armour and carried no shields. From the way they
regarded one another, exchanged whispers, touched hands now
and again as they went about the morning tasks of any camp,
Drann deduced that they were lovers. He was handsome, she
close to beauty; they were well matched. All these people, as
best he could tell, had slept under blankets in a circle round a
fire that now guttered and glowed. They had a dozen horses,
more than were needed to carry them all, tethered just beyond
that circle.

None of this was what set its hooks most deeply into Drann's
attention, and sent thrills of wonder, of trepidation, through
him. No, the thing from which he could barely avert his eyes
was a huge, heavy flat-bedded wagon that stood not far from
the horses. It had massive iron-clad wheels. The beast that
hauled it grazed a short distance further out, and it was no dray

horse but a mighty bull of grey hue, with shoulders like rocks and wide up-curving horns tipped with iron sheaths. It had taken Drann a long time to realise that the wagon had its own driver too, for he – or she, he could not really tell – stayed some way apart from all the others. Had not stirred, in fact, in all the time Drann had been watching, from the side of the wagon. A small figure, hunched down, sitting against one of the wheels, features and form entirely obscured by a very strange hooded green cloak that looked for all the world as though it was made of leaves stitched together.

An odd sight, but not enough to distract Drann from what rested on the bed of the wagon. It was a single enormous block of some sort, at least as high and wide as Drann was tall. Beyond that shape and size, he could tell nothing more, for it was covered over with a heavy canvas sheet tied down all around the edges of the wagon. But Drann knew what must lie beneath, in darkness, in silence. He knew it by rumour, at least. The Clamour.

When folk spoke of the Free, more often than not they did it in soft tones of fear or awe or wonder. As if speaking of something more than mere people and their deeds. There were many reasons for that: the fact that this, alone amongst all the free companies, had been the one powerful enough to persist when the times turned against the rest of their kind; that they had, over lifetimes, humbled many enemies others would have feared to even face; that they fought and died by no one's choice but their own, and were said to do both of those things – the fighting and the dying – better than any who had ever lived.

But most of all when old men, softened by drink, whispered

about the Free in some dark alehouse, the hushing of their voices was because of the Clamour. There were Clevers amongst the ranks of the Free, some said to be amongst the most powerful who lived, but most would hold the true reason for the Free's continuing survival, for the inability of School or King to face them down, to be the Clamour. A Permanence. A thing not of this world. The remnant – or result; Drann was extremely vague about how such things came about – of some fell magic gone awry. Run beyond the control of the Clever who shaped it.

There were few Permanences so awful, so wondrous, so potent, that they became the common currency of ale-talk or children's tales. Now here Drann was, and there just a couple of hundred steps away was one of those few. Everyone, everywhere, knew of the Clamour. He'd heard that it once ate an Orphanidon alive, armour and all.

The thin beard Drann had been trying to grow – with unsatisfactory results – for the last week or more itched. He scratched at his chin with grubby fingers. He had assumed he would by now have a thick, wiry beard, such as Creel himself and so many of the hardened fighting men in the camp sported. Matters had not progressed in accordance with his hopes. As it turned out, the adornments of manhood were not so easily come by.

He was poised thus in mid scratch when a wood pigeon burst up from its roost in one of the big trees some way below him, clapping its way indignantly off into the new day. Drann looked towards the sound and found himself staring into the eyes of Yulan.

The Captain of the Free was regarding him with one eyebrow wryly arched.

"You supposed to be on watch?" the southerner asked.

He was clad just as he had been yesterday, but on foot now and with sword safe in its scabbard. Still intimidating, though. Still reeking of composure and capability. He had a heavy sack in one hand, and an expectant expression as he awaited a reply from Drann, perched atop the rock.

And Drann, finding himself tongue-tangled, could only nod in confirmation. He had no idea how Yulan had come to within touching reach of him so entirely unnoticed.

"If all Creel's watchers are of the same quality, that'd explain how he got himself into such trouble yesterday," Yulan observed. It might have been accusation, or condemnation, but somehow it sounded a little gentler than that.

Drann was not sure whether Yulan recognised him or not. Did he know that Drann had been there too, had been the one at Creel's side at the end? Perhaps not. Perhaps men such as these did not remember those of less lofty station.

"You know where Creel's tent is?" Yulan asked.

"Yes," Drann managed to say.

"Good. Show me." He lifted the sack at his side and gave it a shake. "I've got some ears for him."

Drann led Yulan in through the crude palisade that he and his fellow labourers had bent their backs and bloodied their hands to make. He saw Yulan casting his eyes up and down its length, but could read nothing of his impression. Unfavourable, Drann would have guessed. The fence looked all too obviously what it was: a lot of trees and saplings felled, sharpened and stuck into the ground at various irregular angles by people who barely knew what they were doing. Even to Drann's innocent eye, it hardly appeared impregnable.

The remains of campfires were strewn amongst the tents. A few still smouldering, most long dead. The lines of horses tethered side by side were silent and listless. Those few fighting men wandering around were sluggish. Even the handful of flags on some of the larger tents hung limp.

Drann marched steadily on, making for the wide white tent near the heart of the camp, where Creel's orange banner and a green truce flag flew – or rather, hung limply like the rest. He put some effort into keeping a straight back and a long stride, pretending he was full of vigour. It took a certain amount of concentration, so he did not notice for a moment or two that his companion had veered aside. When he did, he turned about sharply and had to run to catch up with him.

Yulan approached a weary-eyed lad who was strapping nose-bags to one horse after another along one of the tether lines. The boy looked up, giving every sign of being far, far too early awake.

"I need fodder for my horses," Yulan said bluntly. "The grass up on the ridge there's not even fit for cattle."

The horse boy blinked. Shrugged, as if to express impotence. Drann felt a little twinge of trepidation.

"Enough for a dozen horses," Yulan said levelly. "Two days' worth would be good."

Drann saw the nose wrinkling, the lips forming into refusal. He darted forward, because it seemed like a good idea, and hissed into the boy's ear: "It's the Free."

Which resolved the matter at once. The horse boy rubbed his eyes, opened them wider.

"Sorry," he mumbled. "We'll send some up there. The ridge?"

Yulan nodded mutely, and pointed the way.

As they drew near to Creel's tent, there was brief commotion. Laughter. The first Drann had heard that day. Half a dozen men were leading a mule with a great dead stag draped over its back. Drann and Yulan stopped to let them pass. The hunters were dirty, and clearly tired, but flushed with their success. Not just in the hunt, perhaps, but in the war.

The stag was bigger than any Drann had ever seen around his northern village. Magnificent, with many-pointed antlers like huge splayed claws. A head as big as a horse's. Even in death, it had presence. A dead king, brought down from his wild pasture.

The guards outside Creel's tent did not look nearly as tired as Drann felt. They looked like alert hawks, in fact, staring out with bright eyes from beneath silvery helms. Unfriendly hawks. Drann was not sure how these things were supposed to go, but he guessed it might be his duty to announce Creel's visitor.

"He wants to see Creel," he said, and it did not sound as confident, or apt, as he would have liked.

"Does he?" sneered one of the guards. "Back to your beds. Too early for that kind of—"

Drann flinched and ducked his head down in alarm as Yulan cried out behind him: "Creel! We've got ears for you!"

The guards were not amused, and Drann could see the snarls

gathering around their mouths, but those were snuffed out by a gruff cry from within.

"Let them in, you slow-wits."

And thus Drann to his considerable surprise found himself, for the second time in as many days, in close company with two of the most famed warriors of the age.

Creel put him in mind of nothing so much as rock: short, stout, grey of hair and beard. Weathered. A bit eroded perhaps, but if so, merely reduced to a hard kernel against which all other rocks would break. Entirely recovered, as best Drann could tell, from his misadventures of the day before.

Yulan and the lord of Mondoon faced one another, mismatched in size yet precariously balanced in potent presence. Each had that aura to which so many aspired, and so few ascended: authority, confidence, power. Great men. The tent seemed too small to contain them. Had they been dogs – or desert lions, more likely – Drann imagined they would surely have started to pace up and down, to measure one another.

"Where's my contract-holder?" Creel asked. "I thought you'd be bringing him to me."

"He's dead," Yulan replied.

"You might have mentioned that yesterday." Creel frowned.

"Didn't seem of the most urgent import," Yulan said easily. "He's as dead now as he was then."

"Well, I'm sorry to hear it. He was a good man."

"I'll take your word for it. We told him to stay out of the way. He didn't. They had Clevered arrows."

"Really?" Creel's reserve gave way to a lively spark of interest at that. "Did you bring any back?"

"No. They only had two. One went through your man, the other through my horse. My best horse."

"A shame."

The words were uninflected. Drann could not tell whether Creel regretted the loss of horse, man or the chance to acquire some remarkable arrows.

"It was a good horse," Yulan said.

Creel regarded the mercenary, eyes pinched into a calculating glare. Then, abruptly, his whole face relaxed. A smile – fierce, but a smile – parted his lips, as if he consented to be a part of some joke.

"I'll take your word for it," he said. "Do you want to eat? I can't drink wine this early – this old bone-house of mine wants nothing but sleep if I do – but I've some you can have, if you want it."

"No wine," Yulan said. "I'll take bread if you have it, though."

Creel nodded to one of his attendant warriors, who stepped smartly out of the tent, then gestured for Yulan to settle himself at a small table. No one was paying any heed to Drann, so he stayed quite still and quiet. Hoping to escape notice.

"Your people are safely nested outside the camp?" the warlord asked as he took his own seat.

"The Clamour, you mean," Yulan grunted. "Yes, we'll keep our distance."

"Good, good. Too many tired folks with blades around here to test their nerves, eh?"

Yulan upended the sack he carried, spilling ears like little pickled dainties across the table. Creel regarded them dispassionately. One tumbled to the floor. No one made a move to retrieve it. Drann had to suppress an instinct to step forward, pick it up and set it carefully down amongst its fellows on the table. Somehow, he doubted his intervention would be welcome. In any case, he saw no need to remind anyone of his presence.

Yulan produced a battered, bent manuscript case from inside his jerkin. It was stained, and had part-folded itself about a notch punched through one side of it. He ripped it open down its length, and unrolled as best he could the similarly discoloured and deformed parchment within.

"Sorry about the blood. Your man carried it strapped across his chest. The arrow went through contract and him alike. But you can see' – he held the document out to Creel, who took hold of it – "you can see that he marked down twenty kills before he died. For the other forty you'll have to take my word. There's not a man bearing blade in the King's name left between here and Trumock. We've done as you asked of us."

Creel examined the fouled contract intently. He showed no distaste, that Drann could detect, at the blood soaked into it.

"Can you do that?" Yulan asked. "Take my word?"

Creel folded the parchment and tucked it inside his jerkin.

"I've heard men attach all manner of calumny and offence to your name, but never the betrayal of a contract, or lying about its completion. And I'd say you won more than a little of my faith with your work yesterday, wouldn't you?"

It was only now, noting a faint softening in Yulan's shoulders and hands, that Drann realised the extent to which the Captain of the Free had been prepared for a different response. He had not been certain of Creel's answer. And Drann had no idea what would have happened if it had been less accommodating.

"Payment's in the pouch," Creel said, jabbing a thumb over his shoulder towards a dark corner of the tent, where not one but several leather bags lay in a pile. "You want it now?"

"After I've eaten."

"Good. Let's break bread."

Creel abruptly swept his arm across the table, sending the severed ears scattering over the rug. One tumbled to touch the toe of Drann's boot before falling flat. He kicked it discreetly away. They reminded him of the pig's ears the butcher in his village sometimes sold by the handful.

The guard who had been waiting patiently by the tent's entrance with a platter of bread came forward and set it down on the table. The lord of Mondoon tore a loaf in half with all the enthusiasm of a ravenous farmhand, and offered a hunk to Yulan.

Whatever was between these two great men, it was beyond Drann's ability to put into simple words. A thing particular to great men, perhaps; incomprehensible to those of meaner standing. Wariness. A grudging regard. Even – though Drann was not at all sure he was not imagining this one – a hint of abrasive affection.

"I've another contract to offer you," Creel said through a half-chewed mouthful. A few crumbs of soft dough escaped his lips and congregated in his beard.

"I told you the Trumock road was likely the Free's last labour," Yulan said. "That hasn't changed. We're done."

Creel laughed. Yulan did not.

"Didn't believe you then, don't now," Creel said.

"We've tested our luck a long time and it's held firm, but it gets to be burdensome. There's more than a few of us'd not weep to leave all this behind, me amongst them; and there's none could easily take my place at the head once I'm gone. I think our time – the free companies' time – is finally passed."

"It passed for all the rest of them a good while back. Not you, though. Not the Free."

"Even us. Our charter's a grant of the Hommetic kings. There won't be any more of them, will there? No more kings?"

"No," Creel acknowledged. "They found Crex a few days ago in the Holden Shaw, hiding in a woodcutter's cottage. Wearing a woodcutter's clothes, the silly goat. His head's spiked and sent to Armadell-on-Lake, arms and legs to four other cities."

"Equitable of you, to share him out. Makes our charter a good deal less certain than it was, though. Will your Council honour it? Enforce it? You and your friends rose up to put an end to the arbitrary exercise of power, didn't you?"

"Depends who you ask. Me, Crex had already taken my brother-in-law's head, and he was better than halfway convinced I was plotting against him. Making the rumour real seemed my best course. But arbitrary exercise of power? I suppose that's the taproot, for some of us."

"Well, that's what's sitting across this table from you. I *am* the arbitrary exercise of power. Anyone who can afford the Free can buy enough power to exercise it just about any way they choose. Is your Council going to rest easy with that?"

"You've more friends than foes amongst the cities," Creel said, with an expansively dismissive shrug. "I doubt you've anything to fear from the Council, or whatever might succeed us."

Yulan smiled, though Drann felt there was more sadness than mirth in the expression.

"And what about the School? They spent decades harrying all the other companies into nothingness. We're unfinished business for them, and believe me, they've tried to finish it more than once."

"Yet it remains unfinished, because you're too fierce and friend-rich for even them to wrestle to the ground," Creel said. "But they're a thing of the Kingdom, anyway. Their word'll not carry the weight it once did. Sided with us in the end, but by all accounts they near tore themselves apart trying to decide between us and Crex."

"They didn't side with you; they decided *not* to side with the King. You'd do well to mark the difference. The School was there – a sapling, but there – before the Kingdom, before even the first of the free companies. Outlasted both, outgrew both, and had more than a small hand in the ending of both. I'll give you a wager, if you like: every penny, every copper bit, of the prize in that pouch over there, that you learn just how much weight the word of the School still carries inside ... oh, six months'd be more than time enough."

"Well, I'll not test my fortune against your judgement. You've the quickest wits of any man on the continent, it's said."

"Not true," Yulan said sharply, and Drann thought he detected just the faintest wince of displeasure at the suggestion. "Not by a long way."

Creel grunted. Leaned back in his chair, chewing a contemplative mouthful. After a moment or two's silence, he shrugged.

Yulan's olive hand, resting on the surface of the table, stirred. The first finger began to tap at the wood. Soft, but regular. It put Drann in mind of the twitching of a cat's tail. Creel did not seem to notice, or care.

"I can't force you to take what I offer, of course. I've a mind this might be a contract you want, though."

"Do you?" Yulan asked with an air of indifference, still drumming that finger, staring into Creel's eyes. "Why's that?"

"Well, the thing is this: it looks like the last stagnant pool of the Hommetic swamp might be ripe for the draining, if I can find some fleet-footed folk with good big spades for the task."

"Who?"

"Callotec."

And at the uttering of the name, everything changed. As if a sudden frost had crisped out of the air to chill and still everything, every breath. Yulan's finger stopped in mid tap, held crooked and motionless. His eyes narrowed as he regarded the lord of Mondoon.

"Not a great threat to your new settlement, I'd have thought," he said, very calmly and quietly. "Friendless, that one."

"Friendless as they come," Creel agreed. "I'll pay well for him, nonetheless. Twice what you'll carry off today. That's enough to give even coin-heavy folks like the Free pause for thought, isn't it? One last pay day to grease your retirement."

"Why do you care so much about Callotec?"

"Well I'm not one for leaving a task only nine tenths done. But more especially, it seems that last loose tenth is on his way to the Empire. There's nobody wants the last man with a claim on the throne sitting in Arnothex making friends with the Orphans. Particularly not if that man's a viper like Callotec. It'd be all but a promise of blood to come. Rivers of the stuff."

Yulan folded his hands in his lap, clasping them together.

"The Orphans acquiring a claimant needn't change much, not even a cousin to Crex; you – the School, at least – still have the Bereaved. They're mad folk in the Empire, but not so mad they'll unlearn their fear of that any time soon, no matter how Callotec tries to goad them."

Creel took another bite of bread, and waved the small hunk remaining in his hand with a flourish.

"A plan that rests upon the sanity of the Orphans is a turd of a plan, Yulan. I don't need to worry about it if I've got Callotec's head on my table, do I?" he said through spittle and dough.

"Who's with him?" Yulan asked.

"Three or four dozen Armsmen, from what we hear. No Clevers."

"Seems like excess to set me and mine on the man, then. Cleaving a mouse with a broadsword."

Creel rocked back in his chair and sighed.

"You use a broadsword if that's what's to hand. My lads are war-spent. I left better than half of them at Caradon, and you saw yesterday what the ones I've got left're worth. Anyway, I can afford you, since I scooped up a nice little treasury at Caradon, so why not?"

"Why not? Because the Free's done, Creel. Most of those who aren't with me here are already on their way to White Steading for the settling of shares."

"But it's the Dog-Lord," insisted Creel with sudden vigour.

"You're telling me that counts for nothing? I don't believe it. I know you better than that."

Drann did not understand the import of all this. He had never heard of any Callotec, cousin to the King, Dog-Lord. But that frost was still on the air. In the leaden, quiet pause, he could clearly feel it. The name meant something, to one or both of these men. Yulan was staring down at his interlaced fingers, lost in thought.

"You haven't asked me where he's running to," Creel said, looking away for a moment.

"You said," Yulan muttered. "The Empire."

"Yes, but what drain does the rat mean to sneak away through? He's making for the Old Threetower Road, Yulan. That's what I hear. He's making for Towers' Shadow."

The Captain of the Free sighed at that. Whatever or wherever Towers' Shadow was – Drann had no more heard of such a place than he had heard of Callotec – it carried great weight for some reason.

"I'll take your contract," Yulan said quietly. "Me. I can only promise you my own sword."

Creel frowned. He rubbed his chin, brushing crumbs from his beard.

"And I'd back your one against Callotec's dozens," he said, "but the contract'll be with the Free. Not just you. Yes? You'll ask them, give them the chance?"

"I'll ask them," Yulan conceded. "But I won't compel a single one of them. The Free's finished, as far as they're concerned."

He extended his hand across the table. Creel stared at it,

pondering, then said, "Agreed," and clasped it in his own. The two lions shared a curt handshake.

"Done, then," Creel smiled.

"How did you get into Caradon?" Yulan asked, and the change in his tone was dramatic. His voice, and the very air within the tent, was entirely drained now of any hint of tension, any consequence to the matters under discussion. It was to be, it seemed, merely two men passing the time in idle conversation.

Drann found his own shoulders easing, and his stance softening; his body responded of its own volition to that change in the timbre of proceedings. He had not realised how tight he had been before.

"Subterfuge or bribery, I'd guess," Yulan went on. "Caradon's walls never counted for much, but you still didn't have the numbers or the machinery to get past them. I thought you'd be about that business for another week or two at least."

"Bribery it was," Creel grinned. "Nothing like a lost cause and a silver-pledge to change the allegiance of folk with nowhere to run. It was a good investment. Turns out their treasury was well stocked. And I took a lot of prisoners, most of them inclined to play friendly now I'm a victor. I look to have added a Clever to my household, which is always—"

"Who? Who's the Clever?"

"You've half an idea already, I can see. I didn't even know he was in Caradon, but I suppose I shouldn't be surprised when you know things I don't. Anyway: the Weaponsmith."

"And you brought him here?"

The urgency in Yulan's voice was startling. The Captain of

the Free leaned forward, set both hands flat on the table. All
that easing of the mood was undone in an instant, as if it had
never been.

"Yes, of course," Creel said, as puzzled at the change in
Yulan's demeanour as Drann was. "Why—"

But the question went unfinished. Yulan surged to his feet,
turning even as he did so. His chair went flying backwards. The
table rocked and shuffled sideways. Yulan ran. The guards in
the tent's doorway had to leap from his path as he vanished, out
into the camp.

Creel of Mondoon stared after his disappeared guest, his eyebrows raised and his lips pursed in surprise. Then he sniffed,
and snapped at his guards: "Get after him, then. See what's
afoot."

The command was given with such sharp authority that
Drann felt himself included by it. As Creel's men sprinted in
pursuit of Yulan, he followed. It was that or be left alone with
the warlord of Mondoon, and that did not appeal.

He felt ears, soft beneath his heels, as he started to run. He
skidded on them, and almost fell, just as Creel snapped out:
"Stop there, boy."

4

The Bloody Man

As a child, Yulan had distinguished himself in but one way from his peers in the rude Massatan village that was his home, at the edge of the sands: he could outrun any one of them. Fleet as a desert gazelle. That was what his proud parents said, in any case. Nonsense, but loving of them to say it. Upon such distinctions are the petty hierarchies of children built, and his pace had won him a perch near the top. He could still remember with the sharpest clarity, as it was his fortune and burden to remember almost everything, how it had felt: those dust-pounding legs, the near-desert sun beating on scalp and neck, the hot air plunging in and out of his chest.

In later life it took rather more to mark yourself out from other men. He had done so in sanguinary fashion, but the bloody man he became had more than once been grateful for the speed inherited from the child he once was. He had run, on occasion, for his life. Today, more lives than just his own might be forfeit if he did not reach Kerig before word of the Weaponsmith's presence did.

The camp and its motley inhabitants slowed around him, even as he moved ever faster. It, and they, became a succession of glimpses, still and stiff. A strewing of rocks around which he must flow as fast and smooth as any mountain stream. So flow he did.

Through a thicket of tree stumps, where Creel's men had felled a copse to make their half-hearted palisade. Between lines of tethered horses that snorted and stirred at his fleeting presence. Across – a single long, leaping stride – the ashen, smoking remains of a campfire. Between two men talking to one another; crying vague abuse in his wake.

Another man emerged, stooping, from a tent too suddenly to avoid. Yulan barged him over, staggered, recovered himself and surged on.

He was running for the ridge where he had left the others. Where, he could hope, they still rested and bickered and ate. That it was a vain hope became apparent very quickly.

He saw another figure darting between the tents. Coming in from the edge of the camp, and running as if it mattered. It was not Kerig, but that did nothing to ease Yulan's worries.

"Akrana," he shouted, and she came to an abrupt halt, her pale hair loose and fluttering about her face. Trotted to meet him.

"Weaponsmith's here," she said levelly. No hint of breathlessness. "The lads who brought us horse-feed mentioned it. Kerig's gone for him."

"Which way?"

She pointed into the heart of the camp.

"Wren?" Yulan asked.

"Hamdan's trying to hold her back. Might manage it for a little while longer, but after that . . . "

She did not need to finish the sentence. Nothing would keep Wren from Kerig's side for long; she was his wife, and like him a Clever. Hamdan could not possibly stop her if she chose to go. Not if she reached for the entelechs.

"Get back there and help him," Yulan snapped at Akrana. "Nobody else comes into the camp. Tell Wren I'm bringing Kerig back. Promise her that."

Akrana nodded, turned, and raced for the ridge. Yulan ran in the direction she had pointed.

Sound told him where to go before sight did. Screams and shouting. Then smell. An unmistakable hint of bitter smoke. Overlaying that, almost smothering it, the rich, warm smell of upturned earth, filling the air with an entirely unnatural strength and depth. That – the earth scent – was Kerig, without a doubt. And it told Yulan that he was probably too late. Likely as not, the worst was already happening.

Other men were already heading in that same direction. Drawn to the mounting tumult like buzzards to a corpse. Yulan pushed past them. He burst into a space more open than most of the camp. A tent, large and red and flagged stood at one end of it.

Kerig was down on one knee, his sweating face contorted by effort and concentration, his hands plunged wrist-deep into the ground. Yulan sprinted at him, but looked towards that big circular tent Kerig was facing. It was burning. Not fiercely yet, but that would come soon. It was the source of the screaming. Men were running with buckets of water. Others were standing, staring in horror or amazement at Kerig, the tent or both. They did not know quite what they were seeing, Yulan was sure, but they knew enough to be afraid. Or appalled.

Yulan's mind spun, and he – his self – was almost separate from it, floating above the blur of its movement, letting it run like a wheel. Thoughts were raised and tested and forgotten with his every stretching, desperate stride. As it often did when he most needed it, the rush of detached calculation left behind it a single conclusion for him to seize upon. It might be too late to prevent disaster, but if not, there was only one thing he could do that might change the course of events.

He threw himself at Kerig. Reached for him and hit him about his shoulders, hard enough to fling him sideways and down, tear his hands up out of the ground in a spray of soil. He held on as they rolled and ended on his knees, pinning Kerig across the chest.

"What did you do, you pig-fucking idiot?" Yulan hissed.

Kerig was too disoriented, too shaken by the sudden rupture of his focus upon the entelech, to respond with more than a formless mumble. His earth-stained hands were shaking beneath Yulan's weight. Trying, as if with a life of their own, to dig themselves back into the soil. Whatever the Clever had been attempting, it had been potent. Costly.

Yulan shifted so that he could look to the tent without lessening his hold upon Kerig. Flames were racing up its canvas flanks, flinging out curls of black smoke. It was falling in on itself, causing the crowd milling about to shrink back. Kerig was a Vernal Clever, not an Aestival, so the fire was probably not his doing; not directly, at least. Perhaps someone had knocked over a lamp. But what emerged from the tent assuredly was the fruit of his labours.

A man came staggering out, clad in loose cloth leggings and tunic, with a tied belt of seal hide. That put his home some-where on the Narbonan shore, most likely, and made him a confederate of the Weaponsmith.

The man's clothes, and the skin of his face, were overlaid with a net of thin, thorned stems. Like green veins, exposed by flaying. Where those stems reached his face and hands – just the tips of them, for they would have writhed up from his feet, out of the earth – they had drawn blood. Trails of it marked his cheeks. Beads of it pricked his hands and brow. The sharp-toothed creepers binding his legs were withering and tearing with his every lurching step; shredding his clothes, and no doubt the skin beneath.

Wild eyes gleamed out from beneath the stems clasped like a clawed hand across the man's face, frenzied by fear and pain. They found Yulan and Kerig and sharpened to a stare of pure anger.

"Don't do it," shouted Yulan at once. "Do you know who we are?"

He shaped the cry carefully, making it hard and command-ing but with only a hint of threat. The effort was wasted. There was no sign that the man so much as heard him. At least one of his ears was torn and loose, ripped by the briars, but Yulan knew that was not what deafened him. It was the fury into which his terror had been transformed. A fury that left Yulan with a rapidly diminishing store of options.

"It's over," he snapped at the man, knowing it would not be enough.

He was aware, imprecisely, of other figures emerging from the tent. Men falling or staggering out as it folded down in a crackle of flame and exhalation of smoke. He spared them none of his attention; that, he kept fixed upon the Narbonan closing on him and Kerig. The man fumbled at his belt and produced a serrated knife from its sheath. His thorny bonds kept browning and falling away, now that Kerig's exertions had been interrupted. His paces were becoming longer, more certain. More purposeful.

Yulan lifted his weight from Kerig. He did not rise, but swivelled to face the Weaponsmith's man. He dug his right hand into the loose earth Kerig had disturbed and closed his fist about a handful of it.

"Somebody stop him," he shouted.

A last, futile attempt to forestall the inevitable. The audience had grown, but none showed any sign of intervening.

In his mind's eye, Yulan saw what was going to happen. As with the past, so with the future: he could often see it with great clarity. He played the scene out in his mind, in the space between heartbeats. Gave the world, or fortune, just another moment to avoid it. But the world chose not to. If Yulan did nothing, Kerig was a dead man; that, he could not permit. He squeezed his handful of soil. Tensed his legs. Then moved.

He pushed off on his right leg. Flung the soil at the man's eyes. As the Narbonan spluttered and grimaced, Yulan seized the wrist of his knife arm and forced it wide. Put a hard blow, with the heel of his hand, into his temple. As the man reeled, his legs going soft, Yulan hit him again, on his breastbone. Air fled the man's lungs in a great rush. He fell.

The suddenness of the violence broke the poised moment. Others rushed forward – Creel's guards, onlookers – and crowded round the fallen man, pushed Yulan backwards, filled the space between him and the burning tent with a mass of bodies. He spun and hauled Kerig, by the collar, to his feet.

"You with me?" he shouted into the Clever's face.

Kerig blinked, nodded mutely.

Yulan pushed Kerig away. The Clever was dazed and unhelpfully sluggish. Yulan drove him through the maze of the camp, like a tutor shepherding a brawling, bewildered student towards discipline.

5

Blood And Gold

Wren knelt at Kerig's side as he lay in fitful slumber on a worn blanket. She dabbed at his brow with a folded cloth. Yulan knew her to be amongst the greatest of the Free's Clevers, capable of extraordinary and terrible things, yet her face now was nothing but gentle concern and love. She was the best of them, Yulan suspected. The least flawed. For all that he liked Kerig, he had never thought the man entirely worthy of her devotion; less so than ever, now that he had ventured all their lives for the sake of his own vengeance. But then, Yulan knew less of this sort of love than he would have liked. Desire and passing passion, yes, but not the rooted, pervasive thing Kerig and Wren shared.

It was evening. Yulan could not delay any longer. He had set Hamdan's six archers as a watch along the side of the ridge, all of them looking down upon Creel's camp. That was where trouble would come from now, if it was coming, and Yulan had already given it more time to emerge than was wise. Hamdan and Akrana sat with him beside the fire. Staring silently, as they had been for an hour or more, into the low flames. The air carried the first faint premonitions of autumn chill on it these days. The year was turning.

Hestin paid little heed to warmth or cold. She was wrapped in her cloak of leaves, small and quiet, sitting behind Yulan and leaning against his back. She was not asleep. She hardly ever slept, poor shackled thing that she was. Her charge, the Clamour, was unstirring in its cage on the wagon, beneath that great concealing canvas. It did not sleep either.

"We cannot stay here," Yulan said reluctantly. "Not now. Creel will do what he can to calm things, but it won't hold. He's got a truce flag flying over his own tent down there, and Kerig's trampled it."

"In good cause," Wren muttered without looking up from her husband's prone form.

"In his *own* cause," Yulan snapped. "He promised me – *promised* me – he would set the Weaponsmith aside so long as he rode with the Free. Debts get settled only when we go our separate ways. That's always been the rule. It's how the Free survived."

"Well, it's finished now, isn't it?" Wren said. "The Free?"

She did not sound angry or indignant. She knew, as well as any of them, what Kerig had risked. That she would forgive him for it, defend him in it, was only as it had to be, given her nature.

"Maybe," Yulan murmured.

"Maybe?" Akrana echoed him.

She leaned forward, resting elbows on knees, regarding her

captain with sharp interest. Of course. Amongst them all, she was the one least willing to yield what the Free had given her. She was not done with killing yet, Yulan knew. She would never be, for she sought to heal the wounds of her past with it, and that was a task without an ending. Save her own death.

"Maybe," Yulan repeated. "I've taken another contract with Creel."

Hamdan swore, not angrily or bitterly, just in surprise.

"All my plans for a contented dotage not needed yet, then? Such good plans, they were."

"The contract's mine," Yulan said. "I'll fulfil it, and if there's a purse at the end of it, that'll be shared amongst you all. I don't need, or want, any of you to come with me." He sighed. "But it'll be your choice. I owe you that."

He had their full attention now. Wren had ceased her ministrations and sank back on her haunches, watching Yulan intently. Hamdan was frowning. No matter how he might deceive others, Yulan had never been able to hide his cares or worries from Hamdan. Whether because they were both Massatan, or because they were true friends, the archer saw through every veil.

"Call your boys in, Hamdan. They need to be a part of this too. Everyone should hear it, choose for themselves."

Hamdan twisted round and sent a soft, two-noted whistle into the gloaming. One by one the archers appeared and took their place around the fire. All close to Hamdan.

"So, I've taken a contract," Yulan repeated when they were settled. "The last I'll ever take. After this, we all walk away from White Steading with our shares, the charter's burned. The Free's

at an end. You can all ride for White Steading now, to join up
with the rest. That's what you should do, I think."

He paused, watching the firewood glow and smoke. This was
the moment he had deferred; the choice he did not truly want
to offer. The burden of Towers' Shadow, and the duty towards
that place, was his. So it had always seemed to him. He had neither the right nor the cause to require others to share it. But he
owed them honesty, these people who had followed his every
command these last few years. The closest thing to a family he
now possessed, with all the subtle tensions and human oddities
the comparison implied.

He owed them a choice, and his reluctance to speak of it was
not because he resented that, or doubted it. No, it was because
he knew what was likely to come of it. He knew these people
too well.

"The contract is to take, or kill, Callotec," Yulan said quietly.
"He's running for the border, at Towers' Shadow. I'm going to
stop him."

And no one said anything. Few of them had been there, at
Towers' Shadow. Wren had not even been one of the Free then.
Kerig and Akrana had been back at White Steading, he minis-
tering to the grave, lingering wounds she had taken on the day
Merkent died. Hestin and the Clamour too. But Hamdan, and
some of these six archers, had been there. It did not matter. By
memory or report, they all knew what had happened at Towers'
Shadow. They all knew with absolute certainty, as Yulan did
himself, that their captain would die alone, if that was what was
needed, for the sake of this one last contract.

*

Yulan's memories of the few days it took the world to rid him of pride were as clear as any he possessed; clearer, since they were engraved upon his mind with a precision only regret and guilt could achieve. Dry and dusty days, they were. Days when each sunset put blood and gold on distant clouds, but each morning brought only clear skies and none of the rain for which land and people alike yearned. So it had been for better than two hundred sunsets, two hundred morns. Drought, then hunger, then dying. People dying by the dozens, then the scores, across great swathes of the Hommetic domain.

The School had put a stop to that in the heartlands of the Kingdom. Their Clevers staved off the worst extremities of suffering for those the great and the powerful thought worthy of salvation. Such worth was not recognised along the kingdom's southern bounds. There, in the fringes of Yulan's homeland, no help was offered to blunt the cruelty of that hard year. No Clevers came to call up rain, or fruitful bounty. What came instead were swords and iron-shod horses and men seeking battle. The Free were amongst them.

It was the first contract Yulan had taken as leader of the Free, and – he understood later but not then, not in the midst of those days and deeds – he was hot with a giddying mix of self-import, responsibility, anticipation. He was hungry to prove himself worthy of Merkent's legacy, conscious of the need to show that the Free remained potent. He thought himself fully capable of doing so. Many people had praised his wisdom, his cunning and his fitness for command over the years, after all. He had allowed himself to believe them.

By the standards of the past, it was a small matter: thirty of the

Free, serving as scouts and cutting edge for five hundred Armsmen
sent to hunt down the stragglers of a failed Sorentine revolt. Crex
the King called it a revolt, at least. In truth, like all the trouble
made by the tumultuous Sorentines since they lost their throne,
it was little more than a bloody adventure born of resentment and
rivalries and a surfeit of young men with something to prove. But
they had anointed a bull as totem of their war, which gave their
raiding a certain standing in their own eyes and by their own rituals. So Crex had sent his cousin Callotec, with five hundred men
and a pledge of enough gold to buy the Free's services.

By the time Yulan and Hamdan and Rudran led the Free,
and behind them Callotec and his little army, into the village
of Towers' Shadow, the hard work was five days done. They had
killed close to three hundred Sorentines on the slopes of
Bruman Hill. Another hundred, taken alive, were beheaded
along the stream at the hill's foot. Callotec knelt them along its
bank, one great straggling line of them, and watched as they
were executed one after another. Yulan, standing far away up on
the higher ground where the killing had been more honest, and
less cold, noted that the beheadings began upstream. Many
loosened heads tumbled into the water. Many of the corpses
slumped forward and did the same, entirely or in part. The current took heads and great slicks of blood down the channel,
past those who were yet to die, to gild their anticipation of the
coming sword. Yulan had heard of Callotec's shallow cruelty
before – it was whispered that even Crex despised him – but
only then, at Bruman Hill, did he learn something of it at first
hand. Not quite enough, as it turned out.

There were few Sorentines still on the loose after that, and they were running, not raiding. They ran into the furthest corner of the lands the Hommetics claimed, where the Empire of Orphans was barely a half-day westward and there was nothing at all to the south save the vast territories of the Massatan peoples. Yulan's people. As were those who dwelled in Towers' Shadow. They were not of his kin – he had never set foot there before, or met anyone from the village – but they were of his kind. More settled than most of his folk, living beyond the main territories of their tradition and history, they nevertheless had the tongue and the look and the manner that had been his own until he was old enough to go wandering in search of something more. It was a long time since Yulan had thought of himself having any home but the Free; even so, to see the people of Towers' Shadow and hear them speak was to be invited back into memories that were more good than bad.

Those people themselves, though, were suffering through a present that had little of the good about it. That was clear as soon as Yulan saw the bare fields around the village, with their dried irrigation ditches and delicate swirls of dust dancing on the hot breeze. Far above the great cliffs of the escarpment beyond, dark vultures and buzzards swung in lazy circles. Patient. A handful of children were playing in the arid fields, scratching patterns in the dust. They stopped to watch Yulan and the others riding in. Their eyes, he noted, were sunken, their skin paler than it should have been.

The villagers came out to meet Yulan. Callotec had sent the Free – and Yulan in particular – ahead for just this: to speak to the people in their own tongue, and prepare the way for the Hommetic army close behind.

He dismounted and passed the reins to Hamdan. He bowed his head to an old woman who came forward. She was wrapped in a tan shawl despite the heat and burdened by a heavy, rusted iron key on a chain about her neck. She looked weary, and hungry. They all did. The children who watched from a nervous distance were thin. No men, save the aged. That told Yulan all he needed to know of how things stood.

"You're Massatan," the old woman said, in the language of Yulan's childhood.

"I am, mistress."

"Him too," she grunted, pointing with a blunt thumb at Hamdan, who sat silently on his horse behind Yulan.

"Him too," Yulan agreed. "The men who are coming after us are Hommetics, though. They mean to camp here for a day or two."

"So we thought. Looking for the bull-folk, are they? There are none here. None near."

"Then we and the Hommetics will pass on soon, mistress, and cause you no trouble."

"Do you have food?" she asked, looking him in the eye. Not a trace of pleading, or desperation. Just a quiet question.

"My people and I can find a little to share with you," Yulan said with a regretful half-smile, "but the man behind us, the one with the army . . . it might be best not to ask that question of him."

She nodded and looked away.

"Wolf, is he?" she murmured.

"Jackal perhaps, mistress. But he does bite."

"World's awash with jackals. You look more the lion, fit to keep them at bay."

She turned from him, and started to walk away.

"Your men are out hunting, trading, looking for food?" Yulan asked her.

"Where else would they be? Nothing for them to do here but take food out of the mouths of their children."

Yulan nodded. "It would be best if you told your people to keep to their homes these next few days. Callotec thinks himself your lord, you his people. He might be impatient of any disagreement on the matter."

As far as the Hommetic throne was concerned, the shadow of its authority fell far across the southern lands, but there were no hereditary lords here to enforce the King's law or claim his tithes as they did in other parts of the domain. Tax-takers came only now and again, and some of those who did never went home again. Dead by flood or lion, the Massatans – a people of independent instinct – would gravely and sorrowfully say, or simply lost in the wide reaches of trackless scrub and desert.

The old woman smiled at Yulan, without parting her dry, lined lips.

"Is he your lord, this Callotec?"

"No. But he is the man who pays me, today."

"Spoken like a true Massatan. You talk your own language like an outsider, but there's still some of the south in you after all. Let this man who pays you think what he will." She jabbed her thumb towards the abandoned fortification on a hilltop outside the village. "The Kingshouse has been empty for years, but if they still want to call this Hommetic land, they can. It makes no odds to us."

The Free camped on the hillock, beside the hollow

Kingshouse. Yulan always chose high ground when he could. Callotec arrayed his men on the fields below. Yulan did not know whether he would have done so even if the crops were abundant, but as it was, it hardly mattered. There was nothing to trample save the fine, dusty soil waiting for the wind to carry it off.

The trouble came with the dawn. Rudran, leader of the Free's little band of lancers, shook Yulan ungently awake.

"Up and about," the horseman hissed in his ear. "You'll want to see this, I think."

"See what?" Yulan asked, his throat sore, his lips arid. Even the air was dry enough to rob a man of moisture while he slept.

"See how Callotec's lads are amusing themselves, down in the village."

Rudran was not an eloquent or expressive man. But there was some colour to his voice and face that morning; some anger. That was enough to make Yulan hurry. He buckled his sword on as he bounded down the hill. Even in the day's barely part-formed light, he could see the crowd gathered at the edge of the village. From its sound and its indistinct, roiling motion he caught its flavour, and that made him lengthen his stride. Hamdan was the only one of the Free to keep pace with him, though he could hear others coming after them, more cautiously.

One of Callotec's warriors was flogging the headwoman of Towers' Shadow. That was what Yulan found when he barged his way his through the jeering ranks of Hommetic men. The old woman's shawl had been torn away, her tunic ripped open across her back. She was half crawling, half writhing on the ground as her assailant lashed at her with a knotted rope. Her frail, thin skin was lacerated and welted. There was blood, but not a lot; her age and weakness left little of it to spare for marking her wounds. She was shaking and twitching. Not crying out, but, Yulan suspected, dying a little more with each blow.

He reached out as he drew near to the man with the whip. Took an iron grip upon the man's wrist, and hooked his other arm around his neck. He bent almost double and threw the man over his hips, rolling him on to the ground, face down. He kept hold of the wrist, twisted it and set a foot on the shoulder joint at the root of that arm. The whip fell from spasming fingers. Another twist, just another few fragments of weight, and Yulan would break bone, or rupture that shoulder.

Villagers were running to the headwoman. In the crowd, others were wailing, or raging. Yulan knew what the people of Towers' Shadow wanted him to do. He could not give it to them.

"Oh, here we are," Hamdan murmured, still a little short of breath after the hurried descent from their camp. Yulan looked round.

"Let that man go."

The warriors had silently parted, and opened a path for Callotec to come walking slowly through and on to the clear ground between them and the village folk. He wore a heavy red robe of the sort his rich kind might don when first rising from their bed. His hair was still tousled from his slumber. His narrow chin and sharp nose did not give him a commanding presence, but Yulan caught the scent of danger, and of menace, clearly enough.

"Let *my* man go," Callotec insisted.

Yulan released his grip. His captive groaned and staggered to his feet, stumbling away with a hand clasped to his damaged shoulder.

"They have taken three of my dogs," Callotec said, staring fixedly into Yulan's eyes. "Some boys were seen carrying them off from the stables, in the night."

"The stables?" Yulan said incredulously. "You put your hunting dogs in their stables?"

Callotec might be cruel, but self-indulgence was his more striking trait. From the first, he had treated this campaign as an inconvenience to be tolerated, its rigours offset by an absurd train of attendants, wagons loaded with wine and fine food. And the hunting dogs. Thirty of them, and each standing more highly in Callotec's affections than any man under his command, as best Yulan could tell.

"Why should I not accommodate my hounds as I see fit?" Callotec rasped. "They need respite. Each is worth more than any horse that might ever have rested its legs in this midden of a place. And if even the property of the King's family is not safe from the avarice of these savages, then they are forgetful of their place and duties. I know how to remind them. I will have the thieves, or I will scourge the life from those who think the throne's command carries no more weight than a leaf on the wind."

"No," said Yulan.

"What?" Callotec said flatly.

"Take care," Hamdan whispered in Yulan's ear. "Might not be the moment to pick a fight. Not with the entire Hommetic

Kingdom. We could manage a few dozen, but five hundred's a bit beyond even us, don't you think?"

The anger tightening Yulan's throat was a rare thing. Unfamiliar in its urgency. Born, he later recognised with the boundless wisdom of hindsight, of many fathers; not the least of them his bitter regret and shame at his failure to save Merkent, and his longing to make the Free, inherited from that good man, something he would have been proud of. It all rendered him short of temper and patience. His thoughts, that day in Towers' Shadow, were not as considered, or as quick, as they might have been. But he did, at least, find the presence of mind to swallow before he spoke to Callotec, and to exile all indignation from his face and voice.

"The boys – the thieves – will be long gone by now, fleeing your wrath out into the wilds," he told the King's cousin. "Might be we come across them, in a day or two, out there somewhere. They'll not be found by whipping these know-naughts."

"You think not? *I* think these brown-skins deliver those boys to me, or they pay the price themselves. *I* think they need tutoring in the matter of respect for their betters."

"It might be so, sire, but this' – Yulan waved an arm in the direction of the prone, bloodied woman, without taking his eyes from Callotec's – "will only make it harder to get what you want. It'll close mouths, not open them. I know these people."

"Of course you do," Callotec sneered. "You're one of them. And you think they are not subject to the same laws as the rest of my cousin's subjects. You think their insolence should go unpunished, like your own, because in their abject ignorance they know no better than to behave like pigs."

Yulan had met with mockery before, on account of his Massatan heritage. More than once, when he was young and freshly come to the Hommetic heartlands, he had broken noses in answer to it. It was not something he had needed to do since he joined with the Free. That affiliation, and his own reputation, silenced any barbed tongues. But the depth and completeness of the contempt he saw in Callotec's face woke old instincts. He imagined – saw, in pleasing detail – himself surging forwards, putting a single hard blow in to the side of Callotec's face, just below the cheekbone. It would break or dislocate the man's jaw, perhaps knock loose some teeth. Certainly, it would put him down. Callotec was not the sort to withstand even a single strike. But then, he did not need to be. He was of Crex's blood. Untouchable, and he knew it.

"There are other ways to punish whatever insolence has been shown," Yulan said tightly. "Ways that need not turn the whole village against you. Against us. Our business is putting down a revolt, after all; not fomenting a fresh one."

Callotec glared at him. He did not look away. Heartbeats of silence passed. Villagers, warriors all waited, and watched.

And Callotec fluttered a dismissive hand.

"So be it. If the whip's not the answer, so be it. Only dogs, eh? Of no great consequence. That's what I'm to think?"

"That's not—' Yulan began, but Callotec had swung away, his robe swirling about his ankles.

"Enough," he snapped over his shoulder. "Enough. I'm tired. I slept badly. I'm going to rest."

The warriors drifted away in their lord's wake, back out into the fields they had claimed for their camp. The villagers closed around their damaged, wounded headwoman. Yulan knelt at her side. Her eyes were closed, the lids trembling. She breathed thinly. She had bitten through her lip, and there was blood all over her mouth and teeth.

"Jackals," she whispered, faint as a mouse in the grass.

That evening, Callotec came to the Free's camp. Yulan and the rest were seated in one great circle around a fire they had set, all of them save the few standing guard out in the dusk. They had cooked flatbreads on stones at the fireside, and ate them with a paste of ground nuts. No one had been speaking much, and Callotec's sudden arrival at the edge of the circle of firelight ensured no one would be doing so now. At his appearance, Yulan and many of the others made to rise; a great shuffling of feet.

"Stay where you are," Callotec muttered, holding his hand up. "Eat."

Yulan nodded in curt gratitude, but set aside his bread in any case. Whether by his own invitation or not, Callotec did not seem like a man to be casually disrespected.

"I have decided to forgive you your earlier impertinence," Callotec said, and Yulan could hear clearly enough the lie of that, buried just beneath the words.

"I am grateful, sire," he said, getting to his feet. Sitting in this man's presence was probably no wiser than eating, he guessed.

"Good," grunted Callotec. "Now, I require your service, and that of your men. There's word that the Sorentines, what remains of them, are in a valley half a day north. Turned back towards their own lands, if it's true. I want you to go and put eyes on them, bring me word of their strength and direction."

"All of us?" Yulan asked doubtfully.

"All of you. My men are wearied. They've done their part in finding the shepherd who told us this. Now it is for the Free to test the truth of it, and discover its meaning. That's what you're here for, is it not? It's what I'm paying you for, is it not?"

It's Crex who's promised to pay us, Yulan could have pointed out. But the contract was between the Free and Callotec, even if the gold was Crex's.

He had thirty men: Rudran and his lancers, Hamdan and his archers. Not one Clever, for the task and the enemy had not demanded it. The Sorentines, if they these days even had any Clevers amongst them save a few walking-witches, had never been inclined to use them in war. They preferred their fighting done with iron and sinew, and thirty of the Free should not need any Clevers to meet whatever such materials these Sorentines had left after Bruman Hill. Unless Callotec was knowingly sending them into a furnace. Which, Yulan grimly reflected, was not out of the question.

That was not what really concerned him. He had boundless faith in the abilities of the men he commanded, and no small amount in his own ability to lead them. On any ground, so long as they had the freedom to move and fight as they chose, he knew they should overmatch ten times their number of ill-disciplined, half-beaten Sorentines; and could escape a greater number, if it came to it. No, what worried him, and set his every instinct for trouble on edge, was the question of what might happen between Callotec's warriors and the people of Towers' Shadow while the Free were half a day away.

There was the contract, though. There was the duty to fulfil it, and to win for the Free their first gold-prize since he had become leader. An open breach with the royal family would be a disastrous, perhaps fatal, beginning to make. Crex's own cousin was issuing an instruction, and was not the sort to acquiesce in its refusal. So many times, Merkent and others had praised the sharpness and nimbleness of Yulan's wits, and yet no insight came to him there beside the Kingshouse at Towers' Shadow. He felt impotent. Bereft of choice.

And so he and his thirty men rode out, in search of the dregs of a rebellion that had already failed.

They found the bull in a vale of wispy yellow grass, treeless and open. It was folded down, as if it had settled there to sleep. There was an evening light on it, stretching its shadow out over the ground. Its blood had put a deeper darkness on to the grass around the stump of its neck. It had blackened there, and dried to a crust.

Yulan stood by the bull's severed head. A huge and heavy thing, with horns almost as long as his forearm. It lay tilted slightly to one side. The eyes were gone, and most of the tongue. The carrion birds that had claimed them soared overhead, waiting for these intruders who had disturbed their feasting to depart. Yulan flicked a hand to ward the swarming flies away from his face.

"What do you see?" he called out to Hamdan, kneeling a dozen paces away.

"There were maybe fifty of them," the archer said thoughtfully. "Perhaps a dozen mounted. They all moved off northward after they killed the bull. Not hurrying."

Yulan wiped his fingers over his brow, smearing away sweat and the dust of a long ride.

"Bring your bow boys in, then," he said. "I think we can call this done."

Hamdan straightened and whistled, the piercing note lancing out across the wide valley. His men, dotted across the whole expanse, searching like him for footsign, turned as one and began trotting back.

"No point in chasing them once they've killed the bull," Yulan muttered to himself as he leaned down and took hold of one of the horns.

He lifted the bull's head, permitting himself a fleeting grimace at the great bony weight of it, and carried it back towards the horses. So it was, and had always been, with the Sorentines: they made a bull the totem of their war, and when they judged that war done – won, lost or simply no longer of interest – they killed the beast and went back to their homes.

Yulan rested the head across his horse's shoulders.

"Perhaps the sight of this will persuade Callotec that we're finished," he said to Rudran.

"Perhaps," the big man said gruffly. "You seen that yet?"

He twisted about in his saddle, pointing back the way they had come. Back towards Towers' Shadow. Yulan looked, realising as he did so that all of Rudran's men were already faced that way, staring at the horizon.

A thin column of pale smoke was rising into the sky, far away. Going straight up.

"That stupid thrice-bastard," murmured Yulan, feeling a knot clenching in his chest. Knowing, in his deepest bones, that he had become part of something terrible. "How long's that been there?"

"Just started," Rudran grunted. "But we're a long ride away."

The Free came down upon Towers' Shadow from the north, riding horses all but spent. They came in the first of the day, with the morning's cold, sharp light on their flanks and the angry yellow glare of flames before them.

Half of Towers' Shadow was already gone, sent into black ruin by the fires. A few cottages were still alight, pouring out smoke that churned and swirled above the village. The Hommetic army was scattered all across the fields surrounding the village. Not arrayed as warriors might be for battle, but strewn like a disorderly crowd observing a contest or fight. They stood in small groups, some cheering or laughing, others simply watching in silence. They stood amongst bodies, some of them.

There were old men, dead, at the edge of the village. They must have come out to defend their homes. Old men with pitchforks and crude spears and skinning knives against Callotec and his army. Women had died too, Yulan saw as he rode into the village. His nose burned with the stench of smoke and ash and death, and it sickened him as it never had before. It made him feel weak. He had the bull's severed head sitting before him on his horse's shoulders; one hand on the reins, one hand resting on the bull's brow, between the horns. His fingers were pressing ever harder against the skull, he realised. As if they wanted to gouge their way through the bone.

He looked into the face of a Massatan woman slumped against the blackened stub of a roof timber. She looked just like his mother's sister. There were arrows in her chest, and stomach, and mouth. He slowed his horse to a walk, feeling it trembling from exhaustion beneath him. Thought that perhaps he too trembled, for other reasons. He could hear the crackle of flame, and the dull excitement of the warriors around the village, and people crying, people wailing. And the yipping of dogs, those accursed hounds of Callotec's. They were here somewhere amongst the houses, but he could not see them.

The headwoman's body was in the centre of the village, stretched out on the ground. She must have been dragged from her sickbed. She had been trampled by horses. Her corpse, ignored as it lay there, was misshapen. Crushed. Yulan could see the imprint of hoofs on the bandages her whip-wounds had been bound in. He could see the shape of hoofs in the hollows and dents punched into her back, her skull.

Callotec was standing close by, with a dozen or more of his guard. He was surveying the wreckage of Towers' Shadow, with a crude smile upon his face. He turned this way and that, spun about, and then saw Yulan coming.

"I found them, those little thieves," Callotec shouted. "Do you know what they did with the three dogs they stole from me?"

Yulan knew. He had known from the moment he heard of the theft. But he said nothing. He let his horse drift slowly closer to Callotec.

"They butchered them," Callotec spat. "And ate them. Hounds bred over generations by my family to be the finest hunters in the land. Hounds worth more than this entire village. They *ate* them."

"They are starving," Yulan said dully, though he knew it would do no good.

"Starving?" screeched Callotec. "Then I've rid them of some mouths to feed, have I not? I've saved them from their hunger."

"You have done enough."

"And who are you to tell me so?"

"I am Captain of the Free," Yulan cried, and he flung the great bull's head down at Callotec's feet. Then he leaned down, stretching as close as he could to this cousin to a king, this butcher who dressed like a lord. "And in their name I say you have done enough here. That head tells you this war is over. You should listen to its message, and I'll open your ears to it if you make me. You might have five hundred men at your back, but I have the Free and I'll gladly test the two in the balance if that's what you want."

He was aware of Rudran and Hamdan and all the rest spreading out beside and behind him. They formed a line. He heard blades unsheathing, arrows slipping from quivers. He saw Callotec's eyes flicker from side to side. A gust of hot wind sent a curl of smoke writhing down around the bull's horns. The hunting hounds were snarling and yelping, somewhere not far away. Demented, to Yulan's ear; just like their master and his blood-maddened host.

"Which side of the scale do you think is the weightier, king's cousin?" Yulan said. "Thirty of the Free, or five hundred of your dogs? Which side do you think has more men on it who truly know how to kill, and how to die with honour if need be?"

Callotec gave a snorting, strangled laugh, and backed up a few quick steps. His guards thickened about him. Yulan curled his lip in contempt.

"The Free have never been party to this kind of madness," he spat at Callotec. "You'd not have done it had we been here. You'd do well to remember that, now that we are."

Callotec's glare was as laden with hatred and fury as any Yulan had ever met. There was nothing behind those eyes but pride and utter indifference to the sentiment or fate of others, he suspected. The man was worthless, and thought himself precisely the opposite.

"Oh, I yield, great Captain, if that's what you want to hear," Callotec cried at last, with an exaggerated flourish of his arms. "Does that make you feel like a fell and terrible warlord? It should not. I remain a royal cousin, and you just a brown-skinned savage like these peasants here. It's done. I'm done here."

He took a few steps forward and kicked the bull's head with the toe of a fine polished boot.

"We can go home," he snapped. "No one welcomes that prospect more than I."

An eruption of growling and snapping made Yulan turn. A writhing knot of Callotec's hunting dogs had spilled out from between two houses that had survived the flames. They were fighting, all of them trying to fasten teeth on to a thick, pale stick.

"Get your dogs out of the village," hissed Yulan.

But even as he spoke, his vision was tightening upon the object over which the dogs fought. The sounds of the moment – the crackle of fire, the voices of anguish or glee, even the deep-throated snarling of the dogs themselves – fell away from him, and for an instant he was entirely alone, cut off from everything save the sight of that child's arm. It had been torn off at the elbow, leaving a stub of bone and trailing tendon and muscle. Along the length of the forearm, the skin was shredded, hanging in tatters. Some of the fingers were gone.

Slowly, heavily, Yulan turned towards Callotec.

The King's cousin bared his teeth, taking steps backwards into the protection of his swordsmen. He held his arms out, spread his palms.

"What?" he said. "It seemed a fitting kind of justice. Dogs must eat too. Half a dozen Massatan brats made for a fine—"

Yulan stabbed his heels into his horse's flanks, and the animal surged forward. He set his hand on the hilt of his sword. But then his horse was twisting and veering to the side, as Rudran lunged in and pulled the reins from his grasp.

"Not the moment," the lancer hissed to his captain.

Yulan blinked, barely understanding what was being said to him.

"Us dying'll not mend anything, no matter how many of them we take with us," Rudran insisted, staring deep into Yulan's eyes. "There'll be another day for the mending."

Yulan breathed, felt the smoke in his chest. He hung his head, and let his sword slip back into its scabbard.

The Free did not travel the same road as Callotec's men away from Towers' Shadow. Yulan did not trust himself, or Callotec, or anyone, to keep even a hateful semblance of peace. So as the Hommetic army crawled back along the Old Threetower Road – a derelict highway, but the only route even half fit for their wagons – Yulan led the Free up and away over rough ground and older, fainter trails.

He stopped his horse on a rise in the rolling hills, the last from which they could see Towers' Shadow, and looked back to the dark, crippled village in the distance. The others rode on in dour silence, save Hamdan, who waited.

"I brought him here," said Yulan quietly, to himself as much as to the archer. "He made me his herald."

He knew, even then, that this was a guilt, and a shame, he would never shed. His bitter anger might fade. The knowledge that this, his first endeavour as leader of the Free, had brought no honour to their name, and fallen far short of what Merkent would have wanted, might be accommodated. Might even make him a better captain, if he could learn from it. But there would never be anything, no future deed or glory, that would undo or answer his utter failure of the people of Towers' Shadow. His own people. He could have guessed what might happen – not its detail, but its shape – if he had allowed himself. For that, there would be no forgiveness. Not from his own heart.

One night in the wilds, still days from their destination, he cut the hair from his head. He shaved his scalp, leaving only a single long horse-tail that he bound up into a topknot. No one asked him why. He was grim and silent through all that journey, and something in his mood made everyone fearful to approach him. So no one asked him, and no one knew, why he left his black hair on the ground by the remains of a campfire, far from anywhere. No one knew except Hamdan, and he did not need to ask. He was Massatan too. He recognised and understood the trappings of penitence.

Yulan saw Callotec only once more after Towers' Shadow. He would have made it never if he could, but the creature cornered him in a gilded passageway of Crex's palace. There were great bay windows looking out over the lake, where bones were said to lie thick beneath the waves. Callotec was lurking in one of those bays. Lurking in ambush, Yulan realised, and could not help but reach instinctively for his sword as Callotec stepped out in front of him. But the noble's only weapon was a venomous tongue, not a blade.

"So you came not just to take the King's gold, but to whisper your bile into his ear, did you?" Callotec said.

"I took only one third the gold we were promised," Yulan said through clenched teeth, "and would have taken none, if I could have done it without punishing my men for a failure that was all mine."

"But you thought to punish me, didn't you?"

Callotec jabbed a finger at Yulan's chest as he spoke. It would have been easy enough to catch it and break it backward. But all Yulan wanted was to be gone, and to banish this man from his sight for ever.

"Crex mocked me, and called me Dog-Lord, and told me I'm to command a Kingshouse out on the Narbonan shore," Callotec snarled.

"I'm sure you'll thrive there."

"It's exile, and you know it. You have cost me my standing, my . . . everything."

"I have?" Yulan had to fight the anger rising within him. "No. The King asked me what I had seen, and I told him. That is all, sire."

"And he takes the word of a sell-sword over that of his own family. He lets your malice persuade him to injustice, to my dishonour."

"He takes the word of the Captain of the Free. And he hardly needed persuading, truth be told. He did not seem overly surprised that the man he sent to quell a rebellion came close to starting another one. Angry, but not surprised. I think it pleased him, sire, to be given the chance to rid himself of you, your cruelty and your worthless indolence."

The barbs, the acid, Yulan put into his voice were unwise but the fury roiling inside, against himself as much as Callotec, would admit of no restraint. He was tired, and feeling Merkent's loss as keenly as if it had happened yesterday, so he goaded the man.

The blush that coloured Callotec's face, and the quiver in his lips, told him that his contempt had found its mark. He was surprised, though, at how quickly Callotec mastered himself. How sharply his eyes narrowed and gleamed with fell malice. He spat at Yulan's feet.

"Enjoy your moment, sell-sword. You've done nothing, and changed nothing. I'll tell you a secret ... no, not a secret. A promise. Tides ebb and flow, but they do not change the nature of the sea. I am of royal blood, and nothing you can do will alter that. The tide will bring me back, and lift me up again." Callotec leaned close to whisper, and though Yulan longed to back away, he did not. "When it does, know this: I'll see you on a gibbet like the peasant you are, and I'll go back to Towers' Shadow and finish what I started. I'll go hunting with a hundred dogs next time, not just thirty, and they'll be the best fed hounds in all the land by the time I'm done. I'll see every man, woman and child in that cesspit dead, and burn every shack I left standing, and I'll plough the offal and bones into the ground with the ashes. And I'll take greater pleasure than you can imagine in doing it."

"You won't do any of that, Callotec," Yulan said coldly.

He brushed past, and walked slowly and steadily away. His footsteps echoed from the flagstone floor and the bare, hard walls.

"You think not?" Callotec called after him, almost shrieking. "I don't make promises lightly."

Yulan stopped. His anger, Callotec's madness, the smothering weight of those few days at Towers' Shadow; it was all like cloying mud at his ankles, trying to pull him back. Refusing, utterly, to let him go. He turned around. Walked back to stand close to the Dog-Lord and stare into his glittering, mad eyes.

"Nor do I," Yulan said. "And yes, I think you will never do any of those things, because I will not permit it."

He walked on, out into the streets, where the stench was of manure and dirt and workshops, and sweeter by far than that of the palace.

Yulan did not look at those around the fire. He did not want them to see anything in his face, or eyes, that would sway the choice they made. Because he knew them as well as he knew anyone in the world, he knew – or at the least suspected – what each one of them would say, and why. He wished it were otherwise, but he could not make it so by will alone.

Hamdan spoke first, of course.

"Well, I'll be going along. Cannot think of anything I'd rather be doing with my last days with the Free, and that's the purest truth you ever heard on my lips."

He said it lightly, as if Yulan had proposed that they go gathering apples in an orchard. The ire was in him, though. Yulan knew that better than any of them. He had never doubted Hamdan's response to this. Even if it had not been Callotec, and Towers' Shadow, Hamdan would have said the same thing. Yulan suspected they would never be parted, the two of them; and if they were, it would likely not be by Hamdan's choice.

The other one whose response he had been certain of was Akrana.

"I too," she duly said.

Because she did not want the Free to end, Yulan knew.

He looked at the archers, one by one, and one by one they nodded. Hamdan had taught them their trade, led them for years. Their loyalty to him was unquestioned. This too Yulan had known would be as it was. Which left Wren, and Kerig, and there Yulan's certainty failed. These two had more to lose, more to seek elsewhere, than the rest. They had been ready to walk away from the Free with the least regret, for they could imagine a future for themselves with a clarity, and a joy, that Yulan envied almost beyond words.

Wren smiled at him. She absently set a hand on her husband's arm. Glanced at his sleeping face.

"I don't think I need to wake him," she said. "He'd only say it was my choice, in any case."

One or two of the archers chuckled at the truth in that.

"And he'd say he would go with you. We both would. You've been the best leader the Free's ever had, Yulan. Just two men dead in all the time you've been captain. You've made us rich, you've kept us alive, you've outgrown what happened at Towers'

Shadow. But perhaps you need to go back there. If so, we'll go with you. Of course we will. There'll be time enough for tilling the earth after one last ride."

"Someone's coming," Hamdan observed casually. "Doing it clumsy and alone, so not a worry."

From the gathering darkness, a slight figure emerged clutching a leather parchment case in both hands before him, with a spear folded into the crook of his arm. It was the youth who had guided Yulan down from this ridge earlier, to Creel's tent. Who had been at Creel's side in the fighting the day before. He stood there outside the circle, uncertain.

"Well?" Yulan asked, already guessing the answer.

"Lord Creel sent me," the youth said hesitantly.

He held out the scroll case, as if it were some badge or pennant that would explain everything. Which it did, in its way.

"He says I'm the contract-holder. I'm to go with you."

As he stretched his arms out, his spear slipped from its lodging at his elbow and fell to the ground. He hurriedly bent to retrieve it.

Akrana snorted. "So we're riding with children now?"

The newcomer blushed with either anger or embarrassment – perhaps both – as he straightened.

"I'm not a child," he protested, but even he did not sound as if he entirely believed it.

6

On The Road To Harvekka

On the road to Harvekka, men – the King's men – had been gathered. They had been gathered and stripped of their clothes and hung from gibbets. An old cart track curved away from the cobbled road, and there, at the point where the two separated, twenty freshly made gallows were clustered. A nasty little copse.

They had been big men, most of them. Warriors. Armsmen of the King. Strong-limbed, but now loose and reduced by death. Birds had found them, and taken from them much that was soft. Eyes, and lips; cheeks and tongues. Manhood. Time and the weather had begun to remove what the birds had not yet claimed. A darkening and a diminishing and a rotting was under way.

Morue, Mistress of the School, looked up into one of those corrupted faces. It was difficult to say, in the dimming twilight and through the mask of corporeal decay, but she thought she had known the man while he lived. Not a warrior this, if so; a tithe-tallier. A scratcher with quills in the King's service. If it was indeed the man she remembered, he had been rather timorous, but lively of mind. Possessed of a wife and three children – and where might they be now? she wondered. Harmless in himself, but a burden to those who drew his attention. They had taken the opportunity of revolt to unburden themselves. The tithe-tallier hung there amidst the swordsmen, his discoloured corpse swaying very slightly beneath the gentle breeze.

Morue turned her horse away and moved on towards Harvekka. Angers, once set free, found many places to set their claws. It was in their nature. It was also profoundly regrettable, but that which was regrettable could not always be prevented. Sometimes it might even be necessary, as a purgative.

She would have commanded her Clade escort – multitudinous, as befitted the times – to cut down the corpses and give them burial or cremation, had the day not been short and their destination still a long hour away. They had left Armadell-on-Lake with the dawn, and would not reach Harvekka before darkness was gathering. A draining journey, more normally completed in two full days. But the School, and therefore she as its mistress, was required to be in all places at once during these fraught days. She had, long ago, been told that the sandfolk of the distant south used the same word, with an obscurely different inflection, to mean both change and danger. It was not an absurd idea.

By twisting about in the saddle and scanning the horizon, she could have counted three titanic columns of dirty brown-black smoke climbing the sky. The sharp, dry scent of them was draped across the land. The village of Surmet was burning, half a dozen miles inland. Behind, towards Armadell-on-Lake, the jetties and float-houses along a stretch of the Kurn River were still smouldering, as they had been for three days now. Ahead, something was on fire in Harvekka.

The road at last began to descend from the low hills and twist its way down on to the coastal lowlands where Harvekka stood. A man awaited them there, at the first sinking of the track. His feet rested on the cobbles, his backside on the thin grass. A long sword lay across his knees. He was carefully weaving strands of grass into a cord or bracelet. He had a handsome face, though it was dirty with soot and perhaps blood.

The front half of his scalp bore only a dense, dark stubble. From the rear half woven braids hung, matted and heavy, to his shoulders. Each braid was weighted with a single stone bead, some of them white, some black. It was a style affected by the corsairs of the Mule Isles, but this man was no corsair.

In the roadway before him lay a body. Another was in the grass behind and beyond him. His horse, its mane braided and beaded just as his hair was, stood close by that second corpse, quietly cropping the meagre sward. Its reins hung loose. He had not bothered to tether or hobble it.

Morue raised a hand to halt her retinue. She let her horse advance at its own leisurely pace until it drew close to the man at the roadside. It stopped then, not at her command but because it did not like that body lying in the middle of the road. It had little experience of the dead; until recently, at least.

The man looked up. The beads in his hair tapped gently against one another.

"Mistress," he said placidly.

"Sullen."

He rose, letting that meticulously crafted rope of woven grass

fall away, taking his sword in one hand and the halter of
Morue's horse in the other. Looking into his face, now that he
was close, Morue could see that there was indeed blood on his
cheeks. Not his, of course. It was never his. The man who commanded the School's Clade had a gift for shedding the blood of
others, and preserving his own.

"What happened here?" she asked him.

"Robbers. They're a plague in these parts now. They thought
me just another straggler, easy of the taking. I did try to convince them otherwise, but . . . well, as you see."

"You should have brought some of your men with you,"
Morue muttered, a trifle irritated. She could guess just how
little Sullen would have exerted himself in the avoidance of violence. "If you had been accompanied, there would have been no
need for this."

Sullen shrugged. "I thought you might appreciate discretion,
so I came alone."

The Mistress of the School exhaled wearily through her nose
and stared ahead, down the road. Beyond the yellow, brown,
green patchwork of fields, gridded by irrigation channels and
canals, Harvekka was an irregular encrustation upon the coast.
She could see, now, that the tower of smoke there was rising
from somewhere near the docks.

"Is the city safe?" she asked.

Sullen looked that way too. He patted the flat of his sword
against his leg absently.

"Safe enough. The rebels have won; the King's men are dead
or gone, hiding or turning their coats. What happens next is
getting decided."

Which is why I'm here, Morue did not need to say.

"Good." She glanced back over her shoulder, to ensure that none of her companions, none of Sullen's own Clade men, were within earshot. "And what of other matters? What of *the* other matter?"

"They've not been found yet," Sullen said flatly, as he said almost everything. "It is . . . frustrating."

"Frustrating? If we don't find them, and soon, ruin follows." She flicked an arm out towards the city on the shore. "Everything might burn. All that's happened these last few months will have been for nothing, and will be *as* nothing to what comes after. So, yes: frustrating. You might call it that, Sullen."

She was distracted by an abrupt groan, tenuous, like a thought only partway become sound, rising from the longer grass away from the road. She saw a dark shape there, moving very slightly. Without that faint movement, she would not have seen it at all, or would have thought it just a rock. As she watched, and as Sullen turned to look, an elbow crooked up out of the grass. Someone trying, and failing, to lift himself up.

"It seems one of your assailants survived your acquaintance," Morue muttered.

"No," said Sullen. "He's dead, sure enough; just hasn't understood it yet. I loosed his guts from his belly. Please excuse me for a moment, Mistress."

He strode towards the crippled man, hefting that long blade.

Morue averted her eyes, watching the smoke rise from Harvekka. Sullen was a regrettable man. Profoundly so. But necessary. So she chose to believe.

7

House-Dog's Puppy

Creel's contract-holder – Drann, his name had turned out to be – was no great rider. No rider at all, really. Yulan was not surprised. Farmers such as this boy's family must be might have a horse for hauling a plough or a wagon, but not for riding. That would be a waste when they seldom had anywhere more than a few miles away that needed the going.

Probably ridden a plough horse's broad back now and again as a child, Yulan would guess. Just as probably, never laid foot or buttock on stirrup or saddle. As a result, he was no doubt already, less than a day out from Creel's camp, being assailed by a wide range of discomforts. Yulan wondered if the youth knew just how far those discomforts might in time ascend towards the heights of real pain.

It was a poor choice on Creel's part, this selection of contract-holder. The lord must have had his reasons – he was seldom short of them for anything he did – but this journey would be fast and hard, which meant Drann would find it, and the Free, unforgiving. For all the preoccupations crowding Yulan's head, he could spare a little corner of it to feel briefly sorry for the boy. He had the look of a hoper, a longer. One of those who thought the Free something wonderful. Something for him. He would discover the untruth of that soon enough. Of them all, Hamdan was the only one who might give him a welcome, and that would be for reasons to do with other times, other people. The Free was no place for hopers.

Especially not ones who really could not ride with even the slightest hint of grace. Or facility, Yulan thought wincingly as Drann swayed one more time in the saddle, or confidence, stability; without any attribute, in fact, that might be of value in a horseman save a certain mulish persistence. He would fall off eventually. That, or he would aggravate his long-suffering mount beyond its patience – and they had given him the most imperturbably patient one they had to hand – and it would be off and away, flinging him into a gully and racing for freedom. After a couple of hours, Yulan beckoned Akrana, and when she drew up alongside him, he whispered blunt instruction to her. Without comment, she trotted on ahead, and without explanation, without even looking at him, attached a cord to the halter of Drann's horse, and led both it and him on the end of that tether.

Yulan could read Drann's indignation in the stiffness of his back and his refusal to so much as look at Akrana, as if she might disappear should he ignore her for long enough. Poor lad. No doubt more than a little unsettled by her, too. No shame in that. Yulan had known great warriors, great bluff oafs, to be cowed by Akrana's cold and haughty indifference. She tended to leave folk feeling drenched in chill contempt merely by looking at them.

Between Yulan and Drann rode Kerig and Wren, side by side.

"I'll not have a thing to do with goats," Kerig was muttering. "They're foul, stinking beasts with the temperament of spoiled children."

"You'll have a natural affinity for them, then."

"Oh, steady me before my laughter pitches me off this nag."

"Why are you so cruel to me?" Wren moaned with a petulance that Yulan recognised as playful, flirtatious. "We'll have enough land that you'll never need to see my goats. Not even hear them. Why can't you just let me have what I want?"

"Because *I* don't want a wife who smells of goat," Kerig muttered darkly.

There was a muffled thump as Wren punched him playfully in the shoulder. You might think the excitements of Creel's camp had never happened, that no harm had been done, to hear the two of them chattering.

But then Kerig laughed, and the laugh turned into a hacking cough, and then into a long, gloomy silence. The harm was still there, in more ways than one. Kerig had reached deep into the entelech in his attempt on the Weaponsmith, and paid the price. It would be days before he was hale and hearty again, and even then some small part of him, his vigour and life, would never return. That was how Clevers did what they did.

And it would be more days before Yulan allowed him to think he was forgiven his indiscretion. He knew why Kerig needed the Weaponsmith dead. He approved it, as a cause. But not when it endangered all of the Free. Not when it set personal desire over duty to the company. Some things had to wait until later, until there was no one else to be caught up in the turbulent wake of debts being settled. Yulan would have one or two of those debts to settle himself, even after Callotec was tidied away.

That, of course, was the grit in Yulan's eye. The nagging, accusatory whisper deep in his skull, probing away in there as it searched for weakness. He had allowed these eleven people – twelve, if Drann counted – to be caught in the wake of his own debt. They all thought they had some stake in setting right what had happened at Towers' Shadow, in the name of the Free and its honour. Yulan had never shed the notion that the debt, and the penance it required, was his alone. Yet he was their captain, and they chose to follow him now; thus he must lead, and must bring them home safe to White Steading. That must be his entire purpose, and he set his mind to concentrating upon it to the exclusion of all else. The Free had made him who he was. He owed it, its every man and woman, everything. There was nothing he would not do to bring it and its people safely to its final willing dissolution.

Drann could hardly believe that he rode with the Free. A house-dog's puppy amongst wolves. Not just any wolves; *the* wolves, whose like had never been seen. He only hoped that he could get through the day without coming loose from atop his lurching horse and cracking his head open on the ground before their very eyes.

Wolves and monsters. He could hear the constant creak and rumble of the wagon that bore the Clamour, grinding along at the rear of the little column. Pebbles cracked and popped beneath its iron-shod wheels. Drann had still not seen the face of the driver – Hestin, he now knew she was called – for it stayed all day in the shadow of her leaf-made hood. He had heard not a single word, no sound of any kind, emerge from that shadow. Not that any of the Free seemed inclined to talk to him, or around him.

He had somehow expected banter, even merriment. Adventurers embarking upon a new adventure should give some little sign of excitement, surely? Apparently not. The mood was subdued, purposeful rather than anticipatory. Kerig and Wren teased and taunted one another a little. Once or twice, Drann had met Hamdan's eye and received a more or less warm smile or nod from the archer. Other than that, he had to confess, he did not feel entirely welcome. It was disappointing.

"Stop there, boy," Creel had shouted.

Drann's heart had trembled at the cry. He should never have been there, in that tent, witnessing those exchanges. Terrible punishments would follow, he was certain.

"You're the lad who didn't run away, aren't you?" Creel said, squinting at him.

It did not seem a hostile regard. Not yet, anyway.

"Yes, sire," Drann managed to say.

"The one who lay on top of me when some whore's whelp was trying to gut me. The one who felled himself with a tree."

Drann nodded.

"What are you doing here?"

"He . . . the Captain wanted to know where your tent was," said Drann, as if that explained and excused everything.

Creel grunted. He pulled a sheet of parchment from inside his jerkin and spread it on the little table. He unfolded a small square of leather, to reveal a smear of black ink. Carefully, he rolled the ball of his thumb in the ink and then pressed it to the bottom of the parchment, leaving a smudged, indistinct print there. Then he took a ring from his left hand, delicately gathered ink upon the embossed design that adorned it and made that mark too.

"Might be you saved my life, up on that knoll yesterday," the lord of Mondoon said, just as Drann was starting to hope he had been forgotten or dismissed.

"I don't think so, sire."

Creel glared at him.

"Idiot. Wit-short peasant. A lord muses that you might have saved his life, and you dispute it? Did your mother raise a buffoon? If she was here, she'd scold you for such wanton spitting in the face of fortune, wouldn't she? She should. She should."

"Yes, sire," agreed Drann, far too alarmed and bewildered to think of anything more apt.

Creel rummaged amongst the sacks in the corner of the wide tent. Drann could hear the clinking of coins, stirring in their beds. The lord of Mondoon produced a tubular case. He rolled up parchment he had marked and slipped it inside. Then he strode over and slapped it against Drann's chest, holding it there expectantly until Drann recovered himself sufficiently to grasp it himself.

"Might be you saved my life," Creel repeated gruffly, "so you get to be my contract-holder to the Free. It's a reward, of sorts, though it remains to be seen whether you'll thank me for it. But there's this: the contract-holder gets a little taste of the prize, once the work is done. A *very* little taste, mind you. Big enough to make a farm boy happy, though. His whole family, most like. Now do you think you saved my life back there?"

"Yes, sire," Drann said. "I think I might have done."

"Good. Now you listen close," Creel rasped into his face. "This contract doesn't leave your sight. It's what gives the Free the right to do what they're going to do. Anyone questions that right, you show them this, you tell them the Free are acting for me. All lawful, all paid for, in accordance with their charter."

"I understand."

"Say it like I'm supposed to believe it, boy. You're there to vouch for the Free on my behalf, so say it heart-strong if you're going to say it at all."

"I understand."

Drann was not entirely convinced he did fully understand the responsibility being bestowed upon him; but he *was* entirely convinced that now was not the moment to parade his uncertainties. He had no idea whether or not he could refuse this duty, but it hardly mattered, since he did not want to. To ride with the Free, after all, would be the stuff of childhood dreams. Unimaginable.

"Did you tell me your name yet?" Creel demanded.

"I'm not sure, sire. It's Drann."

"Is it," Creel grunted. "Unmemorable sort of name. Perhaps you did tell me before. Anyway, you and Yulan bring me Callotec – alive and whole or just his head, I don't much mind – and return the contract to me. I pay. That's all there is to it. You'll find me in Armadell-on-Lake, likely as not, conferring with my dear and loyal friends on the Council."

"Yes, sire. Uh . . . are they going to do it, though? It sounded as if—"

"Oh, they'll do it all right," Creel said dismissively. "Yulan will, therefore the rest of them will. Sharp as he is, even he doesn't grasp how doggishly they'd follow him anywhere. You go up there . . . oh, around dusk, I should say, and present your-self. They'll be making ready by then."

Drann nodded.

"No later, mind," growled Creel, wagging a stern finger at him. "I don't want them or you anywhere near here by dawn. I can smell trouble making itself, the way Yulan ran out of here. It's always making itself when the Free are about."

Which, Drann had thought then and did now as he rode along with the Free, was entirely as it should be. Troubles should surely flock about the Free like crows about a dead lamb, or they would not be worthy of their reputation. He did not know what was going to happen, but that it would be bigger and grander than anything his short life had offered thus far must be beyond doubt. And if it was truly to be the last ride of the Free, he had somehow, by blind good fortune, found him-self a part of history, and of tales to be told by Old Emmins yet to come.

He just hoped he would not fall off his horse in front of them all before the great events began to unfold.

The Free camped by a stream, beneath a canopy of soft, graceful trees. The exhaustion that overtook Drann as he half fell, half dismounted from the horse was as numbing and dumbing as any fever. It left him shambling about the campsite like some drunken sheep, unable to help in any meaningful way. Not that the Free needed, or wanted, any help. They worked in silent, practised unison to tether and feed the horses, set a fire, lay out bedrolls, refill empty water skins. As soon as Drann recognised that nobody cared what he did, he sat in the grass, drifting into a grateful doze.

He stirred from it only when someone pressed a hot, dry meal-cake into his hand. He muttered thanks, but was too bleary-eyed to note who had given it to him. He regretted that, since it was the first small generous gesture any of them had made towards him. He would have liked to know whose it was. He knew all their faces now, save Hestin's, and most of their names.

As he blinked and cleared his vision, he realised he was sitting with the Free in a great circle about the crackling fire. Embers of gleaming ash were rushing up into the dark sky. More meal-cakes were still baking on flat stones propped up near the flames, filling the air with their nutty, smoky aroma. No one spoke. They ate, or drank, or watched the fire. The sharp heat flushed Drann's face even as he felt the cool night at his back.

That warmth and that meagre ration of food sent Drann sinking back into a dreamlike cocoon. Only fragments of what came after reached him; passing glimpses of the moments he was living.

Wren dancing, amidst tendrils of smoke and glimmering fire-sparks, to the trilling tune of a flute played by one of the archers. Smiling as she danced, a smile of weightless pleasure. She seemed then as beautiful as any woman Drann had ever seen, with her pale skin, her loose brown hair. Others laughing, clapping. Though he could not be sure, Drann thought he laughed too, for it seemed a wonderful thing to him.

Lying, later, on his side beneath a rough blanket. Plagued by aching limbs, but knowing it was not the pain that had roused him from incipient slumber, but some sound. Hearing it again, and seeing the dark, squat shape of the Clamour's wagon out just beyond the reach of the dwindling firelight. A guttural, snuffling rasp of sound – perhaps a breath rattling through spittle – coming from beneath those canvas covers. Drann shivered, and rolled stiffly over.

Opening his eyes, the fire more glow than flame now, looking across the circle of sleepers to see beyond that glow a shape, and a movement, that his sleep-fuddled mind could not at first explain.

It was Wren, astride Kerig; the blanket draped across her shoulders hiding all but her face and hair, and she rising and falling, swaying. Drann watched, and dreamed himself seeing another dance. Wren's head turned slowly, and though he could not see the detail of her eyes, he knew she was looking into his. And she shook her head slightly, gently. He rolled again, to face out into the night once more, and as he went, he saw Kerig's hand rising smoothly, touching her mouth, slipping a fingertip between her lips and turning her back and down to him.

Drann woke to strange sounds and a cold dew. The moisture beaded his brow. He wiped it away and lifted himself up on his elbow. It was movement enough to make his body sing with stiff agonies, every muscle protesting at the mere suggestion that it should do something. He made a self-pitying sound and sank back. The grey, lifeless light told him the day had barely begun. He needed, by his estimation, another five or six hours of sleep to feel even part rested.

He could hear finches twittering in the bushes along the stream, but that was not the sound he found strange. Nor was it the rustling and clattering and muted conversation of the Free as they quickly and efficiently broke camp around him. Behind all that, separated from it, was a rapping of sticks, stamping of feet, grunts of exertion.

He turned achingly on to his side. On the grass at the very edge of the stream, Yulan and Akrana were sparring. They moved more quickly and more smoothly than Drann would have thought possible, and though they wielded only wooden clubs they did so with a violence that looked more like battle than practice. Their feet slid and stamped on the dew-slick grass. Yulan was naked to the waist, his pale brown skin overlaid with sweat. His arms and torso were hard, sculpted from smooth stone. Marred here and there by old scars. His single length of hair was unbound, falling to his back.

Akrana matched her captain in concentration and force. Every bone-bruising blow he sought to land on her was met, parried, returned with equal conviction. Never in his life had Drann seen a woman who was also a warrior, let alone a warrior of such evident ability. He could not tell which was the better fighter. Both seemed unnaturally accomplished to him. Each seemed utterly committed to doing the other violence.

Hamdan kicked Drann in the backside.

"Don't admire the scenery, lad. We don't catch this Hommetic weasel before he crosses the border, you could be a slave of the Orphans this time next year. That or dead as a throat-cut sow. They like making corpses even more than they like making slaves. Lazy's not the game to be playing now."

The man was a good head shorter than Yulan. He had a good deal more black hair, though; flat and tight on his head, neat and short about his chin. And his voice, for all it had the same rounded accent as the Captain's, bore a good deal more humour and verve.

Drann struggled to his feet, hobbled by his rebellious body's resistance. As his blanket fell away, the morning's still cold air took hold of him and he shivered. Even that hurt.

He inadvertently caught sight of the very horse upon which he had spent so many painful hours the previous day. It had an oat bag strapped over its muzzle, but to his suspicious eyes it appeared to be, very clearly and pointedly, watching him. Its gaze, Drann decided, had a baleful quality. His heart sank.

Hamdan laughed. He slapped Drann on the back, which pushed him into a forward stumble and a further chorus of muscular agonies.

Yulan came to them, wiping sweat from his chest with his bunched shirt.

"Want to reach Curmen well before nightfall," he said to Hamdan. "You ride on ahead and make sure there's no surprises for us there; and that we don't come as too much of a surprise to them. Make sure Ordeller's got a feed ready for us and for the horses. We'll be no more than an hour behind you."

"Ha! Ordeller. The Ape's Mother. You'll like her, son," Hamdan told Drann. Then to Yulan: "I'll take this one with me."

Drann, though still bleary-eyed, saw the flicker of doubtful reluctance in Yulan's normally composed face quite clearly.

"Akrana can keep an eye on him here."

Drann felt a twinge of despondency at that, and was pleased to see Hamdan roll his eyes.

"What's the boy done to earn such cruelty? Look at him. He's on the verge of death already. Poor broken thing. I'll take him along, teach him a bit of riding. Having the contract to hand might do no harm in smoothing our way into Curmen, anyway. You know how nervous folks get when we turn up unexpectedly."

Yulan shook his head, regarding Drann through narrowed eyes. Drann was uncertain whether any response was expected of him, but he gave a little nod just in case it might make a difference. He saw no sign that it did.

"I'll take good care of him," Hamdan insisted stubbornly.

Yulan yielded. He slung his crumpled shirt across his shoulder.

"Be sure you do. If you get him killed, I'll hear about nothing else from Creel for the rest of my days."

Hamdan gave a small exclamation of triumph and made to clap Drann once more upon the back. Drann dodged clumsily out of the way. From somewhere at the back of his belt, Yulan produced a little leather coin purse that he threw to Hamdan.

"To calm the townsfolk's nerves, if you need it," he said.

Drann was permitted barely enough time to eat a few dry biscuits and to check that the contract stayed secure in its case, bound to his belt. It was not the most comfortable place to keep the thing, but it felt imprudent to tempt ill luck by doing as

Creel's last contract-holder had done and strap it across his chest as it was really meant to be carried. That had not ended well for the man, after all.

Then it was back into that torture chair of a saddle. The day ahead was a dismal prospect, but less so perhaps if he spent it in Hamdan's company rather than that of Akrana, the Clamour, and the rest of the Free.

Kerig and Wren came to give Hamdan's horse a farewell pat across the haunch. It was only then, when they were close, and he looked at Wren's fair face, that Drann remembered what he had seen the night before. Their silent lovemaking by the fire. They were married, he knew; even so, it felt strangely illicit. He did not know whether he blushed at the memory, but he averted his gaze.

"Tell Ordeller I'll want no fleas in my bed," Kerig instructed Hamdan, who grunted in soft derision.

"I'm not saying a word that'd suggest there are *ever* fleas in her beds. She might set her ape on me."

"And you, lad," Kerig said. "If Hamdan's talking too much, pretend to fall asleep. Not likely to quiet him, but at least you won't be expected to say anything yourself."

The Clever looked sick and pale, as if he was prey to some common ague or fever. At least he was not coughing for now. That sound had been an accompaniment to much of the previous day's ride.

"Throw stones at him, if the sleeping thing doesn't work," Wren offered.

They were both talking to Drann, and yet not. Neither of them looked at him. He was simply a tool for the goading of their fellow. Not included in the jest, merely the means of its delivery.

"May lice feast in your lower hair, every one of you," Hamdan said happily as he turned his horse about and rode away.

8

Feet In Water

"It's not that they don't like you," Hamdan said. "They don't . . . well, they don't care enough one way or the other to feel either liking or its shadow. Don't let it fret you. Just stay out of every-one's way and all will be well."

Hamdan had proved to be just as loquacious as Kerig had foretold. The hour since he and Drann had parted company with the Free had been filled with an all but unbroken flow of talk, much of it an idle, if enthusiastic, commentary upon their surroundings. Drann did not mind. It distracted him from his unremitting aches and sense-dulling weariness.

Their surroundings were not of the most interesting sort, however. Rolling hills, given over to rough grazing, with scat-tered clumps of scrub and woodland; cut through now and again with little streams that were more rock than water. There was not much to be said about it all that could not be said in a minute or two. That was why Drann eventually started asking about Hamdan's comrades.

"I'm pretty sure Akrana doesn't like me," he insisted.

"Well, you might be right in that," Hamdan conceded, unperturbed. "Don't worry about it, though. More rattle than fang, Akrana. Although truth to tell, she's got fangs sharper than any. Just that she tends not to use them. Hibernal Clever, she is, but much prefers the sword. Kerig and Wren, though? Strongest Clevers the Free's got, those two; and that means strongest Clevers pretty much anyone's got, these days. They'll show it, too, if there's need."

"They don't seem so fierce."

"Do they not? You'd have run like a rabbit from Kerig if you'd met him before he fell in with Wren. Only wed a year, and she's already gentled him. Anyway, most folk – folk of your sort – would judge any Clever, no matter how gentle, worth running from."

Drann knew what sort of folk Hamdan meant. Farmers. Villagers. Folk who knew everything there was to know, every single little secret, about the patch of land they lived on, and the people they saw every day; and hardly anything about the rest of the world and its inhabitants save what they had heard from stories and rumour. In Drann's case, those stories and rumour were largely the tales Old Emmin used to tell him, and they had indeed taught him a little fear, but also curiosity, wonder. A kind of ambition too, he supposed. The desire to experience things for himself.

The only Clever he had actually seen, before the Free, was a walking-witch who turned up in the village when he was around eleven or twelve. She stayed just a couple of days, mending a few sick animals, cleansing the sour water one of the farmers had tapped when he sank a new well. After that, she disappeared. It had been whispered that someone – jealous, perhaps, of the services she had sold others – reported her presence to the School, and she had slipped away before their Clade could arrive and take hold of her. She had seemed harmless to him.

"What happened in Creel's camp?" he asked Hamdan. "Yulan went rushing off as soon as Creel mentioned some Weaponsmith, and it seems . . . it feels like something happened. Nobody's told me."

The archer grimaced at him.

"None of your business, at a guess."

There was a shutting of the gate in the words. The closing out that Drann was starting to expect from the rest of the Free, but had dared to think was not going to happen with Hamdan. It irked him.

"Never mind, then. If I'm not allowed to ask . . . "

"Oh, don't come over like a scorned suitor. The cloak don't fit. Nor does that arse-feather fur you've got on your lip and chin, by the way. You should scrape that off, and try again when you can grow hair the way it's meant to be grown."

It was not cruelly said, but still Drann instinctively put his hand to his chin, feeling the unsatisfactory soft stubble there. Removing it would feel like defeat. Leaving it, now, would feel like volunteering for mockery. The defeat would be easier, he knew.

"Beards don't make warriors," Hamdan went on amiably. "Anyway, I'll tell you, if you can keep the knowing to yourself. About the Weaponsmith, I mean. That was the old Kerig.

The fierce one. Do you know what the Weaponsmith does?"

Drann shook his head glumly, still preoccupied by the matter of beards, still scratching at his chin.

"He crafts weapons, obviously," Hamdan continued. "Other Clevers do that, but the ones the Weaponsmith makes are Clevered in a particular way. They're . . . bonded somehow to the one they're meant to kill. He cooks their victim's death into them in the forging. A long while back, before Kerig had even joined the Free, a man had the Weaponsmith make a particular arrow. Then that man used it to kill Kerig's brother. Never heard all the whys and wherefores."

Drann frowned.

"Shouldn't Kerig be after the man who did the killing, instead of the one who made the arrow, then?"

Hamdan regarded him as if he was being wilfully and absurdly dim-witted.

"That man's been dead four years, son. Some might have left it at that, but Kerig's one who knows how to share a grudge around."

There were bodies on the track. Scattered across and beside it, half hidden in the grass like debris strewn by some retreated wave. A fox went bounding away as the horses approached. It stopped and turned its head to stare suspiciously at Drann and Hamdan before trotting more decorously into a clump of bushes. Crows took less fright at the riders' approach; they hopped heavily from their feeding perches. Flicked their wings as if in indignation at the interruption. There were vultures overhead, idly circling.

Unless Drann looked closely, which he resolved not to do,

the corpses might pass for boulders, or abandoned baggage. The stench, and the sound, could not be so easily recast by his imagination. He covered his nose and mouth with one hand. There was nothing he could do to stop his ears. The hum of flies was all about. If he closed his eyes, it could have been the insect drone of a hay meadow in high summer.

Hamdan was unperturbed by either sound or smell. He looked around, apparently curious, as they passed through the field of the dead.

"Quite the fight," he mused. "Two or three days ago. Shame nobody told them the war was all but done. Crex's Armsmen on the losing side, I should say. It's not Callotec's boys, more's the pity. Wrong badges."

He glanced across to Drann, and gave a dry smile at the sight of him with his hand clasped across his face.

"Does it smell bad?" the archer asked. "My nose stopped paying much heed to certain scents a long time ago, sad to say."

He leaned down as his horse stepped over a corpse, and tugged a broken spear out of the body. He regarded its point, and then sniffed and sent it spinning away into the grass.

Disturbed by the arrival of the spear, a great lizard – a good deal longer than Drann was tall – went lumbering away from one of the bodies, its massive tail scything back and forth. Drann grimaced. Of all the carrion beasts that haunted armies, the lizards were the ones he found the most repellent. Creel's warriors had told frightful tales of what happened to those left injured on a battlefield, unable to defend themselves, when the lizards found them.

Drann was suddenly struck by the strangeness of it all, as his

horse picked its way carefully around dead men. Lives and
memories that were gone like floating seed heads on the wind;
just meat now for the lizards and crows and foxes. There would
be people somewhere – perhaps hundreds of them – who did
not yet know that their father, husband, son was dead on this
hill. Maybe they would never know when and where they died.

"What was his name?" he asked Hamdan quietly. "Creel's last
contract-holder who got killed?"

Hamdan regarded the sky with wide-open eyes, pinning his
lower lip with his teeth for a moment. He closed one eye. Then
snapped it open again, shook his head and returned his gaze to
the road before them.

"No. Can't remember."

"Really? Did you not speak to him?"

"Not overmuch. Didn't take to him. He was an older fellow,
short on good humour as far as I could tell."

"You do know my name, don't you?"

Hamdan frowned at him. Bit at that lower lip again. The
frown deepened as his memory delivered nothing to his tongue.
Then he shrugged. Drann's spirits fell abruptly and unexpectedly, as if tripped by a half-buried stone in his chest.

Hamdan laughed.

"Ha. What a fine face, like a scolded pup. Drann, son. Your
name's Drann. You're going to be the butt of every jest if you
don't learn to dress your hopes in a mask now and again."

The archer's mirth tricked Drann into overconfidence. He let
himself think that because Hamdan had told him about the
Weaponsmith, there might be more stories to be mined from
those rocks.

"What is it about Towers' Shadow?" he asked lightly. "What's this Callotec to Yulan?"

And that was what finally got Hamdan to stop talking.

The cart track dipped down to ford a narrow, rock-strewn river. On the other side, beyond a fringe of trees and bushes, the ground rose towards the town of Curmen. The modest buildings of pale, almost yellowish stone were starkly silhouetted by the low sunlight at their back. As the horses came to the water's edge, a sandpiper went jinking and darting away up the valley like an erratic, low-flighted arrowhead.

Hamdan drew to a halt and allowed his mount to dip its head and drink from the chuckling river. Drann looked questioningly at him. The archer was watching the opposite bank intently.

"Might be a little problem," he murmured.

"What is it?" Drann asked, but Hamdan was already swinging out of the saddle.

"Sit tight. Hold these reins for me, would you? Folk tend to find a man on a horse a bit more worrying than a man not."

Drann was alarmed to find himself thus responsible for two horses, but both animals were placid. Entirely insensitive, it seemed, to the tension in the air.

Hamdan stepped forward into the river. The water foamed and spluttered about his ankles. He walked slowly, in a rut generations of cartwheels had ground into the riverbed, both hands raised above his head. Drann saw that he held in one the little leather coin pouch Yulan had given him.

"Not meaning any harm," Hamdan called out to the bushes on the far side of the channel. Still advancing, feet feeling the way carefully, keeping his eyes fixed on the riverbank. "Just looking to put a little coin in someone's hand."

The screech of a buzzard overhead snatched Drann's gaze upwards for a moment. He saw the bird circling high, a dark quill-stroke against the sky. When he looked back down, every-thing had changed.

Men were coming out from amongst the bushes, right there at the point where the track climbed out of the river. Four of them. Three men and a boy, in fact. Everything about them was instantly familiar to Drann. He had never set eyes upon any one of them before, but he knew them.

Rough and rugged clothing that had softened over years of use. Faces dried by sun and wind, worn and blunted by labour, shaped by the lives they had lived. Spears – simple, wooden – meant not for killing men, but for leaning on when you had walked half the day, and for fending off wolf or cat or bear. Farmers and shepherds in other words, like those Drann had lived amongst all his life.

Only the boy, who was perhaps twelve or so by Drann's guess, had not yet been weathered by the world. And only he carried not a spear but a sling, hanging loosely at his side with a rounded stone cupped in its fold.

"Good day to all," Hamdan said cheerily as he walked on through the river. But he twisted his head over one shoulder and hissed back at Drann: "If that lad with the sling starts winding up, fall off your horse. He's not going to miss you sit-ting up there like a sack of corn."

Drann blinked, feeling suddenly heavy and fixed upon the animal's back. Feeling, in fact, much like a sack of corn.

"Don't come no closer," one of the townsfolk rasped at Hamdan, who kept smiling but ignored the instruction.

"After nothing but trade and a bit of talk, you have my word," the archer insisted. "In sore need of both, come to that, so we'll pay well."

"Nothing to sell you. Last few months, your kind's emptied our stores for us, stolen half our flocks. Trampled every field. Burned our barns. Killed our people. So you stop where you are!"

That last was shouted, the man's voice peaking and straining. Hamdan did stop. A couple of paces from the men, still ankle-deep in the river. Lips still locked into a determined smile.

"So you've had enough, then," he nodded. "Taken up spears. I'd do much the same in your place, no doubt. But I'm not here to take anything, only buy. And I really would like to talk to—"

"Nothing to sell, nothing to say," the leader of the townsfolk cried, and himself took a step closer to Hamdan, coming down to the water's edge. His spear was levelled now. Its point trembled, etching on the air the powerful emotions its wielder struggled to contain.

For a moment, there was no sound but the gurgling of the river and the sifting of trailing willow boughs by the gentle breeze. Hamdan was a statue, arms outstretched in submission. It did nothing to dim the spearman's ire.

"You brave bastards with your armies and your swords. You've ruined us. My children are hungry. You think I'll sell you what food I have left?"

To Drann, he looked to be on the brink of tears. Drann had seen his own father weep once, after the King's tax-takers found the barley he had hidden away. Not when they made him bleed in punishment for his crime, but afterwards, when they had carted that secret store away, and left him with only the prospect of a hungry family. Drann suspected there were few things worse for a loving son than to see his father weeping. He wondered, fleetingly, whether that youth with the sling was son to this near-broken man.

"I understand," Hamdan was saying, still with a light, almost merry tone. Drann was not sure he did understand. Perhaps he did not see quite what Drann saw.

"If you'll let me explain who we are," the archer continued, "you might—"

The farmer jabbed with the spear. Even Drann could tell it was a half-hearted, clumsy gesture. Hamdan leaned aside, but the spear point did not quite reach him in any case.

"Oh, now. Don't be doing that," Hamdan said sternly. "Really. Don't be doing that."

The farmer gathered himself and took a step nearer. His teeth were bared, in fear and fury alike.

"Hamdan . . ." Drann said, urgent but too quiet.

Again the spear darted out. What happened then was too fast for Drann to quite understand, until it was already done. Three men and a boy, all armed, against one man with only his hands, and with his feet in water; and it was finished before Drann had taken four breaths.

Hamdan seized the shaft of the spear as it came towards him and pulled sharply. The farmer took a staggering step forward. Hamdan planted a boot firmly into the man's crotch. In the same movement, his free arm flicked out, his fingers opened and the bag of coins darted from his hand straight to the boy slinger's face. It hit him on the bridge of his nose, his efforts to avoid it merely planting him on his backside, sliding him a little way down the riverbank.

As the first spearman was falling, Hamdan was already surging up out of the water, spray pluming about his legs. The other two men he faced were moving, but too slowly, without decision. Hamdan knocked one down with a blur-fast pair of strikes to the centre of his chest. The second managed to turn, and even begin to run, but Hamdan tripped him and pulled the spear from his hands and cast it aside.

When Hamdan turned to face the boy, Drann wanted to cry out, to tell him to stop. But there was no need. Hamdan seized the boy's collar with one hand, his sling with the other, and growled into his face: "Stay still." The boy obeyed.

The three men were all on the ground, in varying states of distress. One by one, with pointed detachment, Hamdan broke their spears across his knee. He wiped his hands on the breast of his jerkin and turned to Drann.

"It was good advice. The falling off your horse bit. You should have taken it."

Drann nodded.

"Don't look so miserable, son," Hamdan said. "People who can't fight shouldn't start fights. Might be a useful lesson they've learned today. Now, go fetch the rest of them, would you? Think you can do that without coming unshipped? Quick as you like. I've got wet feet."

9

The Clamour, That Permanence

It was only as he rode into the tiny, shabby town of Curmen that Drann realised he had been looking forward to arriving there. Arriving anywhere, in fact, in the company of the Free. He had, without actually thinking about it, been hoping that people would see him riding amongst them and think him one of their number. Look upon him with the same awe that he had assumed must greet Yulan and the rest wherever they went. He only realised all of this because the reality of the experience so completely dashed those unconsidered hopes.

The Free were greeted not with adulation or awe, but with grim silence, suspicious eyes. It made Drann uneasy. None of the others seemed at all concerned by it. He could only guess that the scene had been repeated so many times, in so many places, that it no longer troubled them. Perhaps – a darker thought this, more discomfiting – they no longer compre-hended it, or whence it came.

"Where are you going?" asked a tall, long-limbed man who walked alongside Yulan's horse.

The chief man of Curmen. Not one of those who had challenged Hamdan at the ford. Those three, and the boy, had been released as soon as Drann brought Yulan and the rest to the river. Yulan had given them the pouch of coins before they disappeared. He told them it was in payment for the spears Hamdan had broken, though it was ten times what such simple weapons could be worth.

A well-meant gesture, Drann did not doubt. But you could not mend crippled pride with unasked-for coins; that was salt, not salve, to the wound.

"We'll bed down in Ordeller's lodging house," Yulan told the town's headman without looking at him. "Stable our horses there. We all of us need a good night's rest."

The man cast an uneasy glance at the Clamour's wagon, grinding its way up the unevenly cobbled street with Hestin sitting, as ever, still and silent at the reins in her cloak of green leaves.

"That too?"

"That too," Yulan confirmed, staring straight ahead. "Best spread the word that your people should keep away from the stables tonight. We'll set a guard. Pay the stabling fee to you as well as Ordeller tomorrow, if there's no trouble."

Curmen was a sorry old town, bedraggled but clearly come from better times, like a little lord whose lands and wealth had been frittered away through drink or coin games. It had a wall of sorts still about it, gappy and robbed of most of its good stone. The buildings were solid enough, made from the same rock as the surrounding hills, but worn and tired.

Drann knew vaguely that Threetower had once been a trading place and busy border crossing when the Hommetic Kingdom and the Empire of Orphans had briefly attempted a sort of peace. It had not lasted long. The road from here to there had no doubt lost its traffic, and dragged Curmen down into decrepitude with it. Now, somewhere out in the gathering darkness, the last of the Hommetics fled along that same road, seeking refuge and perhaps an avenging army in the very empire his ancestors had for so long resisted.

The lodging house to which Yulan led their little column embodied the town's reduced circumstances. The tall building had finer windows, a finer roof of slate tiles, than those that surrounded it; one or two of those windows were cracked, several of the tiles loose and all of them stained and pitted. The adjoining barn was big enough to accommodate more travellers' horses than the place must ever see now.

While Hamdan and his archers saw to the stabling of the Free's mounts, and the hiding away with them of the Clamour and its wagon, Yulan led Drann and the others inside. Ordeller awaited them there, and she was a sight to behold.

Tall and prodigiously broad, she had a jowly face as softly full as an overbrimming water skin. Everything about her was eye-catching – from the garish red skirt to the many-coloured ribbons tied through her hair – but none of it could hold Drann's attention when set against her companion: a large black-haired ape that sat on one of the tables.

It was a beast unlike anything he had ever seen. He had heard of them, of course. Strange creatures, near-men some called them, that hailed from the forests far to the south, beyond the Massatan sands, beyond everything. He could not guess how one might have arrived here.

Its face was uncannily human, its eyes in particular. Its fur was grizzled, just as an old man's might be. Greying about its cheeks, its temples, and across its shoulders. Those liquid, intelligent eyes were a touch rheumy.

The creature sat there, loose and comfortable, upon the table and chewed at an apple. Once, it met Drann's fascinated stare, and returned it for the briefest of moments before losing interest and looking away.

"The brown boy and his crew," Ordeller cried with a capacious grin, offering Yulan a slightly mocking curtsey. "The honour'll make me dizzy. Catch me if I fall, Captain; catch me do."

"Feed us first," Yulan said. "If you're going to faint away, do it after."

Ordeller had always been one of Yulan's favourites. Just as people had overpraised his own wit, down the years, many missed the depth of Ordeller's. She hid it well, of course. That was a part of her gift and her usefulness. People thought her just a mildly strange, solitary woman letting a lodging house rot away beneath her feet. Even if she was truly just that, Yulan suspected he would have liked her. But she was a good deal more.

She sat with them about the largest table, though she did not share in the bread and stew she had set out. There was no one else. No other eaters or drinkers or weary travellers. Ordeller had closed up and barred the doors for now. Until the talk was done.

"You've come for a piglet, got yourself a boar to fight instead," she said ruefully. "One with big gutting tusks, at that."

"Meaning?"

"Few dozen of the King's men passed by, right enough, just a couple of days back. Killed two shepherd boys and four of their flock, the whore-bastards. That'd be this Callotec, I guess. Thing is, another couple of hundred folk arrived over the hills from the south. Joined up with them. They're all camped not three hours west along the old road, in the broken lands."

Yulan's heart sank. A twist in the weave. He had brought the Free to fight a handful, and found hundreds instead.

"You're sure?" he asked, knowing the answer.

"Sure as sure. What you pay me for, isn't it? My thinking parts've not turned to shit since last we met. It's been a time, but not that much. I've had one or two brave lads take a look. Keep an eye. Three hundred or more, no doubting it."

"That's a shame," murmured Wren, almost wistfully.

"That it is," Yulan grunted, glancing at her then turning back to Ordeller. "The Kingshouse at Towers' Shadow still ungarrisoned?"

"Far as I know," Ordeller nodded.

"No more friends for Callotec between here and the border, at least," Yulan mused. "Nothing to stop him, either."

"You can catch him easy enough," Ordeller said. "When the trading stopped up at Threetower, the road looked more like an invitation for the Empire's army than a tit to be sucked at, so the Hommetics had parts of it torn up, dug up, ploughed. It's a slow old way to go, these days. Well, you know that, I suppose. Like as not, that's why these King's folk chose it; none'd think to seek them this way. They've got wagons and all sorts with them, so they'll not be out of sight for days yet."

Yulan made no reply. He sank back in his chair and set thumb and forefinger to the bridge of his nose, pinching thoughtfully at the skin there. He stared absently at the ape. The apple had long ago vanished down its gullet; seeds and stem, every little bit of it. After sitting for a long time in quiet contemplation, scratching at its folded legs, it had carefully lowered itself to the floor and wandered into a corner. There it now sat, picking at loose plaster on the wall with a single, hooked finger.

"Should he be doing that?" Drann asked quietly; his attention had evidently been similarly distracted.

Ordeller looked round and growled in displeasure. The ape regarded her with seeming disdain, but it did shuffle a little away from the wall. It wrapped its arms about itself, hunched its shoulders and sat with its back to the assembled humans. Sulking.

"We bore the Emperor," Ordeller observed.

"Any trouble waiting for us here?" Yulan asked softly. "In Curmen?"

"Not likely," Ordeller said. "No friends, that's sure – they'd drop me in the drowning pool in the next valley if they guessed I was one of yours, I expect – but they're too frit, too ground down to raise a fist against you."

"They for King or Council?"

"Neither. They're for being left alone by all the blood-crazed bastards wandering the land. Not meaning any offence to you blood-crazed bastards, of course."

"I'll take Hamdan up the road, then," Yulan said, suddenly resolved.

Since the day he left Towers' Shadow, it had become a matter of importance to him that he should never act without care, never without a second, and a third, plan to fall back upon if the first turned to dust. It had made him a better captain. No matter how he longed for haste, he would not permit the man who had taught him that lesson to now make him unlearn it. Not with lives to be lost if but a single foot stepped wrong.

"Take a look at Callotec for myself," he went on. "Three hours?"

Ordeller shrugged. "For me. You two lively boys, riding the way you can? Less."

Yulan twisted towards Akrana – "We'll be back before then, but if not, be ready to move at dawn' – then to Ordeller once more: "You have birds?"

She looked affronted. The rainbow of ribbons in her hair gave a little shiver of indignation.

"Of course. That too is what you pay me for, isn't it? If I'm working too hard or well for your coin, you be sure to tell me. Wouldn't want to make the rest look like shirkers."

"Where are they for, the birds you've got?" Yulan asked.

"White Steading, Armadell, Sussadar."

Again Yulan looked to Akrana.

"Rudran'll still be at Sussadar, won't he? That's the only one close enough to make any odds."

She glanced upward, towards the black beams criss-crossing the ceiling, recovering memories.

"Rudran and . . . fifteen or so lancers," she said at length.

Yulan sucked his teeth.

"Sixteen, I think. It'll have to do. Send your Sussadar birds, Ordeller. All of them, to be certain. Tell Rudran to come here with all speed. Every man he has to hand. You write out the messages, I'll put my mark on them before Hamdan and I ride out."

Part of him hated to do it, though he took care to hide that. It was not something the rest needed to see. Dragging more men into this endeavour went against his every starting intent. But he had to have choices. People died when choices ran out, and he did not mean to let that happen. He might not need Rudran and his lancers – there was still that hope – but if he did, and they were not within reach, that would be when the dying started.

A sudden clearing of a throat drew every eye to Drann, the contract-holder. He shrank a little beneath such sharp attention, but to his credit rallied and managed to get the words out without too heavy a cargo of nervousness.

"Isn't three hundred a . . . a few too many? Even for you? Even with another sixteen lancers?"

Yulan said nothing. Akrana snorted.

"No, it is not," she said, not troubling to conceal her contempt. "We are the Free. All things are possible."

Yulan and Hamdan rode out while Drann was in the room Ordeller had given him, leaning over a bowl of cold water, scraping the fur of his nascent beard away with a knife. He heard the clatter of their horses' hoofs in the street outside, a dwindling tattoo beaten out on the cobblestones.

He stared at the flecks of hair floating in the water. In the flickering candlelight they looked like dust cast over the surface. He felt none of the regret he had half expected. As it turned out, from the moment Hamdan had condemned his attempt at a beard, he had lost interest in it.

He was deeply tired, and deeply pained by muscles that riding had somehow, mysteriously, both softened and stiffened. But he knew he could not sleep. Not yet.

He went downstairs, and found nothing and no one but Ordeller's black ape. It sat squarely in the middle of the table at which the Free had eaten, testing some indistinct stain on the wooden surface with its lips. It looked up when Drann entered, but found him less interesting than the stain. For all its age, it looked a little too big and strong for his comfort. He did not trust its lack of interest in him enough to linger. Instead, he went out into the dusk. Perhaps the air would bring on sleep.

Curmen was quiet. A little way down the street, a woman was shaking out a blanket on her doorstep. His nose told him that someone nearby was roasting a spice he did not recognise. He could hear children shouting, somewhere behind the row of rude houses opposite. It did not amount to much life for a town this size. The people were fearful. Wearied by what they found outside their doors in these times.

Drann stood in the middle of the street. Akrana was out here somewhere. She had shown no interest in finding a room, washing away the day's dust, with the rest of the Free. Had gone instead, grim-faced, to stalk Curmen's streets and alleys and keep a roving watch upon the place and its people. Drann could not imagine her ever being at ease.

A soft sound made him look up. High on the roof of the lodging house a trapdoor had opened. From it one, then another, then a third white dove spilled out, brushing the air with wings and splayed tails as they climbed up and away from the town. They turned, the three of them, in a rising spiral up into the darkening sky, then arrowed away, like pale stones loosed from a sling.

Ordeller's birds, gone to summon more of the Free's strength. Drann had no idea how far they had to journey. He had never heard of the Sussadar for which they were bound.

"Drann, is it?"

He looked round.

One of Hamdan's archers stood by the stable's huge doors. He nodded at Drann and beckoned him over. Drawing closer, Drann realised that the man could not be a great deal older than he was himself. The shortbow and quiver strapped across his back, the sword at his hip, the hard set of his jaw added years to him, though.

"Lebid," the archer said by way of introduction. "Can I ask a favour of you?"

"I suppose so," Drann murmured.

"Stand here for me, long enough that I can beg some fodder from Ordeller. Not a morsel's passed my lips since we got here, and my guts'll be rising up and throttling me if I don't feed them soon."

"I've no weapon," Drann said, feeling inexplicably foolish. "Left my spear up in my room."

Undeterred, the archer at once slid his sword from its scabbard and proffered its hilt to Drann. Who had never held a sword in his life.

"I wouldn't know what to do with that," he said.

"You won't have to do anything." There was just a trace of irritation in the man's voice now. "It's for show. Trust me, no one's going to kill you before I get back."

Drann raised his eyebrows at that, but the archer summoned up a grin.

"Jest! No one's going to kill you at all. They wouldn't dare. Just take a few moments of my watch while I hunt down some scraps, that's all I ask. Is it so much? I'm no good to anyone if I drop down from hunger."

His own dull weariness could not be unique, Drann knew. For all that they seemed accustomed to it, the Free must be suffering from the demands of the last few days just as he was. He shrugged, and took the sword in his hand. The sensation was so strange and surprising that he paid little heed as the archer trotted towards the lodging house with murmurs of gratitude.

He wondered absently what his father and mother would think, to see him standing here in a distant town, holding such a blade. It would sadden them, he thought, especially his mother. But he could not say precisely why he felt so sure of that.

The snorting of a horse from within the stables distracted him from his reverie. The wide doors stood just a fraction ajar. Stepping closer, he was taken for a moment back to his village, transported by the soft exhalation of the stable. It smelled as only stables did. Straw and dirt; horse sweat, horse dung. A hint of warm dampness. Familiar, to Drann. He had hidden in the horse shed more than once, when fleeing parental wrath or injustice.

As he eased himself between the doors, taking care not to make a sound, he recognised that this was a good deal more than a mere shed. It was almost dark within, but he could see that there were stalls for better than a dozen horses – all now occupied by the Free's mounts – and old cartwheels resting against the walls, sacks of feed and bales of hay. The roof was higher and wider than any barn he had seen, with ropes hanging in loose-bellied festoons from pulleys and rafters. Somewhere up there, in the deepest shadows, he could hear little birds warbling softly to one another.

The Clamour's wagon stood in the centre. An indistinct shape that Drann took to be Hestin was curled on the filthy straw beneath it, folded into her green-leaf cloak. Asleep, as best Drann could tell. It was not such a bad place to sleep, he supposed: the warmth, the comforting sounds of horses and birds, the darkness settling in through the plank walls. But an odd choice, when there were beds to be had just a few strides away. Further evidence, as if Drann really required any more, that Hestin was cut from a different cloth than the rest of the Free. She and the Clamour were somehow two parts of a whole, in which the others did not entirely share.

He edged closer to that wagon, and its silent, canvas-shrouded cargo. It was a cage that lurked beneath that cover, the meagre light leaking in showed him. One edge of the canvas had caught on the metal grille beneath, hooked up just a little. It felt like a trap, but if so, it was not the kind that could be avoided, for no one – no one who had dreamed for even a moment of a world beyond village and fields, at least – could refuse a chance to set eyes upon the Clamour, that Permanence

which, after perhaps the Bereaved and the Unhomed Host, was
the most famous, the most feared, in all the world.

Drann paused, even so. Caution gave a last, delicate restrain-
ing flutter as he listened for any sound emerging from that great
cage. Not a breath, not a stirring. Hestin was still; the Clamour,
it seemed, was still. If he did not look, he would regret his cow-
ardice for the rest of his life.

Close now, he could hear breathing. A toing and froing of air
like a sluggish wind stirring lakeside reeds. It was not human
breathing; too deep and broad for that. He bent, peering in
through the narrow aperture the hitched-up cover had opened.

The darkness within was all but complete. He could make
nothing out. There was heat, though. Faint washes of it upon
his face, keeping pace with the ebb and flow of that breathing.
And a strange, dense scent of . . . something. Rot, soil, sour air.
Some admixture he had never met before, but that was unmis-
takably animal.

He reached for the edge of the canvas sheet, thinking to lift
it just a fraction higher. He noticed that his hand trembled, and
let it fall back to his side. Reached instead with the tip of the
sword. Holding his breath, he shifted the wagon's heavy cloak,
opened a slightly bigger window into the cage. And looked
inside.

Still he could see nothing. Just hints in the blackness. Shapes.
He leaned closer.

His eyes sharpened. Learned the shadows. And he saw, dimly,
fingers resting upon the grubby floor of the cage. Broad, blunt
stubs of fingers, calloused and bloated and blotched; thrice the
size of his own. Like lumps of decaying wood. He could not tell

whether those fingers bore nails, whether the rest of the hand and arm were as disfigured. As inhuman. His heart was shaking in his chest.

One of the fingers twitched. A hand seized his ankle.

Drann cried out as he lurched away from the wagon. The canvas covering fell back into place. He fell over, thumping down on to straw. The grip upon his leg was loosened, and he scrambled towards the door, stumbling to his feet. He looked back and down and saw Hestin, almost out from under the wagon, staring at him.

He could see her face more clearly than seemed right in that gloom. Her old, creased face from which glared unnervingly bright and transfixing eyes.

"He does not sleep," she said, her voice rough and thin. "Nor I no more."

Drann stumbled out into the street, feeling almost sick with alarm. He blundered into Akrana. She was standing there with one hand on the shoulder of the archer who had put Drann here. Lebid looked humble, scolded. He avoided Drann's frightened gaze. Akrana pushed him away as she prodded Drann's chest, looming almost a head over him.

"Do you even understand what it is?" she snarled into his face.

"A Permanence," Drann mumbled. "Everyone knows about Permanences. The Clamour, the Bereaved. The Dembine Stone, the Silent Gyre, the Unhomed Host."

"You know nothing but names," Akrana snapped. She was pushing him back. "Nothing worth the knowing. If you did, you would not be sneaking about like some wit-short child, trying to get a look. You would be browning your trews at the thought of having to sleep within a hundred paces of the thing. How old is she?"

"Hestin? I . . . I don't know."

Drann backed into one of the stable doors. His heels bumped against it. The sword fell from his grasp. It rang on the street.

"How old?" Ankara demanded.

"Forty? Fifty?"

"Twenty-four, more or less. That is the price she pays to keep the Clamour from taking the head off every curious idiot like you who wants to feel the breath of a Permanence. More fool her. But fool or not, you will not make mockery of her sacrifice again. If you do, I will cut your stupid head from your stupid shoulders myself."

The Seventeenth Captain Of The Free

Kites stood above the ridge on taut strings. A whole flock of them, immensely high up, no more than smudges against the night sky, trembling upon the wind. They strained against the bonds that anchored them, and Yulan could hear their lines thrumming. As he ran beneath them, weaving his way between the lines and the low cairns from which they rose, it felt as if a host of wide-winged birds was hanging there above him. Watching him.

There was, he knew, a corpse within each of those cairns. The folk of these rocky canyons and hills held the human soul to be principally an expression of the Vernal entelech, as was the wind that coursed about these craggy heights. So they sought to unite the two after death, setting a kite to ride the currents of the sky above each stone-encased corpse. When the string broke and the kite tumbled away on the wind, so too would the soul, returning to the formless substance of the entelech from which it sprang.

It seemed no more foolish, or improbable, than any of the many other notions about such things Yulan had encountered in his travels.

Hamdan ran a little behind him. Just as sure- and soft-footed on the uneven ground, even in this meagre moonlight. Just as steadily untiring. They had left their horses in a hollow on the flank of the long ridge, safely hidden from prying eyes. The beasts needed the rest after the gallop from Curmen, and a horse was in any case no way to come unnoticed upon a hostile camp in such a landscape.

They reached the last of the cairns and kite cords, and the rugged, exposed ridge ahead began to sink towards a confluence of gorges. Down there, on the flat ground, was where Ordeller had told them to expect Callotec and his band. Yulan dropped into a crouch behind a boulder and whispered to Hamdan when the archer joined him.

"I'd have a watcher up here somewhere if I was Callotec."

Hamdan nodded. "Only a fool'd not."

"I'll go on. Take a look."

Again Hamdan nodded.

"You watch from here," Yulan murmured. "I run into trouble, save me."

"Of course." Hamdan grinned, his teeth catching just a hint of the moon's pearly white light. "Every time."

Yulan left him there, amidst the cairns, and went on alone. He did not run now, but crouched low. Stole across the stony ground, passed stealthily from sheltering rock to concealing crevice. The precious wind that blew – he had known it could be trusted as soon as he saw and heard the kites from down below – carried off every slight sound, brushing it out over the bleak, serried folds of land that stretched beyond sight. All he could hear, aside from the wind's own restless sigh, was the dull murmur of the kite strings behind him.

He sent his breathing and his heart into a steady, slow rhythm. Sent his mind into still concentration. Worked his way methodically closer to whatever awaited him.

"Yulan's the seventeenth Captain of the Free," Kerig said, stretching his arms, fingers interlaced, above him. "Best of the lot, some say."

The act of stretching, and the bend it put into his back, made the Clever cough. He hacked up some phlegm, and wiped it away with the back of his hand. Drann saw, in Wren's face, the fleeting passage of concern. Kerig smirked, though.

"It's easing," he said. "I'll be back to my best in a day or two."

Husband and wife sat opposite one another, Kerig with his feet up on a bench, Wren hunched forward over a Land board. Drann sat at an adjoining table. He had not been invited to join the two Clevers at their own, and knew better than to assume a welcome. Especially since he had so angered Akrana. But she was still out there somewhere, haunting Curmen's streets in the night. Perhaps these two did not yet know of his transgression. Whatever the reason, Kerig was unexpectedly willing to talk.

"He can run longer, and faster, than you or me or any one of us," the Clever went on. "Think deeper and sharper. Kill a man quicker, quieter. Most things, most deeds, Yulan's better at than anyone you've ever met, farm boy."

"If you say so," said Drann, cupping his bowl of soup with both hands contemplatively.

He had hoped for beer, to quell the nervous, queasy agitation that his encounter with the Clamour and Hestin had left rattling around in his stomach. Ordeller stood there, even now, over at the counter, tapping a new cask of the stuff. The ape was perched atop the counter, leaning down, extending its long lips to touch the tap even before Ordeller had got it in place. She pushed the animal away now and again, but her shoves lacked conviction.

As it turned out, the Free adhered to a strict sobriety when working under contract; a fact that surprised Drann, who in his brief attachment to Creel's army – and despite the old warlord's strictures – had seen more drunkenness than in all his previous years. He did not know whether he was expected to now share in the Free's self-denying discipline, but it seemed the safest course. So he made do with soup, and the warmth of the fire crackling in the grate.

"Takes someone special to lead a hundred . . . well, to lead a hundred of us," Kerig mused. "Being the kind of folk we are, most of us."

"A hundred?" Drann said. He was distracted and wary of antagonising anyone else tonight, but not so much that he would refuse the chance to learn of the Free. He had never found wariness a natural or easy companion. "I didn't know you were so many."

"Ha. You thought it was just us few you're lucky enough to ride with?"

"Well, no. I know there's—"

"There's better than a hundred. A dozen Clevers, fifty or so fighting men. Almost the same again working for a wage: stewards, traders, housekeepers, armourers. And then there's plenty like Ordeller, just for the watching and for being sure there's a friend around wherever we beach ourselves."

"Kerig, close your mouth, for the love of mercy," snapped Wren. "Have you gone soft-headed, to think this boy needs to know every secret of the company?"

Kerig frowned, and shrugged. "Not telling him secrets," he said, a little sulkily, but he did have the grace to look regretful.

Drann guessed it was his improving health that had loosened his tongue. The Clever's cheeks had recovered a lively hue, and his eyes glinted with restored vigour. It had, apparently, made him want to talk; to give that bodily renewal a voice. Drann just happened to be the closest pair of open ears. He was not foolish enough to take it as a sign of acceptance.

Wren extended a long finger, rested its tip atop one of the crudely carved beetle pieces and fixed Kerig with a meaningful gaze.

"What?" he asked.

"If you paid more heed to the game, instead of wasting breath on the boy, you'd not be losing."

She slid the wooden beetle to its new position on the board and sat back. She looked satisfied. Drann had no idea whether Kerig was really losing. He had never played a game of Land in his life. It was not meant for the likes of him. His gaming hadn't gone beyond the throwing of knuckles on a plate, and even at that – which as best he could tell was entirely a matter of luck – he had lost a good deal more than he had ever won.

"He's distracting me," Kerig muttered, hooking a thumb towards Drann.

"It's not the boy doing all the talking," Wren said.

"I'm not a boy," said Drann quietly. "I'm seventeen years old."

Wren smiled at him.

"Of course you're a boy. There's nothing wrong with being a boy. It just feels that way because of the company you're choosing to keep."

Two great boulders rested against one another, like wearied men slumped shoulder to shoulder. Their posture left a gap between them, at their base. A window, through which Yulan stared, stretched out on his stomach. What he saw troubled him.

There was, as he had expected, a sentry posted above Callotec's camp. Only the man's head and shoulders were visible, projecting around the side of an overhanging slab of rock. A careless eye might easily have read them as merely a part of that rock.

The watcher was sitting not quite atop the ridge – wise, as he would have been too easily sighted there – but just a little way down its flank, presumably above the spot where his comrades were camped. What troubled Yulan was that he could not see that camp. The floor of the canyon running along the foot of the ridge was clearly visible. But where he took Callotec to have pitched his tents, down there amidst the scrub that lined the Old Threetower Road, there was only a great obscuring bank of sickly grey fog.

It pooled limply, utterly unstirred by whatever breeze reached there. Like a pale scar on the night's air. Tendrils of it – thinner and more sharply coherent than any fog had a right to be – rose up the walls of the canyon, twining themselves amongst the rocks and crannies. Yet even they did not move, did not rise or fall or drift. They simply clung to the slopes as if anchoring themselves.

No fire smoke climbed out of that fog. No sound escaped it. Yulan had seen no other mist since leaving Curmen. The weather was not fit for the making of such a vapour. It did not belong. It could only be the work of a Clever.

He had seen such workings before. They were most easily achieved using the Autumnal entelech, and Wren had done so in service of the Free. To conceal, confound and confuse; just as was intended here and now.

Reason enough to be troubled. More than troubled. There were not supposed to be any Clevers with Callotec. So Creel had said. So Yulan had believed. When you fought Clevers, no plan could be relied upon with certainty. No ruse could be trusted to work. Others had learned that to their cost often enough when facing the Free.

His ambitions for the night rearranged themselves, and fixed with narrow precision upon the unfortunate sentry perched above the fog's fringes. He had no intention of venturing down into those obscuring mists, so he needed someone else to tell him what lay there. He needed a tongue.

Yulan twisted, looked up the ridge's backbone. The forest of kite strings was barely visible now, no more than a suggestion of movement in the dark air. Somewhere there Hamdan would be watching and waiting. The archer was as safe a pair of eyes and hands as could be wished for, even when prey to remembered grief.

Unspent grief. Not that there were many other kinds, in Yulan's experience. It might diminish, or slumber, or even transform itself into something else, but it was seldom entirely extinguished. Any echo of its first cause might be enough to give it a stir. An echo such as a youth whose age matched that at which a son had died.

Yulan remembered Hamdan's son. Not well – he had only met him once, years ago – but enough to know that Drann was not greatly like him. Just alike enough in years to call up an instinctive sympathy, perhaps even affection, in the archer. Yulan had seen it in Hamdan's eyes almost as soon as Drann walked into their camp. It was another reason for his regret at Creel's choice of contract-holder. Others might not mark it, hidden as it was by Hamdan's customary good humour, but Yulan could see it clearly: the rising of buried pain. He felt it too, on behalf of his friend.

But Yulan also knew Hamdan well enough to know that nothing – no memory, no sorrow – would distract him from whatever was needed tonight. Their shared origins in the dry, vast Massatan lands through which the Hommetic Kingdom's imprecise southern border ran had inclined them towards friendship from the start; better than a dozen years of shared service in the Free had made it deep, and fortified it with trust and reliance.

Yulan edged sideways, out from the concealing shelter of those boulders. Bent almost double, fingertips brushing over the rocky ground, he worked his way forward, eyes never straying from the dim outline of the unsuspecting sentry up ahead.

"Used to be many more than a hundred, of course," Kerig murmured. "More than five times as many, back in the wild days before the Hommetics crowned themselves. That's why Crex and his line were always fond of us; the Free did more than any other company to put the first of them on the throne, way back then.

"Precious thing, royal gratitude. Only thing that stopped the School snuffing us out like they did, one by one, all the other free companies. Not that they haven't tried, now and again."

"But you're fighting against Crex now," Drann frowned.

"Times change," Kerig said with a shrug. "The buttocks burnishing the throne change. Crex was losing what little mind he ever had, if you ask me; becoming an inconstant friend, if you ask Yulan. You know where we were two years ago, almost to the day?"

Drann shook his head dumbly.

"Fifty miles deep into the Empire, just twenty of us, hunting slavers who'd stolen some of Crex's subjects. Fighting the secret little war between Kingdom and Empire that neither'll admit to, and neither wants to use their own folk to fight. We lost two men that day, the only ones who've died under Yulan; killed ten times that many and more. And when we come back to Crex, he robs us of half our prize because he's somehow got it into his soft head that those we didn't kill bribed us to let them go."

This was what Drann wanted to hear more of: the fell deeds of the Free.

"Is that when the Clamour ate an Orphanidon?" he asked eagerly.

Kerig looked at him as if he had drooled soup down his chin.

"What?" The Clever grimaced.

"The Clamour doesn't eat people," Wren said with mock gravity.

"Oh," said Drann.

"And we're not idiots enough to carry it deep into the Empire," Kerig said, rolling his eyes. "Anyway, we only took the field against Crex once it was plain he'd lose. Yulan's always known how to pick the winning side in a fight. No better man to lead us, like I said."

"He's no Clever, though," Drann said. "Yulan, I mean."

"Ha," laughed Kerig. "No, he's not that. Captain of the Free's never been a Clever. Not once in the eighty years of the company."

"Sulleman Var," Wren said placidly as she pondered the choices the game board offered her.

"What?" blinked Kerig.

"Sulleman Var."

"Oh. Yes, all right. There was one once. But only once, and not for long. Before our time. And the exception doesn't change my point."

"Does a bit, I expect," Wren smiled. "What was your point, anyway?"

"Never you mind. You just try to find some move or other to save yourself from humiliation. Point is that there's precious few Clevers would make a decent leader of something like the Free. Do you even understand what it is we do?"

"Clevers?" Drann said. "You ... make magic from the ent-elechs."

"We make magic from the entelechs." He imitated Drann's northern accent. "Horse's piss. You, the air you breathe, the fear or lust or joy you feel, this table' – he shook it for emphasis, which earned him a foul glare from Wren as she reached to keep the Land pieces from skittering across the board – "everything's made from the raw stuff of the four entelechs. Everything is a pattern arising from them. You understand?"

Drann nodded. The soup was cooling in his bowl, but he paid it no heed.

"So what we do," Kerig went on, "is make new patterns. We take the formless entelechs and give them form. Thing is, it's a river that flows both ways. For us to put more pattern into the world, some has to be lost. Something has to go back. And the place that pattern's lost from, more often than not, is us. Our bodies, our minds, our souls. Know what that means?"

Drann shrugged.

"First, we're mean with our magics. Inclined to the selfish. You've met Akrana. Hibernal. Mighty talented. Could unmoor the seasons, overturn the day's light, if she wanted. She's too fond of her life and vigour to do it, though."

A warning hiss from Wren, sharp as a snake, made Kerig flinch.

"Anyway," he continued, with less enthusiasm, "not good traits for a leader, selfishness, meanness. Second, we don't last long. No Clever's ever lasted more than six or seven years in the Free. Too punishing. We die, or we turn our shares in for coin and go off to live a slower, quieter life. What little life we've got left once the Free's done with us."

"Why do it then?" Drann asked quietly.

"Ha!' Kerig leaned back in his chair. "Because life's meagre fare in these parts, unless you're a royal or rich as one. So long as we're in the Free, we go where we want and do as we please, because we've a hundred of the fiercest, most fearful friends you could ever wish for, and none'd dare gainsay us. If we live to leave the Free, we still go where we want and do as we please, because we're rich. That's why we do it. Wouldn't you, if you could?"

Drann did not know the answer to that.

The guard would be an Armsman, if Callotec had any sense at all. The King's elite cadre had been as fine a set of warriors as any outside the Empire, outside the Free, until it was scattered and devoured by the last few months of fighting. Callotec would almost certainly have gathered up a few of that elite in his flight, and was unlikely to trust any but one of them to stand watch over his encampment.

It took two years to train an Armsman. Yulan had never had a day's formal training in his life; but he had spent better than half that life doing violence to others. Not practising or miming the deed, but doing it. Its methods and necessities were as much a part of his body as muscle and bone. He dropped on to the reverse haunch of the ridge, finding a long, low path that brought him across sharp rocks and then back up to a place where he could climb, slow and careful as a stalking cat, above the Armsman's station. He lay there for many steady heartbeats, spread-eagled upon the flat crown of the low crag below which the man was keeping watch. He was, for that span of time, alone beneath the immense star-strewn sky, the wind rushing over him. It felt good.

He measured his movements forward to the lip of the crag in the smallest of increments. As he went, he felt softly for any loose pebble or rock fragment tucked into a crevice. There were few, but he only needed one. When he found it, he folded it into the palm of his hand and eased himself on.

He poised himself at the edge of the overhang, balanced against the wind, looking down upon the sentry ten feet or so below him. The man was sitting on a rock, blowing into his hands to warm them. Tongues of that malign mist reached up close to where he sat, lying thick and sluggish.

Yulan flicked his little stone out into the darkness. It tick-ticked invisibly amongst the scree and boulders. Not loud, but loud enough. The sentry came at once to his feet and set one hand to the hilt of his sword, the other to the horn hanging at his belt. He took a pace forward, bending to peer out into the night.

Yulan dropped on him. He fell on to the man's shoulders and back, locking an arm about his neck, and knocked him down. Their fall made more noise than he would have liked, but it could not be helped and changed nothing of consequence. He already knew time would run against him in this.

They writhed and rolled together in the darkness, on the high, hard ground. The Armsman was strong; Yulan was stronger. He kept a tight, crushing lock about the man's throat, and held the wrist of his sword arm firm. He could feel the panic in his captive's increasingly desperate struggles. Legs scythed back and forth over the ground as if mimicking flight.

With his free hand, the Armsman at first tried to push himself up, but finding Yulan's weight too great, he clawed and pulled at the arm around his neck. That availed him no more, so he began to scrabble for the horn. Yulan let him do so. The man would have no breath to wind the thing even if he freed it.

As they slid lower, their legs, now entwined as Yulan sought to quieten his prey, reached and then sank into a tendril of the mist. Here at its very upper limit the vapour seemed all the more unnatural, for it was not – as it should have been – fraying and wisping away on the air, but dense and formed. Like milk contained in an absurdly shaped glass vessel.

The Armsman's resistance was ebbing. The strength of his arms slackened; the flailing of his legs diminished and became erratic, driven more by fading instinct than urgent will. The horn, released from his belt, slipped from numbing fingers on to the ground. Yulan had no time to savour his imminent victory, however. Just as the Armsman's vigour dwindled, the mist suddenly acquired a vigour of its own.

He felt its touch, even through his boot. Foot and ankle of the leg that had sunk furthest into the mist were abruptly held, as if they had plunged into sucking, gripping mud. And the grip was tightening. The Armsman was not yet entirely subdued, still weakly stirring, so Yulan could not spare a hand to drag himself away from the fog. He tried to kick the trapped leg free, but that only strengthened its bonds, for the mist resisted and reacted and thickened. It was not trying to drag him in, merely to hold him; and that it did, sure as a snared rabbit.

Yulan sensed the fear flickering into life at the very edge of his awareness, but paid it no heed. The time was not yet come when fear might serve him. His mind worked in its fast, calm way. Callotec had clearly acquired the aid of at least one highly accomplished Clever. The mist had not taken hold of Yulan's opponent. It must recognise him in some way. Know him. To make a cloud such as this was not the work of an untrained walking-witch or a novice. The School, like as not. And that was one enemy he would not – could not – set the Free against in open conflict.

He lay still, acceding to the mist's restraint, and put all his weight and strength into crushing the sentry towards unconsciousness. Gradually, the man stopped moving. Went limp in Yulan's embrace. He did not soften his hold for long moments yet, counting off heartbeats until his experience told him his victim was safely dulled but not yet irreparably harmed. Once sure of that, he rolled away.

That twisting did nothing to break his leg free of the mist's grasp. It twisted with him, coiling like solid smoke around his ankle. Yulan sat up and pulled a knife from its sheath at his calf. He did not know whether he would have dared to reach into the mist, had it been high enough to hide that knife, but was grateful the decision was not needed.

He slit the hide ties around the top of his boot and tried to pull his foot free. The mist pulled back. Yulan cut deeper, sawing at the boot itself. The soft, thin leather parted. He returned the knife to its place and tried to peel the boot down his leg. He gave his fear just a little freedom then, letting it run through him, through his arms. He strove to haul his foot out and free. It came. The boot was crumpled and engulfed by the mist. Swallowed.

Yulan scrambled to his feet and dragged his insensate prize back up the slope a short way. Then he stood, tall and still, and listened to the night. He heard nothing beyond the wind, but did not trust that silence. He took the Armsman's sword from its sheath and rested it gently against a rock, then slung the man over his shoulder and began to trot, unevenly and uncomfortably, back up the rising ridge.

The harsh ground was unforgiving to an unbooted foot. Yulan had gone without shoes for much of his childhood, but that had been on sand and dust and hot, smooth rock. His feet had, in any case, softened since then, cosseted. He would be bleeding by the time he reached the horses.

As he worked his way up and along the ridge's rough backbone, he stopped now and again to look back. Even for one such as him, the labour was punishing and he was grateful for the occasional brief respite. The last time he did it, though, staring back along his moonlit trail, he saw distant figures moving. Running. Coming closer. He did not look back again after that. There was no point.

"Yulan's more dangerous than any Clever, anyway," muttered Kerig as he distractedly pushed one of his beetle pieces across the Land board. "That's why the School so loathes him; maybe that's why Crex came over all doubting. Yulan's their better, and they all know it."

"He was born to lead the Free," Wren murmured, staring at the game. "That's what Merkent said. That's why he marked him as his successor."

"Merkent was your captain before Yulan?" Drann asked.

Wren only nodded, but Kerig said: "He was."

"What happened to him? Is he living that rich-as-a-royal life somewhere?"

"No," grunted Kerig. A bitter snarl suddenly twisted his face. "He was killed. He was betrayed. We all were."

"Who by?"

"Sullen. The School's butcher. Ow!"

Kerig clasped a hand to his brow, covering the spot that Wren had hit with a hard-thrown playing piece. The little wooden beetle bounced off his skull and went skittering away beneath a nearby table.

Ordeller's ape looked their way from its perch atop the serving counter. It stared at them for a moment, then towards the table beneath which the playing piece had disappeared. In slow and considered fashion, it lowered itself down from the counter and came on its knuckles in search of the lost beetle.

"That's it," Wren snapped at her husband, true anger now colouring her cheeks. "You've gone giddy like a loose-tongued child, just because you don't feel like death's got hold of your balls any more. This boy's got no place hearing things like this."

Kerig wrinkled his nose. He slid his feet off the bench and dropped them to the floor, leaned forward still nursing his stung head.

"What does it matter?" he muttered. "If the Free's no more after all of this is done, what does it matter?"

"It matters because we're not done yet, and there's some things you'll not be talking about even after we are. We hold together. You know that. All stand, or all fall; but we don't tell tall tales to those who've not made the same promise. Now, go find that piece before the ape does, so I can—"

"I didn't want to play any more anyway," Kerig said, more than a touch sulkily.

"Because you'd lost," Wren grunted.

"You imagine so if it makes you happy," Kerig snorted.

Yulan could dimly see, up ahead, like a rock amongst a hundred others, the shape of Hamdan standing, bow drawn. He had retreated some little way back amongst the swaying kite cords and the cairns from which they rose.

"Stand your ground," the archer shouted across the rumbling wind as Yulan came beneath the invisible shadow of the first kites. "Stand still, you fool."

He sounded irritated. Unreasonably so, felt Yulan, labouring half shod and beneath a considerable burden on unreliable ground. But he did not hesitate. He sloughed the unconscious Armsman from his shoulder and spun about.

Five of them were coming at him, strung out one behind another. The wind buffeted them, the lurching strings of the kites above swung at them, but they came on intently. Yulan drew his sword. Settled his stance. The pain in his foot was forgotten.

An arrow snapped past his ear, close enough for him to hear the hiss of its feathers, feel the cut of it through the air. It hit the first of his assailants in the chest and went through the thin leather tunic. Not deep enough to pierce the heart, but deep enough to make the man fall clumsily forwards and smash his face on a projecting rock. Teeth scattered like unseated pearls.

The next of them sprang over his fallen comrade, and landed badly. His lead foot slid on loose stones and robbed him of his balance. He veered sideways and ran into one of the tight kite cords as it swayed lower. It strained across his shoulder and neck, and staggered him.

Another arrow, flashing across the corner of Yulan's eye to smack itself into the palm's width of exposed flesh in the man's throat. He went backwards with blood already at his lips.

The man's fate caused Yulan to reconsider. The kites offered little safe room for swordplay. He dropped his blade and crouched to pluck the knife from his ankle sheath. A little too slowly, as it turned out.

A rangy man rushed him, block-headed iron hammer already raised and readied for the crushing blow to come, shield carried carelessly wide. Yulan drove up and forward without his knife, lunging out to meet the attack rather than await it. That gave him the fragment of surprise he needed to drive the heel of his hand into the man's chin with all the strength of arm, shoulder, thighs.

The impact jolted through him. It did much worse to his opponent. The man's head snapped back like a breaking twig. Yulan felt the jaw dislocating, heard neck bones parting, moving. The corpse fell like a sack of lead. Yulan let his rising movement carry him on, over the slumping body; he caught the dead man's hammer as it fell from lifeless fingers.

The last two had learned from the demonstration of their quarry's nature. One had learned fright, and was already sprinting back the way he had come. An arrow leaped over Yulan's shoulder and went sighing away into the night in pursuit of that fugitive. Yulan did not bother to track it. Hamdan was not given to mistakes.

The other had learned caution, or been bred with a greater store of it. He came on carefully, round shield held across chin and throat and chest, sword close. A sterner test, then.

Yulan rolled his wrist as he advanced, measuring the weight of the hammer. It was well balanced. A horseman's weapon, really, crafted to dent armour and break the bones beneath. Made to meet the threat of the Empire and their shining Orphanidons. Not to his taste, but it would serve.

He held his opponent's gaze with his own. Looked into his eyes and did not blink. He dropped a shoulder, lifted the hammer. The man tipped his shield up, just a fraction; he could not do otherwise. He slashed at Yulan's exposed flank, but Yulan was already sinking sideways, squatting away from the strike. The hammer hit the side of the swordsman's knee hard enough to tear its insides.

The man howled, but to his credit did not quite fall. He hopped wildly backwards, struggling to keep his one good leg beneath him. Yulan rushed after him, pulled the top of his shield down with one hand, smashed hammer to helm with the other. That first blow was enough to send the helmet clattering away amongst the rocks, and to put the man on his back. The second stoved in his temple and killed him.

Yulan let the hammer fall beside the corpse. He had never much liked the things. A sword could answer more questions than a hammer, in most fights. He heard Hamdan coming out from the darkness, picking his way around the dead. The archer was unstringing his bow.

He prodded the unconscious sentry with the toe of his boot. "We asking questions instead of looking for ourselves?"

"We are," Yulan confirmed. "We'll put an hour between us and Callotec, then loosen his lips."

"Best hurry along, then," Hamdan said placidly, already turning away. Already heading for the horses.

Yulan lifted his unshod foot for a moment and squinted down at it. He could feel the lacerations, the flow of blood.

"A fine idea," he called after Hamdan, "but it'll need you to play packhorse for our prisoner. I'm a little lamed."

Drann found sleep elusive, despite the dreadful weariness pooled in limbs and head. He had allowed himself too much time with Kerig and Wren, seduced by the stories he was told, the half-secrets glimpsed. Sat there too late into the night, until exhaustion turned into something else, something that resisted the needed slumber.

It might also have been that the bed was too soft, too comfortable. He had been without a bed of any sort for a long time now, and the one he had known before that had been crude by comparison with those Ordeller provided.

He rolled and twisted, trying to quieten the insistent workings of his mind. He saw again that bloated, blunt finger in the cage, the piercing stare of Hestin's young but old eyes. What kept sleep at bay in the end was the muffled sound of voices. Just as he was slipping away, the thoughts in his head blurring into the fancies and absurdities of near-dream, he heard people talking in the next room. Kerig and Wren.

Most of it was indistinct, but fragments came clear to him. Single leaves wind-blown from the talking tree.

Kerig saying: "He's barely said a word to me since Creel's camp."

Wren: " . . . forgive you. Yulan's not cruel . . . "

It was not the ebullient, effusive Kerig of earlier. This was a weary man, burdened. Letting show, Drann supposed, truths he would trust only to a loved one.

"I'd do it again . . . my brother . . . "

"I know."

Drann felt guilty at his intrusion upon these moments. The tones, the words, were too heartfelt to be meant for uninvited ears. But he lay still and quiet. Listened.

" . . . my love . . .' – Wren, this – " . . . I'll always walk with you. All the way. Even if no one else . . . "

Whispers, then, that Drann could not make out, until Kerig, trying not to laugh: " . . . leave the goat-breeding to our grand-children, when I'm not around to smell the things."

And silence, which was what finally shamed Drann into rising from his bed. It was an intimate silence, and he had no desire to witness it; nor whatever sounds might eventually disturb it. He went stiffly to the door, his weariness cruelly engulfing him like a smothering cloak now that he had given up on sleep for the time being. The passageway outside was utterly dark, but he remembered where the stairs were. He even remembered, to his surprise, that one of the steps about halfway down creaked mightily; he managed to avoid it.

Ordeller was slouched in a chair, feet up on a table. Snoring. Her ape had somehow folded itself into the next chair, its arms wrapped about its head, legs curled up into its stomach. It too slept. Drann rubbed his eyes. He was at a loss. He wandered across to the serving counter and leaned over it, debating whether beer would help or hinder slumber. A loud snuffling and snorting behind him brought him sharply upright. He turned to find Ordeller regarding him with an odd expression.

"Miserable times, aren't they?" she said, her voice still thick and a little indistinct with sleep.

Then there were horses outside in the street, their hoofs loud in the night. Footsteps hurrying to the lodging house. The door burst open. Yulan and Hamdan entered, faces taut with exhaustion and concern. Yulan was hobbling, one foot booted, the other bandaged.

Ordeller struggled out of her chair, the noise of her ascent rousing the ape, which lifted its head and blinked at the people disturbing its rest.

"Are the rest of them abed?" Yulan snapped.

Ordeller and Drann both said, "Yes."

"Wake Akrana. Let the rest sleep a time."

Drann was not sure whether the command was meant for him or Ordeller. He hesitated; she did not. As she vanished up the stairs, Drann watched Yulan slump into a chair and lift his wounded foot to examine it, grimacing.

Hamdan's face was fixed in a fell scowl. The archer unslung bow and quiver from his back and threw them down on to a table with unwonted violence.

"What happened?" Drann asked.

"The Bereaved," Hamdan snarled. "Callotec's got the Bereaved."

PART TWO

When Drann Was Eleven

When Drann was eleven, the crops failed. A blight killed the barley in the fields, rotting it where it stood. No farm was spared. No one had the stores to go without the harvest. Without barley to sell or eat, hunger was promised.

That promise made everything hard. It made tempers short, words sharp, hearts tired. Not for Drann, who being eleven was too distanced from notions of consequence and future hardship to feel their weight, but for his parents, whose moods darkened. And for Old Emmin, who was ailing by then and perhaps made fretful by thoughts of things still darker, and more final, than the family's hunger. It all set an unhappy air over the cottage.

One morning, Drann's father came in from a long night spent awake at the side of their one cow. Trying to ease the bad birthing of her calf. Trying and failing, for the calf was dead, the cow exhausted, fragile. Perhaps dying.

Drann listened to his mother and father shouting at one

another for a time; not shouting about the calf, but about everything else. About the small burdens of their lives. It made Drann anxious, so he fled from the sound and went out into the village.

There, he fell in with Kurl and Martan, the only village boys near his age. Drann was an only son. He had two sisters, Emmin and Trae. For a time, he had had a brother. Rellick. Rellick had died in his fifth month and, just like that, Drann had become once more an only son. Kurl and Martan were not as brothers to him, but they were friends; good ones, more often than not.

That day, they took to playing a game of warlords. There was, on the southern edge of the village, a little humpbacked stone bridge over a stream. It had gone without repair for a long time, and was used only to drive animals to and from the fields now and again. For the boys, though, it could be the huge bridge across the Kurn at Karnolan, where Hugent, first of the Hommetic kings, won his crown with five thousand men against thrice their number.

No one wanted to be Hugent, of course. Whatever love there might once have been for the Hommetics had been squandered by his successors. But Drann was more than willing to play the role of Roluman, Captain of the Free; the red-haired, unnaturally strong giant of a man whose company won both day and throne for Hugent. Kurl and Martan were to hold the bridge against Drann's assault.

He lobbed some little sticks at them, a cloud of arrows. He advanced with a bigger, stronger one in his hand, the gleaming blade of Roluman's famed sword. He stretched as tall as he could, to be that giant, that hero. It felt much better than being himself.

Kurl went dutifully down, beaten to the cobbles by Roluman's martial prowess. Martan, though, broke faith with history. For whatever reason, he did not feel like losing that day. He and Drann battled back and forth on the span of the bridge, breaking and splitting their stick swords. Eventually, Martan threw his aside and grappled with an increasingly indignant Drann, pinning him against the low parapet.

"Drann!"

The angry cry made the boys spring apart.

Drann's mother was standing a short way up the track towards the village. Her face was flushed with anger, fists on her hips.

"What are you doing?" she shouted. "Get back here."

Drann let the shattered remnant of his sword fall. Martan was edging away from him, attempting to disappear.

"I'm Roluman," Drann said.

He knew it was the worst possible thing to say. Perhaps that was why he said it. His tongue had never acquired as much discipline as some would wish.

"No you're not." Almost a screech, that. "You're nobody but you, today and every day. You're the boy who's going to help your father get the pig's shed mended. That's who you are."

"Let him be."

Drann's father was coming down the path behind his wife. He looked as wan, as tired, as diminished as Drann had ever seen him. It was the first time in his life his father had ever looked small to him.

"Let the lad dream, one day at least. This life'll set itself to taking that from him soon enough. You think it needs our help with that?"

His wife scowled at him, and the glare carried a fury that Drann had not seen pass between his parents before.

"Well do you?" his father demanded.

They left without another word, to Drann or each other. He watched them go in silence. Uncertain what he should feel, or think, or do. He thought to himself that he would not let life take from him the chance to be Roluman, or whoever else he might want to be. And he did not know why that thought, as he watched the receding backs of his round-shouldered parents, made him angry.

Because he did not know where that anger came from, or what to do with it, he did what was easiest. He became once more Roluman, great Captain of the Free, and fought with Martan. Beat him. Bloodied his nose and bruised his ribs.

12

The Mistress Always Wins At Land

The School's Home stood a quarter of a mile inland, on the south-western fringes of Harvekka. A market street, almost deserted, was upon one side of it, open fields golden with unharvested grain on the other. Between town and country, the Home. The School's greatest holding here in the south, the place of its founding and its modest beginnings more than two hundred years ago.

The Spiral Garden, the famous ornament that ascended the oval building on a continuous rising terrace, normally put at least a faint smile on Morue's face with its profuse greenery and ebullient flowers. Its presence, in unchanging defiance of the cycle of seasons, was a rather indulgent piece of ostentation. A constant visible reminder of the School's continuation. And of its power, since it required diligent and selfless Clevers to keep a garden abundant even through winter.

Morue had herself played an occasional role in that achievement. She was a Vernal Clever, attuned most closely to that

entelech that came to prominence in the spring months and
shaped much that was green and vital. That was what it took to
make the Spiral Garden grow: the Vernal entelech, tapped and
shaped to bestow unseasonal life.

Today, as she walked amongst the bare, unattended market
stalls towards the Home, she could not summon a smile. Not
even as she caught the scent of jasmine drifting down from the
Garden. Continuation. That was the difficulty. The Garden
declared it, yet she was one of the few who knew how unsafe
that declaration had become of late. A mere two months into
her rule as Mistress of the School, and already she was wondering if she might be the last to hold that office. Pity everyone
living in these formerly Hommetic lands, should that prove the
case. There was not much time left to save them.

Lurro, her manservant, hurried to get ahead of her and pull
open a side door.

The great stairway of the Home echoed the Spiral Garden
outside. It coiled up the inner wall of the building. Morue
climbed it slowly, favouring her sore ankle. She had slipped on
a step the day before and twisted it. That set a wart of irritation
upon her mood, for it felt too much like the injury of an old
woman and Morue did not – would not – consider herself to
be old. Her mother had lived to seventy-five, her father almost
as long; at fifty, she could tell herself she had time aplenty yet.
Of course, neither of her parents had been a Clever. They,
unlike their daughter, had not had to pay the punishing toll
that path exacted.

Lurro walked at her side. She might have taken his arm to
steady herself, but that was a concession – to him, to her age –

she was not willing to make. Her walking staff was concession enough.

Past the refectory, the scholars' hall, the dormitories. Up and up. The Home was quiet. Teaching and training were much reduced, these last few weeks. There were Clade guards on the stairs, scattered up them like statues, but the thirty scholars spent much of their time out of sight in safe, inactive seclusion. A sad state of affairs, given the School's origins. It had begun, long ago, as a place for the finding and training of Clevers. That it had, over the many years since, accumulated more powers, more influence in all manner of areas did not to Morue's way of thinking change the fact that the scholars remained at its heart.

There had been thirty-five of them when the first spark of what had become the Council's rebellion was lit. Two had simply disappeared, carried off by the chaos. Another had slipped out one night to explore the exciting, tumultuously transforming world, and duly been killed in a riot. One – to Morue's profound shame – had died in an entelech-fuelled brawl between rival gangs of scholars when the world's transformations had birthed factions within the School itself. And the last: she had been executed for that murder. Slain by the very School that had sworn to train and nurture her, for that was what the law required, and in matters relating to Clevers, the School was law, judge, executioner.

Atop the Home was Morue's own apartment, reserved for the Mistress or Master whenever they were visiting. Her predecessor's taste had been in a luxurious vein. She found the array of rugs and silks, tapestries and gold that greeted her as she entered more than a little distasteful. She had much reduced the ostentation of the main residence she had inherited, in the School's Keep at Armadell-on-Lake, but had not yet found the time to do the same here.

Sullen was waiting there, sitting in an elaborately carved ebony chair. His uncouth presence was a dissonant note amidst such finery, with his half-braided hair, his worn warrior clothes, his great sword resting against the arm of the chair. He looked nothing like the disciplined Clade men he commanded.

He did not rise when she entered. He was presumptuous. But then, he had earned a degree of presumption.

"Mistress," he said quietly.

She nodded, and handed her staff to Lurro. He took it and the Land set he carried under his arm to a closet. Sullen watched him as he passed. The two men did not like one another. That did not concern Morue. Although he could exude a certain charm and air of reason when he so wished – he could hardly have commanded the loyalty and service of the rest of the Clade otherwise – she had never encountered anyone who truly liked Sullen, and if she ever did, she would most likely suspect them of some derangement of the senses.

"You've been playing Land again?" Sullen asked.

"Yes. With Krurtik."

She found it fattened up Krurtik's sense of importance to be seen playing Land with the Mistress of the School. He was a crude man, formerly castellan of Harvekka's Harbour Tower, but like others such the revolt had elevated him. He was, by default, now master of Harvekka and a member of the rebel's Council. The School required such friends if it was to survive and retain its influence.

"Did you win?" asked Sullen.

"The Mistress always wins at Land," Lurro said as he closed the closet doors.

"You can leave us, Lurro," she told him.

"You're certain, Mistress?" he asked with a little bow.

"Yes."

"One of the—' Sullen began as soon as Lurro was gone from the chamber, but Morue held up a stern finger of warning.

He waited silently while she arranged a stool before her own chair, and unwrapped her headscarf to make a cushion. She lifted her leg with both hands and set it gently down upon that soft support. She sighed with relief, and then gestured for Sullen to continue.

"One of the Free – a Clever – killed a man," he said.

"That is hardly unheard of," Morue observed.

She was disappointed. When she'd received Sullen's request for her presence, she had hoped it would be some matter relating to the Bereaved. Hope was too small a word for what she had felt, in truth.

"He did it in Creel of Mondoon's camp," Sullen went on, "under a truce flag and without the protection of a contract."

"Ah. Well, the truce flag's neither here nor there; that's Creel's concern, if he sees fit to enforce it. But for the rest . . . Did this Clever use the entelechs?"

"Seems so. Man died of burns."

"Which of the Free was it?"

"Kerig."

Morue wrinkled her nose.

"A Vernal. It is unlikely he would use fire."

"Man's dead, and burned, nevertheless. Seems clear Kerig caused it, one way or another."

Sullen's voice was entirely flat. Disengaged. Yet Morue knew he would, in this matter, be most acutely interested. He was, after all, the only man living who could truthfully say he had killed a Captain of the Free. His deeds would have made him famous – infamous, more aptly – were they not a secret known to only a handful. The struggle between School and Free had never been treated, by either of the contestants, as a fit matter for public discourse. Both had too much to lose, should they forfeit the King's favour, or allow themselves to be drawn into open, unrestrained conflict. Sullen had risked all of that at White Steading.

Every nuance of the human soul, every subtlety of the personality it displayed, was an expression of the four entelechs that had woven themselves into its form. When they were unbalanced in some way, it was rarely of great consequence. A slight preponderance of the Aestival in a soul might breed a hot temper; a moderate excess of the Vernal an ebullient, light-hearted manner. On those rare occasions when a more profoundly unbalanced soul arose, there was seldom much that could be done. In most cases collapse, utter degeneracy, madness, ungovernable misery would be the result.

And then there was Sullen. A man possessed of a soul so unbalanced it all but beggared the imagination. An embodiment of unfeeling cruelty and viciousness. Most carrying such base savagery within them would be ruled by it; defined, in their deeds, manner and thought, by its insistent demand for expression. Quickly destroyed by it.

Sullen was different. He had somehow – Morue had no idea how – harnessed that void at his core without diminishing it. He had turned what in others would be a deforming burden into a tool that he could wield in service of a sharp and calculating mind. It made him amongst the most valuable of all the School's servants. Morue's servants. He was no Clever – none of the Clade that he led were – but without him, she would never have emerged victorious from the struggles within the School unleashed by the rebellion. It had been, until Sullen decided to take Morue's part, a struggle conducted through debate, argument, conspiracy. Sullen changed that, and delivered her victory over the corpses of her opponents. Most of them, at least. Sadly not all.

Had he not done so, Kasuman would be Master now, and the School would have become a dull and compliant adherent to Crex's cause. The King would very likely have unleashed the Bereaved against his own people, with the School's connivance. That, Morue remained certain, would have been a disastrous crime. One worth a great deal of savagery to avert. One not yet averted.

"What of the Bereaved?" she asked quietly.

The faint, instantly suppressed twitch of irritation at the corner of Sullen's eye did not go unnoticed. He resented the change in topic. He was not wholly imperturbable, though his voice remained a study in tranquillity.

"No trace. No new word."

Morue stamped her good foot. The effect was somewhat diminished by the thick rug overlying the floorboards.

"All else is distraction," she snapped.

"Better than five hundred of the Clade are out hunting. There is little more to be done, unless you want me to tell the Council that we have lost the Bereaved. They would be delighted to join the search, no doubt."

"And the School would be swept into history overnight," Morue growled. "What need have they for us, if we do not have the Bereaved? It would become a prize for whatever petty warlord found it. And how long then, do you suppose, before its plagues were feasting on these lands? Or perhaps the Orphans learn of our weakness and descend upon us before anyone even finds the Bereaved. They are watching, you may be sure; and nobody – not even you, Sullen – would find conquest by the Orphans to be anything but a waking night-mare."

Sullen shrugged.

"You know more of such things than I do, Mistress. I concern myself with the immediate. I understand the importance of finding and killing Kasuman, retrieving the Bereaved. All that can be done to further that cause is being done. There is nothing else, without more men. A great many more men."

"And now you want to challenge the Free with what men you have left," Morue muttered.

It was not as easy as she would have wished to master her temper. It was fear, she knew. Fear for the future of the School; for the future of the people it existed – in her mind – to protect. Since the first days of the Hommetic Kingdom, the Bereaved had been the one and only sure protection against the Empire of Orphans. Its appalling capacities had been the Kingdom's armour, kept and husbanded by the School. On behalf of the King, some – kings amongst them – had assumed; on behalf of the people, Morue had always thought. Now it was lost to them, stolen away by the very man Morue had warred with for leadership: Kasuman.

The rightful Master of the School, by many accounts, but hopelessly misguided in his fervent loyalty to Crex. He had traded adherence to the people, the School and their interests for adherence to the King. That Kasuman had not already unleashed the Bereaved, now that he had carried the Permanence away, was a source of constant surprise to Morue. She awoke every day expecting to hear word of plague, of corpse fires, of death unbounded. The absence of such word gnawed at her gut almost as much as its arrival would.

"I thought," Sullen said quietly, "that if there was even a chance of hamstringing the Free, you would not be the one to let it pass."

"In other times, you would be right," Morue said irritably.

Her irritation, her anger, her every sentiment was wasted on Sullen. The man was impervious to the moods of others. She was not sure he even recognised their gradations sometimes.

"Whether I'm here or not makes no odds to the finding of Kasuman," Sullen persisted. "Let me go to Creel's camp. I'll find out what happened."

She stared at him. He stared back, unblinking, with those dead eyes. Had he not done such service to the School over the years, and to Morue herself more recently, she would have been rid of him before now.

"You've told me many times the free companies were a

canker in the kingdom," Sullen said. "The worst threat to lasting peace. That extinguishing them, one after another, was the School's greatest contribution to that peace. There's only the Free left. The only Clevers outside the School's command or discipline, thanks to that charter of theirs."

"Please do not goad me with my own words," Morue said. "And you and I – you more than anyone – both know that their charter did not stop us pursuing them, when times were more predictable. When our position and power gave us the freedom to act, even without Crex's approval."

Sullen smiled. Much as a corpse-eating lizard would smile, Morue suspected.

"The Free are my only failure, Mistress. The only time I have failed the School. I might remedy that now. Their charter may be no more, since the royal line that issued it is extinct. But if Kerig has killed a man without the protection of a contract, he's put himself beyond that charter in any case. He's just another Clever committing a crime: under our authority, for trial, judgement. Execution."

"If the Council permits our continuing exercise of that authority."

"They can't withhold a permission we don't request. If we act as if we retain authority, we retain it. That's in the nature of times such as these."

It always troubled Morue when she was reminded that Sullen's pretended lack of subtlety was just that: pretence. Even she could now and then be lulled into forgetting how sharp was the mind behind those impassive eyes.

"I will not permit the School to be trapped into open war

with the Free, not when there is so much trouble already bearing down upon us. The Clamour overmatches us no less than does the Bereaved, in hostile hands."

"Perhaps," Sullen said levelly. "I only ask to go to Creel's camp. Establish the truth of what happened. Make a show of the School's right to address such matters."

"Whom did Kerig kill?"

"One of the Weaponsmith's followers. It's the Weaponsmith who asks us to intervene, not Creel. When one Clever invokes the School's laws against another, we must act, must we not?"

There was a dark determination within him that Morue did not entirely understand, could not imagine herself into. None but a fool, she thought, would want to live even a moment in Sullen's head. It made it impossible for her to fully trust him. Yet she needed him and his ferocity. At least until some kind of peace and order was restored.

And he was right, in the end, that the Free were – and would always be – a challenge to that peace and order, and to the secure authority of the School. The mercenary companies had ever been a malign influence, an open invitation to violence and ambition for anyone who could afford their services. The Free, the last of them, more so than any other by virtue of its sheer power.

"The Free will be gone from Creel's camp by now, I imagine," she murmured.

"Not beyond our reach. Kasuman's assassins fell short of perfection. Sestimon Trune still lives, after all. Time's past when he might have tracked Kasuman for us, but if I can get him to the camp quickly, the traces are probably still fresh enough that he could point the way to Kerig. His wounds are all but healed. He would probably survive the journey."

"You will not engage the Free in battle," Morue said sharply. "Not for the sake of a single Clever."

Sullen shook his head, the beads in his hair sliding over one another.

"I'll find out what happened. If there's guilt in the air, I'll find out where the guilty man is."

"And if there is any word of the Bereaved, you will go at once in its pursuit."

"Of course, Mistress. At once."

13

Ifs Are Hares

Just outside Curmen, uphill, stood a mean little farmhouse. Its fields of grass, marked out with old walls of yellowish stone, were greener than the dry turf cloaking the hillside. There were no animals to be seen in them, though. It was nothing but sense, to hide precious animals away when the land was thick with folk eager to carry them off. Drann could imagine his father doing the same. Likely *was* doing the same, with what few animals the family kept, in that faraway village in the north.

But it was not cows or sheep that Drann and Akrana sought now. It was horses. Ordeller had said there might be some here. Yulan wanted them. He had sent Akrana to get them, and Drann along with her because everyone else was busy readying for what would be a fast, hard march.

The sun was a sliver, edging over the eastern horizon. Drann's eyes were already leaden – he had stolen just an hour or two's sleep in the last part of the fraught night – and the dull, cold air was working hard to drag them closed entirely. He was glad he had his spear, only because it gave him something to rest a little of his weight upon, to push himself forward with.

Even Akrana, stiff and stern as ever, betrayed hints of her weariness in the dark shadows beneath her eyes, the slight sluggishness in her movements. She was not entirely inhuman and invulnerable then. She was not talking to Drann, either, and for that he was not sorry.

They advanced slowly up the narrow, rough track to the farmhouse door. Partly from tiredness, partly from caution. Akrana had unbuckled her belt and carried it and her scabbarded sword in one hand. Drann could smell smoke, and just make out the thin trail of it snaking above the house. Someone was awake, and cooking or warming.

"Go and look in that byre," Akrana whispered, pointing with her sword towards the run-down cow shed around the corner of the house.

Drann made his way there, glancing nervously through a window as he passed – seeing nothing but the glow of candle-light – and stumbling a little on the uneven ground. There was a shuttered aperture in the near wall of the shed. He lifted up the shutter and peered in.

"Four horses," he said as he walked back towards Akrana.

"Fit for riding?" she hissed.

Drann shrugged. He was far too tired to feel anything like nervousness at her curt manner. That would be entirely too much effort.

"They're not farm horses," was all he said.

That was evidently enough for Akrana. She rapped, hard, on the door with the hilt of her sword. It shook in its frame. She gestured for Drann to stand back, and retreated a few steps from the threshold herself. Side by side, they waited. Akrana set her hand on the sword hilt, but did not draw the blade. Not yet.

"Do you want me to mend that for you?" Kerig had asked quietly, regarding the bloodied bandages about Yulan's foot with raised eyebrows.

"No," Yulan grunted. "I don't want you spending yourself. We might have greater need of your strength soon enough."

He was carefully peeling away the bandages as he spoke. Fresh ones, which Ordeller had ripped from one of her bed sheets, lay beside him on the table, waiting to be applied. His wounds hurt. Less than some he had acquired in the past, more than others.

It was still three hours from dawn. Candles burned around the room, giving a little light. Ordeller loitered by the door, listening for any sound out on the street. All of the Free – save Hamdan's archers, who all now stood guard over Hestin and the Clamour in the stables – were crowded around a single large table. Ordeller had brought them bowls of soup, warmed up from the leftovers of yesterday. No one was drinking it. She did not seem to mind. She sat alongside Drann at a separate table. No one had told the two of them to keep their distance, as far as Yulan knew. It was right, though. This was for the Free only, now.

"I trust his fear," Hamdan was saying. "He was fit to weep once we convinced him who we were. A few pokes with a knife and he was longing to tell us everything he knew."

"Which was not enough," Yulan grunted, winding one of the

clean bandages about his foot, "but it's what we've got."

"The Bereaved, though?" muttered Wren. "I can't believe it."

"And I do," said Yulan. "We know the School turned in on itself, fighting one against another over whether to help Crex or not. We know that the ones who thought not won the day. If they hadn't, I'd never have taken a single coin from any of the Council."

"If they hadn't, the whole Council'd be dead," snorted Hamdan.

"Maybe," Yulan acknowledged. "The war would not be over, that much is certain. I'd thought that those who lost the argument within the School were all dead, or imprisoned. Evidently not. Clevers, and Clade, and the Bereaved. All camped there with Callotec. That's what our tongue said."

"Do we know how many Clevers?" Kerig asked dolefully.

Yulan shook his head.

"Not many. But at least two hundred warriors; Clade, and as many of the King's levymen as they could round up along the way. All running for the Empire for want of anywhere else to run."

Ordeller's ape had climbed silently up on to the table. It investigated the nearest of the abandoned bowls of soup, stirring its finger in the thick broth. The ape smelled bad, Yulan thought. Ordeller hissed a warning from the far side of the room and the animal retreated regretfully back on to the floor.

"Why isn't every army in the kingdom busy turning over rocks, hunting through every copse, if the Bereaved's got loose?" mused Wren.

"Because the School hasn't told anyone," Yulan grunted. "I'd heard the Clade had companies roving around, but thought it just some unsettled part of their internal squabbles. If anyone but them lays hands on the Bereaved, who knows what will happen? The School would certainly lose their standing, perhaps everything. And the Council might go to war with one another over its possession. Anyone who holds it might think the mere threat of it entitles them to a throne."

"Probably does," Kerig muttered.

"It's Kasuman, most likely," Yulan went on quietly. "He was chief amongst those who wanted the School to stand behind Crex. If you go four generations back, he's got Hommetic blood in him. He's the only one I can think of who would have the fire in his belly to actually break the School apart, and the cold stupidity to steal the Bereaved away."

"Stupid enough to let Callotec use it, though?" Hamdan asked. "Or deliver it to the Orphans?"

"Probably," Yulan sighed. "I imagine Callotec expects the Empire to let a tame king – him – sit in Armadell after they've wasted the land. He might convince Kasuman of it, if he needs convincing."

Akrana snorted. "King of Ruin, if the Orphans dance over everything first."

"Or King of the Dead," Yulan said. "He wouldn't be the first to think either of those a better title than King of Nothing."

He set a fine bone pin to hold the new bandage in place on his foot, and carefully pressed his sole to the floorboards. Testing the pain. It was bearable. The least of his concerns now.

"Listen," he said wearily. "Listen. This is not what we came looking for. This is not what I promised you, when I offered you a choice back at Creel's camp. Everything's changed. Creel's not paying us to fight three hundred men and the Bereaved."

"But if we win the Bereaved as well as Callotec, we can name any price we dream of," Hamdan said quickly. "Every power in the land will want to treat with us, and grovel at our feet. Even the School."

"Yes," Yulan conceded. The truth of it was too obvious to deny.

"If they carry the Bereaved into the Empire, there'll be thousands of Orphanidons on the march the next day," Akrana said. "Uncounted deaths, by plague and sword."

"I know," Yulan nodded. He spoke gently. He knew what that thought, that vision of the future, meant for her.

He sighed. Too much, weighing upon them all. Clouding what had seemed simple. And none of it going to the heart of what he wanted to say.

"I've served the Free for twelve years," he said at length. "It's given me a place to belong. You have. I didn't know what I was searching for when I walked up out of the south, until Merkent found me and showed me. That I became Captain when he . . . when he died was a greater honour than I ever deserved, or dreamed of."

Hamdan made a show of dissent, about to protest the question of what was deserved or not, but Yulan silenced him with a raised hand.

"I have tried to be worthy of that honour, and to live up to the traditions of those who went before. But in truth, I've known for years that what I really needed to be worthy of was you. All of you. There is more loyalty, more courage, more honour in the ranks of the Free than I have seen anywhere else. So many times, wielding such power, it might have fallen into cruelty or tyranny. It never did, because it has always been something more than all the other free companies ever were.

"And it was over. We found an ending for ourselves, because the time had come to seek such a thing. I think it was a good ending. So this needs to be said: you do not have to do this. None of you; not any more. It will not be done easily, if it's done at all. When it was just Callotec and a few Armsmen, sword and arrow might have sufficed. Now it's different. It'll take the entelechs."

He looked at Kerig, at Wren and last of all at Akrana.

"It would take everything we have, short of the Clamour. I hope short of the Clamour. So I say again: you do not have to do this. I go on because I choose to put myself between Callotec and Towers' Shadow, whatever the circumstance. Only for that."

They regarded him in silence. The only sound was the heavy snuffling of the ape, settling in beneath the table.

"I go where you go," Hamdan said at length and pushed back his chair. "I'm going to check on my boys in the stable. Make sure all's well with Hestin."

As the door closed behind him, Akrana rose as well.

"Nothing's changed," she said. "Nothing important. We go on. We honour the contract, and give Creel Callotec's head on a table."

Kerig and Wren were looking at each other, not at Yulan. Wren's hand rested over Kerig's on the table. Yulan thought he detected the slightest of squeezes there. A moment of silent comfort, communication.

"Go home," Yulan said softly to them. "Go make your farm, raise a family."

Wren smiled at her husband and then turned to Yulan.

"We're not done with this family yet. One last war for the Free."

Yulan shook his head a little. He felt strangely calm, faintly sorrowful.

"Do you really not know why we're doing this?" Wren asked him. "All of us. Even Akrana there, though she'll deny it with every breath. For you. Because however much you think you've been striving to be worthy of us, we know you surpassed that mark a long time ago."

Yulan did not know what to say to that. He had to swallow to slow the emotion that rose in his throat.

"A couple of hours' sleep for everyone," he said briskly, getting to his feet. "Then we ride hard. Ordeller?"

The matron of the house looked up.

"Does anyone in the town have horses fit for riding? At the pace I mean to set, we're going to be crippling ours if we can't find some spares to take along."

"Only ones I know of – by rumour, not certain – are out at the Maralon farm. Heard tell they came into possession of a few some weeks back. Nobody knows how, and they've got them hidden away if they've got them at all."

"I'll need them," said Yulan. He waved Kerig and Wren away from the table with expansive sweeps of his arms. "Sleep, all of you. Two hours."

Drann made to follow the rest as they filed up the stairs, but Yulan beckoned him over.

"Akrana tells me you were poking around the Clamour's wagon," he murmured.

The guilt that paraded itself across the youth's face might have been comical in another place, at another time.

"I suppose so," he said. "I just—"

"Don't do it again."

"I won't. Akrana said she'd cut my stupid head off."

"Well, I probably wouldn't let her do that, so that's not the reason you won't do it again. The real reason is that I'm telling you, and that you're hopefully not quite as stupid as Akrana seems to think. Agreed?"

"Agreed," Drann said emphatically. Then, more tentative: "She called it 'he', not 'it'. Hestin did. When she spoke, it was . . . strange. Jumbled."

Yulan sighed.

"The Clamour's the pure substance of the Aestival entelech, here in an impure world where it doesn't belong. Rage is an aspect of the Aestival, so Hestin's there, spending every moment of every day quieting that rage, dispelling it. It takes everything she's got. Not just her body. Her mind. She's losing it all, piece by piece.

"Now, I've got a question for you. You can wait here for us, or go back to Creel if you want to. I'll not insist you come with us, and there'll be no shame if you choose not to."

The question clearly took Drann a little by surprise. He frowned in consternation and glanced out of the corner of his eye at Wren disappearing up the stairs.

"Do you not need a contract any more, then? Or a contract-holder?"

"I don't know," Yulan confessed. "I might."

Drann shrugged.

"Then I'll come with you."

"That's not the wise answer."

"Probably not. But I'll come, a bit further at least."

"Then go and try to find some sleep. You'll be needed in the morning."

Drann had come close to pleading with Yulan not to send him at Akrana's side to the Maralon farm in search of the rumoured horses. But he had known it would serve no purpose. No one was questioning any of Yulan's instructions now; and someone had to go with her, after all.

So now he stood at the Clever's side, leaning on his spear at the door of the farmhouse in a dawn still miserly with its light and warmth. He stared down at his own feet, mind too dull to admit any thought. He noted that the stitches around the sole on his left boot were fraying. Might come apart any day now.

The door opened so abruptly and loudly that he took a startled step backwards. Akrana, of course, did not. Even when a stream of abuse spilled out and over her.

The shawled woman delivering the torrent was short and stocky, head shrunk down on to her shoulders. She was old. The two tall youths who peered over her were too young to be her sons, Drann thought. Grandsons, perhaps. This would not be the only farm that was missing a generation these days.

"We need your horses," Akrana said into the flood of invective.

"What horses?" snarled the grandmother. "Get a stick, boys, and chase 'er off."

One of the young men disappeared into the farmhouse. Akrana puffed out her cheeks in frustration.

"Get the horses," she said to Drann, and then leaned down towards the old lady. "I have a fistful of coins here for you, Mother. We will take nothing without paying for it, but be sure we must take what we need."

"Coins ain't worth more'n shit to me," the woman shouted. "Who's got anything to sell these days?"

Akrana glanced at Drann, who was still standing there, both mind and body heavy. Neither knowing what to do.

"Would you go and get the horses out of the barn," Akrana snapped at him.

And the lash of her anger did move him, send him sluggishly over towards the byre. He watched the confrontation in the doorway as he went, though. The old woman was glaring after him, her wizened face knotting into a scab of fury.

"He's stealing the horses, boys," she shrieked. "Stop him!"

That put a little life into Drann's stride, and he darted into the dark, enclosing shed and began unhitching the animals. The place smelled of cows, but there was no stock in here now save the horses. He had no idea how he was supposed to lead or manage four of them. For want of anything else to do, he carried on as if he knew precisely what he was doing, gathering all the long ropes by which they were tethered into his free hand and walking backwards. Trying to ease them from their places and out into the dawn. To his surprise, the animals did not resist.

As he emerged into the yard, he could hear the argument still raging. On one part, at least. It seemed that Akrana had given up on talk.

"You can't take them! I don't want your coins. You can't eat a coin."

She was trying to push past Akrana, but the Clever stood her ground, and set her sheathed sword crossways across the doorway. Someone had found a way out, though, for Drann heard a door clattering open at the back of the farmhouse. The noise must have disturbed a flock of crows on the field round there, for a great flight of them came raucously up, croaking their way into the sky and rolling over the roof like a ragged cloud of black leaves.

The birds swirled low over the yard for a moment, before rushing upward and scattering and speeding away over the hillside in a loose, spreading flock. Heading into the rosy blush tinting the clouds on the eastern horizon.

One of the youths was coming down the narrow path at the side of the farmhouse, staring at Drann. He had an ugly-looking cudgel in his hand. Drann blinked at him, looked towards Akrana. She was pushing back against the other grandson, who had stepped in front of the old woman.

"Let go those horses," the approaching youth shouted at Drann, brandishing his club.

"We do need them," Drann called out despondently. "I swear, if you knew why, you'd let—"

"Let them go!"

Drann hefted his spear, holding it clumsily as if he meant to throw it. He did not expect much to come of the gesture, but his opponent stopped.

"Best to just take her coin," Drann said.

He had never thrown a spear at anything but a straw bale. What little hunting he had done as a youth had been with snares, sling or fish trap. To his surprise, fear leaked into the farm boy's expression, replacing anger. He was afraid of Drann, and of his apparent intent. No one, as far as Drann could remember, had ever been afraid of him before.

"Take the coin," he said again. "It's the best you can hope for out of this."

He began to edge away, easing the horses across the yard. No one was going to try to stop him, he realised, but he kept the spear up just in case.

Akrana sprang back from the doorway, tossing a pouch of coins as she went. It burst open, and spilled a tinkling tumble of coppers on to the threshold, the cobblestones. That distracted the farm folk, but it was her sword, swept from its scabbard and held ready, that ensured they would not follow. She backed away from the house. Turned and walked beside Drann down the track, watching over her shoulder all the way.

The old woman's shouts pecked at them. Soon enough the door was slammed shut, and although that did not stop the complaints, it at least dulled them.

"They didn't seem to have anything but the horses," Drann said, as they headed slowly for Curmen.

"And where do you guess folk like that got riding horses from?" Akrana grunted. "No coins changed hands to make that happen, to be sure. Stolen, or looted from a battlefield. They have their profit."

"Like she said, they can't eat coins, though," Drann said stubbornly. "What if this was your farm? Your family?"

"I have neither," Akrana said, and Drann knew he should heed the threat in her voice. He chose not to, because what they had done left a sour taste, whether it had been necessary or not. Because he was tired, and frightened.

"But if—"

Akrana whirled on him, and pushed him back against the low wall bounding the track. She snatched the horses' tethers away from him with one hand and pressed the other flat against his chest.

"If?" she snarled into his face, close enough to make him shrink away. "A meaningless question. Ifs are hares, starting from your feet as you walk a path. Chase the hare, lose the path. Just as with the past and the future. They are not real. There is only the now. That is where you live. You do what needs to be done now, in this place, in pursuit of this task. Don't concern yourself with ifs."

He nodded mutely. That was not enough, it turned out, to drain away Akrana's fury.

"You know what it means if the Empire comes here?"

He could feel her breath. He could feel her spittle on his face. It seemed more than his questions deserved. He had – not a new experience this – said the wrong thing at the wrong moment.

"You know what it means to all these peasants you care so much about?" she shouted at him. "It means things a thousand times worse than having to sell a few horses, or having an empty belly. It means half the men being slaughtered. Any of the rest — men and women alike — who are unmarried going off into slavery. It means every child under the age of two, every one of them, being carried off to be raised a servant of the Empire. Any village that resists is burned; everyone in it, without exception, killed. You know how they kill people, the Orphans?"

Drann shook his head quickly, though of course he did. He had heard stories. Everyone had.

"They spit them. Whole families together, dying slowly on stakes in a circle. Always in a circle, facing one another. That is what it means, for the Bereaved to cross the border into the Empire. Within a month of that moment: a thousand forests of stakes, across this land, with families on them like split fruit. You think these people can stop that happening?"

She flailed a hand, the one still clutching the ropes, in the direction of the farmhouse, hidden now behind the rising ground and the long, low walls.

"No! They cannot. They are just little farm folk, fretting over a few horses. But we are the Free. We can change things. So we take their horses, and we go to fight. You think I care if they hate us for it? I do not. Their hate is too small a thing."

She lurched away from him, and strode off, dragging the horses after her. Drann waited for a moment, leaning against the wall. Puffed his cheeks out in relief.

"I am not afraid of their hatred," he heard Akrana saying as she marched downhill. "You make a gaol for yourself from it if you want to. I will not.'

14

Take My Son

Yulan knelt beside Hestin on the seat of the Clamour's wagon. The Clever held the reins in limp hands. Her cowled head dipped down and forwards. The great grey bull was quiet between the shafts. The metal capping its horns caught fragments of the daylight seeping between the closed doors.

There was no one else in the stables. The rest of the Free were outside, mounted. Ready. Waiting in the street. Yulan was alone, with Hestin and with the Permanence she had given so much of her life to. Given so much of the time that might have been hers.

Her leaf cloak was green. She was in control, of herself and of the Clamour.

"Can you hear me, Hestin?" he asked quietly, lips close to her ear.

She said nothing, but made a noise at the back of her throat. A sort of humming groan. An affirmation.

"I am sorry to ask this of you," Yulan said. "I think you will know – I hope you will remember – that I would not ask it if there was another way. Perhaps it's my failing that I cannot think of one."

He shifted a little to ease the discomfort in his foot. He was wearing a new boot to replace the one he had lost, and it was still stiff and pressing hard on his wounds.

"We have to go far and fast, Hestin. Some of the way across hard ground, I think. We are hunting a dangerous quarry now. We must get ahead of them. There will be no stopping to rest. I have more horses than riders, so I can spare them some of the punishment. But you cannot be parted from the rest of us, so your bull must keep pace. It will need your strength. Can you do that, Hestin?"

Again, that muted, neutral sound. Again, the guilt. Only twice in his life had he truly felt without choice. At Towers' Shadow, and when he first met Hestin. She had been a beautiful young woman then. Soft, but strong. The only one who seemed able to subdue the Clamour and end the devastation it was spreading. She had wanted to do it, and he had agreed, because he had no other answer to the need. So he persuaded Merkent to take her and it into the ranks of the Free, and to this day he did not know whether he had saved Hestin or condemned her. He had, at the least, assisted in her willing sacrifice, and her ruin. If he thought it would remove the necessity of that sacrifice, he would gladly surrender his life. He would die for any of the Free – he was not sure how many of them knew that, and it did not matter – but none more so than this girl who was herself dying to save everyone, everywhere, from the Clamour.

"Two days, and the night in between," he whispered. "No more than that, I hope. Your leaves will tell me if you falter, and I promise you I will stop if that happens. I will not let it wake. Even if that means our quarry escapes us."

"I know," she whispered. "This thing. All things, in you."

He put his hand on her shoulder. He could feel the bone there, beneath the thin covering of woven green leaves.

"This is the last of it," he promised her. "After this, we go away, you and I. We find peace somewhere. Somehow."

She made no reply.

"Let's go, then," he said softly, and climbed down to throw open the stable doors.

People watched from their windows as the Free rode out of Curmen. Some few came out on to their doorsteps, or into the street itself, but most preferred to keep a little more distance. They watched in silence, and in that silence the rumble of the Clamour's wagon was overbearing. It echoed from the walls, feeding on itself to become pervasive, as if the whole town was groaning.

Ordeller stayed out of sight. Pretending, no doubt, that the company had left her lodging house in a filthy state, near-beasts that they were, and that she must spend half the day setting it all to rights.

He had known Ordeller longer than most of those he now rode with. All of them, save Hamdan and Akrana, in fact. Before he had become Captain, he had been Merkent's right hand, and that had meant looking after the company's web of watchers and listeners and tellers, strewn across the kingdom and beyond. Ordeller was one of the best. He had more than once tried to persuade her to move somewhere she might be of greater use to the Free – Armadell-on-Lake, or Harvekka, perhaps – but she had only ever shaken her head ruefully, and told him that the Emperor would not enjoy the change of habit. He was, she judged, too old an ape to take to city life.

"Send Rudran and his lancers on after us," he had said to her as they parted. "But only by their consent. You'll make them understand what it is they're riding into, and that there'll be none who think the less of them, whatever happens?"

"I will," Ordeller said. "And luck to you, brown boy. I think you might need a little dusting of it this time." And then something more, that had heartened him: "Might be with you already. Feels like the first storm of the season's on the air to me. It'll be short – the early ones always are – but it'll make a mire of the Old Road. You'll be the only things moving fast up there, if you crack the whip hard."

He rode just a little behind Drann as they worked their way out of the town. He watched the contract-holder, curious about the likelihood of him staying in the saddle once the pace quickened, but paid more heed to the townsfolk at their windows, at their doors. Caution was seldom wasted, and he could all but taste the sour hostility.

Because of that caution, he saw the woman and youth coming before Drann did. They emerged from the last building, a workshop built up against the remnants of the town's wall, and strode quickly, purposefully towards Drann. Yulan kicked his horse forward, but even as he did so, he understood the two of them, their manner and mood, and the alarm that had briefly stirred in him fell away.

The woman was swaddled in ragged, dirty blankets. The youth – her son, Yulan did not doubt – was lean but strong, carrying a pitchfork. He did not carry it as if he meant to use it. Their faces spoke not of anger, but of more complicated emotions. Weary hope, Yulan might have called it if required to name it.

"Take my son, sir," the woman said, reaching for the halter of Drann's horse. "Please. He's a good—"

"Take him?" Drann asked in puzzlement as his mount came to a rather reluctant halt.

Yulan slowed his own horse and drew up alongside Drann.

"Let him join you," the woman implored. "He can fight. There's nothing for him here now. His father's dead, my purse is empty. He wants to go, don't you, boy?"

She looked at her son, and he nodded, staring up at Drann with contrived firmness, putting on the mask he thought would please the Free. Trying to look fierce. But Yulan could see the fear and uncertainty beneath the paint.

"Oh, no," Drann murmured. "I'm not . . . I'm not—"

"We've no place for him," Yulan said loudly, to spare Drann.

It was not hard to read Creel's contract-holder. There was nothing in him that Yulan had not seen before in others encountering the Free: the like and dislike, teetering as one side or the other of the scales was pressed down. The desire – longing, in some – to join, and be a part of, something that they nevertheless half thought cruel and violent and ruthless. Any pleasure Drann found now in being mistaken for one of the Free would bring its own sharp shadow of troubling discomfort.

Mother and son turned their attention to Yulan. She looked

anguished at his refusal. The boy did not; not so much, at least.

"I'm sure he's all you say," Yulan said, "but believe me: you don't want him riding with us. Not today. Pitchforks won't suffice."

The Clamour's wagon went grinding along, passing out through the wall and into the fields.

"Please . . ." the woman said.

"I'm sorry," Yulan told her. "I'm doing you a kindness. Both of you. I can promise you that."

And he reached across to tap Drann's horse on its rump, nudge it onwards. They rode away, and left Curmen behind them. When Yulan glanced back, as they followed the road down towards the first valley of the broken lands to the east, the woman and the youth were still standing there, watching them go.

The rain came just as Ordeller had prophesied, and it came as if it deeply resented having been held at bay through the dry summer months. It had a great deal of fierce displeasure to vent, and it beat the land like a drum.

The Old Threetower Road quickly betrayed its diminished nature. It had once been clad in smooth cobbles, raised and graded to shed water into drains along its flanks. Now, many of those cobbles were gone, or cracked or sunken, and the drains were blocked or in places deliberately broken. Water pooled. It raised dirt from crevices and holes, spread it over the road as mud.

The low bund between the road and the little river that accompanied it was breached in many places. If the watercourse rose much, it would spill through.

All of this was good, to Yulan's mind. He needed the road only for a little while. After that, there was the older drover's way that climbed up and around the ragged, canyoned ground ahead. That, he hoped, would carry the Free ahead of Callotec's more cumbersome column. So long as they could bear the pace he intended for them, and so long as Callotec kept crawling up the unhelpful road, through unhelpful weather.

Hoods came up, capes on, and the rain pounded out its thrumming song on them, and on the canvas draped over the wagon. The horses dropped their heads. The huge bull hauling Hestin and the Clamour broke into a leaden trot now and again to keep up. The wagon thumped and shook through potholes and ruts. It was made to withstand such harsh treatment. And the bull could sustain it for even longer; for as long as Hestin could feed it vigour from the entelechs.

They had done this only once or twice before. Requiring from Hestin anything that might distract or detract from her unremitting focus upon the Clamour was not safe. Not something to be lightly done. It demanded a close watch, and Yulan gave it that. He rode alongside the wagon. He paid more heed to Hestin, and her cloak of green, than to the road ahead. If trouble was to come now, that would be where the first sign of it showed.

Hamdan dropped back to fall in beside him.

"Shall I take a couple up ahead, then?" the archer asked with a slightly rueful smile. Rainwater was dripping from his nose and from his bearded chin.

"Just to be sure," nodded Yulan. "They'll likely have outriders at their back, now they know someone's paying attention to them, but with any luck they're more interested in moving on. Look for stone markers, three of them climbing up on your left hand. That'll show us the turn off the road. Don't go beyond that; we'll find you there. Be careful."

That last was not a thing he needed to say, and seldom did.

Hamdan brushed the rain from his bow, and trotted off into the storm with a pair of his archers. They would be an unpleasant surprise for any eyes Callotec had sent back down the road. Mounted archers were not a thing well known in these parts. Hamdan had brought the habit north years ago from their homeland in the south, and found most of the Free's opponents pleasingly unprepared to meet it.

Not that arrows could win the battle to come. It would be the Clevers who delivered any victory. Their willingness to sacrifice some part of themselves when it was needed.

Kerig most of all. He was a troublesome sort, not always to be entirely relied upon – he had proved that well enough at Creel's camp – but Yulan had no great doubt he would play his part. Reluctantly, perhaps, but well in the end. With any luck, whatever faint guilt he felt at his self-indulgent antics outside the Weaponsmith's tent might make him a little more pliable. And Wren would do what she always did: that which was needed, to serve the purposes of the Free.

Akrana was always the one, of all the Free's Clevers, about whom Yulan felt least certain. She was, he was reasonably confident, more than a match for Kerig and Wren, though everyone assumed those two to be the company's most inventive, potent Clevers. Her profound reluctance to employ her skills had concealed that from most people. That and her remarkable facility with a blade, to which she turned with vastly less reluctance.

Much of it was rooted in her past, of course. She had been taught anger, and isolation, at a cruelly young age. She rode best alone. He would need her in what was to come, though. One more sword – however skilfully and ferociously wielded – would not win them the day. One more Clever might.

She would answer the need if it came, he believed. If for no other reason than that it was the Orphans who would gain the most if Callotec and Kasuman and the Bereaved reached the border. Akrana had, after all, seen the Empire kill her family on stakes when she was only five years old.

The standing stones were there, as he remembered, to mark the place where the droveway climbed up and away from the Old Threetower Road. Two of them were, at least. The third and highest was lost somewhere on the high ground, veiled by the sweeping rain.

Hamdan and his archers were waiting by the first of the stones, at the edge of the road. They did not look overly happy, slouched there on their sodden horses. There was no shelter to be had here.

"Nothing," Hamdan grunted. "No sport for us."

Yulan was glad of it. He would as soon see neither hide nor hair of his quarry until he was ready for the meeting.

The marker stone was as tall as Yulan, atop his great horse. As he looked at it, he saw, almost weathered away but still faintly legible, the carved symbol of the long-gone Sorentine Kingdom: a bull's head, with sharply recurved horns. The Sorentines had been crude and wayward – still were, the unruly rump of them in the valleys – but they had put great store by an ordered net of roads and tracks. Their waystones had once covered all the land. Few remained.

He watched Hestin's bull haul the heavy wagon off the road and begin the long, wet climb up towards the rain clouds. A needle, for the world to prick him with, that he should be returning to Towers' Shadow in the company of a bull, with bull's heads marking the way. Those inclined to think in such ways might have called it an ill omen. Yulan was not, and did not. He took it only as a bitter reaffirmation of his need to finish what he had started. He did not know how many people now lived in Towers' Shadow – a hundred? Two? – but he knew how many would live there after Callotec had swept through on his way to exile.

It was always the way with such ancient tracks that they found, as if by animal instinct, the easiest line through even the least forgiving terrain. The slope up which the Free now went looked unpromising, for it was the beginning of the broken lands of bare rock and sharp crags that covered perhaps half the distance between Curmen and Threetower. Somehow, the droveway made it hard but not impossible, skirting the worst of the scree, cutting across the steepest stretches, revealing hidden gentleness.

Had it not been for the torrential rain, it would have seemed the most modest of feats to make that ascent. Though even then, and even with Hestin's aid, it would have been asking a great deal of wagon and bull. As it was, more than once it took firm shoulders and strong legs to heave the wagon's wheels over some stubborn rock.

The Free, when they emerged on to higher, flatter ground,

were a sorry-looking assembly. Drenched and wearied. It spoke to their resilience that there was no lingering, no great catching of breath. The droveway offered them a long, flat path out towards gentler, thinly grassed hills beyond, and one by one they took it. Pausing for only a moment, one or two of them, to spill some of the water from their capes.

Yulan did the same as he crested the top of the climb. Spared himself the briefest fragment of time to shake his shoulders and lift his injured foot from the stirrup. It was sharply painful, protesting at any weight he put upon it. Nothing he could not bear for now.

The sound of the Clamour's wagon coming up behind him caused him to turn, to see how the bull was faring after its cruel exertions. Spittle was trailing from its great wide mouth, and he could hear the snorting of its breath even through the muffling rain. Its stride still looked strong, though; its head was not falling too low.

Then he looked to Hestin, hunched up on the seat behind the beast, and he saw the mottling in her cloak of leaves. The dullness, here and there a hint of browning, that had taken over the formerly luminous green. And he was afraid for the first time since they had left Curmen.

"Halt!' he cried into the storm, loud as his voice would bear.

He sprang from his horse and ran, splashing, slithering, for the wagon.

No, no, was all he could think. *Don't let this happen*. Nothing, not Callotec or Towers' Shadow, perhaps not even keeping the Bereaved from the hands of the Orphans, would be worth the loosing of the Clamour. *Don't let me have made this happen.*

15

Hope On The Air Yet

"Halt!' Drann heard Yulan shouting behind him, startlingly loud and sharp.

His horse had already begun trudging of its own volition after Kerig and Wren and some of the archers who were heading out, with the few spare horses, along the thankfully now flat droveway. He hauled on the reins, more firmly than he should have done, and the animal came to an unsteady halt, clearly unhappy.

Drann was no happier. For all the protection of the cape he had been given when the rain came, he was as wet as he could ever remember being. His body, which so long as they had kept to the Old Threetower Road had pretended to be growing accustomed to riding, had collapsed into all its habitual aches and pains once the punishing climb away from that road began.

He tried to turn his horse around, to see what was happening behind him, but it had clearly run out of patience with his inept handling and refused to move. Carefully he twisted around to look over his shoulder. The movement scattered raindrops over his eyes. He wiped them away.

Yulan was down from his horse, running towards the Clamour's wagon, which had just come up over the top of the slope and was trundling slowly on. Drann could not see anything amiss. Nothing to cause the alarm he had caught around the edges of Yulan's cry.

Others evidently did, for Wren suddenly came galloping back past him. Her horse pounded through a puddle on the track as it went by, and sent fountains of water splashing across Drann's leg. It made him no wetter than he already was, though it did add an unappealing spray of mud to his attire.

He made to dismount, thinking that this chance to move his legs, perhaps bend and stretch some fresh life into them, was too precious to waste. It would hurt, he knew, but it would be a better kind of pain than the steady stiffness that was in them now.

"Stay in your saddle," snapped Hamdan, appearing suddenly at his side.

Drann froze in mid movement, inelegantly poised half out of his seat. Hamdan's voice held none of the light good humour he had come to expect.

"Stay in your saddle," the archer said again.

He was staring fixedly at the wagon, at Yulan as he climbed up on to the seat beside Hestin.

Drann slumped glumly back down. He looked, and saw Yulan leaning in to say something to Hestin, who was as unresponsive as ever. Wren, still mounted, was leaning down, apparently trying to look into Hestin's eyes, or hear some whisper.

"What's happening?" Drann asked.

"Her cloak look the same to you?" Hamdan said.

Drann squinted through the blurring rain. He supposed Hestin's strange garment did look to have lost some of its lustre. The vividness of the leaves, to which he had grown accustomed, was lessened. That might be a trick of the deceptive rain, but not the browning he thought he could see in some of those leaves. As if autumn had breathed on a few of them, and set the edges to curling and brittling.

"Means she's struggling," Hamdan said dolefully. "Means the Clamour's stirring."

"What should we do? Should we help?" Drann asked, fully sharing now in the wider trepidation.

"We stay on our horses, and if it comes to it, we run. Nothing the likes of you and me can do, if the worst happens. That'll be down to Hestin and the rest of the Clevers. Not much they can do either, probably. If we have to go, I'll take your reins. You just try not to fall off."

Drann groaned, because he could think of nothing else to say. As they watched, Yulan was holding Hestin's hand, murmuring urgently into her ear. Wren had straightened, and was waving at the rest of them to move further away.

The huge shrouded cage on the back of the wagon shook. Just once, as if some convulsion had passed through the monster it contained. Wren's horse sprang away from the wagon and almost threw her. Yulan did not react, concentrated entirely upon Hestin. Hamdan said nothing, but quietly led Drann away.

They went perhaps a hundred paces. Far enough that the

rain swallowed up the wagon, hid most of what was happening. Drann was not overly sorry for that. Whatever curiosity he might retain about the Clamour, it no longer included a desire to see it for himself.

They waited, all of them save Yulan and Wren, huddled together in the downpour. Drann found himself imagining what it would be like to flee on horseback, through this storm, across this ground. He had a glum feeling that it would be a brief flight, whether Hamdan was holding the reins or not. He could imagine himself, all too clearly, pitched from the saddle, sprawling down into mud and puddles. Flailing around there as something terrible came howling down upon him out of the rain.

Wren came slowly into sight, riding towards them. Not fleeing, Drann was pleased to see, even though he did not know whether that meant anything.

"We rest for one hour, Yulan says," she reported as she drew to a halt before them. "No more than that, but Hestin needs it. Getting the bull up here took too much out of her."

Hamdan laughed suddenly, and slapped Drann wetly on the back.

"Looks like you're not dying today after all, son. That's a pleasant surprise, eh?"

They set oat-laden feed bags about the muzzles of the horses, arranged the animals in a rough line and squatted in the lee of them. It made hardly any difference to the remorseless rain, but it was a little more restful than riding doggedly on. Just a little.

Drann crunched thoughtfully at an apple Hamdan had given him. Acquired from Ordeller, it seemed. Drann wondered whether the Emperor had been deprived of some of his preferred fodder. He doubted the ape took such disappointments with indifference.

"Is the Clamour going to . . ." he began, only to realise he did not know quite how to phrase his question. "Is it going to fight, when you catch Callotec?"

"The Clamour's more threat than weapon," Hamdan said. "You ever see that thing out of its cage, you be sure to wet your breeches right before you run, because there's a good chance it'll be the last thing you see. It'll mean the threat's failed, and all other hope is spent. That's not where we are now."

He lifted his chin and sniffed ostentatiously at the water-thick air, then grinned at Drann.

"I smell hope on the air yet, don't you?"

Drann did not know what to say to that either, so he shrugged.

"Trust me," Hamdan nodded. "I know the scent of hope. We've not outpaced it yet. Not quite."

"You've a sharper nose than me," muttered Kerig, sitting a short distance away.

"Of course," agreed Hamdan lightly. "I've a sharper everything than you. Just ask your wife."

Kerig growled. It was not angry, not confrontational. An echo of their habitual barbed banter. But neither of them had quite the belief, or the lightness of spirit, to pursue the exchange.

They rode on, into the night and beyond the storm's will to hound them. The rain faltered and then fell away. The day's light did the same.

No one in their right mind travelled far in darkness, as best Drann knew. But he supposed that was more out of fear of wild beasts, or robbers, than anything else. Few ill-wishers – whether beast or man – would earn fear from the Free.

The moon, unshrouded now that the clouds had rolled away to unleash their angers elsewhere, gave light enough for the trail ahead to be seen clearly. It did not give light enough to dispel Drann's own tiredness. He was dimly aware, in an unconcerned way, that his head was nodding in time with his horse's stride. That his hands were slackening on the reins. His eyes narrowed, moment by moment. It felt as if it would be a great and unreasonable exertion to force them open. When he allowed them to at last close, a tremendous, releasing relief washed through him.

Then Yulan was pushing him upright in the saddle.

"You've two choices," the Free's Captain said gruffly. "Share a horse, tied to the back of the rider. Or share the Clamour's wagon. Neither's much of a bed, but you might get some sleep. More on the wagon, I should think. It's one or the other, because I'll not have you slowing us."

Drann looked back. The bull was there, not far behind him, still pacing strongly, unnaturally on. Hestin was calm and quiet. Her cloak was as simply green as ever.

"Is it safe?" Drann asked bluntly, not at all interested in trying to conceal his unease.

"As much as it's ever safe, yes."

But for his deep-rooted craving for sleep, as demanding as the most desperate hunger, Drann suspected he might never again dare to get within ten paces of that ominously silent cage.

At that moment, though, he was starting to wonder if, and how quickly, uncomplicated exhaustion might kill a man. And he would overcome almost any fear for the promise of some time, however brief, spent away from the back of a horse.

He wedged himself in between two bales of bedding at the back of the cart. Perilously close to the edge; so close that a deep hole in the track might be enough to bounce him out. As close as he was willing to get to the Clamour.

He slept in fragments, jolted and shaken back to wakefulness over and over again but never dragged entirely out of sleep's grasp. Even when he felt someone forcing themselves ungently into the narrow space between him and the cage, digging out their own tight sleeping space, he did not wake far enough to tell who it was. Given the sharpness of the elbows being employed, he fuzzily thought it might be Akrana.

In some of that disturbed sleep, he had the vague sense that he was dreaming of his mother and father and sisters. Even of Old Emmin, though she had been dead several years now. None of it stayed with him for more than moments, and even while it did, it felt oddly like someone else's dream. All of it was shaken away by the wagon's juddering progress.

He was finally, irrevocably woken by the unpleasant sensation of his unknown sleeping partner climbing over him, standing briefly on his head. Drann yelped in protest, and waved a protesting arm before sitting groggily up. It turned out to be Kerig. The Clever dropped to the ground and walked away, entirely ignoring Drann.

Drann grumbled a little more, to none but himself, as he looked around through narrowed, crusty eyes. It was daylight.

He was surprised; he must have slept longer, and sounder, than he would have thought possible.

The wagon had come to a halt on the brow of a low hill. The grass here was longer, the hill a patchwork of wind-bent scrub and glades. It had not been grazed by stock in a long time. They had entered wilder lands, where few people dwelled.

Drann clumsily levered himself out from his nest and jumped down. It turned out to be a less than good idea, as his left leg had not yet joined the rest of his body in wakefulness. It was numb right through, as good as absent. Certainly not paying any attention to his commands.

He lurched and wobbled around, barely staying upright. The wet, clinging grass did not help. His leg tingled and burned and protested as life slowly returned to it, and he hissed his discomfort. He was glad that no one seemed to be paying his performance any heed. Those of the Free not eating appeared to be asleep, stretched out on blankets on the damp ground. Drann's stomach rumbled its own very clear response to the sight of Hamdan pulling apart a flatbread. His hunger wetted his mouth. He hobbled over to the rest of them, rubbing at his thigh.

Hamdan saw him coming, and sent a hand-sized piece of the flatbread spinning across the air towards him. Drann was not quite awake enough for that, and tried to catch it, juggled it, and dropped it into the grass. He retrieved it, and brushed flecks of dirt and stem away before taking a bite. He limped over to stand beside the archer, not wanting to sit down for fear that his leg might seize up again.

The Free had chosen their resting place well, screened from

most views by clumps of ragged thorn bushes. Drann noted
that Akrana and Lebid were not amongst the others. Standing
watch somewhere, he assumed. He wondered, faintly guilty,
whether Lebid was being worked harder than the rest now, in
punishment for his – and Drann's – mistake in Curmen.

"How long are we resting for?" he asked through lumps of
chewed bread.

"Just a couple of hours," Hamdan told him. "You've slept
through the first of them already, mind. We made good time in
the night. However many times we swap the horses around,
though, they need some rest; and Hestin's tired."

Drann looked over to the wagon. Hestin was sitting on the
ground beside it, her back to one of the great wheels. Wren was
kneeling there, holding a water skin to Hestin's lips. That leaf
cloak was green enough, but not quite as bright as Drann
remembered it.

"Why does she do it?" Drann murmured. "Ruin herself like
this?"

"Somebody has to. She chose to be that somebody.
Otherwise the Clamour'd be raging around, tearing the world
to pieces. Like a never-ending storm. That's what it was doing
when we were sent to put an end to it. Kill it. Way things
turned out, it likely would've killed all of us instead if Hestin
hadn't turned up. Tamed it, joined us."

"You couldn't kill it?" Drann said, wondering what kind of
power could overmatch the Free.

"It's a Permanence. Pure entelech. It only *looks* like a real
thing, a thing you can touch or fight. It's not like you or me, or
that bush over there. It's essence, a little bubble of the raw stuff,

risen up to spend some time in our world. Not sure anyone could kill it." Hamdan shrugged. "I don't know enough about these things to say. Just be glad that Hestin does what she does, so none of us has to try."

"Yes," said Drann. "Yes."

"They're coming," Wren suddenly called from over by the wagon.

She was standing now, looking back the way they had come in the night, shielding her eyes against the low sun with her hand. Drann tried to see what it was that had caught her eye, but could not. Around him, the Free were getting to their feet; some just waking from their dozes. Yulan walked slowly towards Wren. He had a rough woollen blanket draped across his shoulders, and a heaviness to his tread. Even such a man as he had his limits, Drann realised with a distant tremble of concern, and they were being tested.

They came over the crest on magnificent horses, as big as any dray horse or plough-puller but built for the charge, not the steady drudge work of the fields. The sunlight struck flashes from the metal blades of lances, and set shimmers dancing on chain vests and bright helms. The horses stepped high, held on tight reins. They wore stiff leather scales on their faces, nets of chain ringlets across their chests, more leather, part covered with brightly coloured cloth, over their hindquarters.

Drann had never seen such men at close hand. He had not known there were any such in the kingdom, save Crex's own Armsmen.

The lancers rode in double file, their leader ahead of the rest, alone, though there was nothing in his dress or his mount's equipment to mark him apart. Rudran, Drann assumed. He did not look to be more than thirty years old, but he was a big man. Wide-shouldered and long-backed, with a dense red beard.

"There you are, son," Hamdan said, rising to his feet beside him. "Didn't I tell you there was hope on the air yet? That's hope riding in on big horses, that is. Can you smell it now?"

"I suppose so," Drann said, and more or less meant it.

Rudran and his band did look like men fit to meet any challenge. A fearsome kind of hope, which struck Drann as the only kind likely to be worth much in the coming days.

16

Simple Men Doing Needful Things

Creel of Mondoon mistrusted all things in matters of campaigning and war. Allies, weather, assumptions. Promises and pledges; predictions and perceptions. All of it, he thought, essentially a conspiracy designed to trick or lull him into careless error and horrible defeat. He would be the first to admit that it made him less than soothing company for those who rode with him. But then he would contend that it made those who rode with him a good deal more likely to enjoy a long life than they might otherwise do. More often than not, they seemed inclined to agree.

It all meant that Creel, while at war, constantly expected something unexpected and probably unhelpful to happen. On the one day he had let his guard slip and rashly trusted assurances of safety, he would have died but for the Free. Since then, he had redoubled his commitment to doubting everything and anticipating imminent disaster.

As a result, he would not have named it a surprise when a

vaguely harassed-looking messenger came, in the midst of the chaos that breaking such a large camp entailed, to tell him that the School Clade had arrived. Unannounced, uninvited and already going about some unexplained business of their own. Not just any of the Clade, either. Sullen, their loathsome commander.

Creel gathered enough of his household guard to match Sullen's reported strength – twenty-five men – and strode purposefully through the disappearing encampment. Tents were being folded away, the ashes of fires kicked over and extinguished. Horses were being hitched to carts. Men were hurrying to and fro, some carrying stores, some weapons or saddles.

There were already many riders and walkers silhouetted up on the high horizons. Creel's army was, with his consent, scattering. He would take only two hundred men to the gathering of the Council at Armadell-on-Lake. The rest – untrained levies, the volunteers, the farmers – had no desire to go anywhere but home now that the war was won, and they had too little value to him to make opposing that desire worthwhile. Two hundred should be enough to match or exceed whatever force the other members of the Council would bring with them to Armadell. He would not appear weak or inconsequential, and that was what mattered. All the better if he could slap Callotec's head on the table when they met, and paint himself the taker of the last Hommetic life.

Creel knew, with the long experience of having lived inside his own skin, that if he allowed himself reflection, he would envy those men departing for their homes. Their wives and families. He had his own, waiting for him back at Mondoon, and he craved their comfort and company, and the sedate quiet of his faraway keep. That was where his heart resided, with them and with those walls. All else was distraction. Lost time.

But he could not permit such thoughts to ingrain themselves. He was caught up in the current of events, and if he did not ride it, and seek to guide it, he would drown. As so many others had already done.

"That horse is lame," he shouted at an unfortunate handler leading a string of animals past. "If you're too wit-short to see it, find someone who can, and knows what to do about it."

Not a surprise, that the School should intrude upon his plans, but annoying. He had expected, especially after his exchanges with Yulan on the subject, that they might stir from their passivity now that those with the heart to do so had finished with the bleeding and the dying and the winning. Carrion birds come to see what spoils they might pick from the Hommetic carcass, perhaps. One more set of ambitions and pride to overfill and unbalance the already too small boat that the members of the Council had grudgingly consented to share.

"Could you not at least have found out what they wanted before coming running to me?" Creel growled at the brow-beaten messenger, trotting along at his side in an effort to match his determined pace.

"They would not say, lord. Sullen would not say. Only that he had to speak with the Weaponsmith."

"*My* Weaponsmith," Creel rumbled.

In that part of the camp given over to the Weaponsmith and his modest entourage, there was no sign of preparations for departure. That annoyed Creel still more. As did the sight of those twenty-five Clade warriors, with their clean and fresh blue tunics. A pretty little army that would have been useful in the war, had they not been safely sequestered in their barracks.

The Weaponsmith had the grace to look faintly alarmed, perhaps even guilty, at Creel's approach. The man with whom he stood in deep conversation did not. Sullen. Creel would have liked to know a good deal more about the School's butcher than he did; but then, that was a sentiment shared by almost everyone, so far as he was aware.

He had never met anyone who knew exactly where Sullen had come from, how his slow ascent to the leadership of the Clade had been achieved or justified. It was just possible that his famed expertise with a blade and his equally famed ruthlessness were explanation enough, but that had always seemed a touch unlikely to Creel. It occurred to him that he should ask Yulan about it, when next they met. The Free always seemed to carry around with them more knowledge, about more things, than was entirely reasonable.

"The lord of Mondoon," Sullen said, in his toneless way, and gave what might pass for a bow in undemanding circles.

"I know who I am," Creel grunted. "What I'd like to know is what brings the Clade into my camp, and why I'm coming so late to the knowledge."

"The affairs of the School," Sullen said simply.

Creel loathed the absurd styling of his hair. Half cropped, half braided, and burdened with those silly little beads. A ridiculous affectation, in imitation of corsairs. Sullen had no corsair blood in him, as best Creel knew.

"That much I could have guessed," he said. "I was hoping for more daylight than fog talk."

He looked to the Weaponsmith, thinking a little weight applied to him more likely to be fruitful than that wasted upon the impervious Sullen. The Weaponsmith was a big man, easily a head taller than Creel, with arms reminiscent of tree trunks, grey hair tied tight back in a horse-tail, and a lean, stern face. But Creel knew he was not as resilient as he appeared. There was a vein of weakness, compliance that ran through the Clever. He had an instinct for submitting to those with the authority or determination to face him down.

"Let us show Mondoon what this is about," Sullen said placidly, before any cracks could appear in the Weaponsmith's facade. "It will save everybody some time."

He led Creel to a litter, set upon the grass – what muddily remained of it after the trampling of the last few days – close by. A white sheet was draped over it, but the shape was unmistakable. A corpse. Creel felt the first intimation of gloom, rather than the irritation that had dominated thus far. His mind was not the most agile, but nor was it sluggish. He could guess the direction, if not the detail, of what was about to happen.

Sullen bent and pulled back a corner of the sheet.

Creel looked at the dead man. He did not know him, but even if he had, he might not have recognised him. Terrible burns, which had exposed and cooked the flesh, covered half the face. There was an odd blotching and bruising on the unburned cheek and chin. Sullen covered the dead man up quickly.

"What is it I'm meant to understand?" Creel muttered.

"He was killed by a Clever. Kerig, one of the Free."

Creel turned on the Weaponsmith, who quailed just a little.

"I thought there were none dead. I was told – you told me – that none had taken any fatal wound, all would recover. The business with Kerig was cut short, before it could become a crow feast."

"So I thought," the Weaponsmith said, recovering a little of his poise. Perhaps buttressed by Sullen's steady, expectant gaze. "I was wrong. This man died of his hurts. That made it – makes it – a matter for the School. I am entitled to expect my rightful—"

"Oh, hush," said Creel. He turned to Sullen, who was almost smiling.

"I am satisfied there is something that bears examination here, lord," Sullen said. "Something that it falls to the School, the Clade, to examine, by duty and law and tradition."

Creel glared at him. The man was dirty from his journey. His garb was more fit for a levyman than the holder of high martial office. But he was no fool, Creel knew. He was dangerous. And he could surely not be here without the consent of the School's Mistress, Morue. That was enough, just, to persuade Creel that his anger must not reach his tongue.

"I have bought the Free's services," he said tightly. "It's of no concern to me what discussions you have with them after they've completed their—"

"We will be riding out shortly," Sullen told him. "I have a man here who might follow their trail, but only if it is done soon, and fast."

He gestured towards the silent gallery of Clade warriors with a loose hand. Creel looked there, and saw amongst the tall, erect fighting men one who was, by contrast, stooped and older and clad in a simple brown cloak. Pale and pinched of face. He looked unwell.

"What the Free are doing needs doing," Creel growled, still staring at that odd little man. "You interfere with it, you aid no one."

"Not our intent, of course. We must ask questions, that is all. Clarify matters. If a Clever kills a man, it falls to the School to pursue the truth, and justice. It has always been so."

Sullen spoke with all the calm confidence of one knowing he would not in the end be gainsaid, whatever rough waters he might encounter along the way. And he was right, Creel had to grudgingly acknowledge.

If he had his way, he would see the Council unpick some of the tendrils of power and influence the School had extended through the land over the years. The finding and training and guiding of Clevers was one thing. A valuable thing, for which the School had first been founded. The exercise of absolute and separate justice in all that related to Clevers, the levying of taxes on river trade, the provision of wayhouses for message riders, the keeping of records of land ownership: these and more, that the School had gathered unto itself over the decades, were different. They bloated the School's coffers and its pride.

But nothing could be done now. Creel knew that. Not today. The ground in which seeds of change might sprout had not even been ploughed yet. And the School was easily strong enough to resist any ill-judged assault, should they choose to do so. They had Clevers, after all, and the Clade. And the Bereaved. They were still needed.

"If you keep the Free from their task, you hasten the closest thing left to a Hommetic heir into the hands of the Empire," he said stubbornly. If he must yield, he would not do so gracefully.

"Where he's as likely to be hung from a gibbet as fed wine and sweetmeats, I'd think," said Sullen. "But nobody will be kept from their task, in any case. Questions only, I said. Do I look to have come with an army fit for fighting the Free?"

That, Creel had to concede. Twenty-five of the Clade would not be compelling Yulan into doing anything he did not want to do.

"The Weaponsmith will accompany us," Sullen added.

Which tested Creel of Mondoon's restraint to its outer bounds, and just a hand's width beyond.

"He's my man," he snapped. "Taken into my household at his own request. He's coming with me to Armadell."

He included the Weaponsmith himself within the compass of his ferocious glare. The Clever looked distinctly uncomfortable. Sullen, predictably enough, was unmoved.

"Given his peculiar talents, you'll understand that the School has long taken a close interest in this new member of your household. His liberty to do as he does is ours to determine, in law. While he served the King, the balance was in his favour. Now . . . well, we will have to see. For now, it is his wish that he accompany us."

The Weaponsmith only nodded nervously in response to Creel's angry, silent question. The lord of Mondoon stood there for just a moment more, stewing in his frustration. Then he concluded that he was achieving nothing but sharpening the appearance of his defeat in the eye of every observer. He spun on his heel and stamped away.

"They were making for Curmen, and the Old Threetower Road, I understand," Sullen called at his back.

"You understand whatever you like," Creel muttered. "I've got a march to prepare."

"Well, we have our own means of finding the way, as I said."

Creel did glance back, briefly, before disappearing into the comfortably familiar churn of his army of simple men doing needful things. He saw that feeble-seeming man who had stood amongst the Clade warriors kneeling on the grass. Pressing his hand flat to the ground. Closing his eyes. He looked to have an ugly welt of a scar, fresh-looking, around his throat, like a raw torc.

Some Clever trickery in the making, no doubt. So be it. The Free had a good deal of that to call upon themselves, if needed. Yulan was a match for Sullen. Hopefully.

17

Two Ends To A Spear

Yulan could all but smell the weariness draped over the Free like a deadening blanket. Unlike most of the others, he and Hamdan could sleep on horseback. Not well or long, but better than not at all. It was a habit and a talent passed down through generations from their distant ancestors, horse lords who had supposedly ruled all these lands and more long, long ago. Before even the Sorentine dynasty arose.

Such were the meagre inheritances of a lost dominion: a people, strewn along the desert's edge, who could breed horses and sleep as they rode, and use a bow like no others; but in more years than not could barely feed their families. It was not much for those who had held sway over countless thousands to pass on to their descendants. No less than most kingdoms provided for their latter kin, Yulan suspected.

The Sorentines had kept their primacy for centuries, yet their people were now a discordant, disorderly scattering of clans in a few valleys. The Hommetics had had their brief moment of

glory, bright indeed for a merchant family that had won control of Armadell-on-Lake more by luck than judgement amidst
the chaos of the Sorentine collapse. It had taken them close to
fifty years of warring to win themselves a wider kingdom, and
not much longer than that to lose it. To pass into extinction.

Yulan's people had at least survived, even if in poverty.
Should he live long enough to return to his homelands with the
booty his service in the Free had won him, he would be the
wealthiest man to walk that hot, dry ground in many years. He
did not know if that would ever happen. It certainly would not
until he had answered what had happened at Towers' Shadow.
Until he could pass a day without seeing, clear as if it was there
before him, a child's arm in the mouths of dogs.

But even then, if he outlived the Free, and lifted the burden
of Towers' Shadow from his shoulders, there were other things
he meant to do — had to do — before he could turn his path
southward.

A day and a night after Rudran joined them, they had come
far and fast over hard ground. Yulan was tired, right down to his
deepest bones, so he knew that the rest of the Free must be
beyond the limits of their endurance. They had taken turns
eking out what little rest they could on the wagon, but that,
Yulan knew from experience, was about as unrestful as sleep
ever got.

Hestin's cloak had never quite recovered its full green lustre
after that climb up from the Old Threetower Road. The bull
marched stolidly on, but there would come another moment,
soon, when she could not make it do so without loosing her
grip upon the Clamour.

Yulan judged they must be ahead of Callotec's column by now. Unless it had scattered. Unless Callotec had run for the border and left behind all the wagons, all the levies, and the Bereaved. That, Yulan thought, would be the wise thing to do. It would be what he would do, if riding in Callotec's saddle. But he did not think it was what Callotec would do. He thought Callotec would first want to fulfil a promise he had made long ago.

And as Yulan thought these things, thought that the time had come to rest once more and ready themselves for the greater test to come, a burned-out farmstead appeared there by the trail. Rudran and half his lancers were riding ahead to flush out any trouble that might be awaiting them. They whistled back when the ruined building came in sight, to call a halt. Yulan trotted his horse up to join them as they examined the place from a cautious distance.

It had been prosperous once, that much was clear. Burned not long ago. A few weeks, perhaps a couple of months. The walls still stood, in part, but the roof was gone and the stone had been blackened by the fire. There were dead animals – the bones of them, at least – outside. Scraps of gristle and withered flesh clung to the bones like wilted leaves. It was all the scavengers had left.

"Shall I take a look?" Rudran asked.

He was a simple, solid man. Not much given to talk, or to laughter, or to any vigour of emotion. Devoid of any ambition save to lead the finest, most disciplined little band of lancers he could. A good and safe man to have at your side when what needed to be done was clear, and difficult, and likely bloody.

"We need a place to rest for a few hours," Yulan said. "Why don't you just ride up there and see if it feels restful to you?"

"I will."

He said it, yet he did not spur his horse on ahead. He regarded his Captain steadily, from beneath thick, reddish eyebrows.

"You want to know what makes you a fool, Yulan?" he asked at length.

"By all means," Yulan said, entirely surprised that such a question should come from this placid rock of a man.

"Thinking there's any one of us, man or woman, that'd not follow you out here, to do this thing. What was it about, Ordeller saying over and over when we reached Curmen that we could turn back if we wanted?"

"I thought it right."

"It was wrong. You don't think every one of us who saw what Callotec did there wants to make things right just as much as you? I told you back then there'd come a time for mending, and here it is. It's never been just you waiting for the day to come. Even the ones who weren't there. They all want to wash the Free's name clean of that memory."

"I don't . . . I didn't think I could ask anyone to die for it."

"Anyone except you, you mean," Rudran grunted. "Fool, again. Did it never occur to you that half the Free would die for any cause you chose to name? Not for the cause, but for you."

"Lorin was forty-two years old," Yulan said distantly. "Joined the Free before I'd even left my village. Had a scar on his cheek he took from a horse thief's knife. Had a wife in Sussadar and one in Armadell-on-Lake, and loved them both. Died under his horse when it broke a leg on the charge. Manadar was twenty-five. As good with a throwing knife as any I've ever known. He wanted to see everything the world had to offer, and had made a good start on it. Played the reed flute every evening, near enough, and was less good with that than with the knife. A slaver's mace to the side of his head."

"They died in the Empire, two years ago," Rudran nodded. "What of it?"

"I remember them too well. I don't want to see anyone else dying. Not when we all thought the Free was finished with and all had new lives to be forging."

Rudran grunted. "Best shed that, I'd say. We're in it now, all of us willingly. You've got the best of the Free here with you, and if you want to bring it out in one piece, it's time to think war, not peace. If you're not willing to risk lives, more than likely you'll lose them. No half-measures. We need you thinking hard and clear. There's a lot of dying to be done; you want it to be them, not us, you set your mind to killing, not keeping people alive. Now hold this, would you?"

He passed his lance across to Yulan, who, being distinctly unused to the feel and balance of such an ungainly weapon in his hand, took a moment or two to get to grips with it.

"Rather you didn't drop it," Rudran murmured.

He reached behind him and freed a long-handled, metal-spiked cudgel from its bindings. Another weapon Yulan found unappealing, but one Rudran could – unusually for him – wax adoring about. The methods and accoutrements of mounted battle were, in fact, the only things that normally seemed to much enthuse Rudran.

The lancer took a couple of his men slowly up ahead. Yulan watched them circling the wrecked farmhouse and its out-buildings, leaning to peer through windows and doors. He understood what Rudran had said, perhaps better than the man did himself. Before he had become Captain, Yulan knew he had been fiercer, harder. More dedicated to the business of slaugh-ter. That he had changed was as it should be, he still thought. A leader had to have more strings to his bow than that.

But what Rudran wanted was the old Yulan back, just for this one venture. And he was probably right. There was going to be blood fit for wading in soon. It was time to forget why or to what purpose, and bend his mind to only one end: ensuring that it came not from the Free but from their enemy.

Rudran was brandishing his long mace in the air, swinging it in wide circles to summon the rest of the Free on.

Yulan turned in his saddle and called back: "If you're want-ing sleep, now's the time. Rudran's found a fine accommodation for you."

While the others saw to their horses, and laid out their blan-kets, Yulan stalked around the farmstead.

Flies and beetles still busied themselves about the meagre remains of the animals. A few cattle, a few goats, Yulan judged from the bones. Behind the house was a walled garden. Cabbages and kale withered and rotted where they grew, since those who might have harvested them were dead, or fled. The air of abandonment was heavy. Miserable, but precisely what Yulan had hoped for. None had been here, he guessed, since whatever had brought about the place's destruction.

The inside of the farmhouse was a ruin of fallen, charred roof timbers and tumbled stone. Perhaps a grave for unseen bodies. So the Free took to the grass outside it, by the edge of the track that had brought them here.

Kerig and Wren were already asleep, together on a single large blanket. She with her arm draped across his shoulders. He snoring unquietly. Both of their faces were so utterly peaceful that Yulan could not help but smile. The knowledge of what he would soon require of them chased the smile from his lips.

Hamdan was helping Drann to untie the cords holding his bedroll. The knots had tightened, after their wetting and drying in recent days. Yulan walked over to them.

"You should get yourself a spare water skin, and food for a day or two," he said to Drann. "We'll not be travelling together for much longer."

Crestfallen disappointment swept across Drann's face.

"You're not going to leave me behind?"

"Only for a time. You'll not be alone. I need to—"

"What if they want to see the contract?" Drann said earnestly, tapping the scroll case at his belt.

"No," Yulan said. "Callotec'll not be asking to see any contracts. Not with three hundred men at his back, and the Bereaved in his train. This'll be warring, not reading."

"I can help. I can fight."

"No," Yulan insisted. "Your only task now is to come back with me to Creel after all this is done. I'll have no place for those that can't look after themselves in what's coming."

"I can! I know how to use a spear. Creel drilled us in—"

"In how to stand a charge, a hundred or more of you together, I'd wager. That's how lords use levymen, untrained men. A mass of you, quilled like a porcupine. That's not the kind of fight we're riding to."

"You might need every spear. There's three hundred of them and only—"

"Enough!' Yulan said it sharply, not out of anger, but out of the certainty that he could not spend time freely now. "Akrana. Test this boy."

She was sitting cross-legged, rolling her shoulders to loosen them, but rose at his call, and walked purposefully towards Drann.

"I'll do it if you want it doing," protested Hamdan, but Yulan steered him away with a gentle hand upon his arm.

"You've other business to be about, my friend," he said.

And that was true, but so was his desire to see Drann tested. That was what would teach him the wisdom of caution, and of humility, amidst such perilous times and company as these. Perhaps save his life, if it drained a little of that bravery. Hamdan, Yulan knew, would not give Drann such a test. He did not have it in him.

"It's time for you to go," Yulan told the archer as they walked together towards the horses, Hamdan glancing back, frowning, over his shoulder. "I need you to find Callotec for me. Find me my ground; my time and place."

Hamdan sighed, but nodded.

"We'll keep to this course for as long as the trail favours us," Yulan continued. "Send one of your bow boys to find us and guide us in, once you've the measure of it."

"You want me to leave one or two of them with you?"

"Two, yes. They'll be looking after Kerig and Drann."

He threw an arm round Hamdan's shoulder.

"Don't worry. I won't let her hurt him."

Behind them, the sounds of a sparring match were just beginning. Yulan was pleased that Hamdan resisted the urge to look back.

"You're limping," the archer observed.

"Huh. I thought I'd hidden that better."

"Not from me. That foot going bad?"

"It's not going good, that's sure," Yulan grunted.

In truth, it burned and throbbed. When he put weight upon it, cruel little darts of pain came trembling up through ankle and calf. He hadn't taken off his boot in some time. When he did, he doubted he would find anything beautiful.

"It doesn't matter," he said. "Won't be a problem, soon enough."

"Is that so?"

Yulan nodded.

"Don't get seen, and don't get killed," he told the archer.

"Never do, do I?" Hamdan smiled.

"Not so far. I'll be needing a lock of your hair before you go. All of you, and the horses."

"Ah," Hamdan said wryly. "Poor old Kerig. There's going to be unsweet words spoken of you hereabouts soon, then. Not sure I'm sorry or glad to be missing that."

Drann had twice gone to levymeets, where all the men of fighting age in a few villages were gathered together to prove they had spear or bow to bring, should their lord ever call upon them. At those raucous gatherings, they had been given some training in the craft of battle. Notionally, at least. In Drann's little experience, they were as much about bartering and arguing and gossiping and, once the lord's men had disappeared, drinking as anything else.

But then, when he joined himself to Creel's army, there had been true training. Hard. Two drills a day for a week or more. Just as Yulan had said, though, that had been all about fifty or more men marching and kneeling and sprouting spears. Not about trying to stand alone against an ill-tempered Clever with a ferocious gift for swordplay. Drann knew he was going to lose, fail whatever test Yulan thought this added up to, and did try to say as much to Akrana. But she was not listening.

She was trying to kill him; or would have been, had she not restricted herself to the use of a wooden sparring stick, pulled from her saddlebag. She certainly seemed to be trying to hurt him, and to Drann's untutored eye that looked, and indeed felt, much like trying to kill.

She came at him in a flurry of blows that appeared wild and uncontrolled, yet somehow set his spear dancing around uselessly, rapped out a cacophony of knocks on its shaft. And on his knuckles, which made him howl and drop the spear entirely.

Akrana slid her foot under the spear, midway along its length, and lifted it. Held it balanced there on the top of her foot, just off the ground, then flicked it up to him. He caught it, out of instinct rather than desire. He glanced at his knuckles as he did so. A couple of them were bleeding.

"There's no point—' he began, but she was already advancing on him again.

Drann shuffled backwards, and as he went resolved himself to at least show that he was no sheep to go meekly down. He was fairly certain that he could not so much as scratch Akrana unless she allowed it; little harm could come, therefore, of fighting as if he meant it. Might as well earn whatever bruises she meant to inflict upon him. Perhaps, if he got improbably lucky, he might even—

Akrana rushed him, hissing like a delirious snake. Alarm made him jump back, and he caught his heels on an anthill bulging out of the short grass. Fell hard. Akrana sprang up and over the hummock. He rolled wildly to avoid her boots as she thumped down precisely where he had been sprawled.

"You are slow," she said.

More or less everyone Drann had ever seen was slow compared to Akrana. He had no interest in discussing it with her, and suspected it was in any case a mere distraction intended to result, one way or another, in further pain or humiliation. He scrambled to his feet, and gave an exploratory lunge with his spear. She knocked that aside easily enough.

Later than he would have wished, he remembered what Hamdan had done to the man who jabbed a spear at him outside Curmen. He decided to make no more attacks, feint or otherwise, himself. Let her come to him. He thought Creel's trainers had said something of that sort when trying to make fighters from the motley mass of farm folk that had been drawn beneath his banner. Something about spears being good for holding your own ground, not for taking another man's.

Drann set his feet, tightened his grip on the spear, held it hard in against his hip. Levelled its point at Akrana's gut. She closed with him more cautiously this time, swaying that club from side to side. Drann watched it, tracked its every movement, and then suddenly thought that might not be a good idea and snapped his gaze up to Akrana's face. There was nothing to read there. Not so much as the faint echo of emotion. Just concentration. Intent.

Beyond her, Drann could see Hamdan and his archers riding away. Yulan was standing, watching the sparring match with his arms folded. Drann tried not to let any of that intrude upon the more painful business immediately to hand.

He did not retreat. He let Akrana come closer and closer. It troubled him a little that she just kept coming. He was not sure what he could do about that, short of sinking the spear into her stomach. She spared him too much confusion over such matters by suddenly springing sideways, crouching as if to fling herself at him. When he swung the spear around to keep it between the two of them, she reached out an alarmingly fast and long arm and seized hold of it, and pushed it on along the arc of its movement, and then down.

She drove the spear point into the earth, took a couple of long strides straight towards him, leaped and kicked him, hard, in the centre of his chest. So hard that it felt like having a stone block dropped from height on to his ribcage. So hard that he could not breathe. So hard that he lost hold of the spear, went reeling and fell on his back.

Akrana stood over him, staring down not with the contempt he half expected, but rather with an odd kind of empty distance in her eyes.

"You are of no use to us," she said.

Anger boiled in Drann, surging up to his lips. Ready to spill. He bit it back. Shaped it.

"Can I get up now?" he asked.

She reached down, he reached up and they clasped one another's wrists. She dragged him to his feet. Drann wiped his hand across his face.

"I might not be of any use, but at least I had a better reason than just gathering coins for joining the war. I was fighting because our lord seized half my family's land, that we've held for three generations, and Crex's court said that was just. Because the royal share of the tithe doubled in two years and when my father hid some of our barley from the tally-takers, they split the skin on his back with cord whips. Because men from Hudrin fort got into a fight at my village's beer shop, and came back two nights later and burned it, and killed the man who brewed the beer. He'd not even been part of the fight. And nobody flayed the skin from their backs, the men who killed him."

"Not true," said Akrana, entirely unmoved by what Drann had thought a rather fine speech. "What you were really fighting for was Creel of Mondoon's place at the table where the spoils will be shared out. In any war, there are only ever a few who truly win. It sometimes seems otherwise, but it is just that: a seeming."

She turned and walked away.

"And what are you fighting for, then?" Drann called after her, still angry.

"The joy of it," she said without looking back, and without any trace of joy.

"She's done you a service," Yulan said while Drann was pouring a little water over his battered knuckles, trying to brush grime and blood from them. "Remember how easy that was for her. How fast."

"Am I supposed to thank her?" Drann muttered.

"You might," said Yulan sharply. "And you might want to remember that she started her life, a very long way from here, with less than you did and she's lost more of it. All of it, on stakes planted by the Empire in her village. Whatever she might say, or think, she fights for more reasons – and darker ones – than just pleasure or coin. Everybody does. You would do well to think of that before getting into arguments about such things with those who actually know how to use a sword."

Drann stared over at Akrana, who was checking her saddle, tugging at the straps. She did not look like someone come from poverty, with her tall, straight back and strong arms. Her sword and warhorse. Perhaps she did, though, behave like someone who had lost everything that mattered.

"Next time," Yulan told him, "try to remember there're two ends to a spear. It's not just the sharp end can be useful in a fight. But remember this first: a contract-holder only has one responsibility that matters. To stay out of the way, and not get himself or anyone else killed."

18

Oh, Joy

Within a couple of hours of Hamdan's departure, Drann realised that the mood was changing. When the time came to ride on from the shell of a farmhouse, the Free were quiet, measured in movement and speech. They loaded their supplies on to the wagon, packed them away into saddlebags. They took a last little food and drink. Tested the saddles and the laces about their boots and the slide of sword from sheath. They did not smile, or goad. They barely looked at one another.

It unsettled Drann, but he fell in with it. He borrowed the mood.

They rode on more slowly. They were waiting, Drann understood. Waiting for Hamdan, or one of his men, to come to them and bring word that the battlefield awaited.

The land changed. The rises and hollows over which they rode were less pronounced. The grass was thinner, drier; the earth in which it grew finer and lighter. The sky was wider, stretching to far horizons that showed only the same endless undulations. Grass, rolling hills, a scattering of trees and shrubs. Nothing changed, in whichever direction Drann looked save one.

To the west, towards the Empire, there was higher ground. Dark at this distance, a grey line running between sky and earth. Cliffs, Drann thought. And atop them, so vanishingly faint and small that he could not be entirely certain he did not imagine them, a little stand of three pillars. Three towers. Standing upon the border between an empire and a kingdom that they long out-aged. He knew only scraps of history, but he thought they were Sorentine, those towers. They must be.

Not that it much mattered who had built them. He would get no closer to them than this, as far as he could tell. Everything would be settled without him, out of his sight. He should be glad of it, that he would have no part in whatever slaughter might take place. Neither the giving nor the receiving of it. But somehow the gladness refused to take hold.

Of one thing he could be glad, though. He was starting to think he might have learned how to ride. His horse no longer seemed quite so inimical. It even did what he asked of it, with rein or heel, more often than not. His body no longer sobbed inside after a few hours in the saddle. It was not much to take from this grand adventure, but neither was it entirely nothing. There were only a handful of folk in his village who could ride a horse properly, so far as he knew.

The pounding of hoofs announced the return of one of the archers. The man came arrowing in from a long stand of scrubby trees, bursting out from amongst them at full gallop. Grass and dust flew in his wake.

He came to a skidding halt in front of Yulan, his horse blowing hard.

"They're close," Drann heard the archer say. "And we've got your ground for you."

Yulan only nodded and stood in his stirrups to survey the land around them with careful attention. Drann did not know why he did that.

The Captain of the Free turned his horse about and rode slowly down the length of the little column, past Rudran and his proud lancers, past Hestin and the Clamour. To the end, where Drann rode with Kerig and Wren, two archers behind them.

"Kerig," Yulan said, "I'll be needing you now. You stay here with Creel's lad, and a couple of the bow boys. And a fistful of hair."

"I knew it," Kerig moaned, rolling his eyes.

It was Wren's reaction that startled Drann, though. She glared at Yulan, and slapped her thigh so violently it could only be because she would rather have struck her captain.

"Come on, Yulan," Kerig said, almost pleading. "It's not the season for me to be trying that. If I do it while the Vernal's running so feeble, I'll be a wreck for days. Weeks. If it doesn't kill me."

"Telling me things I already know is no kind of argument," Yulan said. Drann could not remember seeing him so cold, so stern. "And you didn't seem too concerned about such matters when you were trying to kill the Weaponsmith."

"Hatred's a powerful motivation."

"That, I know. But you'll have to find something else to serve now. This needs everything, from all of us."

"Yulan—' Wren began, but he silenced her with a stare that matched her own in ferocity.

"There is no other way. Not short of opening the Clamour's cage. You think that would be the better choice?"

That Wren thought it at the very least a choice worthy of more consideration was plain in her face. She did not look away, did not flinch from Yulan's fierce certainty. She had iron in her. More than Drann had realised. But then Kerig spoke.

"Well, I'd need a tree," he said glumly. "A big one."

Yulan pointed. Perhaps two hundred yards ahead of them, some way from the trail, there was a soft, smooth hillock. Nothing grew upon it save the wispy, sere grass that cloaked all this land. Nothing except a single tall, spreading tree on its very crown. An oak of some sort, Drann guessed.

"Oh, joy," muttered Kerig.

They gathered beneath the shade of that great tree, and a strange ritual was enacted. Drann and the two archers – one of them Lebid – who were to stay there with him stood apart. They were mere audience to what followed.

Everyone dismounted. They stood in a line, each beside his horse. Kerig went silently from one to the next, to the next, with a knife. From each of them he carefully cut a few strands of hair and bunched it all together in his hand. The same with the horses: he cut hair from their manes.

When he came to the wagon, he neatly took a tuft from the bull's tail. The beast turned its heavy head to stare menacingly at him, but by then he was climbing up to sit beside Hestin. With gentle hands, he eased the Clever's hood from her head, folded it down on to her shoulders.

It was the clearest sight Drann had yet had of Hestin. The most painful, now that he knew her to be not so very much older than he was himself. Forty years of hard labour could not have produced a face more worn, more wearied. Nor forty years of hunger skin so sallow. Kerig delicately cut a frond of her limp, thin hair, then lifted back her hood. Hestin never once showed any sign that she even knew he was there.

When it was Yulan's turn, he turned his back on Kerig. Reached up and unpinned the knot of slick black hair atop his bare head. The single long lock fell heavily down. Kerig cut away its end. To Drann's eye, he seemed a little less gentle with that cutting than he had been with others.

Kerig reached Wren. The last in line, the closest to where Drann stood. He took a snip of hair from her horse's mane. Then from her. He looked down at it, packed in there with all the rest in his hand.

"There's a lock I'll not be letting go of," he murmured. "Not while there's life in my fingers."

"Oh, there's life enough in your fingers for a long while yet, my love," Wren told him, brushing his cheek with her fingertips. "Believe me."

They embraced. Wren pressed her face into Kerig's neck.

"This will be the last time," Drann heard her say, muffled and soft.

"You'll get no argument from me on that," her husband said.

Before the rest of them left, Yulan pressed a fold of calfskin into the palm of Kerig's hand.

"Hamdan's hair, and the others," he said. "Everyone who's not here."

Kerig took it wordlessly. He turned away and walked over to the tree and sat down beside it. Yulan watched him for a moment or two, thinking thoughts Drann could not guess at. Then he turned away, and sprang up into his saddle.

First Rudran's lancers went trotting away, then Yulan and Akrana riding alongside the wagon. Then, last and slowest, Wren. She was the only one of them to look back. Kerig held up his one free hand, palm outwards, fingers spread. Wren did the same. Then she let it fall, and turned away and rode after the rest of the Free.

Drann sat in glum silence. He watched Lebid and the other archer tethering the eight horses Yulan had left with them. He watched Kerig clumsily wrapping a long cord around his wrist. The hand in which he held all that hair stayed firmly clenched. Drann wondered if he needed some help, but the Clever did not ask and Drann did not offer. He felt young, and ignorant. Not a part of the Free. He never would be that, he was coming to realise. He felt less regret than he would once have expected.

Kerig spread his hand against the tree trunk, splaying his fingers over the coarse bark like a flat spider. The loose ends of the cord looped around his wrist hung down. They coiled in the sere grass.

"Tie me to the tree," he called to Drann.

Who at first was not quite sure what he meant.

"Tie the cord around the trunk," Kerig snapped. Irritated. Or frightened; which was a much more unsettling thought.

Drann hurried to do as he was told. The bole of the oak was massive. Two men, linking hands, might have been able to encompass it. The cord was long enough for him to bring its two ends together on the far side of the tree from Kerig, but not by much.

"Tight," he heard Kerig saying. "Do you know knots? It needs to be tight."

Drann did know knots. He pulled the cord taut, and closed the circle with a knot he doubted anyone would part without a blade. Returning to Kerig's side, he could see that the Clever's hand was held tight against the tree, pressed as flat as the uneven bark would allow. It could not be comfortable. Kerig did not seem troubled by it. He sat there, cross-legged, with an oddly placid expression upon his face now. He was looking at his free hand, resting in his lap; or at the fistful of hair – human and horse – it gripped.

"Important, the knot," the Clever murmured. "I pulled loose once, a few years ago. Almost got Merkent killed." He looked up and fixed Drann with a wry smile. "That would have been an unfortunate claim to fame, eh? Getting the Captain of the Free killed. Of course, he was dead anyway inside three or four months. At least it wasn't my fault, though."

Drann nodded, unsure of what to say. Rather than say nothing – and in his usual disregard for that part of his mind that told him saying nothing would be a fine choice – he resorted to the first obvious question that occurred to him.

"It's going to hurt?"

Kerig rolled his eyes.

"Sorry," Drann said quickly. "Foolish question, I suppose."

"Foolish as they come. It's beautiful here, don't you think?"

Drann had not considered it. Now, gazing around, he supposed that Kerig was right. The sun was creeping down from its

zenith, and illuminated the hillock with the kind of flat, dry
light that would be better suited to midsummer. It lacked the
fierce heat of that season, but the deep shade cast by the tangled
canopy of the great oak tree was still welcome.

The tree was a lonely thing, standing there atop the rounded
hill. For a hundred paces in any direction, off down the gentle
slopes, there was no other vegetation save the thin yellowed
grass. Patches of almost bare earth here and there, so desiccated
that Drann imagined any breeze would raise dust. But there was
no breeze. Just the blue sky, the stately tree, the whining song
of grasshoppers.

The horses were listless, but quiet. Lebid and his fellow
archer were silent too. Lebid lay on his back in the grass, arms
cupped behind his head, a long stem of nodding grass tall in his
mouth. The other went from horse to horse, lifting one hoof
after another to check for stones or splits.

It was beautiful, Drann supposed. Absurdly calm. A gentle
moment.

"Won't be quite the same when I'm done," Kerig said.
"When Yulan's done."

"Is he punishing you?" Drann asked.

"You think I'm in need of punishment?"

To that question, Drann was reasonably certain, there was no
good answer. For once, he allowed good sense to lock his lips.

"Maybe he is," Kerig said softly, without bitterness. "But he's
doing what needs doing, as well. If I had done nothing to
offend, chances are I'd still be here. Tied to this tree. Short of
letting loose the Clamour, this is the Free's greatest trick. *I'm* the
Free's greatest trick. You should account yourself lucky that

you'll get to see it. Few have. Only done it twice before. It's not the kind of trick a man can play many times without running out of life. Especially when it's not his season. So, yes," he gazed off into the distance with unfocused eyes, "this is going to hurt a great deal."

"I'm sorry," Drann said, for want of anything better.

"Give me some water," was all Kerig offered in reply.

Drann held his water pouch to Kerig's lips. Some of the water spilled over the Clever's chin. It fell on to his tunic, and stained it darkly.

"Now get me a strip of cloth," Kerig said afterwards. "There'll be a shirt in one of those saddlebags over there you can tear up. You need to bind my hand closed so that I don't lose hold of this hair."

19

The Long Three Hundred

They left Hestin and the Clamour and three of Rudran's horsemen in the lee of an overhanging rock face. The horsemen dispersed themselves to mount a watch, but in truth they were not there to stand guard. The Clamour, and therefore Hestin herself, would not be endangered by anything that might stumble across them out here. It was the Permanence itself that needed watching. There was to be violence; there was to be much shaping and twisting of the entelechs. These were things that could, on occasion, disturb the Clamour and test Hestin's control over it. It was only the crudest of wisdom to have some folk on hand to bring warning, should the worst happen.

When they parted, Yulan noted that Hestin's cloak of leaves had a healthy green to it. It was not taxing her overmuch to keep the Clamour quiescent. She did not seem overly tired, or ill. With even the most modest of good fortune, nothing would go awry.

The high ground flanking the Old Threetower Road was

more rugged than that they had recently traversed. Knolls of bare, cracked and layered rock burst from the short sward as if they were boils blistering on a giant's back. Between them the ground was undulating, punctuated by sudden dips and rises.

Without the Clamour's wagon to haul, they could move quickly and with a good deal of shelter from prying eyes. Yulan was not, in any case, much concerned with concealment. Hamdan and his archers were still out there, scouting. Hunting. Any out-riders Callotec had scattered to guard the line of his march were unlikely to raise the alarm before an arrow stilled them.

If the Clevers that now rode with Callotec were somehow keeping more subtle watch . . . well, there was not a great deal to be done about that. It seemed unlikely, though. That sort of continuing exertion while on the move was beyond most Clevers; certainly those accustomed to the gentle life of the School. It was punishing. Very few were able, and fewer still willing, to make the sacrifices required.

They found Hamdan sitting on a rock, close to the little valley through which the Threetower Road ran, quietly smooth-ing the flights of his arrows with his lips. His fellow scouts were still mounted, passing a water skin from one to another. They held the reins of not only Hamdan's horse but two others.

"He had two riders up here," Hamdan said as Yulan and the rest drew near. "Not very good at their business. Didn't even see us coming."

"Another two likely over there somewhere, then," Yulan said, jabbing his chin towards the high ground on the far side of the valley. "Best to get on with things, just in case they've got better eyes."

"They'll be looking the other way, but yes." Hamdan cupped a hand to his ear and raised his eyebrows in exaggerated expectation. "I don't hear them yet, but I think our guests should be here at any moment."

Yulan vaulted down from his horse and waited for Hamdan to carefully slot his arrows back into their quiver. The two of them went forward alone.

The last few yards they covered on their bellies, sliding on the dry grass, easing themselves up to the point where the high ground dropped sharply and suddenly.

The slope down to the roadway was precipitous, but smooth and grassed. The shallow river that had carved the valley was little more than a trickle. The road ran on the near side of the riverbed. There were only some thirty or forty paces of flat, open ground between the foot of the slope and that riverbed, with its jumble of rounded rocks. A few thorn trees dotted the line of the watercourse, but other than that there was no shelter. It would make for a good killing ground.

Some way down the road, Yulan could see Callotec's band approaching. They looked to be, as he had hoped, thinly stretched out.

"Three hundred, give or take, like Ordeller said," Hamdan was whispering beside him. "No more than a third of that mounted, the rest walking. Three wagons, and close to a dozen mules carrying supplies."

"Order?" Yulan asked as he pushed himself back from the skyline.

He trusted Hamdan to have done his work well; there was no further need to see it with his own eyes.

"At least fifty Armsmen marching up front. Swords, from the look of it. Then two score or so of riders. They've got the best horses, the prettiest helms and robes, so I'd guess that's Callotec and Kasuman and their hangers-on, whatever Clevers they've got. Then the wagons, each with a driver and guard and a couple of lancers riding alongside."

Yulan got to his feet and brushed dirt from his knees. He flicked little specks of it from his fingers as he and Hamdan walked back to their horses.

"That where the Bereaved is, you think?" he asked. "On one of the wagons?"

"The second, I'd guess. There's a passenger there, all caped and hooded and hidden. Size of a boy."

Yulan patted his horse's massive neck. The animal was immensely strong. Not as fine as the one he had lost on Creel's last contract, but good enough for what was to come.

"Try not to put any arrows in it, then," he murmured to Hamdan. "Might get ugly if you prick a Permanence."

"Wouldn't dream of it." Said with a smirk.

"And after the wagons?" Yulan asked.

"Mules, with handlers and guards. Then better than a hundred on foot, spears and bows. Most of them look to be levy, not Armsmen. Some School Clade in there, though. Another fifty or so lancers behind them. A long way behind. Rearguard."

Yulan glanced up, and blinked against the sun. It was low enough to serve its purpose. The Old Threetower Road was almost in shade. If Callotec and his men looked up as Yulan and his crested the top of the slope, there was a good chance they would be gazing into the full glare. It would last only for a moment or two, but the smallest advantage was worth the taking if offered.

The battle to come took shape in his mind. He did not have to sink much effort into that shaping. It came to him almost unbidden, as a pattern made by shadows on a wall might suddenly take on a recognisable form. He could simply see what was possible, what was not. What would likely follow if he chose to do this, or that.

"I'll take Rudran and the lancers into the hundred behind the wagons," he grunted, swinging up into the saddle and turning his horse about. "Scatter them, keep their archers out of it. Akrana and Wren can deal with the rearguard. You and your bow boys shoot for Callotec, and anyone around him. Anyone who looks like they might be a Clever."

"What we always do," Hamdan said with a grin.

"What you always do."

"You want us to keep one or two Clevers alive, for looking after the Bereaved?"

Yulan thought for a moment, then shook his head.

"Bereaved's not like the Clamour. Doesn't need someone who understands it to keep it quiet all the time, as far as I know. To use it, maybe, but we'll not be using it. So, no: kill as many as you see fit."

They trotted back to where the others waited behind a rocky outcrop. No one interrupted while Yulan curtly issued his instructions; no one's attention wavered. Not even Wren's, though he knew she would have other thoughts on her mind.

He watched her and Akrana more closely than the rest as he spoke, even so. If things went awry, it would be them, if anyone, who might avert complete disaster. He saw nothing to worry him. He trusted them.

Hamdan returned to the edge of the gully with his archers. They lay flat on the ground, only Hamdan himself sliding forward far enough to peer down at the road. Yulan and Rudran and the riders lined up further back, well out of sight. Fifteen of them, strung out. The horses were restless, quiet but uneasy now that they sensed something imminent. On their right, perhaps thirty paces distant, stood Akrana and Wren.

Altogether, a score or so of the Free, and three hundred awaiting them in the valley below. It would be brutal, Yulan knew. But they should win. If his people were better than Callotec's — and they were — they would win. If Kerig was strong — and he was — they would win.

He reached down and freed his knife from its sheath on his calf. He held the tip of the blade poised above the ball of his thumb and watched Hamdan. He felt his heartbeat, marking off the moments. Pacing out this last little stretch of quiet. It paced, and paced. Slowly.

Hamdan, without looking round, raised one hand and gave a casual, almost dainty, beckoning flutter of his fingers. Yulan sank the point of his knife into his thumb. Blood swelled out, a delicate red orb. He returned the knife to its place; sucked away the blood. Then kicked his heels into his horse's flank.

Yulan and the riders crested the skyline in the same moment that the archers' first arrows took to the air. The fifteen horsemen plunged down the slope, loosing screams to sharpen the pounding of hoofs. It was like falling, Yulan thought; plummeting like a stooping hawk.

They came so fast, so sudden, that heads were still turning, weapons still being drawn, alarms still being cried, as the fifteen crashed into the side of the long three hundred.

The waiting became uncomfortable. Partly because of the unresolved tension between knowledge and ignorance: Drann knew something was going to happen – something significant – but not what it would be. Not what it would be like to witness it, live through it.

He settled, eventually, just a few paces away from Kerig and his tree. The Clever had apparently lost all interest in talking, and lapsed into an inward-looking silence. His eyes had closed. His lips still moved, soundlessly. It looked as though he was reciting, over and over again, some memorised passage. Preparing himself, perhaps. Whatever he was doing, it had no room for Drann in it any more.

Kerig's last audible words had been to the tree, not Drann: "Sorry about this, old timber."

So Drann sat, with arms folded across his raised knees and chin resting on arms, staring out over the dry grasslands.

As the sun slowly descended towards the western horizon, the light had deepened and become less harsh, raising a softer orange-yellow from the thin grass and dust. It was not a colour Drann had ever seen in his homeland, up in the hills on the north-western fringes of the Hommetic domain. There, it was all green grass, grey rocks. The white of snow on the high ground. It rained too much for anything to ever dry to this pale ochre hue. On balance, he preferred those dank hills; there was something just a little too wizened and barren about this desiccated terrain.

A little too dust-bearing. That was what he saw then: a thin plume of dust, arising from some indistinct, moving source perhaps two or three miles away. A moving source that was coming closer. Horsemen, Drann realised almost at once. Coming true as an arrow, straight for that hillock, its solitary tree and the four of them. Coming fast.

He scrambled to his feet, turning towards the two archers, but they had already seen the same thing. All their languid indolence was gone as if it had never been. They were stringing their bows.

As they drew nearer, Drann guessed there must be thirty riders. At first he thought they might be a happenstance, but they were galloping, and even Drann knew horsemen seldom galloped unless driven by some pressing purpose. And they were following neither track nor ebb and flow of the land. They were coming straight for the very piece of ground upon which Drann stood. They stank of intent.

"Who is it?" Drann called to the archers.

They paid him no heed. They stared fixedly out, watching the riders. At best, they seemed to Drann uneasy; at worst, afraid.

When it started, it started quietly. A gentle preamble to what was to come.

"Ha," Drann heard Kerig saying softly behind him.

He twisted round to look. The Clever was looking at the thumb of the hand in which he held all that shorn hair.

"Here we go," Kerig said.

His tone was conversational, inconsequential, but Drann could clearly see the tightness that entered his expression. The slight pinching of his brow and narrowing of his eyes. Drann got to his feet and walked over.

When he got close, he could see a pinprick of blood on the ball of Kerig's thumb. It looked like nothing. An insect bite. Kerig sucked the blood away.

"What happened?" Drann asked.

"Stand back," Kerig said, still calm. "Can be dangerous for onlookers, this."

Then he winced sharply. Gave one of his feet a little shake.

"And that's Yulan's foot. Hope he's happy now, bastard that he is."

A low creak sounded from the tree above. Drann backed away. Not far. He watched as Kerig flexed the arm that was tied to the tree, bending a little stiffness out of the joint; rolled his head around his shoulders. Closed his eyes once more.

Drann glanced at Lebid and the other man guarding the horses. They were both staring at Kerig now. The threat of the approaching horsemen was briefly set aside.

Lebid waved at Drann, beckoning him away from the tree. The urgency of the gesture was striking, and irresistible. A little puzzled, Drann walked further towards the horses. That was why he had his back to Kerig when the Clever cried out the first time.

It was part cry, part scream, in truth. It made Drann spin on his heel. He was in time to see a great wound spring open on Kerig's face, the skin flicking apart as if slashed with a knife from chin to cheekbone. Flecks of blood flew. The Clever straightened sharply; his head rocked back.

Drann started to run towards Kerig, hearing the archers

shouting behind him. He had taken no more than a couple of strides before he saw the long cut closing up, sealing itself as if it had never been. Kerig's whole body trembled. His hand, as much as the bonds that held it against the tree would allow, clawed.

And the tree boomed. The sound came from somewhere deep inside the bole. A crack zigzagged across its bark, just above Kerig's hand. It ran perhaps a quarter-way around the trunk. Drann stopped, and blinked.

Kerig suddenly hunched over, folding down around a point on his left side. He blew out a great gasping gust of spent air. A dark flower of blood bloomed on his shirt, the fruit of some grave injury to his flank. And in the instant it appeared, he jerked upright again.

A hole burst open in the tree trunk, as if some invisible fist had punched through from within. The eruption sent fragments of bark and splinters spinning out. Drann ducked instinctively as one, the size of a finger, flashed past his head.

He recovered himself, and turned back to Hamdan's men.

"What's happening?" he shouted to them.

"What's supposed to happen," Lebid said.

"Except they're not supposed to happen," the other muttered, glaring at the tight knot of riders drawing rapidly closer.

20

The School's Butcher

Yulan's great horse bucked and reared amidst a knot of his enemies like a ship in the grip of turbulent seas. He hacked down, first to one side then the other, at heads and arms and shoulders. They still reached for him, some of those hands and spears, not yet understanding what they faced. He cut them away.

The wound in his left side, where one of the first spears had punched in, was already gone. The searing, startling pain of its arrival carried away, just as the rending of his flesh had been, just as the older wounds to his foot had been; all that harm flying, a formless bird, across the distance from him to Kerig, sitting and suffering beneath his doomed tree. Yulan could spare no sympathy for Kerig, though. Not now. When it was done, when the Clever's sacrifice had bought them their victory, then perhaps there would be time to acknowledge it. Now, that sacrifice must be used, not mourned.

Callotec's column was a snake, struck in its flank by Yulan and Rudran and their few riders. It writhed and tightened and twisted in unthinking response to the blow. Uncaring what injuries might be inflicted upon him, Yulan could watch its throes.

The mules were scattering, some of them already splashing into the stream, dragging their handlers with them. The wagons tried to push forwards, even as men from the head of the column turned to rush back and confront the assault. Hamdan and his bowmen up above the road were dropping riders from their mounts, putting swordsmen on their knees. As Yulan watched, an arrow darted into the shoulder of one of the wagoners and set him sagging sideways. He dragged on the reins as he slumped, and the wagon skewed across the road.

Rudran's lancers were wheeling in unison amongst the great fraying crowd of their foes. An arrowhead of hawks, plunging through a disordered flock of songbirds. Their first charge, down the steep slope and across the flat ground into the unready ranks, had been brutally successful. Men had gone down beneath their horses, died on their lances, been thrown violently aside. Already they had cut clean through the spine of Callotec's column, and now turned in neat array to fall on it once more. Some were casting aside broken lances, raising their long, cruel maces. No words or signs were needed, for these men were as well trained as any horsemen anywhere.

Yulan was not a part of Rudran's arrowhead. He fought, and rode, alone in their wake. He felt his horse stagger. A knife or sword had opened a long cut on its shoulder, scoring a ragged line through its hide. He saw the edges of that rough wound already knitting back together, as its burden was visited instead upon Kerig. He slashed down at the Clade warrior who had inflicted it. His sword did not cut all the way through the padding on the man's shoulder, but the blow was hard enough to break the collarbone beneath. Yulan heard its clicking snap, even through the tumult of battle.

Hoofbeats told him that Callotec's rearguard was coming up. He glanced that way, as another fleeting stab of pain in his thigh recorded a knife's stab. A mass of lancers – Armsmen from Armadell-on-Lake itself, the red blaze on their breasts told him – were charging, lances levelled, horses already at full gallop. They made for a fearsome sight, but Yulan felt no fear. He trusted Wren and Akrana, watching from somewhere up on the high ground, to do what was needed.

The forelegs of the lead horse plunged deep into the road surface. Hard-packed earth suddenly turned to sinking sand as loose as liquid, sucking down cobblestones and hoofs alike. That was Wren. The first horse, and then another, pitched forward. Their legs broke as they went down. Their riders rolled and were trampled, bringing down more. Lances were falling from hands, their wielders crying out and clasping at their own eyes. Blinded, Yulan knew; and that was Akrana, and the Hibernal entelech she used, marking them. The charge at once began to slip into churning disorder. A wave breaking and collapsing before it reached the shore.

Yulan's horse burst free of the assailants surrounding it, and in doing so set many of them to flight. Dozens more were already scrambling to get away from Rudran's men, across the stream, over the wagons, even up the slope towards Hamdan's bows. The warriors of the School's Clade stood firm, but the rest were not minded to die today.

A Clever had climbed on to the seat of one of the wagons, and was holding both hands towards Yulan, fingers splayed. Every Clever had different habits in their use of the entelechs; this one was evidently of a showy, ostentatious sort. Ill suited, like most of the School's people, to the immediate demands of battle. An arrow transfixed his neck and he toppled leadenly from his perch.

Clade spearmen were gathering between Yulan and the wagons. Panic did not yet have hold of them. They were trying to make a hedge of shields and spears, curved across the line of the road. Yulan knew he needed disorder if the Free were to carry the day, if he was to reach Callotec. He drove his horse at those half-formed ranks. Several of Rudran's men came in tight array after him, knowing the same thing.

The horses broke in amongst the spearmen, and for long moments the chaos of battle spread its wings over them all, gathered them into its embrace. Fragments of shield flew. Spears broke, horses stumbled. Men fell, howled, spat spittle and blood. A spear went up into the neck of Yulan's horse. The animal slumped to its knees, and Yulan rocked forward in the saddle. He loosed the reins and reached to pull the shaft free. That was one thing that could sometimes undo all of Kerig's protective work: a weapon that remained in the wound it made.

He tore the spear loose, more concerned with speed than care, and the horse shook. Yulan felt its strength coming back to it at once, though. It began to rise. Someone threw themselves across his back, clawing at his neck. The horse lurched down again. Then Rudran himself was there, clubbing Yulan's assailant away. The lancer was grinning fiercely, eyes a little glazed, a little distant. An arrow was lodged in his shoulder. He pulled it out and threw it aside.

Yulan's horse surged up, and bounded forward of its own accord. It brought him hard up against one of the wagons. A Clade spearman ran at him and tried to impale him against the wooden sideboard. Yulan bent flat against his horse's neck and the spear rasped across the small of his back, cutting through his jerkin and his skin. There was no space for the swing he would have liked, but he managed to put enough strength into his sword arm to sever fingers from the spearman's hand and to break the shaft beneath them.

Yulan straightened. Someone was leaping at him from atop the wagon. He caught the glint of a knife. An arrow sprang down and smacked home, but too late to stop the leap becoming a fall, carrying the man into Yulan. His foot came loose from his stirrup under the impact; he was borne down beneath its weight, and knew that if he did not let it take him, he would be left trailing from the other stirrup, caught in it. And so he kicked himself free and fell with the arrow-shot man to the ground.

He rolled away at once, came up in a crouch, sword still in hand. They ran at him as dogs might to a lamed deer, but found him a harder prey than they thought. Kerig's sacrifice bought him an abandon; freed from that need to guard himself, he could attack, and fling himself at his enemies, and look only for the openings that would allow him to kill them. They cut him and pierced him. The pain came and went, the wounds came and went. But he killed them. All that he could reach.

His horse had waited for him. He turned to it and set foot to stirrup, ready to throw himself up on to its back and ride for Callotec, and for any who stood with him beyond these wagons. But behind him he heard the clatter of metal on metal, the beating of hoofs. He looked.

Some few of the rearguard had come unscathed through the nightmarish obstacles Wren and Akrana had set in their path. Very few, but enough to draw half of Rudran's men into a swirling melee of horse against horse. And as Yulan watched, one of those marvellously armoured and becostumed horses that his lancers rode took a scything sword blow to the side of its neck and staggered, reeled. It twisted its head, its legs went from under it and it crashed down on its side. And did not rise. Its blood continued to flow.

Alarm clenched tight in Yulan's chest. He swung up into the saddle, kicked his horse towards that struggle. The lancer was trapped, one leg pinned by the huge body. His helm had fallen from his head. Yulan made for him, distantly aware that his name was Hurdan, that he came from a shore village near Harvekka, that he had joined the Free just two years ago.

Hurdan worked his leg out from under his dead horse, and scrambled to his feet. He bent to pick up his mace from where it had fallen. He and Yulan spotted in the same moment the Hommetic rider coming pounding towards him. Yulan raked his heels across his horse's flank, but the distance was too great.

He saw the sword come down, almost lazy, in a great smooth

arc. He saw Hurdan's head rock backwards at the blow. He saw him sway for a moment. Turn his head slightly, so that Yulan could see the huge bony crevice that had been punched into its side. Then fold down, knees buckling, arms limp. Fall straight down, to the ground.

Yulan cut halfway through the rider's neck as their horses swept past one another. He heard the body fall behind him, but did not look. He stared down at Hurdan. Who was dead. Whose wound had not healed in the moment of its receipt.

And Yulan knew they were in the direst trouble, and that they might not get out of this narrow valley alive.

Piece by piece, moment by moment, the oak tree was dying. Being rent apart. Every wound that made Kerig cry out and tremble was fleeting, its lasting effect sent into the timber, and the branches. The whole canopy shook and shivered. Leaves fell as if beneath the most tempestuous of winds, but there was no wind.

Once, to Drann's queasy horror, Kerig's arm, the one bound to the tree, suddenly cracked and bent where there was no joint. That loosed a true scream from the Clever's mouth, but the arm righted itself in an instant, remembering and returning to its whole form. The tree, though, took that wound and made thunder of it. Spat gouts of pulverised wood from a huge split in its trunk. Shed a rain of leaves.

Drann had retreated to stand beside Lebid and the horses. There were too many branches falling, too many eruptions of splinter and bark. He could not tear his gaze away from Kerig, but was content to keep his watch from a distance.

Lebid was not watching Kerig at all. He was staring at the thirty-odd riders now cantering up the slope of the hill.

"I'm thinking this is going to be bad," he murmured.

Drann looked then. It took him a moment or two to understand what he saw. Blue tunics, most of those men wore. School Clade. At their head came three differently attired. One was slight and clad in a dull cloak. Slumping in the saddle, Drann thought. Looking a little unsafe. The second a huge man, with neck and shoulders and arms like stone blocks and long grey hair tied back. The last of them all leather and hide, gloved in black, with a huge sword at his side. There was something odd about his hair that set Drann to squinting. It looked as though some strange, weighted braids were dancing about the back of his head as he rode.

"Go," Lebid hissed to his fellow archer. "Ride for Yulan. Fast as you like."

The other man did not dispute or hesitate. He hurriedly untied one of the horses – the nearest, for he did not trouble to find his own – and leapt into the saddle. He pounded away, low over the animal's neck, without so much as a backward glance.

Two of the Clade horsemen peeled away from the rest, angling their approach to pursue the archer. The man with the odd hair called them back. Drann heard him quite clearly, even at this distance.

"Let him go," he shouted. "We'll not be long delayed here."

"Who is it?" Drann asked Lebid.

"Sullen. The School's butcher."

"What are they doing here?"

"Nothing good," Lebid said dolefully.

"Do we fight, then?" Drann asked.

The men were close now. He could hear their horses struggling for breath. See the foaming sweat on their necks and flanks. They had come far and fast, these Clade men.

"No, we don't fight," Lebid rasped. "If they try to kill you, you can fight if you like. They try to kill me or Kerig, you leave well alone. Nothing to be gained."

He unslung his bow from his back. Held it up high above his head, so that Sullen and the others could see it held no shaft. Not that they showed any interest in either Drann or Lebid. They drew their horses up just outside the shadow of the tree's canopy, and stared at Kerig's suffering, the tree's convulsions.

Kerig's head had sunk low, his chin tucked in to his chest. The wounds still came – a gash spat blood from the back of his neck even as Drann looked, but was gone again in the blink of an eye – but he responded less obviously to each succeeding one. He no longer cried out, but moaned and swayed unsteadily. His body rocked as if struck by unseen blows raining in from every side.

Sullen leapt down from his horse and walked slowly towards Kerig.

"And here, indeed, is the very man we seek," he said, then called back over his shoulder, "You have a remarkable gift, Sestimon. Quite remarkable. It's no wonder Kasuman sent someone to cut your throat."

His voice sounded lifeless to Drann, with none of the rise and fall, the passion, those words might have carried coming from another's lips. It gave no clue as to Sullen's mood or intent.

His actions did, though. He kept moving towards Kerig, turning to walk a few paces backwards as he did so.

"This is the man you accuse? Just to be certain, you understand," he said to the big grey-haired man waiting amongst the Clade warriors.

And that man nodded.

"This man is to answer to the School for recent events," Sullen said to Drann and Lebid, sparing them no more than a dismissive glance. "It is nothing that concerns you."

But Drann found it did concern him. His body responded before his head could sort things into order. He hurried to set himself between Kerig and Sullen. The tree creaked and cracked at his back. Leaves drifted down.

Sullen stopped.

"Put that spear aside and get out of my way," the School's butcher said quietly.

Drann wanted to, in a way. It sounded a fine suggestion. Yet his feet stayed planted where they were, and his hands stayed clasped about his spear. Not for Kerig's sake so much as that of the Free. He did not perfectly understand what was happening, but he understood enough. Somewhere, not far from here, the Free were fighting. And bleeding. And what Kerig was doing here, with his body and with this tree, was as best Drann could tell the only thing keeping them alive.

"You can't take him," he heard himself saying. "Not now. The Free are—"

"Undone," whispered Sullen and came towards him. The long grass parted about his shins. Grasshoppers scattered from his path like pebbles flicked by invisible fingers. Falling leaves spun about him as if a thousand pale butterflies were tumbling dead from the sky. Drann did not know what to do.

He gave a jab with the spear, when it seemed that Sullen was going to barge right into him. It was not meant to strike home, merely to warn. To stymie the man's remorseless advance. Even as he made the thrust, Drann remembered what Yulan had said about there being two ends to a spear, and he snapped the butt around in a low swing. He thought he might catch Sullen in the knee. He did not.

Sullen swayed without breaking stride and stretched out a gauntleted hand. It caught and closed upon the spear's shaft. His other hand lashed round and struck Drann a backhanded blow on the face that sent him sprawling, breaking his own grip upon the spear.

His ears rang to the echo of the impact. He had to blink to clear his vision. His thoughts turned to mud as he tried to rise on legs unmoored from his will. Sullen kicked him in the ribs. Drann rolled on to his hands and knees, spittle – perhaps a little blood – trailing from his mouth. Sullen broke the spear across his back.

Drann slumped down. Pain burned in his spine, burrowed dully into his kidneys. He tasted dirt. Suddenly Sullen's hand was on the back of his head, clenched in his hair, grinding his face into the dusty soil so that he could hardly breathe.

"Stay down," the School's butcher murmured, frighteningly dispassionate. "If you're who I think you are, it's not your fight, is it? There's no one here you should be giving your life for. But make no mistake: I'll take it if you offer it."

A resounding, cracking boom burst from the tree. Through

narrowed eyes, Drann saw a weaving fissure race up its flank, spitting out shards of wood and flakes of bark that pattered into the grass by his head. It made even Sullen start, and Drann was able to twist and spit dirt from his mouth and get a good breath in.

Kerig was sagging, swaying. Wounds flickered across his body, opening and closing like eyes. Bruises flowered and vanished in the same instant. His clothing was sodden with blood. The injuries pulsed through him, through his arm, and into the tree. They tore it apart from within. As Drann watched, a branch split from the main trunk and slowly wrenched itself free, leaving a ragged stump. It crashed to the ground. Dust was writhing from the rents in the tree's bole; the stuff of its innards, pounded into a fine mist.

Sullen straightened, his beaded braids swaying heavily. Drann rolled on to his side.

"Might be a whole flock of birds to be knocked down with a single slingstone here," Sullen said thoughtfully, perhaps to himself. Then, quite clearly to Kerig, who equally clearly could not hear him: "I do know what this is, don't I, Kerig?"

He turned to the Clade warriors, many of whom were staring in uneasy fascination at the violent death of Kerig's tree.

"Cut that Clever loose," Sullen said. "Bind him and get him on to a horse."

"No," Drann grunted.

He would have cried it out loud, but the pain in his flank and back was like a tight band, squeezing the air from his chest. Sullen gave him another, desultory kick in the side and walked away.

"Gather up these horses, too," Drann heard him shouting.

"A few fresh mounts'll speed us on our way, and slow Yulan and his boys nicely. If any of them are left alive after this."

Yulan whistled. Over and over again, turning his horse about, ducking an arrow that skimmed low over his head. He held a spread hand straight up in the air, and answering whistles and a horn came, sharp over the cacophony, from up there atop the slope.

As one, like the most ruthlessly trained hunting dogs, Rudran's men broke away and rode at full gallop. Those couple who still carried lances cast them aside. The signal was for instant retreat, and they all knew it. Yulan went with them, riding down those in his way.

The trap was now against the hunters, for that short but steep slope that had carried them down into Callotec's flank was cruel to those who wished to climb it. The ground crumbled beneath the clawing hoofs of the horses, and stole from them all their strength and speed. An arrow went into the back of the man next to Yulan, right in the centre of it, through some flaw or chink in his chain vest. He arched, and gasped, and fell sideways. The spearmen who came boiling in their wake swept over him, and closed about him. Stabbing and pounding. Fethin Fiveson. His name had been Fethin Fiveson, the distant, still part of Yulan's mind thought.

He pumped with his arms, driving his horse on and up. He could see Hamdan and the archers standing now, starkly exposed, at the crest of the rise, sending arrow after arrow darting down. His horse was faltering, betrayed by the sliding ground beneath it. He shouted into its ear.

Out on to the high ground he came, his horse trembling and ready to drop. He looked back. The whole column of warriors – what remained of it – was a seething mass, streaming to the foot of the slope, up it. Hungry for the Free.

"Wren!' he shouted.

She was running towards him, and he could see in her face that she understood what had happened, and what it meant. There was no time for that now. Only for what he and Wren had agreed might be needed, if all went wrong. She would be ready for it, he hoped.

"Wren! We need you."

He pointed down the slope, at the furious host coming for his blood. Wren stopped, and scowled at him, then nodded. She dropped to her knees, pressed her hands to her face for a calming, centring moment, then set them one atop the other on her thighs. Yulan spun and called out to Hamdan.

"Kill the carthorses. Wren has the rest."

Hamdan did not even acknowledge the command, but he adjusted his aim. All the archers did, and a hissing flight of shafts went skimming down in search of horseflesh.

Yulan dropped down from his horse and knelt, that he might be a less tempting target for any arrows climbing up. He watched as the first of the Hommetic spearmen came slithering and scrambling to almost within touching distance.

"Quickly would be good, Wren," he said calmly.

Even as he spoke, the whole face of the incline gave a great convulsive heave. It flung men into the air as a bull might shiver to flick flies from its back. Wide slabs of thin turf came loose and slid down the slope, carrying a tumbling mass of warriors with it. The movement spread rapidly wider and wider until all the land was sliding away, the ground shaking beneath. A great slip, that piled all of Callotec's men back to the foot of the slope in drifts and exposed scars of pale rock.

"To your horses," Yulan shouted, backing away. "We ride!"

And then he had to dart forward again, to catch Wren in his arms as she fainted away.

21

The Eye Of The Bereaved

One of the carthorses was dying on the track. Enormous, lying there on its side, its strength ebbing away with every bubbling, bloody, wheezing breath. Its dark flank heaved, the arrow that had gone deep in there and pierced its lung quivering. A second shaft was sunk into its neck and had released a wide pool of blood across the road.

Another of the animals needed to haul the wagons was already dead. Callotec's men were cutting it free from the harness. It had fallen there, dropping in an instant, when an arrow went in through its eye. That had been either a lucky shot or the work of an absurdly gifted archer. Callotec was minded to think it the latter, given the identity of their assailants.

"The Free do not abandon a fight just because their first attempt is rebuffed," he murmured to Kasuman, who stood beside him regarding the great dying horse.

"Agreed," the Clever said, equally quiet. "We are short two carthorses. Three of the mules have run off, with everything they carried. A good thirty of our men are dead, close to twenty too sorely hurt to move from here. Two of my Clevers are arrow-shot to death. You truly think we have the strength to fight the Free all the way to Threetower?"

"Everything you say is true," Callotec conceded, hiding his contempt with difficulty. "But we still outnumber them by ... what? Ten to one? Only three of us need to reach the border to claim victory, Kasuman. You, me, and ... "

He nodded discreetly towards the wagon upon which sat the Bereaved, anonymously cloaked.

"That's true, I suppose."

"Of course it is," snapped Callotec.

He curled his lip in distaste. Distaste at everything. The indifferent cruelty of a world that had stripped him of all he had once possessed, and left him standing here in the wilds of a lost kingdom with only dead horses, a fell Permanence and timorous allies for company.

Callotec had fought, as he was bound to do, for Crex and the throne as long as any sane man might. With that cause lost, and nothing on the horizon but death – hard, unkind death in all likelihood – at the hands of the rebels, he had fled. As any sane man might. There was nowhere the traitorous Council could not reach him save the Empire, so it was towards the Empire he went. And hoped, in his secret heart, to finish on the way that which he had once left unfinished at Towers' Shadow. Callotec had no great desire to be a subservient king swept to the throne by a raging army of the Orphans, strewing his future kingdom with the corpses of his future subjects. But it would serve.

As would Kasuman and the Bereaved. The Clever had

pledged fealty, called him the rightful, if uncrowned, king. Brought him two hundred men to fight his way to the border and safety. Now that the Free – Yulan – hunted him, whatever faint chance remained of reaching the Empire alive relied upon keeping close to hand every single sword Kasuman had brought with him.

"We might be able to do it," Kasuman said softly, as if catching the scent of Callotec's thoughts on the evening air. "Unless they loose the Clamour."

A flicker of dark movement amongst the rocks on the far side of the stream caught Callotec's eye. A lizard. A mottled corpse-eater. Nosing about there. Already sensing the feast awaiting it upon this field. The vile thing should be readying for its winter sleep by now, but the abundant table laid for it and its kind these last few weeks had kept them awake, hungry, deeper into the year than was usual this far north.

Callotec bent and scooped up a loose cobblestone from the road. He pitched it towards the huge lizard, putting all his bitter frustration into the throw. The stone clattered harmlessly off the rocks, part of it erupting into a cloud of splinters and grit. The lizard writhed sinuously around and disappeared into some crevice or hole.

"You there!' Callotec shouted at the nearest of his Armsmen. "For the love of mercy, silence this horse. Its moaning repels me."

The swordsman drew a long knife and did as he was commanded, quickly and quietly. He and Callotec shuffled backwards to keep their feet out of the blood that pulsed thickly from the horse's opened throat.

There was some disturbance amongst the men labouring to pull one of the heavily laden wagons out from the rut into which its panicking horse had dragged it. Callotec and Kasuman both turned and looked that way.

The effort to free the wagon had been overtaken by pushing and shoving. An argument had taken root, and prospered amidst the shock and fear of the battle's aftermath. Grown towards brawl. Levymen were exchanging abuse with a pair of Callotec's Armsmen who had gone to lend their shoulders to the task. One of those Armsmen was sent sprawling backwards, spat out from the fractious knot. The warrior fell, and cursed, and came to his feet again. He made to draw his sword.

"Stop that," Callotec called out.

As he walked towards the wagon, the ten or more levymen concerned arrayed themselves to meet him. One of their number, unarmed, came forward. He did not look, to Callotec's eye, as submissive as was appropriate to the moment. The approach of several of Kasuman's Clade warriors – formerly of the Clade, Callotec supposed was more correct – did draw a slightly more nervous glance from the levyman, but his courage withstood the test.

"We're thinking we'll be going home," he said – almost shouted – without preamble.

Callotec nodded. "Indeed?" he said.

"I'll not fight the Free for any man. None of us will."

"You've already beaten them!' cried Callotec, spreading his arms as if to summon the evidence of their bleak surroundings. "Did you not see them fly from the field?"

He knew that the tale told by the scene around him did little to strengthen his words. Men dragging bodies off the road, piling them to await the carrion-lovers since there was not time, and too few hands, to dig graves and no wood for the making of pyres. Others tending to the wounded. More gathering the supplies that had spilled from wagon or mule in the confusion.

"You don't think they'll be back?" the levyman shouted. Callotec had a poor ear for accents, especially those of peasants, but he thought the man to be from Armadell, or somewhere near it. "You don't think they'll make bone and meat and shit of us all? And in any case, I'd as soon die now as become a slave of the Orphans. You think my family'll thank me for taking that to the Empire?" He nodded as he said it towards the Bereaved, sitting on one of the wagons, unmoving and silent as ever.

"You are a subject of the Hommetic king!' Callotec shouted, his meagre stores of patience long exhausted. "Here stands that king, and he commands you to see him safe to the border."

"Aye?" the Armadell man muttered. "I see no crown on his head."

"Then you are treasonously deaf and blind."

Callotec could feel the black fury rising in him. The flood that he had never been able to resist when it came. Never wanted to resist, in truth. The levyman could not see it. He spat in the dirt at Callotec's feet.

"World's got nothing but treason to it, these times."

"Maybe so, but it still carries a price," Callotec said, suddenly cold and calm.

He turned away, spoke sidelong to the nearest of the Clade men standing behind him.

"Take hold of the traitor."

They rushed in before the levyman could do more than cry out in surprise and anger. Some took hold of his arms. Others faced his fellows, hands upon the hilts of their swords. For a moment it seemed that threat might not be enough. That a general slaughter was about to begin. But the levies had not quite so far outrun their senses as to think they could best what faced them. They did nothing as their spokesman was dragged away by his captors.

Callotec walked back to Kasuman.

"An example is necessary," he told the Clever.

"Sire?"

"The Bereaved. Nothing less will do." Callotec felt calmer now that he was set upon the course. "Close to a third of what strength remains to us is of his sort. If we allow these notions to foul their heads, we'll never get them out."

"Perhaps . . . " murmured Kasuman.

"They doubt my rightful crown. I will prove it to them, and there will be no more treason after that."

"Prove it?"

Callotec smiled. "The Bereaved, as I said. Its possession and its use has ever been the most potent symbol of Hommetic power. That is something they cannot contest, or dispute."

Kasuman hesitated, and Callotec marked that and would not forget it. But in the next moment the Clever turned away and beckoned the warriors to bring their captive after him. Callotec was satisfied. Events had their flow, and once it began it was seldom turned aside. Those who thought otherwise, as often as not, would be cast ashore, battered and bruised. Or dead.

Kasuman reached up and delicately, as a mother might lift a sick child, brought the Bereaved down from the wagon. He set it on its feet beside him.

"No!' the levyman screamed as they hauled him closer. He bucked and writhed, but the hands that held him were strong.

Kasuman took the cloak from the Bereaved's shoulders, and it stood there, before them all. A Permanence that few had ever seen, all had known and feared. Even Callotec had never set eyes upon it before, not when it was so exposed. As far as he knew, it had not, in his lifetime, set foot outside the School's Keep in Armadell-on-Lake until Kasuman somehow stole it away. In all the time it had sat there on the Clever's wagon, these last days, Callotec had not dared to draw near to it, let alone lift its hood. Now everyone looked into its face.

It had the size and form of a small child. Pale, smooth, naked, featureless. An imitation of a human, looking as if it had been shaped from soft white wax. It was sexless and hairless, and lacked a mouth and nostrils. The only break in its skin was where its eyes might have been. There were no eyelids; merely thin slits, such as might have been made by gently pressing a blunt blade into its yielding face, and behind them blank white orbs.

"Kneel him," Kasuman said.

The Clade warriors pushed the levyman down on to the ground, one of them punching at his neck when he struggled. From the crowd of onlookers there came a rustle, a stir of indignant unease. One or two voices dared to rise in protest. At that, the rage took hold of Callotec once more and he spun on his heel and shrieked out at them.

"Treason! There has ever been but one answer to it. And now you will see that there are worse things than the Free in this world! There is more to fear than a gaggle of brigands, even one that claims the Clamour amongst its number. Greater powers than you contest these days, greater powers give battle; greater histories are being written than a thousand of your lives might sum to, and it is not for the likes of you to choose whether or how to serve."

Kasuman bent, and whispered into the flat white ear of the Bereaved. His eyes closed. Those of the Bereaved twitched. Still the levyman kneeling before the Permanence cried out for help, his words becoming great choking sobs. Still his captors held him firm, belaboured him with slaps and blows that did little to quell his panic.

Kasuman whispered. The Bereaved trembled. He carefully lifted one of its arms. The fingers of its hand were limply spread. Like white slugs. There were no fingernails. Not a blemish in its pearly skin. Callotec felt an almost ravenous excitement. He clenched his fists at his sides.

Kasuman touched the Permanence's hand to the top of the levyman's head, and at that touch a single black tear sprang from the eye of the Bereaved and coursed, too fast, down its face. Dropped to its shoulder and then ran along the arm, out over one of those extended fingers and into the scalp that awaited it.

At once Kasuman lifted the Permanence's hand away, never once breaking the urgent rhythm of his murmurings. He pressed the Bereaved's arm back down to its side, eased it backwards, away from its victim. The Clade warriors holding the doomed man backed away smartly, too. He looked up at them, his face contorted by fear. His anguished gaze passed from face to face, and found no succour, no comfort. Callotec looked into his eyes for a brief moment, and smiled.

Pinpricks of blood appeared across the man's face. A lattice-work of tendrilous bruises crept across his temples, and down on to his neck. He moaned. A bulb of milky white mucus beaded at the corner of each eye, and swelled and spilled on to his cheek. His lips split, a score of raw wounds opening in but a moment, and he wailed.

Part of Callotec wanted to look away, but he did not. He forced himself to watch, and easily enough found another part of himself to take delirious pleasure in the sight. This, he thought, might be the shape of the kingdom he would found. One where all the timidity that had crippled Crex's reign was replaced by absolute authority, and the absolute will to enforce it. That was how you stemmed revolts before they took hold.

A hush fell across the onlookers as the dying man curled on the ground. Spasms shook his body. He vomited black bile. He folded his hands over his head, hiding his corrupting face from view. Across the backs of those hands, a forest of pustulent blisters bloomed.

The levyman was making no sound now. He grew limp. Not quite still, for tremors still racked his arms. His scalp was sloughing from the skull beneath, sliding down to the ground. The skin on his hands was curling and peeling back, exposing the already rotting flesh beneath. He died, and as he did so the stench of death spilled out from him and suffused the valley.

On all sides men turned away, pressed their hands over nose and mouth. Gagged.

Callotec at last closed his eyes. He covered his own nose. Blinked away tears called up by the astringent stink. It was an extraordinary thing to have witnessed. A wonder.

He was not ready to die yet. His wife had died, with the baby, in childbirth six years ago. Everyone who shared more than the thinnest part of his blood and descent was now dead, or imprisoned. The world and the times had stripped away everything and everyone, and left just him. Alone. The last of his kind and kin.

He would not lie down. He would fight every step of the way to Threetower, if that was what was needed to give him life, and a crown.

"It is regrettable," Kasuman said softly as the two of them walked to the head of the column, "that we have lived to see the day when the Bereaved must be used against our own people."

"They are not our people," Callotec said. "Not any more. Everyone from here to the sea is a traitor, until they bow to their rightful king. The ones who are still alive, after the Hommetic throne has been restored: they will be our people. Only them. Only then."

22

When Yulan Was Not Yet Captain Of The Free

Wren came and went from wakefulness. She was stretched out on a blanket, head propped up on one of her own saddlebags. Yulan sat beside her, because there was nowhere else he thought he could be more useful.

Now and again, he crossed to the tiny spring beside which they had settled, sopped up some of its waters in a cloth and brushed Wren's brow with it. When he pressed the back of his hand to her cheek, she still felt hot, but the fever was diminishing slowly. He thought so, anyway. He had no great knowledge or instinct when it came to such things.

His instinct was for more sanguinary business, and that was what occupied his mind as he sat looking into Wren's pale, troubled face. The means by which he might salvage something from the wreckage of this undertaking. He had an idea how it might be done. Back in Curmen he had been thinking how it *would* be done. Now, it was *might*.

Now he must save the Free, as well as Towers' Shadow. That was what it had come to, the choice he had made while sitting across a rickety little table from Creel of Mondoon far from here. Everything, and everyone, he held dear rested upon the precipice now. His heart shook at the simplicity of it. He had led them all into a storm, which would rage now until its hunger for blood was spent.

He went to wet the cloth again. He held it down in the bitterly cold water for a moment or two, letting it soak up that cooling balm. When he came to Wren, and knelt by her side, he found her eyes open. Looking at him.

"You cannot leave him to the School. To Sullen. You know what will happen."

"I do. And I know what will happen if we go to war with the School over him. You know. We would lose, in the end. There are too few of us, too far scattered. The School would pay a terrible price, perhaps be destroyed by it, but we would certainly be. You know that. Once it is begun, Sullen would never stop."

"No. I don't know it."

He reached to set the cold cloth to her forehead, but she pushed his hand away. He could feel her weakness in that push, but allowed her to fend him off. It wounded him almost beyond endurance, that small gesture. And perhaps he had earned the wounding.

"There's another way, Wren," he said. "The Bereaved. If we have that, we have everything. The School, the Council, everyone would be willing to barter with us then. We hold all the bones in that game."

"That will take too long. And how will you set hands on the Bereaved? Without Kerig, with fewer swords."

That deserved no answer less than true, so he gave it.

"I'm not sure yet. But I believe. It's possible, I promise you. We still have the Clamour."

She pressed her fingers into her eyes, then ran them over her forehead and into her scalp, smoothing back her hair. Exhausted. Despairing. Of all the things he would have wished to avoid, of all the partings he would have wished to forestall, this was the one he had most feared. He had told them to go to their farm. Now he knew he should have forced them.

"We still have the Clamour," she murmured in echo of his words. "That's ... that's not a thing to stake everything on. Would you wager your own life – the life of someone you love – on what happens when you open that door, Yulan?"

He looked at her sadly. She was right. The Clamour might as easily ruin them as win them the victory. It was the last arrow in their quiver, to be used when all the rest were shot. As they were now. So he understood her doubt. .

"It's what we have left, Wren," he said as gently as he could. "It's the best chance – the least poor chance – I have to get him back."

And I want that more than you know, he thought. He would not willingly add to the number of his ghosts. He would set aside almost any other goal, if he could but retrieve Kerig and reunite these two, and send them safely away.

"The best hope for all of us, including Kerig, is to capture the Bereaved. Callotec and Kasuman too, if we can."

He said it softly, but with conviction. Hoping that she would hear in his voice all the desire that went into those few words. She did, he thought. But even if she heard him clearly, it did not meet her need. He saw that, and could not blame her.

She turned her head silently away from him. Closed her eyes, pressed her lips tight together. Holding it in, all of it, for now.

"I'm sorry," he said, and rose to his feet.

It would be too hurtful, too blunt, for him to stay there at her side now. He left the wet cloth folded on the blanket beside her hand.

When Yulan was not yet Captain of the Free, he killed a horse riding from Harvekka to White Steading faster, it was afterwards said, than any man had done before. He hated to do it, for the care of horses ran deep in his upbringing and the traditions of his people, but he did it nonetheless.

Yulan was custodian of the Free's net of eyes and ears and tongues, cast across the kingdom, harvesting knowledge and rumour. It was a responsibility he took seriously, for the Free were fewer than they had been in their days of famous glory but their world had become no less dangerous, no less populated by those who might wish them harm.

Sullen had come to them eight months ago, proved his prodigious martial talents more than once, distinguished himself, even in that short time, as perhaps their finest swordsman. But Yulan had never liked him. The man stank of artifice and affect. Hollow, Yulan's instincts cried out. His surface a lie, though a convincing, impenetrable one.

He had said as much to Merkent, early on. For all his faith in Yulan, the Captain had found no grounds upon which to send away such a potent sword arm. Especially one who came to them from a past life amongst the corsairs. Trouble was brewing along the tangled, island-fringed coast those pirates plagued. There were said to be five towns full of them on the Mule Isles now. The kingdom would soon move against them, by all accounts, and that might mean profitable work for the Free.

Once the sliver of doubt had entered Yulan's mind, it festered. Grew. Sullen dressed and carried himself as might a corsair, but his manner struck Yulan as entirely too self-possessed and informed for one of those wild, unschooled pillagers. So Yulan cast his net. Gave the people he paid the chance to earn their coin. Even sent one of them – brave Harvant – out to the Mule Isles, in the guise of an escaped prisoner. Him, he gave a lot more coin, because that was a cruel thing to ask any man to do.

Harvant had been gone for close to three months. Now he had returned. That was why Yulan went to Harvekka. He would have been there sooner, but Hamdan's son had died, away in the south, and the two of them went together to see to his passing – under the sky, in the beaks of vultures – and to the care of his young widow. So Yulan came to Harvekka a few days late. He would always regret that.

He met Harvant in a seething, stinking drinking cellar near the waterfront. The kind of place where every man, and every woman, looked worth a wager, should a fight break out. No one gave Yulan any trouble. He looked worth a bigger wager than any one of them.

Harvant, on the other hand, looked gaunt and nervous and scarred. Someone had cut a long gash into his cheek, and it had not healed well. He sought no pity, though, and Yulan hid what he felt. He let Harvant speak.

"There was a boy, they said, years ago, who got himself the name Sullen. Wasn't his birth name. They couldn't remember that. And he hated being called Sullen, beat some who spoke it half to death. All the way to death, once, they thought. A fighter, anyway. Nasty, which amongst those folk I can only think must mean savage as the worst bloody beast you ever did meet. He wasn't right, they said.

"But he went away, this lad. Just upped and disappeared, before he was sixteen. Didn't seem like anyone was sorry for that. And not sight nor a word was had of him after, but for one story I heard. Came through several tongues, so no telling if it's true or not, but it'd be a funny sort of whisper to set running without something to it.

"Story's this: a man from the harbour this Sullen grew up in, he was raiding right on the northern edge of the kingdom. Not even sure whether he was inside or outside it, supposedly. After furs, must have been. Not much else to chase up there. Anyway, they got themselves caught out. Ran into Clade swords they weren't expecting; not many, but enough to set them scuttling back to their ships and away. And he reckoned one of those wearing the blue tunic was Sullen. A few years on him, but Sullen still."

So Yulan killed a horse, because he knew Sullen for a liar and a pretender. Much worse than that, perhaps, if he was in the service of the School. He rode to White Steading. By rights, Sullen should have arrived there two or three days before, to attend the annual accounting of shares. Almost all of the Free —

those of them with a claim on a share, anyway – would be there. Yulan had thought it more important to go to Harvekka and meet Harvant, though he had told no one where or why he was going.

The Free had bought White Steading four captains ago, and made that grand farmhouse, white as chalk, into their strong-hold. Its outbuildings had been turned into stables and armouries and dormitories. A stone wall high as a man had been thrown around it, and a wooden palisade and a boggy moat around that. Watchtowers had been erected and spiked pits strewn across the ground before its gate, to make any approach slow and dangerous. Tunnels had been dug, and treasure cellars, that none but a handful knew of.

The farmstead lay beside the wild-watered Fleet River, an impassable torrent of seething rapids at that point. Over that boiling channel, a rope and plank bridge ran from the upper floors of the farmhouse to the low cliffs on the far bank.

The watchers opened the gate for Yulan as he came riding up on his foaming, faltering horse. He leaped from its back in the yard and it fell as he ran from it. He heard its death prophesied in the rattling, snuffling gasping of its breath behind him, but did not look back.

He fought to steady himself as he drew near the door to the barracks. He slowed to a walk, held his arms stiff and still at his sides. Sullen knew he neither trusted nor liked him, but might still be taken unawares if Yulan came to him in seeming calm. Even so, Yulan threw the door open more violently than he had intended. His blood had not cooled quite enough. He pushed his way through the few warriors gathered around the nearest of the cots, ignoring their questions and complaints. There was no Sullen. He asked the men standing there, regarding him with puzzled expressions. They did not know.

He walked out into the yard. The pounding of hammers in the smithy echoed that of his heart, but he strove for clarity. He looked up, and saw Sullen there, on one of the high wooden walkways that connected all the watchtowers to the farmhouse like branches fanning out from a mighty tree trunk. The two of them looked into one another's eyes, as the sounds and doings of the White Steading carried on around them, oblivious. And Sullen must have seen something there, in Yulan's gaze. Another regret and guilt: that single, unguarded moment in the eyes that betrayed him. From which all else flowed.

Sullen ran for the doorway that led into the great white house.

"Alarm!' Yulan shouted as he sprinted. "All to arms! A share of mine to any who takes Sullen!"

The Free, more than any company in the kingdom, knew how to respond to such a call. Coming from Yulan, second only to Merkent himself, it had an instant effect. Weapons clattered. From barracks and smithy and stables, men came rushing out. Yulan was still the first to reach the farmhouse, by some way. He gave himself just a fraction of a heartbeat, in the doorway, to listen for any sound. And he heard it: footsteps, loud on the bare floorboards up above; the clash of blades, the collision of bodies.

He drew both sword and knife, went pounding up the stairs. Akrana was on her knees at the head of them, hand pressed to her side. Blood seeped out between her fingers. She was slumping down already, eyelids fluttering. She said nothing, jabbed her chin down the corridor to show him the way.

At the end of that passage was a wide, near-square hall. The Captain's quarters were on one side of it; on the other, the door out on to the great wooden balcony from which the footbridge vaulted across the Fleet. Yulan slowed, cautious of the corners and angles that might conceal ambush. He listened. He heard them coming just a moment before he saw them.

Sullen and Merkent tumbled together from the doorway of the Captain's rooms. They fell heavily, hard enough to split floorboards. Yulan sprang forward, ready to let knife and sword drop and drag Sullen away from Merkent, but Sullen was already rising, springing away from the Free's captain. Who did not rise to follow him. Who did not reach to stay his retreat.

Sullen bared his teeth at Yulan, his beaded braids swirling as he spun and darted out on to the balcony. Yulan knew he should not hesitate, but he did. He went down on one knee beside Merkent, the man who had taught him more than any other, and earned his respect in a way no other ever had. Merkent's long grey beard trembled as the last of his life whispered out through it. His stomach was opened, sliced from side to side. His blood made a lake, and sank between the floorboards. His eyes twitched and he was looking at Yulan as he died.

Yulan went out on the balcony, quite calm now. Quite controlled. Empty, in truth, of anything save the ambition to kill Sullen. Later, he knew, he would be prey to misery and guilt such as he had seldom known. He chose not to feel them now. Not yet.

The Fleet roared beneath the swaying bridge. It bounded and sprayed, and the mists it cast off wetted Yulan's face as he stood at the bridge's end. Sullen was almost halfway across. The short sword in his hand was shedding drops of blood that were snatched away by the white torrent beneath.

"Guard on the bridge!' Yulan shouted, as loud as he could, but they were already coming. Two spearmen showing themselves at the clifftop to which the bridge led.

Sullen glanced at them, turned back to face Yulan, and smiled. He beckoned him.

Yulan laid his sword carefully down. He needed a free hand to steady himself on that inconstant bridge, and in his mind's eye he could already see the shape of the fight. It would be fast, and intimate, constrained by the lack of space and sure footing. More suited to knifework.

He advanced slowly, deliberately, giving himself time to envisage what might happen. Sullen was, if anything, better with a blade than he was. But Yulan gave himself the edge in balance, speed of movement. An even contest, then. He imagined the next few moments, and took from that imagining the message he wanted: he was going to win. Sullen was a dead man.

When he was within a couple of sword lengths, Yulan pumped his legs to put a spasm into the bridge's wooden planks and rope skeleton. Used it to throw himself forward, even as Sullen was momentarily unbalanced and reaching for a surer hold on the bridge.

Yulan cut at Sullen's swinging sword arm and nicked it, but not badly. They slashed and parried, neither landing a telling blow. All the time the river deafened them, flung up its spray as if reaching for them.

But Sullen was indeed the better man with a blade. He wielded that short sword as deftly, as fast, as if it were but a knife like Yulan's. He flicked aside a darting attack, blade grating across blade, and rolled his wrist to flatten the sword, punch it down and in towards Yulan's stomach.

It was instinct, not thought, that told Yulan what to do; showed him a pattern he might make of the next instant. He took the thrust into his side, welcomed it. It would not kill him, he knew, and it gave him something worth all the pain. It gave him Sullen's sword and his neck. He hooked his free hand around Sullen's sword arm and locked it in there, jabbing the embedded blade deeper still as he jerked the traitor close. He stabbed straight in at Sullen's neck, aiming for the soft point just above his breastbone.

Sullen's other hand flashed up and the knife's blade impaled it. Sullen wrenched it sideways. Yulan used the spreading wide of his arm to lunge his head forward, butted Sullen hard across the bridge of his nose.

Sullen staggered backwards, barely finding a grip on the rough ropes with the hand he tore free from Yulan's knife. The sword pulled out from Yulan's flank, and his strength went flooding out with it for a moment, so that his knees shook. Sullen surged back in to renew their embrace, blood pouring from a split above his nose. It might blind him soon, Yulan thought, knowing he might not stay alive long enough to use that.

But Sullen was hurt too. Angry. The smallest of mistakes, to come at Yulan just slightly too high, with a straight thrust. Yulan dropped back and down, twisted to bring one leg flicking round and take Sullen at the ankle of his leading foot just as he put his weight on it.

Sullen's leg swept out from under him and he went down sideways. His hand lashed against the ropes and the sword was wrenched away, spinning into the river. Yulan rose, one hand clamped across his wound to stem the strong-flowing blood. Sullen, sitting there, looked at him, looked at the spearmen now coming towards him from the other end of the bridge, then silently folded himself, hunched himself, and slipped backwards through a gap in the bridge's ropes to go tumbling heels over head into the river.

The white water snapped him away like a falling twig. Just once Yulan, leaning heavily to keep himself from dropping to his knees, saw a dark leg rolling in the rapids. Then nothing. Sullen was gone. They searched for him downriver, but never found him.

The next day, Yulan was acclaimed the new Captain of the Free, just as Merkent had wished. Never had a prize been more bitterly won.

There was a dense, sprawling mass of trees down in the hollow beneath Drann, clustered around the stream that fell from the spring up here on the higher ground. Beyond that, plains rolled away for perhaps a mile or two. Then the beginnings of a scrubby, scrappy forest. A few trees here and there, growing in number and size. Thickening slowly.

He stood there, staring out, as he had been for much of the time since the Free came to this lonely place. Since they had fled here, truth be told. It had been a measured, careful flight – in part because they were short of horses now – but flight nonetheless. Yulan had gathered them all together, guided them an hour from the Old Threetower Road, and set camp here on a hillock. Beside a huge tumbledown cairn that must mark an ancient grave, or memorialise some great victory or defeat. Yulan probably knew its origins. Drann did not.

Far out, on the edge of the day's last light, he could see shapes moving amongst those scattered trees. Like pale shadows sprung free from their sources, drifting through the fringes of the woodland. Wolves. A big pack, each animal loping along its own trail. Ghostly kings, crossing their domain.

Drann had not seen so many in a long time. Perhaps never. There had been a pack, when he was very young, that grew too large and too brave for the liking of the villagers. Every night brought fresh and rising fear, carried on the howls drifting from the high slopes around the village. So they hunted that pack into nothingness. It took them more than a year to do it. Day after day they went out into the mountains, those mere farm folk with their crude spears and rude bows and thin cloaks, and hunt by hunt, death by death, they slowly killed the whole pack.

He remembered them coming back with bloody wolf skins, severed wolf tails. He remembered their fierce joy and pride, as if they, humble as they were, had slain monsters. Which in their way they had.

"War's always good to them."

Drann looked round, to find Yulan standing at his side. Staring out at those same distant shapes. One by one they were disappearing from sight, fading into the loose forest. Until there was but a single wolf, running on and on alone. Then it too was gone.

"They're the only ones who could say there's no such thing as a bad war," Yulan said. "The wolves. Once they're done with killing each other, the people'll come back, though. Turn to killing wolves."

"What are we going to do?" Drann asked.

"We?"

Because it sounded as if Drann was counting himself one of the Free, he assumed. That had not been what he meant; but then, it had been what he said.

"We're going to give Wren and the wounded one more day to strengthen, and then we're going to kill Callotec and take the Bereaved away from him."

"Without Kerig?"

"Without Kerig. Once Wren's got some of her strength back, she can work wonders for us. And we've still got the Clamour."

There was a terrible hollowness to Yulan's voice, unlike anything Drann had heard there before. And when he looked at the man's face, he saw only sorrow.

"Is all hope spent, then?" he asked.

Yulan glanced at him, the premonition of a frown on his face. He did not quite understand, evidently.

"Not yet," the Captain of the Free murmured. "You should leave now."

That took Drann unawares. It was not a thought that had entered his mind, these last few hours. Perhaps it should have. He had been distracted by memories. Sullen coming towards him through falling leaves. Kerig being dragged away, bleeding. The tree, some little time later, after Drann and Lebid had almost forgotten it, suddenly breaking. Coming down with a terrible mournful cracking, in a cloud of leaves and twigs and branches. Destroyed. Fresh memories, so vivid he doubted he would ever be rid of them.

So it was not a thought that had entered his mind, but he knew his answer to it at once.

"No."

Yulan gave a curt shake of his head.

"We're not fighting for that contract now. What we have to do, we would do whether or not Creel had hired us. It will be brutal. It might become a matter of Free against School. Not a thing to take part in when you don't have to."

"The Bereaved can't cross the border. That hasn't changed, has it?"

"No," Yulan conceded.

"That's what I'd fight for," Drann said. "Not for the Free, or for money. It's my land, my village, my family'll be ruined if the Bereaved's not here to protect them. You can't tell me I'm not allowed to fight for that if I want to."

"No," Yulan said wearily after a time. "I can't. You do as you will."

A sharp clattering sound behind them made them both look round. It was only a few of the flat stones that made up the cairn, come loose and sliding down its flank.

The wagon, the bull, the horses were close to the cairn. The Free – those of them not keeping watch – were scattered about like wind-tossed debris. Some asleep, some sitting staring into air. Mourning their dead and their lost, Drann supposed, though hardly anyone had spoken of that. Perhaps such folk as these did not.

He was surprised to see that Wren had got to her feet. She looked unsteady, with her blanket wrapped around her shoulders. Like someone old. Her voice had not aged, though.

"You'd leave him there," she was shouting at Akrana.

Everyone looked. Not just Drann and Yulan, but Rudran, his lancers. Even Hestin, curled up on the seat of the wagon, shivered.

"I would," Akrana snapped back. "It's what we have to do."

"It's not."

"We can't turn back, set the whole Free to the recovery of one man. Not when he brought it . . . "

She faltered. Even cold Akrana was not quite a match for the words Drann knew had been coming to her lips. But he was not the only one who knew them.

"Brought it on himself?" cried Wren. "That's it? You don't think we fight for each other, even when we've made mistakes? You don't think Kerig would fight for you, whether he thought your trouble of your own making or not?"

Rudran was starting to get heavily to his feet, but Yulan stalked quickly towards Wren, waving the lancer back down. It was a bad day to be Captain of the Free, Drann thought.

23

A Killer In The Heart

Kerig was too close to death to spare much attention for the living, waking world. His body was battered and bloodied, his mind dulled and disoriented. Because of this, he experienced only fragments of his journey into captivity. Towards his death, he recognised in those brief passages of lucidity he was allowed, but he was entirely too angry, too damaged, too lost to worry overmuch about that sort of thing.

He knew that death lay ahead, because in those first terrible moments when his connection to the tree, and to the entelech, and to the Free was abruptly broken, he heard, distantly, as if it came to him through a howling storm, a voice he recognised. Sullen. He heard it, and then was swept away from it as the agonies in his body overwhelmed him. The wrenching plunge as he lost his grip upon the entelech that had been flowing through him was akin to being disembowelled. That pure and potent stuff of which the world was made, which he had been attempting to give a shape in that world, slumped into raw chaos and poured out of him. Taking with it melting fragments of his strength, his time, his soul. Sucking them out and carrying them away to merge them with the endless, formless entelech.

Nothing more came clear to him until some time later. He was slung over the back of a horse, tied there. Thumping up and down as the animal cantered along. It was dark, but not quite night. The sun was gone, the echo of its light still on the shaking, rocking horizon.

There were others riding all around. He knew that from the hammering of hoofs, not by his eyes, for his sight started to fail almost as soon as it returned.

The next thing he was aware of was being ungently tumbled down from that horse. Falling badly and gashing his head on some stone or perhaps one of those hoofs. Blinking in the pitch dark, dust stinging his eyes. Coming into possession of his awareness just enough to recognise how much his experience at the tree had diminished him. What he had done there would in any case have exacted quite a cost; that cost was higher, since he had been interrupted. Disturbed. Run through for a time by an entelech over which he had lost control. He did not yet have the clarity of thought to measure precisely what had been taken from him. For now, he only knew there was absence. That he was less than he had been before in some small way. Many small ways, most likely.

Someone kicked him as he lay there.

"Fresh horses! We're not tarrying for food. There'll be no halts till we reach the Tower."

Sullen. Hatred bloomed in Kerig then; the only thing potent enough to stir him with any vigour. He understood vaguely that they were at a wayhouse. One of the many far-flung places the School kept for the reprovisioning and rehorsing of message riders. It was inevitable, of course, that the whole land might be convulsed and ravaged by war yet the cursed School still found a way to keep its wayhouses working.

Soon enough he was rehorsed himself. Thrown atop a fresh and rested mount. No more comfortable a perch than the first one had offered. He lapsed into unconsciousness once more.

Later, he was lying on the ground. He could not even open his eyes. They were dry and crusted shut. He felt warmth upon his face, though. It was day. Something was touching his also dry, split lips. Something trying, quite gently, to part them. Then it was snatched away.

"No food, no water for him." Sullen again. Not angry, just stern.

"He's not looking like he's got much life left in him."

"Good. Idiot. That's how you get to stay alive around a Clever like him. You keep him close to death. Too weak to call up vines to throttle us all, or fill your lungs with water, or put you on your knees, weeping at some unrequited love that never even entered your thick head before."

Then, muttering into his ear: "You won't die, will you, Kerig? You're tough, you bastard's bastard."

Kerig would have given much, everything he had left, to rise then. Even to roll his head and bite Sullen's nose from his face. But everything he had left was not enough even for that.

In time – how much of it, Kerig could not begin to guess – the sound of the horses' hoofs changed. They were on stone, not dirt now. He managed a few painful blinks. He glimpsed high walls. A gate. Turrets up above him, against a blue sky. Sullen had said something about the Tower, what felt like half a lifetime ago. Haut Terpen, then. That was bad.

They stripped him naked. His body quaked at that, for it felt like having his skin peeled away, so much did it make his flesh and bones protest. Then they hung him up, in some small and dark chamber. They tied his hands behind his back. They looped and tied cords around and under his shoulders. They hauled him up, with much grunting and puffing, until his feet left the ground. He swayed gently, all his weight upon the narrow bonds under his armpits. It was painful at once. It would be agony soon.

More gaps. More darkness and unthinking emptiness. After what he thought might be many hours, perhaps days, water thrown in his face.

He coughed, then groaned as he rediscovered his pains. It felt as though he had bands of red-hot iron strung beneath his arms. As if spikes of that same iron had been driven through his shoulder joints. The groan lifted into a cry, then dwindled.

"Can you open your eyes?" Sullen asked him.

He tried, but it hurt.

"Try harder," the man of the Clade said.

Kerig felt a searing heat wash over one side of his face. Sullen was brandishing a torch at him, he guessed. He could not help but try to twist his head out of the way, and that made him cry out again.

"Open your eyes."

He did. He had to narrow them against the hot glare of that torch. They were in some tiny, stinking room with damp walls and a low ceiling. Sullen stood before him, with a pair of Clade warriors. And another man Kerig recognised. The Weaponsmith.

"You remember my companion, I see," Sullen said. "He's painted you a killer, Kerig. Whether you are or not, there's no doubting it's not for want of effort on your part, so we can call a killer in the heart as good as a killer in deed, I think."

I'll be a killer in deed yet, Kerig wanted to say. Longed to say. But his throat would not allow it. He croaked, like a sickly raven. Let his eyes close once more.

"Kill him and be done with it," he heard the Weaponsmith rasp. "You saw his guilt with your own eyes, back at Creel's camp."

The one man for whom his hatred could find new heights, beyond those which Sullen elicited. For the Weaponsmith, though, his hatred was a cold thing, not like the hot anger he felt towards Sullen. It was cold and deep, as much a part of him as bone.

"Be quiet," Sullen said in that dead voice of his.

"Why—' the Weaponsmith began, but got no further.

"He thinks I should kill you, Kerig. He doesn't understand the game he's joined. You do, perhaps."

Again that surging, biting heat from the torch. Again Kerig flinched, and wished he had not as the cords bit.

"It's not you I want, of course. Or not you alone. I want all of them; Yulan especially. Perhaps fortune will smile on me, and they'll venture your rescue by force. Somehow I doubt Yulan's that foolish, or that fond of you since your indiscretions the last time you got within reach of our Weaponsmith here. Still, I can hope.

"Failing that, I'll have from you a confession, properly witnessed, to all manner of injustices committed by the Free. Transgressions on the part of their Clevers. Once we have that . . . well, you can guess, no doubt. And I'm sure you know I can get such a confession from you."

Kerig refused to know that. He would hope to die before such a thing came to pass, under either Sullen's ministrations or his own. A Clever had more ways than most to end his own life. But he needed some strength, some respite from the constant distracting daggers of pain. He set himself to retreating, burrowing back into the darkest and most silent recesses of his mind. He hoped Wren might forgive him for all of this. And that she might find a way to kill Sullen one day.

"If he seems to be regaining his strength, bleed him for a little while," Sullen was saying to the guards. "Constant watch. Never forget what he is; what he is capable of if you give him the chance."

The sound of a door opening, grating over rough flagstones.

"Come away, Weaponsmith. I need to get some rest. We all do. There will be much to be done in the next days, if all goes well."

24

A Hundred Thousand Wings

The smell of roasting hare made Drann's hunger dance a jig in his stomach. Lebid had shot the thing that afternoon, from a ridiculous distance, as it sped across the hillside. Sent it tumbling head over heels with a single arrow that transfixed it through the chest. The best arrow-work that Drann had ever seen in his life.

Now the hare was skinned and gutted and spread-eagled on sticks beside the fire, dripping its juices to sizzle on the stones beneath it. Its scent had been what woke Drann from an unsatisfactory drowsing sleep. For a moment, he had dreamed he was back in the village, watching his mother serve up rabbit stew. Then he had opened his eyes and found himself somewhere very different, living a very different life.

Everyone seemed to find the hare and its cooking utterly entrancing. Night had come on while Drann slept. Wood had been gathered, the fire lit. The Free had assembled around it – Akrana, Rudran and a dozen of the lancers and archers, at least – and now stared fixedly at the skinned animal. Lost in their own thoughts.

Drann took his place in the circle, and held his hands out to gather in some of the fire's warmth. The air was acquiring that sharper chill that said a lasting change in the weather had begun. Back in his village, the first snows were probably only a few weeks away. Perhaps less.

He had never seen the Free so subdued. So silent. He wondered whether this was defeat.

"Where's Wren?" he whispered to the archer at his side, a little nervous at disturbing the contemplative hush.

"Went down into the trees by the stream," the man grunted without taking his eyes off that hare. "We found a drowning pool down there when we were getting the firewood. Said she wanted to see it."

"Oh."

Drann looked towards the hollow beneath the camp. The moon dusted the canopy with silver, but other than that, the trees were a dark mass.

"Is she recovered, then?" he asked.

"A little," Rudran said quietly. "Way to go yet."

"Has she eaten?"

"Couldn't say. Don't think so."

Rudran did not seem overly concerned. His lack of interest struck Drann as resignation rather than indifference.

"I could go and see if she wants food," Drann suggested. "Perhaps she shouldn't be on her own."

Rudran shrugged. "Perhaps she shouldn't," the man grunted, "but you'll not have more luck telling her that than we did."

Drann hesitated for a moment or two, staring into the fire. Then he pushed himself to his feet and set off down the hillside. Down to that dark and unwelcoming thicket of trees.

He had to kick and crash his way through tangled undergrowth once he got there. If there was a path, he could not find it in the darkness. The woods were not of the sort suited to people. A little bit of wilderness, run rampant and disorderly according to its own whims.

There was a wide pool, nested there amongst the trees. It was ringed by ancient flagstones, between which and over which a dense growth of grass and briars had come up. The moon was painted on its dark, still surface. The reflections of the stars above twinkled in it. Wren was sitting by its side.

"It's a drowning pool," she murmured without looking round.

This was the first Drann had seen, but he knew of them. They had been everywhere, once, and though no one had used them for their intended purpose in a long time, ill rumour and frightening tales still clustered about them.

"The Sorentines made them, didn't they?" he said.

For a long time, he did not think she was going to reply. She sat there, gazing into the darkness of the water. Then she spoke.

"They revered the qualities of the Aestival entelech above all others. Fire, strength, courage. The sun, the summer, the day. Even anger. They thought these things the most valuable, and they thought least valuable that which seemed an expression of the Hibernal. Like still water. So when they had someone to kill, someone they had no respect for, they drowned them. In these pools. They had a lot of pools, since there were a lot of people they were minded to kill."

"I didn't know that," Drann said quietly. "Not all of it, anyway."

He took her willingness to talk as, if not quite invitation, at least permission, and sat beside her at the pool's edge.

"People forget things," Wren said. "There'll be bones down there. In the mud."

She closed her eyes. They tightened, just for a moment, as if tugged by some passing pain.

"Are you all right?" Drann asked, and was at once struck by the rank stupidity and cruelty of the question.

She opened her eyes and glanced at him, sidelong.

"No." She held up her hand, turning it slowly before her face in a shaft of moonlight falling through the branches, as she bent and straightened the fingers. "I think the joints have stiffened. They've changed. It's uncomfortable."

"It won't go away?"

"No. I called up a new shape, a new movement, for the earth from out of the Autumnal. My body sheds fragments of its shape, and its movement. What we take must be given back. So it goes."

They sat side by side, both of them gazing into the water. Seeing nothing but a vision of the night sky. It seemed to Drann that he could as easily have been lying stretched out on the ground, staring up.

He looked back towards the camp. There was nothing to be seen, through the trees and the moon shadows, save the fire burning. An orange lantern amidst the darkness. Now and again its light would flicker and shiver, as someone walked in front of it.

"Lebid shot a hare, you know," he said. "It was running fast. I've never seen such a shot. They're roasting it now. If we're quick we can—"

"I'm not hungry. Thank you, for what you did."

"What I did?"

"When Sullen came for Kerig. I hear you picked a fight with him."

Drann grunted. "Not much of a fight. My ribs still hurt. I didn't really think about it. Just happened. Akrana told me that only the present's real. It's all there is, so you do what needs doing now; getting in Sullen's way seemed like it needed doing, at the time."

"Oh, she wants that to be true," Wren said with a sigh. "She wants to be weightless. Truth is, none of us are. The present's always got the past riding on its back. But she's right, too. Sometimes you just do what needs doing."

She plucked a long, nodding stem of grass from beside her and cast it out on to the pool. It made no sound. Ripples, perfect circles, raced out from it. Trembling away into nothingness across the glassy water.

"Look," Wren breathed. "Fireflies."

She pointed across the pool, and Drann saw that there were indeed a few points of greenish light, bobbing amongst the undergrowth.

"I always liked them," Wren said. "It's late in the year for them, though. Their last dance, poor things."

Drann watched those drifting gleams as they came and went

amongst the trees. It was restful. Something in that dance, whether it was their last or not, was easing to his mind. He heard an owl hooting.

"Take a message to Yulan for me, will you?" Wren said.

"Come and tell him yourself."

"No. This is a calming place, don't you think? Tell Yulan this: it's not his fault. I don't blame him."

"You come and tell him," Drann persisted.

He did not want to walk away from her, and leave her sitting here alone with the moon in the water. Calming or not, restful or not, drowning pools were bad places, he had always been taught. Places where bad things happened; where too many people had died. Something bad had already happened to the Free, he knew. But it felt unfinished.

"Leave me be," Wren said, with less warmth than her voice had carried before. "Tell them – tell Yulan – I'll be back soon."

Drann trudged heavily away through the copse, up towards the fire. He knew no one had really expected him to bring her back with him, but even so, it felt like failure. Everything felt a bit like failure right now.

"No luck?" Rudran grunted as Drann returned into the light and heat.

The lancer was sitting on a rock, chewing at a leg of the hare. The fire had put a flush into his cheeks, to match the rusty red of his hair and beard. A beard over which grease was now trickling.

Drann shook his head.

"Where's Yulan?" he asked.

"Perched on the cairn. Watching our trail."

Drann thought he could dimly see Yulan's form close to the top of that great tumbling heap of stones, an outline darker even than the sky that framed him.

"What about Hamdan?" he asked.

Rudran shrugged. "Have some meat, lad. None of this is your mess to mend."

A large bird of some sort suddenly swept low over their heads, its wings snapping. Gone away into the night even as they ducked.

"What was that?" someone coughed.

"Crow, maybe?" one of the lancers suggested.

Drann noticed that Akrana was lying close by, stretched out with her hands behind her head. Looking for all the world as though she was asleep. If Akrana was sleeping, Drann suspected, everyone else probably should be. From what he had seen, she would always be the last of them to seek rest.

First one, then another bird flashed through the little island of firelight. Silent, these; both of them owls, or broad-winged hawks. Drann frowned. Higher up, there were more winged shapes passing over. He walked towards the cairn, and found Yulan already descending over the loose stones.

Drann turned, not knowing exactly why, to gaze out into the impenetrable night, in the direction of the trees and the drowning pool. Was he imagining that he could hear ... something? The sound of wind amongst branches, even though there was no wind.

Birds were coming in from every direction, he realised. High and low, the sky was alive with them. They passed across the bright face of the moon. The stars winked in and out as they were obscured and revealed, obscured and revealed, over and over again. He had never seen anything like it. And there *was* a wind now, stirring his hair.

Yulan took hold of his shoulder. He looked tense. Tight.

"Where's Wren?" he snapped.

"She's still down there," Drann mumbled. "By the pool. I couldn't persuade her to come back to the fire."

Yulan grimaced, cast an anxious glance up into the bird-crowded sky.

"She asked me to give you a message," Drann said.

"What did she say?"

"Uh . . . she said, she said that it wasn't your fault. That she would be back soon."

Yulan stared at him. Firelight danced over his face. Another flight of birds – certainly crows this time – went flapping past, unseen in the darkness but calling loudly. They were passing, as all the birds had been, from high ground to low. Towards the copse.

Drann could see Yulan's lips moving, but couldn't hear what he said. He thought it might have been: "She'll be back soon."

Then he was gone. Gone that same way, towards the copse.

"What did she say?" Yulan demanded.

"Uh . . . she said, she said that it wasn't your fault. That she would be back soon."

Yulan stared at Drann, but did not really see him. Heard, but paid no further heed to, the sound of wings and bird calls in the night.

"She'll be back soon," he murmured to himself.

Such a small thing to say, but it could mean many things in the world of the Clever. It woke despair in him. So he ran.

Bounding down towards the trees, trusting to luck and moonlight that he would not fall, or break his ankle in some scrape or burrow. Reckless, but if ever there was a moment for recklessness, he thought this was it.

He had set Hamdan to watch her, not thinking the archer could prevent her from doing anything rash, just hoping it might buy him some narrow warning. Time enough, perhaps, to stop it. He knew, by instinct, that the warning he had hoped for was not going to come. That it might already be too late. He had failed her, and all of them.

As he plunged into the dense thicket, the wind raking through the treetops grew ever stronger. Branches rattled against one another. The great sails of leaves roared. The undergrowth tugged at him and thorned him, as if it conspired to keep him from his destination, but he pushed through it.

He found Hamdan at the same moment he came within sight of the drowning pool. The archer was soundly asleep, amidst nettles. He would be profoundly ungrateful for that when he woke. It was Wren's doing, of course. But sleep was not a thing to be made from her Autumnal entelech; it was of the Hibernal. That meant she was reaching beyond what came naturally, easily. It would weaken her, and she had already been weak. Yulan sensed disaster bearing down upon him, upon all of them, like a vast grey wolf loping remorselessly out from a far forest, with cold eyes and ill intent. More ghosts, coming his way.

He went on, to the edge of the pool. Its surface was trembling, disturbed by the gusts of wind churning about above it.

Twigs and leaves were flying now. And above it all, armies of birds were coming in, sinking down towards the trees. Riding and tumbling and twisting in the storm.

"Wren!' he shouted. No answer.

Some way beyond the far side of the drowning pool, the trees seemed just a little thinner. The wind a little stronger. He thought he could see a rain of dark shapes plunging down there. Birds.

He ran around the pool's edge, keeping to the flagstones from which guilty and innocent alike had once been cast to their deaths. He pushed through a screen of bending, flailing saplings. The air itself beat at him, pushing back.

"Wren!' he shouted, both in alarm and to make himself heard over the clattering of wings, the shaking of wind-savaged branches.

She was there. Standing in a partial clearing. She gave no sign that she heard him; remained quite still, arms spread, head thrown back. Above her, a huge spiralling tower of birds was descending.

"Wren! Don't do this," Yulan cried.

The seething gyre came ever lower. Crows and thrushes and hawks, all mixed together, all circling down in a wild storm of bodies that would hide Wren from him in mere moments.

"I have no choice," he heard her cry, though her voice was almost lost in the noise.

Leaves and twigs and feathers were spinning around, pattering against Yulan's chest, stinging his face. He put a hand up to guard his eyes.

"Of course you do," he shouted, taking a step closer. "Help us. If we have the Bereaved, we can bargain . . . "

"It'll be too late."

There were birds between the two of them now, spinning so fast about Wren that Yulan could not make out their forms, only the blur of their abandoned flight.

"You know what they'll do to him," she shouted. Her voice was thinning. "What Sullen will do. They'll kill him, sooner or later. I don't have a choice. I gave that up the day I wed him. Gladly."

"Wren, please," he begged. "Trust me."

She was stretching further up, he thought, pushing up on the balls of her feet, though such was the thickening frenzy of birds about her that he could not be sure.

"But I might save Kerig." He could barely hear her now. His ears were filled by the beating of wings, the groaning of trees, the rain of debris. "And you can save the rest of them, Yulan. I know you can. I do trust you."

He could not reach her. The wind was pushing against him, making him sway. The walls of the bird storm were too thick, too fierce. He could barely see the outline of her reaching form any more. His strength was of no service to him. All his hopes and plans were coming to nothing, and still it was not him paying the price, but others.

"Wren!' he shouted.

There was no reply.

"Wren," he tried once more. But she was lost to him, letting the entelech consume her. Passing beyond his reach, beyond his ken.

A great spinning column of dark birds rose before him now. It writhed up from the ground to far beyond the canopy, to the clouds, sucking in more and more birds all the time. Becoming monstrous. Mists of earth and shredded vegetation surrounded it. Feathered corpses were flung out, falling around Yulan; birds killed by collision with their brethren or with the trees.

"I'm sorry," he thought he heard her say, very soft, very distant. Perhaps inside his head, not out there on the turbulent air.

And the great gyre of bird surged upwards. The ground bucked and flung Yulan on to his back. Debris fell all around him. He lay there, staring up, and watched the churning flock ascend into the sky like a writhing black feathered serpent, tearing itself free of the earth. The maelstrom of birds twisted and turned and raced away over the top of the trees. Out of sight, though he heard it still; the muted roar of a hundred thousand wings.

Yulan rose, a little unsteady. He felt sick. His head ached. Wren was gone. Where she had stood, in the centre of the clearing, were only a few feathers. A few dead birds. An emptiness.

He found the rest of them searching through the copse. Confused, alarmed. Some of them carrying flaming sticks from the fire. Drann was kneeling beside Hamdan, trying to shake the archer awake.

"Leave him," Yulan said. "He'll come to his senses soon enough."

Drann looked up at him. The youth's bewilderment, perhaps fear, was plain even in the muted dancing light of a distant torch.

"What's happening?"

"She's gone to Kerig."

"To rescue him? Can she do that?"

"That's what you people forget," Yulan said, with a bitterness that he knew Drann did not deserve. "Just because the School's got all the Clevers on a leash, because there's been no call for wonders or horrors in years, you think Clevers are workers of little magics. They're not. They're makers of miracles. Shapers of the world, if they're willing to pay the price it requires."

He walked back towards the campfire, almost bowed down by the oppressive weight he felt.

"A lot of people are going to die when Wren finds them," he said as he went. "And maybe all of us, not long after. There's the glory, and the honour, of riding with the Free for you, boy."

25

The Castle At Haut Terpen

Wren was gone. Transformed. Subsumed. Her will drove the vast flock that she and the entelech had together become. Her anger swept it, seething, across the land. Her anger *was* it.

The birds, like the extended arm of a giant, clawed up through gathering clouds and plunged down again, trailing streamers of mist behind them. They rolled, in great spirals, southward in the night.

The host passed over villages and lone cottages and farms. Those who dreamed beneath its path dreamed of thunder and of tremors in the deep earth. Those still awake, beneath the sky, heard its roar and looked up. Some stood and stared. Some fled beneath roofs, behind walls. And all in their turn dreamed strange dreams, if they slept at all.

Southward, and then westward and east. Questing. Raging through the night sky. Searching, hour after hour, for one man. And finding him at last, the whisper of him, the familiar sound and scent and love of him, there beyond a high hill.

The castle at Haut Terpen was one of eight built at the command of Hugent, first of the Hommetics, to fortify his hold upon his newly subdued domain. Not much more than the foundations had been dug when he died. He was not granted the time to enjoy his spoils.

Amyllis, his wife, who ruled for their son until he came of age, saw the works to completion. Every one of those eight castles was built to the same pattern, with tall turreted walls encircling yard and keep, stables and workshops and barracks. One of them was burned and abandoned. Three were sold or gifted to lords or royal relations. Three remained, until the late rebellion, strongholds of the King's Armsmen. One – Haut Terpen – was passed to the School, and became their Tower, to stand alongside their Home, their Keep, their Hall.

The castle was not built atop the humpbacked hill from which it took its name, but at the end of a long spur reaching out from that hill into the floodplain of the Munn River. The spur ended in low but disagreeable cliffs that guarded the castle on three sides. Only along the length of the spur could its gates be approached, and there its builders had cut a trench, deep and wide, over which the track ran on a stone bridge.

It would be a stern test for any attacker, but in all the fifty years or so of the castle's life, none had come. It had stood, in peaceful slumber, watching over the wide wet fields of the Munn, and quietly aged without ever suffering assault or siege. The seventy or more Clade warriors who held it lived lives of modest tranquillity, in the main. The Clevers who visited found it a place of pleasant seclusion, conducive to study and training and reflection. Only on tithe days, when the farmers of the plain brought their tribute to the castle, did it ever become loud or crowded within those walls.

In the first hour after dawn, the birds came around the northern shoulder of Haut Terpen like a vast shadow, sweeping low over the slope. Streaming, in a seemingly endless flood, down towards the gate, and the turrets and the keep. They came without voice, without call or croak, but with a great roaring of their wings, as loud as a huge river in spate.

A spearman, on the walkway between two turrets, stopped atop the wall and watched the impossible, the unimaginable, plummeting down towards him. The sky darkened as the sun was obscured. A surging shadow swept across the whole castle.

At the last moment, when he finally believed that this tempest of birds was not going to turn aside, the spearman ducked down and pressed himself in against the parapet. The feathered storm poured over the wall, over his head, and went twisting and plunging into the yard. A limb of it spun down as it passed and snatched him from the wall, and tumbled him through the air, amidst the birds, tossing him to and fro, rending him. He flailed like a child-thrown rag doll, spat out from the maelstrom to crash against the wall of the keep, thirty feet up. He fell, limp and loose, into the yard, a shower of feathers and of his blood falling with him.

Men were running. There was no thought of fighting this, save a few arrows shot up in desperation that vanished into the mass of birds. The flock swept around the keep, coiling about it like some titanic snake born of nightmare. Battering at the walls, breaking the windows. Dead birds fell by the score.

A lashing tongue flailed its way in through a shattered window. Another reached out from the main body of the host to scour the roof of the keep, driving the two sentries there to their knees and then on to their backs. Smothering them, clawing them, tearing their flesh, battering them with the wind of a thousand unnaturally strong wings. Scraps of clothing and of skin and meat were torn away from them and sent spinning out over the battlements.

Birds plunged into the stables. Horses were thrown down, flung about like lambs. Planks were blown out from the roof and seething columns of birds burst up through the holes. Little corpses kept falling like rain. Across the wide expanse of the yard, the flock settled and spun, dragging down the few men who had not yet found shelter. The well at the centre stood like the eye of a spinning storm, and the birds turned around and around it.

Every window of the keep was broken now, and Wren's fury drove into the building from every side at once. Impaled it. Shook it. From high and low, from every part of the castle, birds rushed inward, a great cloud closing on the keep and tearing into its innards. One room, one passageway after another was filled with the boiling flood. Wall hangings were torn down and shredded, tables and chairs overturned, rent into kindling. Doors were split and splintered and punctured; even the strongest of them, for there was more to this than mere birds, mere claw and beak.

Wren was – had been – an Autumnal Clever, but there was Aestival in this as well. Storm and rage, grief and strength, she had shaped it all into this maelstrom, and given herself over to its wielding. The stones of the keep groaned and trembled. Great cracks ran through its outer walls.

A Clade warrior fleeing down a passage was overtaken, overwhelmed, struck down to the flagstone floor. Fire leapt from the oil lamps lighting the way, crackling and springing from bird to bird, dancing through the flock like orange lightning. It stamped down on the fallen man, a pounding heel of flame, and seared him into the stone. The stench of burned feather and flesh swept through the keep. The fire raced to keep pace with that stink, surging through the flock, spilling blackened, charred corpses in its wake. It came to a great iron-banded door, howled upon its face and made ash of it, and plunged down a spiralling staircase into the bowels of the fortress. An inferno carried on wings. A hot gale blowing in its van, down into the deep places.

In his dark cell, Kerig trembled where he hung. He wept. Dust and webs were falling from the ceiling, shaken free. He could hear, in amongst the rumbling and the clattering, men screaming. He could feel, leaking in around the edges of the thick door, the hot breath of the horror consuming the Clade's castle. His wounds and weakness and pain would not allow him to lift his head, but there was nothing to see in that darkness in any case. And he did not need his eyes to know what was coming. The flowing of fierce entelech was like a lance through his chest.

The door to his prison burst open, tearing free of its hinges, smouldering as it fell. The corpse of one of the guards came with it, flopping like a string-cut puppet. A wash of fiery light spilled into the cell, tingling for a moment across Kerig's naked body, and then retreated. To be replaced by the rustling of wings, the brush of them across his skin.

And the whisper in his ear: "Hold on, my love."

A strength about him, taking his weight. Lifting him, and making him wail as the cords under his armpits were suddenly loosened. The fire that burned in his shoulders then was entirely of his body's own making as the joints moved. Then the ropes from which he hung were cut and he was falling. Limp and helpless, he dropped into her arms. He tried to open his eyes, but could not see clearly. Only the paleness of her face, the outline of her hair. Hair made from feathers.

"I have you," Wren whispered to him. "We're going now."

The sounds and the fury faded around him. His pain thinned, as he thinned. The storm of birds gathered him up and he went with his wife into its heart, and they became it, together.

The birds swept out through every wound in the fabric of the keep, as if it breathed out a hundred black-winged breaths. They towered above it, and knitted themselves back together into a single vast cloud. Churned there. Readying themselves, Wren's will steeling itself and directing itself towards distant horizons for the long flight to come. Until a lone figure ran from the keep's main doors, racing across the yard towards the gatehouse, sword in hand.

"Sullen," the sky raged.

The School's butcher looked up. The cloud of birds thickened, formed once more into a furious serpent that swept down, all its fury reignited. Redoubled, for it carried Kerig's hate as well as Wren's now.

"Sullen!' The unvoiced cry shook the castle.

Sullen veered from his course, extended his stride. He flung his sword away as he ran for the well.

The column of birds arrowed in towards him, yearning for his flesh. Yearning to raise him up into the air and dismember him there, let his parts fall, let him be no more. It came down upon him faster than ever it had moved thus far, but still he reached the well and vaulted over its lip and fell, feet together, arms folded, straight down its dark gullet.

The birds followed, and conjured flame from their memories of the keep to bellow all the way down to the water. Where the flames could go no further, and died hissing, and the birds drowned in their dozens. And Sullen stayed deep and still and beyond the reach of all that fury.

The storm might have waited, longed to wait, for the man to resurface as he must. But the yearning to be gone and for Kerig to be safe overcame the blind, loathing anger and diminished it.

The flock ascended, left the castle at Haut Terpen. Carried its shadow scudding away across the land, around the great mass of the hill and back whence it had come.

26

A Still Greater Weapon

"What happened?"

Sullen regarded the Castellan of Haut Terpen with thinly veiled contempt.

"The Free happened," he observed. "Kerig's wife, I imagine."

They stood together, beside the well from which Sullen had climbed. His clothes were sodden. Drops still fell from his sleeves, and from his beaded hair. The Castellan's tunic was torn, his face a tapestry of fine bloody scratches. He had been caught upon the wild fringes of the flock, but survived.

"She's killed at least ten of my men," he murmured, clearly struggling to accommodate what he had seen. "Maybe more."

The yard all around them was covered with dead birds. Hardly a stone could be seen beneath the layer of corpses. Here and there dead men lay. Horses were still screaming in the stables. One had come staggering out and died close by the well, its eyes gone, its hide hanging in tatters.

"Considerably more than ten, I should think," Sullen said.

"And half your horses. It appears that the School is at war with the Free."

"We cannot defeat the Free," the Castellan said quickly.

"Can we not?" Sullen asked, shaking water from his arms. He turned to face the Castellan. "Tell me why."

"Well . . . the Clamour, of course."

"Of course." Sullen nodded. "The Clamour. But their advantages are much greater than that. Everyone's so afraid of the Clamour, they're half blinded by it. Can't see how dangerous all the rest are. Look at what just one of them has done to your precious fortress, after all. And they have Yulan. But you need not concern yourself, Castellan. We can indeed defeat the Free. We have a still greater weapon to call upon in this war."

"We do?"

"We do. Me."

The Castellan frowned, but Sullen was not a man to be lightly contradicted. Everyone in the School, in the Clade most of all, knew that.

"Try not to worry," Sullen said, smiling dispassionately. "It's always been coming, after all. Past time to end the dance between School and Free. One or other of us was always going to have to yield. I don't think it will be the School."

The Castellan still did not look wholly convinced.

"Look to your men, Castellan. Mend those who can be mended. Ready them. And send out riders, in every direction. Any man of the Clade within a day's ride is needed here. Kran Jurmon should be somewhere near Loom with close to a hundred; White Mar is up in the Munn headwaters with at least fifty. Orlotan has a company to the south-west, as well. We need them all. So too any Clever of the School."

"Ah. Clevers? Most of them are still sequestered in our holdings, waiting out the troubles. I don't think the Clade can command—"

"Don't concern yourself with such things," Sullen snapped.

The fragility of his patience sang loud and clear between the two men. A darkening passed across the Clade commander's face.

"Do as I instruct, and I will ensure we have the proper authority. I will inform Morue of what's happened, and what's required. You find me my men, Castellan. That is all."

Sullen strode away, towards the keep. As he walked, he kicked aside dead birds. Dark drifts of corpses flowed around his feet. Partway across the yard, he found his sword, half buried. He bent down, pushed away dead rooks and hawks and owls, lifted the blade and returned it to its scabbard. He cast an appraising glance upwards, measuring the extent of the cracks that seamed the keep's skin. Satisfied that it was unlikely to collapse in the next few minutes, he entered.

Sestimon Trune was cowering beneath a bed in his chambers. The mattress and pillows had been torn apart, their meadow-grass filling strewn all around. The Clever gave a tiny cry of alarm when Sullen lifted the bed, one-handed, away from him.

"Come out from there. The School requires your services."

Together they went – Sullen firm and purposeful, Sestimon nervous, unsteady – to find the only other Clever in Haut Terpen. The Weaponsmith.

Who was in a cellar where casks of ale and sacks of grain and cheese wrapped in cloth were stored. He was looking worn. The echoes of fright and alarm still fluttered across his face. They eased somewhat when Sullen entered, carrying a flaming torch to send the shadows fleeing.

"Come with me," was all Sullen said, and led the two Clevers up, up the winding stair scattered with dead birds, and one or two dead men. Up and up until they emerged on to the roof of the keep, beneath a sky now richly blue and a fresh breeze that stirred the feathers of the corpses strewn there as well.

Both Sestimon and the Weaponsmith stared uneasily at the two dead Clade warriors lying there. The corpses were more disfigured, more dismantled, than most. Sullen paid them no heed.

He looked out for a moment, across the flat farmlands to the wide, winding Munn River. He lifted his face and closed his eyes, breathing in that breeze. Then he turned to Sestimon Trune.

"The School requires your service, as I said," he began. "You must send word to our Mistress. At once. The kind of word that can leap across the miles and whisper in her ear today."

Sestimon shook his head. It was evidently an instinctive, unconsidered response, which he regretted, for he at once held up placatory hands.

"My exertions these last few days . . . the shock of what happened here . . ."

His voice was thin and reedy, as if the cutting of his throat had somehow robbed him of a part of it.

"Nonsense," Sullen said flatly. "Our need makes it nonsense. You'll do as you must, because Morue must know what has happened. That seems clear to me. Doesn't it to you?"

"It does," Sestimon muttered, dropping his gaze to his feet. To the dead hawk lying there.

"Good. The message isn't long. Inform the Mistress that the Free have today attacked the School's Tower and slain many men of the Clade, and that I will therefore be bringing them to justice. She must prepare the rebels – the Council, I suppose – for that. Ensure they don't interfere. And tell her I may require the aid of the School's Clevers, and will call upon those within my reach. That is all."

Sestimon frowned, tapped his nose with one finger as if testing the solidity, or perhaps the wisdom, of a thought.

"What about Kerig? Should I not—"

"Don't mention Kerig. The briefer the message, the less you'll be harmed by its sending. That's true, isn't it?"

"It is," the Clever conceded.

"Be about it, then. Now."

Sestimon swung a foot from side to side, pushing away dead birds to make a space for himself. He could sweep the bodies aside, but not all of the feathers, or all of the blood. Nor all the fragments of beak or claw. So he knelt in them. He cleared his throat, nervously touched the half-circle scar that adorned his neck. Then cupped his hands together at his mouth.

He blew into his hands, though it was not cold. He rubbed them together, cupped them again. Turned his head to one side and whispered. Turned to the other, did the same again. Then pressed his lips into the cup of his hands and knelt there like that, quite still and silent, for some time.

"You do enjoy your little rituals, you people," Sullen murmured once to the Weaponsmith, but otherwise the two of them merely waited and watched.

At length, Sestimon began to rock back and forwards gently.

He blew into his hands once more. Then spoke, softly but quickly, into them. He snapped his head back and away, pressed his hands more tightly together so that they were sealed.

His arms shook. Then he flung them upwards, threw them out wide, opened his hands. As if to cast his words into the sky. But it was not words that burst forth and flew off eastwards. It was bees. A tiny humming swarm of them.

Sestimon fell back. He set his hands down to hold himself erect.

"How long?" Sullen asked, watching the vanishing insects. They flew far faster than any of their natural kin might.

Sestimon croaked. Shook his head. Sullen glared at him.

"How long?"

"Six . . . seven hours, perhaps," the Clever rasped, and now his voice was not thin and reedy, but near ruined. Near gone. As frail as a frayed twig. He touched his throat, brushing the great scar there with a trembling finger.

"That'll do," Sullen said, and turned to the Weaponsmith. "I wanted you to see that. So that you'd realise what remarkable times we now live in. You understand now that I will do – I must do – whatever I deem necessary. You do understand that, don't you?"

"I do," the Weaponsmith said glumly.

"Good." Sullen folded his arms across his chest. "There is something I require of you. You're going to refuse me, because what I ask may well kill you. That won't do, so to save us all time I'm first going to tell you why you *will* do as I command. The why is this: I know Kerig didn't kill anyone in Creel's camp. I know that you did . . . hush, hush."

He held up an admonishing finger as the Weaponsmith stirred to protest.

"I understand your need to deny it, but we both know you did it. I can read the marks on a man's face, even a burned one. He died not of fire, but from want of air, that man of yours. Long after Kerig was gone, I imagine. Someone knelt by his cot and closed mouth and nose with a strong hand. Something like that. The details don't matter.

"I don't know if it was your hand, but I know it was your intent. And I do understand, believe me; I even admire it. Perhaps it was the only chance you'd ever have to set the law and the Clade against a man who was otherwise never going to stop coming after you. I might well have done the same thing in the same circumstance. Indeed, I *have* done something rather similar in our current circumstance. Something of grander conception, but similar even so."

Throughout this address, Sullen was entirely unmoving. His face betrayed no emotion. His voice remained steady. The Weaponsmith, the taller of them by a fraction, was by contrast growing restless. Like an animal in a cage that was unexpectedly shrinking about it.

"My sympathy, my appreciation, is not to the point," Sullen continued. "Despite it, I will put you in that same cell from which Kerig has been removed, and I will extract from you a full confession that you killed your own man. Then I will myself undertake your execution, by whatever means seem most likely to extend your suffering. I confess, I enjoy it. So you can be sure I mean what I say.

"And once you're dead, I'll make it my calling to find

everyone you've ever spent any affection on and render their lives as miserable and cruel and brief as my position and power make possible. Do we understand one another?"

The Weaponsmith said nothing, but stared hatefully at the School's butcher. His huge hands were at his sides, clenching and unclenching. None of which perturbed Sullen.

"I only need you to do what you've always done. You're going to make me a weapon, more quickly than any you've made before. I imagine its making will cost you the greater part, perhaps all, of what life and strength you have left. It's unfortunate, but there you are."

"You have no right—' the Weaponsmith began.

Sullen took a single quick step forward and struck him, hard but open-handed, across the face. Hard enough to draw a spot of blood from the corner of the Weaponsmith's mouth.

"I have every right. I have the right of judgement, since I command the Clade, and the Clade judges Clevers. I have the right of power, since I have this castle, and warriors below to answer my call, and you . . . well, you're just you. Alone. You have your Clever ways, of course, but by the nature of my employment I am required to study you and your kind. I know that you've refined your talents a lot more than most. You can do one thing, and do it well, but almost all else is beyond you. You could not, no matter how hard you tried, produce any trickery from out of the entelechs quickly enough, or strongly enough, to stop me from cutting your throat this very moment, should I want to.

"And most of all . . . most of all I have the right of will. Because yours is weak, Weaponsmith. And mine is not. I can assure you. Mine is not."

27

Permanence

The sky was stained black, out there near the horizon. A moving stain that spread and flowed. The wind came far before it, stirring the grass and brushing over Yulan's scalp. It smelled bad to him, of ash and flesh.

He could not look away, as the dark storm cloud of birds rolled ever closer. None of the Free could. They halted in their march, and every head was turned. Every eye watched the coming tempest. No one said anything. The only sound, on that high road, was the rustling of the grass, the gusting wind that buffeted about them.

Yulan and a few others were on foot, walking behind the wagon. The rest stayed on their horses. Stared. The birds came on and on, a sheet of them that stretched itself across the sky and dimmed the light of the sun. The noise mounted as they drew near. Wingbeats, harsh calls, the rumbling wind.

Then, as the leading edge of the immense throng reached the point above where Yulan stood, the birds rushed together. The multitude made itself into a huge rope, or snake. The serpent of birds put a great coil into itself, folding and turning. Then it plunged, punched down at the ground not thirty paces from Yulan. A dizzying fall of birds, like dark water, hammering at the earth. Some died, some veered up and away, scattering. Grass and soil were churned up, sprayed out.

"Oh, Wren," murmured Yulan, but nobody could hear him.

He stumbled at the shaking of the ground. The horses around him quailed, and nervously backed away. He heard, quite clearly, a groan and a shifting of great mass from the Clamour's cage.

The turf was stripped away. Rocks were exposed. Still the birds came, the whole immense flock of them plummeting down. Yulan had to narrow his eyes against the veils of dry soil that were being thrown up. Its dusty scent was mixed in with the stink of death and fire and feathers that the flock brought with it.

They began to spin, the rooks and thrushes and hawks and owls, churning around just above the ground. Thickening, so that there was only a dense mass, seething there. Then, just as suddenly, they were done, and the whole flock erupted away. Birds, great and small, sped in every direction, waves of them skimming so low that Yulan felt their wings on him.

He saw a naked man lying on his side in the bare scar the birds had etched into the hillside. Kerig. Pale, thinned, bruised and bloodied, but alive. Heaps of feathered corpses lay about him. Yulan and Hamdan ran forward, side by side. Kerig was already trying to rise when they reached him, but he was too weak. When he set his weight through his legs, they crumpled and he thumped back down.

Yulan was dimly aware that birds still thronged the sky, sweeping back and forth overhead. But he could not look away from Kerig. He was utterly changed from the man who had settled himself beneath that tree so little time ago. He had been made frail, and feeble. Wounded.

"Where's Wren?" the Clever rasped, scrabbling blindly about on hands and knees.

Yulan threw a cape over him, held it down over his shoulders and back. Knelt at his side.

"Wren?" Kerig coughed, faltering.

He slumped into Yulan's arms. His captain cradled him on his knees. There was so little of him left. Yulan was worried that he might harm the man, for he barely knew what his arms were doing. Only that he wanted to hold him, keep him safe.

"Make space for him on the wagon," he shouted.

Rudran jumped down from his horse and ran to Kerig, reaching down to lift him from Yulan's grasp. But Kerig cried out at his touch and lashed his arm around, flailing impotently. Yulan saw pain in Rudran's face as he shrank back. The big, gruff man wanted to help, but did not know how. Much like Yulan himself.

"Let him be," Yulan said.

And he rose, and carried the weeping Kerig in his arms like a babe, and set him on the wagon. Hamdan brought bandages and water to tend to him, and when other of the archers came to help, he herded them away like so many overcurious children.

"I'm sorry," Yulan whispered to Kerig.

"Look," Hamdan said quietly to him.

Yulan looked up. The birds were massing again. The survivors, still in their thousands, were knotting back into a churning, formless flock.

"Is it not over?" he heard Drann murmuring in bewilderment. "Where's Wren?"

Yulan said nothing. Just watched the sky. Akrana came to stand beside them, gazing up just as they did. A shadow seemed to be there, in the heart of the flock. Not just the darkness of the birds' bodies, but of the air itself.

"What's happening?" Drann asked of no one and everyone.

"Wren's gone," Akrana said without looking at him.

"What?"

"She overreached," Yulan told him dully. "She's gone away, into the entelechs. This is a Permanence."

Such dreadful loss, to speak just those few words. All he had wanted to do was bring them safely through this. Never had he fallen so far short of any ambition.

"We should go," he said. "Quickly."

He walked away, calling out as he went to get everyone moving. Even he could not help glancing upward at the appalling, extraordinary thing taking shape. A multitude of birds, of every kind, writhing in the air. A Permanence.

"It will be a bad one," Akrana said. "Born from anger, violence. They are always bad ones. Someone will give it a fell name one day, perhaps years from now. Perhaps lifetimes."

"What do you think it will do?" Yulan wondered.

"Fly, I suppose. Fly, until the world comes to ruin and wreck and all that ever was has gone back whence it came."

Yulan looked this way and that. For as far as he could see,

there was not a house, not a farm. Just the hillsides, the trees, the grass. No one to witness this save the Free. No one to witness the making of this thing that might come to be spoken of in the same hushed tones as the Bereaved, the Unhomed Host, the handful of Permanences that the world held. A great and lasting change.

He wished he had not seen it.

"Yulan's right," Akrana was calling out. "We should go. It will not remember that the one who created it was one of us."

Hamdan rode in the wagon, crouching at Kerig's side and trying to ease his trembling and his moaning. Yulan walked behind in the wheel tracks. It took an act of will not to look back, and watch the birthing of that monstrosity in the sky.

With each step he took, grief filled him. Tears pressed at his eyes, demanding release. He did weep a little. And as he wept, other feelings slowly came to take the place of the grief. Not extinguishing it, but covering it over; storing it away to be felt and embraced another day.

He could only be what the moment demanded now. He would match Callotec, Sullen, any who yet lived and would oppose him. Set his terrible will against theirs and visit upon them terrors that they could not yet imagine. If he could save anyone, that was how he would save them. Wren had said she believed he could do it. Now he must find out if she was right, and any who stood in his way would learn that the Free were not done yet. Not so long as his heart still beat in his chest.

PART THREE

28

When Drann Was Seventeen

When Drann was seventeen, he went to war. It was not the decision of a moment, taken in haste or high passion. It came slowly, gathering itself over days and weeks and awaiting the circumstance that might call it forth. That circumstance was made of Armsmen, mud and death.

The war began not as war but as rumours, spread over months, of scattered strife and quarrels. A riot, it was said, in such-and-such a city, over bread made from bad grain. Another city, elsewhere, shutting its gates against the royal Armsmen when they came to take the leader of its watch into custody. The Far Men of Haut Werl, bandits who had plagued those parts for years, learning bravery and overrunning a Kingshouse, slaughtering its garrison. A lord, at last, raising the banner of revolt in Mondoon.

Word of each of these things came to Drann's village, but it came late and faint, like so many fragments of a broader tapestry fluttering on the breeze. There was no one there would speak Crex's part. He was not a well-beloved monarch. Their lord – no more well-beloved – did nothing. Mustered no levies and proclaimed himself for neither one side nor the other.

Life went on. War happened elsewhere, though part of Drann longed for it to come close, that he might see it. Perhaps taste it. Unseasonal rains came and turned half the fields into quagmires. Killed or battered or bent the crops. That was of more concern to most of the villagers than war.

Then one bright day, a long column of Armsmen passed through.

"Stay behind your doors," they cried as they rode. "Any man on the path will be cut down. By royal command, none may pass a night anywhere but under their own roof, unless called to bear arms in service of the rightful king. Any in breach of this command shall be guilty of treason, and meet its punishment. Stay behind your doors!"

Drann watched them pass, peeking out through a crack between the planks of the door. Tall men, with pennants and spears and horses clad in royal insignia. Magnificent, had they not been servants of a loathed rule. Had the words they shouted not brought repression and restraint.

After they had gone, disappearing no one knew where, it turned out they had not merely ridden along the village's one good track. They had crossed the fields behind the cottages. Churned them up and broken down the rough fences and gates that separated one holding from another.

Drann cursed them and their kind, and flung the broken remnants of their own fence around in impotent rage. His father said nothing. Simply stared at the damage for a time, and then set to mending it. They laboured side by side, ankle deep in the sucking mud that rain and the Armsmen had made of the field. Even when the bright day became a cloudy one, and it began to rain again, a misty drizzle, they worked on. Hammering, digging, staggering about in the boggy earth.

When they were almost done, a whole day that was to have been spent weeding the barley field wasted, there was a wailing in the village. Despairing grief given such heartfelt voice that Drann winced to hear it.

Martan was dead, it turned out. He had been Drann's friend – of sorts – when they were younger, but the two had spent less time together as the years turned. He had disappeared days ago, perhaps weeks. Drann could not be sure. No one had known where he had gone; or no one had told Drann, at least.

Now everyone knew. Martan had gone to the war. Walked away from the village, alone, without even a word to his parents, and found his way to the army of Creel of Mondoon, many miles to the south. And died there, in a battle that was won, but in which he – and those parents he had left behind – lost everything.

And that night, after he had eaten the broth his mother set on the table, and helped his father restore an edge to the digging blades they had blunted, Drann took up his spear and told them he was going to fight.

"Why?" his mother asked, aghast.

"Because nothing'll ever change if we don't fight for it," he told her, feeling both foolish and wise. "*We'll* never change if we don't fight."

"You're not going anywhere," she told him.

"I am."

His sisters stared at him, both fear and surprise in their regard. Drann looked to his father, not knowing what he might say or do. The man was shaking his head, slowly.

"You'll not get the change you're dreaming of that way," he said.

It was not said angrily. It did not even sound – so Drann chose to believe – quite like refusal or forbiddance. Rather, it sounded . . . small. Simple.

"You can't make yourself a warrior or a winner of wars just by wanting," his father said.

"I know," Drann replied, not certain he entirely did know, or believe it. He spoke softly and modestly, matching his tone to that of his father. "But I can't make myself anything but sorry and shamed if I hide away here while there's others doing what I want to do."

"You're not going," his mother said again.

She was snatching empty bowls away from the table so violently, so hastily, that one spun from her hand and shattered on the hearth. They all stared at the broken bits of pot.

"Take my spear," his father said into the silence. "It's better than yours. Be sure to bring it back."

29

Three Doves

There were three doves in the basket, of the purest white. More simply beautiful than any birds Drann had ever seen. He had not even known they were there, packed away amongst the bedrolls and feed sacks and quivers on the Clamour's wagon. Packed away beside Kerig, who slept on, swaddled like a suckling child, as Yulan eased it out from behind him.

The basket was small and neatly woven of willow stems. Yulan untied its lid, and held it open just enough for Drann to peer inside. To see those three pristine, immaculate white doves.

"Ordeller's?" Drann asked.

"Yes, her own. They'll make for Curmen the moment we give them the air."

Yulan laced the basket closed once more, and tucked it under his arm. One of the doves within was mewing to itself.

"What message are you sending?"

"One that'll set every bird the Free has, anywhere, flying

within a day or two. Telling our people to scatter. Look to their own safety."

"All of the Free?"

"Every man and woman," Yulan nodded. "The School may come for them. Those of them it knows about, anyway. We can't be sure what Wren did, not until Kerig's fit to talk, but it will have been ugly. Bloody. She might even have killed the commander of the School's Clade."

"Sullen," Drann said miserably.

"Well, you can find a grain of fortune even in the deepest shit pit, if you reach far enough down," said Hamdan, falling into step beside them. "Sullen meeting his end'd count as a decent-sized grain."

"It would," agreed Yulan, "but he's not one to call dead until you've seen the corpse lying at your feet. Whatever's happened, we'll have the whole School, Clade and all, hunting our people wherever they are. It's what they've wanted to do, most of them, for years. Decades."

Yulan sat, with a hide spread across his knees on which to lean, and scratched out the messages to Ordeller. While he did it, Drann stood and gazed at the three towers on the horizon. Now larger, but still indistinct. They must be truly huge, he was coming to understand. Taller by far than any tree he had ever seen, or could imagine. As he frowned at them now, trying to squeeze some clarity from the distant sight, he realised that they were horned. Unlikely as it seemed, they sported at their very pinnacles curving ornaments like the horns of bulls.

Hamdan caught the line of his gaze.

"Sorentine," the archer said. "They did like their bulls.

There's a whole empty town a few miles past those monstrosities, the Threetower that cursed road runs to. Kingdom and Empire alike just upped and walked away from it, when they decided they didn't want to be friends after all. Straddles the border, so anyone who wanted to hold it would have to fight for it, and neither of them liked that idea."

"And Towers' Shadow?" Drann asked.

"Beneath them," grunted Hamdan. "Before them."

He clearly did not want to talk of that.

One by one, the doves came out from the basket. Yulan clasped them tenderly in his big hands while Hamdan fastened the messages to their legs. The archer muttered in irritation as he struggled with the delicate task.

"You need seamstress fingers for this."

But he did it, and Yulan threw the birds into the air, where their wings snapped out and they hauled themselves up and away. Everyone watched them go, those pale shapes dwindling and darkening off into the distance, bearing ill tidings.

Only when the last of them was out of sight did Yulan drop his gaze. He seemed, just for a moment, to be lost in thought, eyes open but unseeing. Then he looked around him. The muscles in his jaw flexed.

"Everyone gather round," he said, not loudly but clear.

They all did, save Hestin and Kerig. The Free stood, their horses behind them, in a wide half-circle, and waited for Yulan to speak. To Drann, it had the solemn air of ceremony.

"Akrana stays with the wagon, Hestin and Kerig," Yulan declared. "And four of yours, Rudran. Kerig's in no state to survive a hard pace. Nor's Hestin any more. The rest of us, we ride for Towers' Shadow and we don't stop until we're there. Then we turn ourselves about and we find a way to hold Callotec. We hold him until the Clamour catches up."

"How long will that take?" Drann asked.

"Doesn't matter," said Yulan bluntly. "We hold him for how-ever long it takes. Towers' Shadow is not falling to that little butcher who wants to be a king. He is not crossing into the Empire. Neither is the Bereaved. We're taking it, and we're using it to bend the School to our will."

Drann heard no trace of doubt in the words. Not the thinnest vein of uncertainty, or the faintest crack through which the notion of failure might be admitted.

"We're going to find out now whether we're a match for the Free of old," their Captain said to the rest of them. "Whether we've lost what they had, back in those glory days."

"You know what Merkent would say?" Rudran asked. "Stop talking, stop thinking, and do the bloody deed."

"That he would," said Yulan. "That he would. And I'm not going to fail the memory of that grey-bearded old bastard by doing anything less than the bloodiest of deeds. We ride, we turn, we fight. And we live for ever, because what we do these next few days won't be forgotten."

And that was all. That was how it was decided. Drann had somehow expected more, but a change had come over Yulan, and all of the Free. There was nothing to be discussed. They were becoming hard as one of their blades.

He set himself in the saddle, and was pleased that it felt a less hostile place than it had in recent times. He no longer believed that the horse despised him and spent its every waking moment, alone in its horse head, plotting miseries for him. His body no longer felt quite so obviously ill formed for the whole business of riding.

None of that crowded out the knowledge that what was coming would be hard. Quite likely, he supposed, that at the end of it his every fibre would be back in the land of crippling aches and pains. He told himself it could be no worse than the first day or two had been, and tried to think of it no more. He gave the horse's neck a gentle stroke. Then he thought better of it; decided that something more determined, more assertively companionable, was required. So he patted its shoulder, firmly, a couple of times.

"Riding hard," he muttered to the animal. "You be good to me, I'll try to be good to you."

Rudran stood up in his stirrups and shouted out, loud and clear: "You know what else Merkent would have said? Piss on doubt; let's do it anyway."

It was worse than Drann had told himself it would be, and that did not surprise him at all. Through day and night they rode without ceasing. Sometimes walking, sometimes cantering. When they did the latter, Drann just held on, tried to copy the style of those about him, and trusted to the beast – for beast he now feared it to be once more – beneath him to stay on the right course.

They passed lonely cottages, one that even had light burning at its window in the dusk. Whoever was in there must surely have quailed at the sound of horses in the night, and breathed easy only after they had swept on and away.

They crossed streams and rivers. Once, the water was high

and hard enough to churn almost to Drann's feet in the stirrups. He could feel its force, pushing at the horse's flank, making it sidestep and toss its head in unease.

Through grassland and across hillsides, they saw no one as they rode. In the night, when they rode slowly on even though the moon was thinning and sometimes masked by cloud, Drann saw the light of a fire, far off to the south. It was hard to tell, in that bottomless black distance, how great or small it might be. Its direction meant it could not be Callotec, and it was thus of no consequence. But it did make Drann think for a while as he bounced along, hands cramping on the reins, how strange it was that there was a world out there filled with people living their own lives, unaware of all that he was caught up in. People sitting around fires, sleeping, loving one another, while all unknown the Free rode through the night to battle.

30

Dog-Lord

Callotec's meagre little army was much diminished. All the injured who could not walk had been left behind, along with two carts and most of their supplies. He had no need of those who could not fight. It was tempting to imagine that the Free, unseen by any scout for longer than anyone had dared hope, might be defeated. Departed. Callotec did not believe that. Not until he walked across the ashes of Towers' Shadow and into the Empire itself would he believe that.

There were birds flocking in the trees along the riverside. He wished he had a hawk on his wrist to send arrowing after them, to tear them out of the sky. More diverting, certainly, than the downcast company of the man riding at his side. Kasuman was proving a disappointment, as far as Callotec was concerned.

"Why did you steal the Bereaved away from your fellows in the School?" he asked the Clever.

"Because they refused its use when Crex demanded it. Because it, and the School itself, has no just purpose in my eyes save the preservation of the legitimate order. The legitimate throne. I feared they would deliver it into the hands of the Council."

It was what Callotec would have wished to hear.

"Do you still have it, that same fire in the belly that led you to such daring in a noble cause?" he asked.

"I have not lost it, sire," Kasuman said. "I am merely weary."

The man would have to learn a touch more resilience, or at least the pretence of it, if he was to serve any purpose in the new order of things, Callotec thought. For now, he was necessary, though. Allowances could be made, perhaps, until that need diminished.

"Perhaps it would cheer you to educate me somewhat," Callotec suggested.

"If I can, sire."

"Very good. Well, then. There is a village between here and our destination. Towers' Shadow. Have you heard of it?"

"No, sire."

A lie, undoubtedly. A man who would lie to a king would be well advised to perfect the art first. Callotec did not believe there was anyone of any consequence in the kingdom who did not know – or think they knew – the cause of his fall from his cousin's favour. Just as there was no one who did not know that some spiteful souls still named him Dog-Lord when he was not there to hear them. Perhaps it was a well-meant lie, though. A dutiful falsehood, to spare a sovereign's discomfort.

"No matter. I mean to raze it as we pass. A nest of traitors, best burned out. I wondered . . . might there not be a place for the Bereaved in this plan of mine? It was my intent to bring a fine pack of hunting hounds with me when next I set eyes upon the place, but ... well, circumstances have conspired against that intent, clearly."

Kasuman pursed his lips thoughtfully. He did not appear wholly averse to the idea. That cheered Callotec considerably.

"Is that something that might be done?" he pressed.

"It is difficult, sire. The Bereaved is not a thing easily restrained once it is stirred into activity. A single ... execution, such as that of your mutineer ... even that was testing. Any reluctance I might feel in seeing it thus employed arises only from that danger. It might be that attempting something of grander design would invite complete devastation. I could not promise you that such a beginning could be ended."

"The Regent Queen did it, did she not?" demanded Callotec irritably.

"At great risk, yes. Perhaps she, and the School of her time, did not fully understand quite what dangers they courted."

"There are but two tamed Permanences in all the world, and we hold one of them! Are you telling me that we cannot use the thing? What is its purpose, then?"

"Oh, but it can be used," said Kasuman quickly, holding up a placatory hand. "When all else is lost, when there is nowhere else to turn. Then, certainly, it can be used. But its greatest purpose is the possession of it. The promise, in the minds of your enemies, that you will indeed use it when that last moment comes. If they ever doubt that, its purpose and power alike are lost. So be of no doubt: it can and must be used, when that necessity is inescapable."

"And settling the debt of Towers' Shadow is not such a moment," Callotec acknowledged in disappointment.

"Perhaps not?" Kasuman agreed tentatively.

"Very well. We shall have recourse to more traditional means, then. But that will require a little more time. We must hurry on."

He turned about in his saddle and stretched, looking down the length of the column that followed him. It was not an overly impressive sight. Tired and ragged men, soiled by days on the road. But numerous enough for his purposes, he thought.

"Faster," he called out. "You can rest after we reach Towers' Shadow."

The pace did increase a touch. Less than he would have wished, but it was something.

"I'm pleased to see you can still find the fire within when it's needed, Kasuman," he said as they trotted along. "We will need such vigour in the next Hommetic Kingdom."

31

The Doves Had Come

The doves had come to Ordeller in the gloaming. She had not heard them at first, for she was washing down the floor of her kitchen. Scrubbing and splashing away while the Emperor sat on the edge of the cooking hearth scratching his nose and watching her. It was one of his favourite stations, that, when the fire was recently extinguished. The stones kept the heat, and he liked heat. Ordeller suspected the weather of these wild lands did not agree with him. Whatever his distant homeland – she struggled to imagine a place so foreign as to contain his kind in abundance – it was a good deal warmer than Curmen. That much she knew well.

The cleaning done, her back aching as it did more often with each passing year, she carried a dozen tankards and cups out to arrange on the serving counter. It might be a vain hope that anyone would be wanting to drink tonight – trade had been thin before the Free passed through, and positively emaciated since – but she liked to keep up the appearance of a welcome.

That was when she heard the bells tinkling. She stood there, arms laden with the apparatus of drunkenness, and angled her head, squinting towards the stairs. No doubting it. A silvery little jangling of bells.

Her birds, those trained to home here to her lodging house, had been taught to peck a little red-painted square of wood when they were in want of seed or water. From that square, suspended in the dove house, up amongst the rafters, Ordeller had dropped a vanishingly thin, thread-like string. All the way down through floor and ceiling into her own rooms. And at the end of that string were bells. She thought it a rather clever trick, and took pleasure in its success whenever it worked. Upon such small pleasures was a modest but contented life founded.

At the sound of the bell, she sighed and set her load down, all higgle-piggle on one of the big drinking tables.

"I'm going to see to the doves," she called to the Emperor, still occupying his warm hearth throne.

He made no reply. He never did.

Ordeller climbed the stairs slowly but steadily. The higher she climbed, the lower her spirits fell. Message birds, in her experience, as often brought good word as bad, but it was always easier to imagine the latter had arrived, for some reason.

And it had, this time. Word both bad and sad. She sat there in the cramped dove house, up in the eaves, surrounded by dust and feathers and the smell of droppings, and was slightly surprised that as she read the messages Yulan had sent, she felt a little like crying.

She had liked almost all of the Free that she had met. Oh, some of them, like that cold-skinned sow Akrana, took a bit of

getting used to, but in the main she had found them full-spir-
ited and well-mannered. And they paid her more than she had
ever earned from selling wine and ale to the impoverished folk
of Curmen, of course, but that was neither here nor there. She
would have liked them in any case.

Miserable, she went down to her room and laboriously
copied out the message Yulan commanded her to send out on
every bird she had. Tell those who received it to send it on, with
every bird *they* had, until it spread through the Free like a chain
of whispers. *The School is coming. Run. Hide. Set no store by anything but your own safety.*

Yulan was scattering the Free. Perhaps never to be unscat-
tered. What a sad ending, she thought, if ending it was, to
something that had been so grand and glorious. So vivid, in a
world grown drab.

It took her a long time to affix so many messages to so many
fragile legs. On impulse, she kissed the head of each pale dove
as she set it loose through the hatch in her roof. She watched
them flutter away into the twilight, drifting off in all directions
one by one.

Then she closed the hatch and went back down to the
kitchens, where the Emperor was looking half asleep. Folded up
nice and comfortable.

"Sorry, old friend," she said quietly to the ape. "I think we'll
be needing to take a little journey. Nothing to worry about, I'm
sure, but cautious is wise, reckless is not, as my grandfather used
to say."

She frowned as she said it, and wagged a thoughtful finger at
the Emperor.

"Or it might have been my uncle. Long time ago. Anyway, I wonder if that cousin of mine in Linden Grove is still alive. Can't remember his name. Never liked him, whoring pig that he is. But he's got a roof he might lend us for a little while, you and me."

The grey-black ape stirred only a little at all this. He looked at her with eyes barely half open. A great deal more interested in sleep than in what she said.

"Don't worry," Ordeller smiled. "No need to rush. We'll get some sleep in our bones first. Be on our way tomorrow, perhaps."

Ordeller packed what she would take with her that night. Not much. She had ample treasure to buy anything she might need when she got wherever she was going. There was a tiny old cart tucked away in a corner of the stables somewhere. Hardly anything to it but two wheels and a couple of spars, if she remembered right, but it would meet her needs. She would have to buy a donkey, of course. That should not be difficult, given her willingness to pay whatever price was asked.

She slept poorly, finding such a multitude of things to fret over – Yulan's difficulties, her own uncertain future, the Emperor's ingrained dislike of change of any kind – that as soon as she managed to still one of them, the next popped into its place.

She was therefore already in a foul mood when a pounding at her door broke out not long after dawn. She was trying to get a fire started in the hearth, thinking to allow herself just enough time before leaving to warm herself, get herself outside some hot food. The Emperor was lying on his back on one of the tables, interlacing fingers and toes, rolling back and forth on his spine.

Muttering darkly, Ordeller made her way to the door and lifted the bar. The man who pushed his way in – rudely, not waiting for invitation or even pleasantry – was not hard to identify. A Clade warrior. A young one, who looked almost as tired and fraught as Ordeller felt.

"You're the keeper of this house?" he demanded roughly.

"Well, it's a delight to meet you too," she muttered. "Looks like you'll be coming inside, then."

She pushed the door closed. Quietly settled the bar back into place.

"You're . . ." He hesitated, tripped by a faltering memory. "Ordeller, is it?"

"That's the name my mother gave me. If it's changed since, nobody's mentioned it to me. Do you want something to drink or eat?"

"No, no." He frowned at the Emperor, who was far too interested in the behaviour of his own limbs to pay any heed to Ordeller's uninvited guest.

"Pretty, isn't he?" Ordeller said.

The warrior gathered himself, and fixed her with a stern glare that looked very much like something his face was not used to.

"The Free have been outlawed. You're said to have some connection with them."

"What manure is this?" laughed Ordeller. Not that she expected it to do any good. The Clade were not famed for the ease with which they could be dissuaded or distracted from their given task. They liked their orders, these blue-tunicked boys.

"I was just told to take you to the nearest wayhouse. They'll know what to do with you there."

"What to do with me? Is that how you talk to your mother? Would she not slap you round the head for your rude manner?"

He shrugged. A nice little reddening of embarrassment and discomfort to his cheeks, Ordeller thought.

"And how many brave men have come with you to carry this fat old lady off to some cell?"

"There's just me. Too much happening for any more. And I'm not taking you to a cell. Just to the wayhouse."

"Do I look like one of the Free to you, boy?"

"Well, no. But I don't really know what they would look like."

"Not like me, I can tell you that much," Ordeller grunted. "Not with ribbons tied in their hair. You think the Free have ribbons tied in their hair?"

"Don't know," the warrior said, a touch grumpy now. Patience running thin, Ordeller judged. Well and good. Nothing to be gained by playing any more games, in any case.

She slumped down into the chair behind her, going heavily and limply. She pressed the back of her hand to her brow and rolled her eyes a touch.

"Oh, it's too much," she gasped, fanning her face with her free hand. "I can't be standing this." She trembled her lip and squeezed a little tear from her eye.

"Just come away with me, will you?" the Clade man muttered in exasperation. "I don't want to have to drag you."

"No, I'm sure you don't," Ordeller said faintly. She held out her hand. "Help me to my feet, do. I'm feeling so faint. It's frightening, all this."

The warrior clicked his tongue against the roof of his mouth in irritation, but took a step closer and grasped her hand.

"Thank you," she murmured.

And she returned that grasp, as hard and firm as she could manage, and smiled at him and said, loud and clear: "Hurt him."

The Emperor leaped, screaming, teeth bared, at the warrior's back. Hit him so hard that his breath rushed out and over Ordeller. He staggered and she kicked at his ankles to take him down, even as the ape beat him about the head and tore at the side of his face with those vicious teeth.

The Emperor was a good deal stronger than his looks and scrawny arms would suggest, and he had a terrible temper. He clawed and flailed at the warrior's shoulders and neck. The man did try to roll away and rise to his feet, but the strength of the relentless blows raining down upon him would have been too much for all but a few. Ordeller could hear the hollow thud every time the ape's fist hammered on ribcage, and she could imagine what that might feel like.

The man's wild struggles upset chairs and sent a table sideways. He was bleeding from bites and scratches. Starting to shout. Best to put a stop to that, Ordeller thought. It was early, but not so early that there might not be someone to hear.

She took up one of those fallen chairs and got as close to the combatants as their violent contest would allow.

"Off him," she snapped at the Emperor, and the ape sprang away.

The Clade man groaned and started to push himself up. Ordeller hit him as hard as she could across the back of his head with the chair, which broke apart in her hands. A shame, that. She had had those same chairs since the day she first opened the doors of the lodging house. The man slumped to the floor, blood trickling from an ugly wound in his scalp.

Ordeller dropped the stumps of the chair and went to the serving counter, leaning over it and fumbling around blindly on the shelf beneath. She quickly found what she wanted. A long knife, not the sharpest, but sharp enough.

"Look away, old fellow," she muttered to the Emperor as she knelt beside the unconscious man. Then, more tartly, when he did no such thing: "Really, look away now. No need for you to see this."

The ape did as he was told, sitting on the floor, facing the wall. Folding his arms. Ordeller pushed the knife right through the warrior's neck.

When the blood was washed from the floor, the corpse secreted away in the cellar – a dreadful business, that, because the man proved heavier than he had looked – and his horse hidden temporarily in the stables, Ordeller took a few minutes to look around the place. She did not know if she would ever be back, and though she had never been one to set much store by such things, she found she would miss it mightily if not.

The Emperor was morose. Ashamed, she understood. He regarded her with wide, sorrowful eyes.

"Don't worry," she said gently, stroking the coarse hair on his shoulder. "It's wasn't your idea. All mine. And it needed doing, I'm afraid."

She shook herself, straightened her back.

"Poor old Yulan was right. Always is, I gather. So now the Free's done. They run and hide, or they get netted by the fishermen of the School. Sorry way for a thing like that to come to an end, scattering into the shadows. Ah, well. We'll just have to hope Yulan can fight his way out of whatever corner he's got himself stuck in, won't we? Wish him luck. You and me, we put it behind us and close the door. Find somewhere a little warmer to lay our heads for a while. At least we've got ourselves a horse now. What do you say?"

The ape folded his lower lip over his upper and snorted through his nose. Which might or might not have signified assent. Ordeller had no idea, but he did at least look a little less miserable.

She could not, after all, talk with animals. But she had always been good at training them. Always.

32

The First Day At Towers' Shadow

Just before the Old Threetower Road lurched up the escarpment above which the mighty towers themselves stood, there was one last village. It was a modest settlement. Thirty or more cottages, a hall, a couple of barns. Smoke curling up from a few hearths, children running noisily between the houses. Men and women, and more children, bent double, working in the small fields behind the houses. In one of those fields, a man waving a long stick at an oblivious bullock that had somehow got in there and set to its own kind of work on his crop.

Towers' Shadow had changed since last Yulan saw it. It was encircled by a shallow ditch now. The worst of the ruins were gone, only their least remnants left like the stubs of broken teeth smashed out of a rotten jaw. In some places that he remembered flames, there was bare, black earth as if ashes and burned wood had been trodden into the dirt over years.

The Free looked down upon the place from a ridge to the

south. The road ran close by the village, then swept on and up, beginning a laboured ascent of the escarpment.

The fields around the village were thriving. There were springs along the base of the escarpment, giving rise to tiny streams that found their way to one another and merged, making themselves into a tiny river that ran off and away beside the road. Yulan could see the glint of water in the irrigation channels cut from some of those streams. The fields between them were well manured. There were groves of young fruit trees.

He stared and stared at it all, as if by doing so he might convince himself that he was truly here, and that the place still lived. Thrived, even. What his eyes most readily found and settled upon, though, were the surviving scars of those days when the Dog-Lord came.

"Kingshouse," one of the lancers said.

Up on a hillock to the north-west of the village, perhaps a half-mile or more distant, was the little half-derelict fortification beside which the Free had briefly camped. A ring wall, and inside it a tiny keep. Just three storeys tall, each one a fraction smaller than the one below, to make room for a battlemented shooting platform on each level. It had once been said that wherever you went, you were never more than half a day's walk from a Kingshouse, and the venal, arrogant Armsmen who garrisoned them. No longer true anywhere, as it had not been here for years.

Yulan wrestled his eyes from the scene below to look up. The Three Towers themselves stood above him, way up there on top of the escarpment. Soaring. Crowned with stone horns. No windows, no stairs, no parapets. Nothing but vast block after vast block of smooth stone, one upon another, climbing up beyond reason. Black and brown vultures described arcs and circles around them and above them, pushed aloft by some hot wind rising from the flanks of the towers.

"What do you think?" Rudran was muttering.

Yulan shook his head. He could not speak. Not yet. He had thought himself prepared for this moment. Perhaps he would have been, had Wren and Hurdan and Fethin Fiveson not died to bring him here. Now he had to earn the right to mourn them as they deserved. He felt a hand on his forearm, looked down at it and then up into Rudran's eyes. He saw there more that he recognised than he would have expected. It was true: this place held meaning for many more than just him.

"What do you think?" Rudran repeated.

"I think Hamdan and I will go down there," Yulan said quietly.

Rudran nodded. He understood.

They drew a crowd, of course. As the two of them rode through the surrounding fields, along the dirt track, through the narrow gap in the ditch that served as the village's entrance, wide-eyed children rushed forward while their parents held back and watched with more suspicion. Those children, though. They laughed. They reached to touch the horses or lay a hand on Yulan's boot. Every one of them seemed to be smiling. He could not bring himself to meet their eyes. He heard dogs snarling inside his skull. There was no release for him here. Not yet.

A man leaning on a hoe blocked their way eventually. Not at

all aggressively. He just stood there, in the centre of the one track that ran the length of the village, and nodded to them when they drew to a halt before him, that chuckling crowd of children still at their backs.

"Hello," he said placidly.

Yulan dismounted. Hamdan did the same.

"Is there someone who speaks for you all?" Yulan asked. "Headman? Would that be you?"

The man with the hoe moistened his lips and shook his head slowly.

Yulan waited for more to come, but it did not. One or two of the children, braver than the rest, were tugging at his jacket. Only trying to raise a smile from him, he knew. He tried to give it to them, even as their parents, standing at a safer distance, called them away with hisses or tongue clicks.

"Who can I speak to?" Yulan asked.

"Metta," the man suggested.

"And where's Metta?"

The villager looked over his shoulder, dipped his hoe to point towards a woman standing in the doorway of a cottage close by. She was of almost the same age as . . . but Yulan would not allow himself to think of that. She had her hair tied up in a headscarf, and around her neck hung that same great rusted key. A pair of young girls were peeking around the edges of her skirts, staring at these unexpected visitors to their village. They were pretty lasses, with ashy dirt smudged across their chins and cheeks. They had been cleaning out the hearth, Yulan guessed.

"Metta," breathed Yulan. He could barely get the words out. His throat was tight.

"Let's talk to Metta, then," Hamdan said. He sounded little better.

The two of them led their horses slowly over. They stood side by side before Metta. Until suddenly Yulan found himself kneeling. He had not known what he would do at this moment. How he could get beyond it, and turn himself once more into the man he needed to be to save this place from what was coming. Now, unbidden, the certainty came. He knelt, and he bowed his head. A moment later, Hamdan was doing the same thing beside him.

"You're Massatan," Metta said, as another headwoman had said so long ago.

"Yes," breathed Yulan, staring at the ground. "I came here before, Mistress, and terrible things happened when I did."

She said nothing. Yulan did not lift his head. He waited. He would wait thus in silence for as long as it took.

"You had your hair then," Metta said finally.

"I did. I cut it when I rode away from here."

Metta sniffed. Yulan heard her flicking her skirts, the young girls scampering back into the shadows within the cottage.

"Well," she said, "you cut your hair. In penitence?"

"Yes, Mistress."

"Lift your head. I can't see your eyes."

Yulan and Hamdan did so. They stayed kneeling, though. The villagers had retrieved their children and shepherded them off to some other distraction. A handful of men and women remained, a few paces away. Watchful and attentive. It did not seem to concern Metta. She was toying with that heavy key about her neck. The symbol of her standing.

"What do you want from us?" she asked. "Forgiveness?"

Yulan could see no trace of anger, or hatred, in her face.

"No," he said. "I want to fight for you."

"And why do we need you to fight for us?"

"Because the man who burned this place, and killed your women and your children and your old men, is coming back. He will do far worse this time, if he can. He will leave nothing behind him. No stone upon stone, no timber in its place. No one alive. I would fight him to prevent that." And then, because he could not keep it from her: "But I cannot allow him to climb the escarpment, either. Because if he does, he will betray all these lands to the Empire. So whatever happens, even if he tries to flee, I must bring him to battle."

"The man who burned this place before," Metta said, speaking each word clearly and precisely. "Callotec. That is the man you mean?"

"Yes, Mistress."

She stared at him for long moments. She scratched the side of her nose with a slightly grubby fingernail. Then she glanced beyond Yulan and Hamdan, to the villagers gathered behind them. She beckoned them, and led them all – perhaps fifteen, men and women – into her tiny house. The door closed behind the last of them with a firm tap.

"We are to be discussed," Hamdan observed.

He looked around; espied a water trough over by one of the barns, where a couple of thin-looking cattle were drinking.

"Let's see to the horses. We've asked more of them than was right, the last day or two."

They led the two exhausted animals over to the trough, and

gently eased them in beside the cattle to slake their thirst. The horses drank long and deep, until Yulan said, "Enough," and they dragged them away.

Hamdan stood in the centre of the village, raised his arms straight up and crossed them once above his head. The others were still there, up on the ridge above the village, in open sight. At Hamdan's signal, two of them broke away, following the line of the road but keeping to the high, rough ground. Scouting for Callotec.

Yulan and Hamdan tethered their horses and sat with their backs against the wall of a barn. Yulan felt almost nothing now. He existed in the space between two breaths, waiting for the world to happen. He had done what he could. Others would decide his future now. He found that an easy thought to live with.

The sun was warm. Both he and Hamdan angled their faces to feel it.

"It would not be a bad place to die," Hamdan mused.

The door to Metta's cottage banged open and the villagers flowed out. They did not rush, or talk amongst themselves. They came out, and dispersed to their own homes. Metta came last of all and walked over to Yulan. He stood.

"Our women and children will leave. Our men will fight with you. They are eager to meet this Callotec, as so few of them were here when he last came."

Yulan nodded. He felt a tingling in his arms and hands, and a quickening of his heart.

"You need not have cut your hair," Metta told him. "You were not here when the worst of it happened, and you stopped it when you returned. Is that not so?"

"It is. That's why I cut my hair, Mistress. Because I was not here."

"And now you are."

"Now I am."

"Well, then," Metta said, satisfied.

Drann dug. He was surprised at how good it felt to labour like that, with his hands and his back, in a ditch. The ground was hard and dry, fighting him all the way. But still, it felt good. He hacked at it, and battled it, and because he had done such work as this almost all his life, he bettered it.

He took pleasure, too, in sharing the struggle. Some fifteen men or more were working, digging down into the hard earth at the village's entrance, all at Yulan's direction. Watching them, he could see the long days of just such toil that their bodies remembered and had shaped themselves to. They wasted no effort, wielded their tools as precisely as the Free ever wielded blade or bow. It was an honest kind of battle, this, Drann thought, and he enjoyed it as he had never done before.

He listened to Yulan and Hamdan while they fought that same battle alongside him. They were grieving.

"You remember that time Wren laid honey in Kerig's trews to seed them with burn-ants while he slept?" Yulan asked.

"I remember his howling. He reckoned his manhood was going to cook from their stings."

"He'd not let anyone make such mockery of him as she did. You remember what he was like before she arrived? There were those too scared to smile at him sometimes, case he took it into his head to knock their teeth out."

"She was good for him," Hamdan nodded, straightening for a moment to wipe sweat from his brow. "The old Kerig had his uses, though. Helps to have some frightening folk around now and again, when you're plying our kind of trade."

"Oh, we still had Akrana. You don't think she's enough when it comes to softening folks' bowels with fear?"

"Her and what's in the cage," Hamdan grunted. "It's enough."

They fell silent for a time. The rhythmic plunge and scoop and heave of digging was the only sound.

"She was one of the best of us," Hamdan said eventually. "She was one of the ones not running away from anything, not breaking under any weight, not kept awake with nightmares. She wore it more lightly than most of us. Having her around made it rest a bit lighter on all our shoulders."

"I think so," Yulan murmured. "I think she did that for us."

Plunge, scoop, heave.

"I hope she killed Sullen," Drann said, surprising himself as much as anyone. He had not meant to speak.

"With all my heart," Hamdan grunted.

"He's not easy to kill," Yulan said darkly.

The grinding and groaning of overburdened wheels made them all stand tall, and look over towards the point where the Old Threetower Road began its ascent of the escarpment. A hundred paces from the nearest cottage in the village, Drann guessed.

Rudran and his men were helping a handful of villagers haul handcarts loaded with stones from the little ruin at the far end of Towers' Shadow. They would be added to the barricade of timber and rock that already all but blocked the road just as it started to rise. That was the core of Yulan's intent, Drann had more or less gathered without being explicitly told. Block the road, hold the village next to that blockage. That way, Callotec could not flee with the Bereaved for the Empire, should the day go against him.

One or two of the stones on the carts being laboriously wheeled along were odd. They had a rusty red hue that marked them out from the rest. It was too even and distinct to be natural.

"What're the red stones?" Drann wondered aloud, not particularly expecting any answer.

"Sorentine lintel stones," said Yulan without pausing in his labours. "Red and yellow were their favourite colours. Painted the lintel above pretty much every doorway of any consequence red."

"They really were a miserable, soulless lot, the Hommetics, weren't they?" Hamdan mused. "No spirit to them. Look at what the Sorentines did. Livened up executions with their pools, splashed red across their every doorway. Paraded bulls through the streets, and danced with them. Festivals of fire, songs of the sun. They had flair, if nothing else. A bit of life."

"That's the way things go," Yulan said. "Make city merchants with roots no deeper than four or five fathers back, like the Hommetics, into kings and you get a petty kingdom of avaricious cheats. No ambitions or creed beyond their own continuance, getting rich along the way. Make a wild, ancient clan from the hill valleys, like the Sorentines, into kings and you get something with maybe too much spirit to it. Not sure everyone who was around back then enjoyed it quite as much as you think you would have. They'd probably have thought a bit of dull avarice tremendously appealing by comparison."

"Well, I've not much more ambition or creed than my own continuance, getting rich along the way," sniffed Hamdan, "but dull's bad. Don't care what anyone says."

They had refound some measure of levity, Drann thought. He did not understand why, since each passing moment brought closer something that could be nothing but terrible, but from the moment they'd walked into Towers' Shadow, the sombre darkness had lifted a little. From Yulan and Hamdan, at least. Not gone entirely, but eased. The nearest he could come to an understanding, and it was no real understanding at all, was that they were, for the first time since he had met them, in some sense where they wanted to be.

And here he was with them. That, as the first day at Towers' Shadow came to its end, was the part of it he least understood.

33

The Second Day At Towers' Shadow

The second day at Towers' Shadow dawned bright. Yulan watched from the top of the Kingshouse's keep as the sun came up. The place was in a bad state, worse than before. Nothing remained but silence and empty rooms and bare stone walls that had clearly been shedding ever more of their fabric in each of the last few years.

Up on its hillock, the keep caught the sun before the village below. Its stone glowed, as if welcoming the day's return. Yulan closed his eyes, and savoured that first touch of warmth upon his face. He missed the heat of the south, he realised. He had once spent much of a winter in a village where the sea's shore was girded by ice, almost as far out as the eye could see. He had slept, years later, two nights in a hole cut from snow, halfway up a mountain. None of it had taught him to appreciate the cold.

He missed the flat ground, the vast skies thick with stars at night, heavy with the sun in the day. The feel of sand under his bare feet. He felt more clearly than he had done in a long time, standing there on the Kingshouse at Towers' Shadow, that he would like to go back to the place where he had been born. That he *could* go back there, perhaps. One day, but it would not be soon.

The Kingshouse provided a splendid vantage point. Slightly too far from Towers' Shadow and from the road to be of any use in what was to come – Callotec could pass it by, even if Yulan had twice the men to garrison it – but by far the best perch for surveying the ground.

What Yulan saw did not fill him with confidence. Nor did it invite despair. They had done what they could, with the time and hands they had, and fortune would decide all else. Fortune and perhaps the Clamour. Fickle, the pair of them. You could only cast what bones you held, though, and he had cast them. He had done his best to be worthy of Wren and the others who had died, and would yet die. It was not enough, would never be enough; but it was all he could offer now.

The road, at the point where it angled up to climb towards the towers, was heaped with rubble and brushwood. No way past there, for wagons or horses. Pits and ditches had been dug, covered over with staked sheeting or wattle panels, and then disguised with a strewing of dirt and dust. Everyone – Free and villagers alike – was where Yulan had placed them. Nothing more could be done. The waiting was the burden now.

It would be brief, it seemed, for he saw Hamdan galloping in along the road. The archer was bent low to the horse's neck, urging it on with arms and legs. Yulan hurried down through the desolate keep, and out through the Kingshouse's gate. He trotted down the long slope towards the village, and Hamdan must have seen him, for he veered off the road and came cantering to meet him.

Yulan took hold of the panting horse's halter, and raised his eyebrows expectantly.

"An hour at most," Hamdan said. "Must have been marching in the night, brave lads that they are. They've learned a little. Almost all their horses are out wide and well ahead. I'd say you've got about thirty lances and swords coming straight at you up the road. Back of them, Callotec and Kasuman and the Bereaved with all the rest on foot. Not too far back, but far enough you might have enough time to lay out thirty dead for them as a welcome gift. If you're quick about it."

"Quick as I can," murmured Yulan, already running for the village. "Quick as I can."

No room for remorse or grief or doubt now. Not if he was to make the deaths mean anything at all. Not if he was to shield Towers' Shadow against what was coming. There could only be clarity of thought and deed now, until it was done.

Back on the desert's edge, if there was a lion the people wanted to kill, they baited it in with a goat. Sometimes with a runt foal, though that was less common. Lebid was the bait goat today. They dressed him in peasant's garb, and set him on the least impressive of their horses. Its hide had been smeared with filth, its mane and tail tangled with the stuff, but its essential nature – bred and trained, strong and well fed – was only blunted, not truly hidden. If anyone took a sharp-eyed look, they would know it for something more than a roving brigand's mount. Hopefully, no one would have the chance to sharpen their eyes quite that much.

The archer sat underneath a lonely spreading tree, out at the roadside. He was making a passable imitation of a sluggishly somnolent deserter from one army or other, sitting with his back against the tree trunk, his legs stretched out and crossed. The horse was cropping some yellowed grass. It looked as though there were a few tiny dark finches fluttering about and squabbling in the branches overhead. That, Yulan thought, was a nice flourish for the world to grace his illusion with. Another delicately placed semblance of calm and normality.

Yulan was peering through a knot hole in the planked wall of one of the small barns. Up high, on the platforms where the hay and feed were stored. It let him watch over the roofs of the cottages and huts. The first rider he saw was up on the very ridge from which he and the rest of the Free had descended the day before. Silhouetted against the sky, no detail distinguishable beyond the fact that he carried lance and round shield. An Armsman, who took up post there and did not move. Yulan could imagine what thoughts must be running through the mind of that distant dark figure.

He would see a man asleep, or at least lazing, beneath a tree. He would see one or two villagers moving to and fro amongst the buildings. Only men, for Metta had led the women and children hurriedly away into hiding somewhere north along the foot of the escarpment. Nothing, hopefully, to alarm. Nothing to draw him down. Yulan needed to catch as many of Callotec's van in this snare as he could, and that meant no solitary outriders acquiring a sufficient excess of curiosity or courage to spring the trap themselves.

Another hint of movement took his eye up to the

Kingshouse. A second Armsman had arrived there, riding slowly round the outer wall. Staring up at the windows and battlements of the keep, no doubt. Satisfying himself that no one was lurking within. So satisfied, the rider drew his horse to a halt and sat there, just as the first did, watching village and valley and road.

Careless, thought Yulan. If he was one of the Free, that man would be tongue-lashed for not getting inside the Kingshouse to see its emptiness from within as well as without. It was a good sign. Perhaps they thought they had slipped the noose, now that the towers stood there before them. Callotec himself would not be so complacent, but his weary, frightened men might easily convince themselves of a relief so strongly desired.

Yulan realised that his lips had dried a touch. He licked them, though there was little enough moisture to be found anywhere in his mouth.

He could hear them coming now, even through the walls of the barn. That faint, familiar clopping of hoof on road. A lot of hoofs. Lebid would be hearing them too, but he was doing the right thing and not giving any sign of it. Yulan spread the fingers of his sword hand, stretching them. Bunched and unbunched them.

The first of the vanguard came in sight. Riding half a dozen abreast at a fast walk, in loose array. The villagers would begin to doubt themselves and their chances at the sight of such horses, such martial finery, Yulan knew. It did not matter. The Free could dispel that doubt, given the chance.

Lebid was stirring, casually uncrossing his legs, brushing his hands on his breast as he got to his feet. He shaded his eyes from the sun to stare at the approaching company. Nicely done.

The boy might have made a fine mummer, if he had lived his life another way. Had Yulan not known better, he might himself have been gulled into thinking this some ragged wanderer or bandit woken unexpectedly from his doze.

The lancers were closing steadily. Lebid mimed alarm, and took up his bow with an ungentle haste that befitted nervousness. Only one arrow was needed, and he loosed it quickly. A shot that would have set Hamdan fuming at the ineptitude of those he had trained, were it not just as it was meant to be. The arrow arced gracefully out, vaulting across the distance between Lebid and the horsemen, and clattered harmlessly amongst rocks off to one side of the road. Faultless.

The lead riders heeled their horses on, and came cantering. More anger than fear, which was just as Yulan wanted it. He needed the rest – or most of them, at least – to follow, though, and for a few moments it did not look as though they would. Then Lebid was scrambling up on to his own mount, and dragging it round to race for the village. That got all but a few of the lancers interested enough to come after him. Yulan set hand to hilt. He tested his grip upon the strappings of his shield. He could hear those few villagers who had been making a show of themselves running for shelter.

Lebid came pounding up the track and over the tiny causeway that divided the village's ditch. Another couple of long strides from his horse, which had Yulan clenching his teeth in apprehension, and the archer pulled the animal up into a long leap at just the right moment. The landing was good, the rhythm unbroken, but Lebid went only a little way deeper into the village before contriving a more or less convincing fall, half sliding, half flinging himself off to the side and thumping down on to the ground. He really did have potential, that one, if his occasional carelessness did not kill him first.

He was slow to rise. He lifted himself on to hands and knees but went no further. Yulan saw him glancing surreptitiously back between his own legs to see how his pursuers fared. Just as poorly as anyone could have hoped, it turned out.

The first couple of Armsmen thundered in, and did not jump as Lebid had jumped. Their horses went down through the hidden woven mats and into the freshly dug trench beneath. Yulan knew there was grief to be had in this reflection of what Wren had done to these same men just days ago, but he could not allow himself to feel it now. He would not.

Two, three riders were thrown from their mounts. Another fell as his horse veered and stumbled to avoid the suddenly revealed pit. Those who came behind had the time and ground to adjust their path as they entered the village. They flowed around the hole where men and horses were floundering. And found more secret pits, on either side, that caught them as well.

Lebid sprang up and loosed an arrow that set a man rocking in his saddle, before sprinting for the nearest of the cottages. Atop other cottages, on either side of the track, more of Hamdan's bow boys appearing, having been hoisted up there by village men. They knelt on the roofs, and began to calmly pick off those Armsmen who remained outside the village's ditch. Within that ditch itself, two of Rudran's own lancers suddenly appeared, throwing off the sacking and dirt that had concealed them. They had spears bought from village folk, and tried to set them in the belly of any horse within reach.

Yulan turned and dropped softly down to the barn's hay-strewn floor. He looked at Drann, and then at the thirty or so villagers standing behind him. They had spears, and forks and hammers and scythes. They had nervous eyes.

"It's time," Yulan said, then lied: "Half of them are already dead. We need to go fast, if we're to share in the winning."

He threw open the doors of the barn and ran, not looking behind to see how many followed him. He could hear, from their cries, that enough did.

Yulan and his motley band ran from one side; Rudran and his last handful of lancers came pounding from the other, bursting out from the second barn further down the track. Few of them had lances any more, but with shields and flailing maces they still made for a fearful pageant. The sun had come just high enough in the sky now to catch their helms, their mail.

If he could, Yulan wanted to get round the side of the disordered Armsmen, to come to the aid of his two men in the ditch. They were the ones most likely to pay for his ambition with their lives, exposed as they were, but he had thought it essential to stymie any easy retreat for those he had ambushed. He could not get there yet, though.

There were still horses struggling and rolling about in those pits, and men with them, but others had worked their way around or jumped across. Several were already forming up into a rank ahead of Yulan. Caught, thankfully, by indecision over whether to charge ahead, into the village, or try to break out over the main ditch. Yulan rushed them, roaring, hoping that Drann and the villagers would follow.

One of the Armsmen sprang out to meet him, lance dipping

and aiming for his chest. He had his shield up to cover his ribs, but that was a meagre sort of defence. At the last moment, once the Armsman had enough pace up to make changing direction difficult, Yulan rolled forwards and sideways, passing beneath the very muzzle of the charging horse. It was dangerous, since lancers trained their mounts to trample, not avoid, men at their feet, but he cleared those raking hoofs by the narrowest of margins and rolled into a crouch, slashing the horse's flank and hindquarters as it galloped past. He heard it crashing into, and falling amongst, the rabble running up behind him.

More lances were already coming at him. Rudran came rushing in from the side, and barged them away, hammering at them with his great mace with frenzied violence. Yulan ran on, into the heaving mass of horse against horse. He paused as he passed one of the trenches to cut down an unseated Armsman who was trying to climb out. Another, who had already dragged himself from a pit and was limping back the way he had come, loomed in front of him and Yulan punched the boss of his shield into the back of his neck. He jumped over the man as he fell.

A rider was jabbing down into the main ditch with his lance. Yulan darted in and cut the man's thigh open; then, when he tried to wheel his horse about, killed him with a thrust under his armour and into his belly.

A great blow to Yulan's back knocked him flat. He half rose, but glimpsed stamping hoofs coming for him, and instead scrambled and threw himself forward into the great ditch. In the few moments it took him to shake off the dazing impact, and to get to his feet, the struggle was all but done. Fewer than ten of Callotec's lancers were galloping away, along the path and over the fields. Back towards the Old Threetower Road. Arrows sighed after them.

Yulan glanced up to the high ground, to the Kingshouse. Those outriding watchers were gone. They had done the wise thing, the disciplined thing, and left the battle to decide itself while they hastened back to their master with word of what was happening. Around the freshly dug pits, villagers were gathered, stabbing down with spears and pitchforks to kill wounded men and horses. Yulan saw Drann amongst them. Creel's contract-holder was not taking part in the killing. He just stood there, spear in limp hand, watching. He looked bewildered. Each time there was a scream, or a yearning groan from the wounded or dying, he winced as if pin-stuck.

Yulan had no time to worry about Drann, though. At his feet, in the bottom of the ditch, one of his own men – one of those two lancers he had hidden here – was dead. The stub of a broken lance transfixed him. It had gone in above the collar-bone, driven right through him to emerge from his lower back. Yulan bent down and pressed his eyes closed. He tried to lift his chin to shut his open mouth, but the dead muscle and bone resisted.

Yulan climbed from the ditch and stood on the track. He wiped each side of his sword across his trouser leg and sheathed it. He walked slowly back into the village. One of the menfolk lay dead. His head had been crushed by the stamp of a horse, by the look of him. The long-bladed knife he had brought to the battle lay on the ground, just beyond the reach of his stretched arm.

Rudran's great horse set itself between Yulan and the sun, sinking him into shadow. He looked up at the ruddy-faced lancer.

"How did you do?"

"Merelick died in the ditch." Rudran said it without accusation, or sorrow, or regret. It was a mere fact, to be conveyed to his commander.

"I saw," Yulan nodded.

"I've another got a broken arm and ankle. He'll not be doing any more fighting."

"Bind him up and have someone take him after the villagers who went off into hiding," Yulan said. "Get the rest of your men together. Hide them in one of the barns, if you can."

Rudran went without hesitation to do as he was bid. He was not as cold as he could appear, Yulan knew. The gruff restraint with which he conducted himself was his way of excelling at his calling. But already Rudran had lost a fourth part of the few men he had brought out from Sussadar at Yulan's command. Potent feelings would be roiling within the big man, waiting for the time he let them out.

Drann and the villagers were trying to pull dead men out of the pits that had trapped and killed them.

"Leave them be," Yulan called over. "Any lamp oil in the village, any firewater or pitch, throw it in there over them. As much as you can find. Quickly."

He did not wait to see his orders enacted. Hamdan was slithering down from one of the cottage roofs.

"That was better than it might have been," the archer grunted.

"Lebid did well."

"Told you he could be trusted for the task," Hamdan smiled. "How long do you think before the rest of them are running down our throats?"

"Oh, not long enough. And I doubt they'll come running. Callotec's not foolish enough for that. Now he knows we're here, he'll come careful and crafty."

"Well, that's what we need, isn't it? If we're hoping that Akrana's going to come and save us, we need Callotec going slow."

"We do. Just a pity that that means he'll not be making many mistakes. These lancers were the easy part. It's uphill from here. Steep, at that."

34

The Store Of Time

Drann was not sure whether or not he had killed a man. He had stood there, jostling amongst the eager villagers, and stabbed down into the pit with his spear. There had been men and horses down there, trying to rise. He had felt his spear strike something, but in the confusion he could not tell what flesh it was he had pierced.

The feel of it, that impact shaking up the shaft of the spear and into his hands, had in an instant extinguished the fire in his breast. Snuffed it out. Taken him back with wrenching force to the chaos and confusion of the knoll where he had fought alongside Creel. Some foolish part of him must have somehow expected this to be different. It was not. It was worse. He pulled away from the crowd, barely able to see. Stood there still holding his spear but not feeling its weight. He heard men crying out, and felt his face react to the sound, but he was so distant, so numbed, that he did not know what it did.

It was all over quickly. Bodies lying around him. Dead and wounded horses. The smell of blood and bowel. The villagers started trying to pull corpses up out of the trenches they had dug just hours before. To loot them of anything of value, Drann supposed, and did not know what to make of that.

"Leave them be," he heard Yulan shouting from somewhere. "Any lamp oil in the village, any firewater or pitch, throw it in there over them. As much as you can find. Quickly."

Absurdly, ridiculously, the villagers stopped what they were doing and looked questioningly to Drann. *Turn away*, he wanted to say. *Turn to someone else. I'm just like you.*

"Do as he says," he muttered dully instead.

He went with them to scour the village for any liquid that might burn, because to be doing something was better than to be standing doing nothing amidst the dead. He carried flasks of oil back to the pits and spilled their contents over the corpses.

When it was done, he fled. He did not want to be seen, or spoken to, so he went to a well at the edge of the village and drew up water from it. He tipped handfuls of the cold, fresh liquid down his throat. His hands were trembling, he noticed. The water spilled over his chin, down his neck. When he could drink no more, he sat with his back against the hard stone of the well and closed his eyes. Confused and distracted as his mind was, he felt sleep reaching for him.

He was not given the time he craved.

"Here they come," he heard someone shouting, when it seemed to him he had barely sat down, barely shut those tired eyes.

He stretched out his hand for his spear.

Yulan and Hamdan climbed together on to the roof of a hut and stood there watching as Callotec's column came slowly and carefully around the furthest turn in the road and advanced upon the village. There was no point to concealment now. Callotec knew where they were, who they were.

And because he knew who they were, the last of the Hommetics was taking care. His little army drew itself up just out of bowshot, beyond the edge of the village's fields, on the flat ground by the road.

No more than two hundred, Yulan judged. A great many fewer horsemen than before, for which he was grateful, but still more than the Free had. Loose lines of levymen. More ordered ranks of Armsmen and a few of Kasuman's rebel Clade followers. Only one wagon now. That and the mules halted behind the lines of warriors. Beside the very tree under which Lebid had sat.

"Well, don't they look pretty," murmured Hamdan.

Two men rode out from the ranks and went charging, at the fullest of gallops, along the road. Yulan cocked his head on one side and watched them go.

"Going to see if we know how to make a barricade, I suppose." he said.

"Looks so," Hamdan agreed.

The two horsemen kicked up plumes of dust as they raced over uncobbled stretches. They were leaning forward, their heads pushed down on the far side of their mounts' necks. Hamdan glanced down, tapped at the roof with one foot, shuffled the other around a little bit to get a sure footing.

The riders were almost at the bottom of the escarpment, almost at the barrier thrown across the rise of the road. They slowed, straightened, and turned their horses about.

"Show Callotec your reach," Yulan said quietly.

"Happy to."

The arrow was nocked in an instant, the bowstring pulled taut. And held there. Yulan could tell that Hamdan had stopped breathing. The archer tracked the movement of the Armsmen as they began to pick up pace, heading back towards their comrades. At what felt like the last instant before they would be beyond the reach of even a master archer, the arrow was away, singing its soft song as it curved up and down. Hamdan lowered the bow.

"That's one of them," he said quietly. "You want the other?"

As he finished the question, the arrow struck the lead rider in the side, just above his hip. He jerked upright, and his horse slowed. He gripped the arrow's shaft even as his companion rushed past him and away.

"Oh, don't pull it out, you fool," muttered Hamdan.

But the Armsman did, and they heard him cry out even from that distance.

"Fool," Hamdan said again, as they watched him ride back to Callotec's company. He was slumping in the saddle, bending over the wound in his flank.

"Let's get down," Yulan said.

They slid to the edge of the roof on their backsides, and dropped to the ground. Hamdan unstrung his bow and slipped it back into the quiver on his back.

"Listen," Yulan said. "There's all sorts of ways this goes bad if it wants, but the quickest and the worst of them is Clevers. We don't know how many Callotec's got left with him, or what they might be able to do with the Bereaved if they're there. So

I've got nothing for you to do now but find them and kill them. However you like, however you can."

"See a Clever, kill a Clever," smiled Hamdan. "Seems clear enough."

Drann waited with the villagers. He had somehow found himself amongst them, not the Free, and they had somehow found themselves convinced of his place there.

Drann looked at them and saw himself. They looked at him and saw . . . something else. He had done nothing to earn that look in their eyes, said almost nothing to any one of them. Yet they knew he had come here with the Free, and that was enough. He felt like a liar.

They huddled in the doorway of the barn in which they had earlier hidden themselves. The doors were wide open and tied back now. They were not hiding. Nor did they make any great show of strength. There were only about twenty of them left. One had already died fighting Callotec's lancers; more had slipped away as soon as that skirmish was done, not liking that taste of the greater struggle to come. Drann understood that. He could easily have slipped away with them.

Looking from face to face now, he recognised his own fear and inner distress. Their eyes danced nervously around, not knowing where to settle their gaze.

"If we don't fight them, you lose your homes, everything that's here," he said quietly, because he felt that something – anything – should be said. He was startled by the way every gaze was instantly turned upon him. Rapt attention, the like of which he had not attracted before.

"And if you lose your village to them, those men out there' – he jabbed his chin in the vague direction of Callotec's lines – "they're going to go on from here and betray us all to the Orphans, and they don't care what that means. They'll watch all of us, all of you, killed and staked and enslaved, and they'll not shed a tear for it because they think it'll get them what they want."

He could not tell whether his words had any effect, but his voice did strengthen as he spoke. He found himself believing them, even if no one else did.

Yulan watched as Callotec sent one party up to search the Kingshouse. Another went on to the high grounds to the south. Trying to sniff out any surprises. That was fine. It ate up the minutes, and Callotec hopefully did not understand what risks he ran in spending the store of time he held. In all likelihood, he thought Yulan had the Clamour waiting for him here in the village. Had he known the truth, that the Clamour was coming, somewhere out there in the rough land, there would have been none of this waiting and searching and taking measure.

Clouds drifted over. Vultures and crows, called by the scent of those already dead, came low over the village. Some settled in the fruit trees a short way beyond its outer bounds. Some circled. One – a small but viciously hook-beaked pale vulture – settled on a rooftop. Yulan, leaning in the doorway of the hut across the track, watched it. He debated, then kicked a pebble loose from the hard ground at his feet and picked it up. He bounced the pebble off the roof right next to the vulture, and it clambered clumsily into the air once more. He had been trying to hit it, but his throwing arm was not the best.

"Not your time yet," he muttered under his breath.

There was no high ground within an arrow's reach of the village save the looming heights of the escarpment rising behind it, which were thankfully inaccessible to the Hommetics. Thus restricted, when Callotec decided to test the mood he was reduced to sending a dozen or so of his bowmen scampering forward across the open fields. They went from ditch to ditch, bush to bush, trying to lose themselves in the tallest of the crops.

Yulan pinched finger and thumb between his lips and gave a couple of sharp whistles. Nothing came of them at first, but that did not trouble him. Hamdan's men knew their work and did not need Yulan rushing them.

He lost sight of Callotec's approaching archers and guessed they thought they had found the range and gone to ground while they readied themselves. Sure enough, a moment later a solitary arrow came looping up out of a field of grain. A black speck that lengthened as it rose and fell towards the village, landing just a few paces short of the outer ditch.

Before it did land, three more of its kind were in the air. Coming not from the fields but from amongst the cottages there at the village's edge. Answering the challenge. They traced back that first arrow's path, and plunged down through the very air it had climbed. A loose flock of shafts rattled amongst the cottages. Again they were answered by those more precise, more perfectly aimed. This time, there was a cry from out there in the crops. That got Hamdan's archers excited. They always drew encouragement from any reward their labours won.

Arrows flashed out from the village, one after another after another. Each man, hidden in whatever shadow he was, behind whatever barrel, loosed as fast as the drumbeat of his rhythm allowed. That was too much for those in the fields. Yulan watched them scurrying back towards safety, crouched almost double but more interested in haste than concealment this time. Only seven of them, Yulan was pleased to note, and one of those limping badly.

He could see Callotec himself riding up and down the lines of his men, gesticulating. A body of perhaps forty of them – levy, with a handful of Armsmen to lead them – began trotting away. They worked around the furthest edge of the fields, moving to settle perhaps halfway between Towers' Shadow and the low hill on which the Kingshouse stood. Another group, of similar size, skirted the village's other flank, making for a young, shrubby orchard. That took them, just, close enough to tempt a few arrows out. One of them even found its mark. But then the levymen were amongst the bushes, and safe for now.

Three prongs to the fork, Yulan mused. The sharpest of them would be the one to the fore, since the two on either side were mostly levy. Callotec had kept the best of his company by his side, out there on the road.

He ran back from his post, keeping close to the houses. He found Rudran and his few remaining men sitting patiently on their horses in one of the barns. They were passing out dry, floury biscuits. Yulan took one himself when it was offered, though it would probably wake rather than blunt his hunger.

"They mean to come from three sides," he told Rudran between bites. "Won't bode well if they can tie the knot, so we'll need to throw them off. There's around forty of them out between here and the Kingshouse, set to come in that way.

Levy. Can't have them reaching the village. You give me that, and I'll do what I can about the other two."

"Shouldn't be a problem," Rudran grunted.

Which was not true, and they both knew it, without Kerig to fortify them or their mounts.

"When you're done with them, I'd appreciate it if you could come back round and lend a hand with those marching straight up the track and down our gullets," Yulan said.

"All right," said Rudran.

Drann had always imagined battles to be urgent, frantic affairs. Not a moment to draw breath or order thoughts. He rather wished that had turned out to be true, but it seemed that now nobody was in a hurry to fight.

Sitting by the doorway of the barn, his view was obscured. Although he could tell that something was happening, because he glimpsed distant movement out beyond the fields and because he saw Yulan running with some message for Rudran's lancers, he had no clear idea of what it was. Callotec was encircling the village perhaps. That could hardly be anything other than bad.

Yet after that flurry of activity, nothing happened. Some of the villagers set aside their makeshift weapons and lay down in the hay of the barn. Drann wondered if he was supposed to prevent that. His own eyes were heavy, though. He had grown so accustomed to exhaustion and shortage of sleep that his guard was down. He rested his head against the frame of the barn door. Encircled his knees with his arms and interlaced his fingers. It was just warm enough, he thought dreamily. Any colder and he would need a blanket. He slept.

And was shaken awake, an unknown time later, by one of the villagers. The man had such a tight grip of Drann's upper arm it hurt. He hissed into his ear: "They're coming."

Callotec's own third of the attack would move first, Yulan assumed. That would be what the two bands out on either side were waiting to see. So it was, eventually. The ranks of Armsmen and Clade warriors closed up, and came marching forward in decent order.

The other two, lacking the training, would move more slowly and clumsily, he imagined. And so that was too. They were coming at the village across fields, with only the most meagre of footpaths to follow. Irrigation channels to jump or splash across. Well and good. He trusted to Rudran to shield his left flank. The men coming from the orchard upon his right would not be the ones that killed him, killed the Free and Towers' Shadow. It was those Armsmen coming right down the main track who would do that. They were the piece upon which this game turned.

Yulan stood on a handcart abandoned by one of the cottages to get a better sight of them. Sixty, he reckoned.

He whistled three times. The signal for arrows to the front. Hamdan's hidden bows obliged him. They were too few to do more than thin the first rank or two, but they did that well. Men stumbled. Dropped to their knees. Those around them kept coming, with hardly a break in their strides. They began to trot.

Yulan darted across the roadway to join Drann and the villagers at the barn. He knelt amongst them. So few, he thought. All he had, therefore it had to be enough.

"Won't be long now." He smiled at them. "We'll give these Hommetic bastards a sharp surprise and send them off with a kick twixt the legs."

It raised a few smiles in response, but they were false. Much too shallowly rooted to convince. He had not had the time to prepare these people for what was coming, to stir their hearts or sow the seeds of self-belief. They were fragile as frost jewels.

"You want to pat my head for luck?" he asked them.

They stared at him.

"Always works, doesn't it, Drann?" He grinned and ducked his head to show them all his smooth scalp. He slapped it himself, making the noise loud. "Smooth as a maiden's cheek."

"It does work," he heard Drann saying, and was grateful for it, since the youth had looked no happier than the rest of them a moment ago.

Drann gave his scalp a couple of quick pats. That was enough to crack the dam. The villagers shuffled and jostled to get close enough. Rained down slaps and taps on Yulan's head.

"Right, then," he said when they were done. "You're luck-heavy now, for sure. There's going to be fire, and when those folk out there pluck up the courage to step through it, me and Drann are going to make them wish they hadn't. You boys are coming along, and if any one of you gets to them before I do, I'll let you keep this bald head of mine for a trophy to hang on your wall. You won't, though. I'm the fastest runner you ever saw."

He heard Rudran going. Hoofbeats sweeping around, out of sight behind the buildings. He could see it easily enough in his imagination. The maces waving, the horses reaching. Bounding

over ditches, scything through the grain. The spears sprouting
to meet them. He put it out of his mind. He could change
nothing about any of that. Only what was before him, within
his reach.

The first of the Armsmen were almost at the outer ditch.
Almost into the village. Yulan could see Callotec riding at the
back of them. The man was no coward. No fool either, sadly,
as he held a tall shield high to guard his face and body. Two
arrows were already standing in it.

Yulan whistled twice. Waited. Watched the trot become a
charge. Watched those sixty fell warriors come running towards
him.

Flaming rags, knotted about stones, came out from between
the cottages. Every one of Hamdan's bow boys had a better
throwing arm than did Yulan, and not one of them missed. The
pennants of flame dipped down and disappeared into the pits
where dead men and horses still lay. Nothing happened.

Yulan held his breath. You could never be sure how this sort
of thing was going to work. How long it would take. The first
few swordsmen were rounding the pits, Yulan already surging
to his feet, when the flames took. The oil took. Fire licked and
then surged up from the trenches. Thick black smoke vomited
forth. Pitch and firewater and flesh caught light.

Yulan screamed wordlessly and raced for the nearest of his
enemies. Those following him – he was glad to hear their feet
there – took up the howl, as he had hoped. The stinking smoke
made his eyes blur even as he ran. What breeze there was should
carry it away from the village, but the heat was so intense it
churned the air and sent curls of acrid, stench-laden smoke

rolling in all directions. He did not need to see clearly to do what he did.

He spun and slashed, lunged one way and then another. Cut a man across the face, hamstrung a second. He gave himself up to this dance he knew so well and let it possess him and carry him. He was the still and unthinking observer of the carnage his body wrought upon his foes.

Searing heat washed over him, and coils of black vapour swept down towards his face, so he swung about to judge the fate of those who had come after him. He found Drann close behind him, his spear stuck in the belly of an Armsmen who refused to fall, who was lashing out with a sword that cut the air no more than an inch from Drann's face. Yulan stepped up and hacked his own blade into the back of the Armsman's neck.

The villagers were falling back, not out of fear but to escape the foul stench of burning meat and the blinding smoke. They had overrun a couple of Callotec's men, leaving their pierced and ragged bodies in their wake as they retreated. Leaving one or two of their own as well. Drann was still struggling to free his spear from the fallen man's stomach. Yulan stood on the corpse to hold it down and snarled: "Pull harder."

Drann staggered backwards as his spear sprang out from the grip of dead flesh. He drew his sleeve across his eyes to wipe away the tears the needling smoke had called forth. He gagged as bile surged in his throat, not knowing whether it was summoned by the stink of burning flesh or the act of killing a man.

That thought was snatched away, for as his eyes cleared he beheld the smoke coming for him. Not as a formless cloud, but a huge bunched fist. It hit him square in the chest and knocked him from his feet. He flew backwards, arms and legs flailing, and landed hard. Yulan ducked under the sweeping black limb and ran to him, hauled him to his feet.

"It's a Clever," he hissed. "They've still got a Clever."

Together they backed away from the wall of smoke that was no longer rising but swelling and sinking, flinging out thick tendrils that swept back and forth like blind snakes seeking prey. One found the last two laggards from amongst the villagers, slower than their fellows to fall back. It toppled them and writhed around and pounded down on one of them, crushing him to the ground.

Drann staggered forward, still fighting for breath, and seized one of the man's arms that extended from under the black cloud. He pulled, but could not move him. Yulan dragged him away.

"Leave him. He's dead. Can't fight this."

And then, suddenly, they did not need to fight it. Every semblance of form and solidity to the great mass of smoke fell away as if it had never been there. It dissipated. Became once more nothing but the product of the fires, streaming up and drifting.

"Stand still," Yulan was shouting to the villagers. "Keep together and stand firm. You live if you keep together."

Dazed, feeling as if his mind was drifting somewhere close to but no longer within his body, Drann went to stand with them. He could think of nowhere else to go but amongst them. Nothing else to do but hold his spear ready. Yulan stood beside them. He did not seem to be breathing hard. Drann was gasping. The smoke was scratching and burning in his chest.

The first ferocity of the fires set in the pits was dwindling as the oil burned away. The corpses still threw up a few gouts of flame, but that initial conflagration was spent. The Armsmen came through the smoke again.

"Charge them!' cried Yulan, and rushed forward.

Drann went with him. Some of the villagers did too. Not all, Drann was dimly aware, but he could not look back. He ran at a swordsman, missed the mark and watched the point of his spear go wide. The sword came sweeping down towards his shoulder. Yulan's shield caught it before it could strike home. He bore Drann's assailant backwards, through a sweeping veil of smoke and out of sight.

Drann made to follow, but he stumbled on a fallen helmet, his ankle turning painfully. He almost fell. Suddenly there was another of Callotec's warriors rushing down on him, this one bare-headed, smoke-blackened, wielding a cudgel. Drann lurched out of the way and tried to fend off a blow from that wicked club with his spear. It was knocked from his hands, stinging his palms. He grappled with the man, fumbling for a hold on his weapon arm, and to dig at his eyes.

The two of them tumbled down. Drann managed to get a knee across the man's arm, another on to his throat. But he could already tell he was not strong enough to make this work. A hand seized the front of his jerkin and he knew he would be thrown away in mere moments. He glimpsed the rolling helmet, still loose on the ground. He snatched it up and hammered it, over and over, into the face of his opponent.

One of the villagers pulled him off the limp form – dead or unconscious Drann did not know – and pressed his spear back into his hands. They plunged together through smoke and flame, to emerge on to the path where it crossed the village's ditch. And there they found Callotec's men streaming away, Rudran and four of his lancers plunging back and forth through the last of them, laying all around them with their maces.

Yulan was standing in the centre of the track. Three dead men lay before him. Villagers were on either side of him, coughing and retching. One was cheering.

"Rudran!' Yulan shouted. "Rudran! Break off!"

The lancers must have heard, even through the din of their pursuit, for they came galloping back at once. Rudran was leaning low and lopsided, pressing one arm in against his side. Drann sat heavily down.

"Get your wound tended," Yulan said to Rudran. "Is this all of you?"

The huge man only nodded, and rode slowly past the guttering fires, through the smoke and into the village.

"Anyone seen Hamdan?" Yulan asked, looking this way and that.

He sounded calm, but Drann thought there might be a flicker of fear there, not far beneath the surface.

The archer came striding, sodden, up out of the fields. He was covered from crown to toe in mud and flecks of grass and leaves. He was grinning.

"Told me to hunt Clevers, didn't you? Was never going to be able to do that except out there."

"I'm guessing it was a good hunt," said Yulan.

"I'd say so. Everybody was so busy trying to kill you, I got close enough to that wagon out there to try a long shot. Lucky

I was there. Saw someone sitting under that tree who looked a lot like he might be playing some games with an entelech. Couldn't really tell what was happening, since I was breast deep in a ditch at the time, but was it the smoke?"

"It was," grunted Yulan, putting an arm round Hamdan's shoulder. "Might have undone us, if it hadn't stopped as soon as it started."

"That'd be because I put an arrow in his eye."

Yulan gave a little laugh, and one or two of the villagers took it up.

"Back to shelter," Yulan said, and shepherded them all towards the houses.

Drann glanced into one of the fire pits as he passed. He could hardly tell what had been in there now. It was just a mass of charcoaled flesh, all crisped together.

"What happened out on the flanks?" Yulan was asking Hamdan. "You see any of that?"

"Not much. Saw Rudran turn up to lend you a hand, so I'm guessing they won their little discussion. The other lot, out by the orchard, just turned about and ran back for the wagon once I shot a couple of them and they saw the fire. No stomach for it."

Drann could understand that. He would never think ill of anyone who fled in the face of this, he thought. Not all the stories in the world could hide its cruel misery. He took that misery and folded it away, buried it deep inside. Not to be forgotten, he resolved.

They were granted the boon of some small time to bathe wounds, and take food. Count their dead. Four of Rudran's horsemen had fallen to the spears of their foes before they managed to drive them off. Rudran himself had taken a sore wound on his hip. Drann thought he glimpsed bone there, before Hamdan pressed a bandage in place.

Lebid had an arrow in him. Right through the meat of his forearm. He made no sound when Hamdan broke both ends of it away and pulled the stub clean through and out, but sweat beaded across his brow. There were only ten of the village men still willing to fight. The rest were either dead or had slipped away, disliking this taste of what it meant to be the Free.

The sadness was that there was fighting still to do. Looking out over the fields, Drann could see close to a hundred men massing around the lone tree, and the wagon beside it. What he had thought a great victory, as he watched those same men tumbling back from the village, flying for their lives, had been but a staying of the execution. Many of the Hommetics had been killed. Others had flown. Too many remained, he feared. Far too many.

Then Hamdan was laughing behind him. Whooping, bizarrely. Drann made to turn about and see what was happening, but then he understood, and could have whooped himself.

Up on the ridge beyond Callotec's band, a familiar shape was breaching the crest. A wagon with a heavy cargo, hauled by an animal too broad and stout to be a horse. There were riders coming up alongside it. Shouts of alarm and command told them that Callotec and his men had seen these new arrivals too. There was sudden movement, shifting and turning to face both village and ridge.

Up there, two or three of the riders had dismounted. They were busying themselves about the wagon. Loosening and pulling back canvas sheeting, Drann knew. Opening a cage.

35

Witness

The Clamour came down from the hill like a bounding, leaping boulder. Or some knotted thundercloud fallen from the sky. It was too far away for Drann to make it out clearly, but it put him in mind of a vast, grotesque naked ape rushing down on foot and knuckle. And he heard it. Heard its rising, keening call as it came.

A sound unlike anything he had ever known before. Not one sound, but many all woven together like rope. A thick, piercing wail of anger and hunger. It was a dagger, a physical pain knifing deep into Drann's skull. He clapped his hands over his ears, pressed them flat. It made hardly any difference. The cry came through his flesh and bone.

Callotec's men did just as Drann would have done, had he been out there on the flat ground with them. They scattered. In all directions, in disorder. They fled as fast as their legs would work, and it was not fast enough, for the Clamour was lightning as well as thunder. Bursting down upon them and amongst them.

Drann saw bodies flung high into the air, spinning with arms and legs splayed. He saw huge sweeps of those monstrous arms cast aside two, three men at a time. He saw a horse beaten down, first on to its haunches and then to the ground, by a flurry of terrible blows. Then raised up and flung, to break against the side of the wagon.

The Clamour surged this way and that, relentless. Insatiable. A storm had come for those hundred men, and it consumed them. Some tried to fight it. Drann saw men who knew there was no escaping the horror at their backs turn to face it and attack it with blades, wound it with arrows. They went down, all of them. Torn apart. Flung away. Crushed.

The Free gathered, at the edge of the village, and bore witness to this. The Clamour was theirs, after all. One of them, in its awful way. Standing there, Drann realised that this was what he had fought alongside them to bring about. This was what the villagers who had helped them had, without knowing it, died to bring about. This wild slaughter.

The Clamour caught up the wagon, raised it. The horse still harnessed to it was lifted off the ground. It twisted and writhed, to no avail. Horse and wagon alike were beaten against the ground, again and again, until the first was still, the second shattered into a thousand thousand splinters.

"The Bereaved," Drann wondered. "Shouldn't we . . .?"

"Nothing we can do," Yulan said beside him. Loud, to cut through the Clamour's howl. "We go out there, we die at the Clamour's hands just like all the rest."

"Can't Hestin . . .?"

"She cannot control it. She's surrendered that, released it to its natural state. This is the Clamour as it is. That's the peril, always: we can never know, she can never know, whether she can take hold of it again and subdue it. Each time it becomes harder. One day, it'll run free and rage on, doing this and only this wherever it goes. That's what she's protected the world against, these last few years. That's what I make her risk, when I ask her to set it loose."

And by the time that had been spoken, the killing was all but done. There were men running still, back down the road and up the surrounding slopes. A few of them. The Clamour ranged to and fro, hunting them. Wailing.

One group held together. A single rider, with eight or nine Armsmen running alongside him. Surrounding him. Making for the escarpment and the road that climbed it.

"Callotec," said Yulan. "Archers!"

Drann watched them gallop out to intercept that last desperate attempt at escape. He kept glancing nervously back to the still raging Clamour. That was why he saw Akrana, and the four lancers who had stayed with her, coming cautiously down from the ridge. He could just make out other figures hunched behind two of the riders. Hestin and Kerig.

He looked back towards Yulan and the others. Saw Hamdan and the archers, darting out unerringly accurate arrows as they rode, fell one, two, three of Callotec's escorting guards. And Callotec's own horse, in the end. They feathered its neck with arrows, until it stumbled and collapsed and threw the last heir to the Hommetic throne to the ground.

"It's coming," Lebid said.

He was standing close by, arm in a sling, watching not the

winning of the prize they had come so far to claim but the Clamour. He was right. It was lumbering along the track towards the village. Closer now, Drann could see its distorted, cankered face. The growths and pits that marred its blotched skin. The hugeness of it, arms like tree trunks punching down, shoulders like barrels.

He began to back away. They all did. But the Clamour slowed. It faltered. Sank down. It dropped its head and grew still. Silence descended. Drann could hear a bird singing, somewhere high up in the sky.

Akrana brought the Bereaved and a prisoner into the village. The Permanence had a heavy cloak over it and about it. Yulan could see pale skin, though. Naked, wasted legs. It was such a small thing. So fearfully small, to be the cause and object of such terrible slaughter. To have held an empire at bay for so many years.

The prisoner was not a warrior. He had fine features, and a slight build. A Clever, Yulan supposed. Who now slept. Akrana laid him out on the floor of one of the barns. The Bereaved sat beside him. Pliant and inert. Yulan wondered if he should fear it, and perhaps fly from its very presence. It had killed thousands in its time, after all. Far more, many times more, than the Clamour ever had. It was the very embodiment of plague and pestilence, the stuff of which those afflictions were made. Yet it sat there and did nothing and seemed no more frightful than a harmless, maimed child. He could not fear it, because of that and because a strange sort of elation was filling him. A giddiness, as of a man suddenly allowed to breathe after holding mouth and nose shut for too long.

"Kasuman," Akrana said to him, flicking a contemptuous finger at the slumbering Clever. "I found him with the Bereaved, hiding behind that tree out there. Whispering in its ear, so I thought it best he should sleep. I was inclined to kill him, but that might be for you to choose."

Looking at her now, Yulan saw that her face was tight with concentration and effort.

"Keep him asleep," he said. "Can you do that?"

"For as long as you like. It is not hard."

He was not certain how much faith to put in that claim.

"It might be we'll be bargaining with the School, now we hold the Bereaved," he said. "Perhaps Kasuman can be a part of that. Perhaps they'll want him too. Keep them well separated, though. I'll have Rudran and Lebid watch over the Bereaved in one of the cottages. They both of them need to stay still and quiet for a while in any case."

Yulan rubbed his eyes and rolled his shoulders. They felt loose. His next thought put a cord of tightness back into them, though.

"But we need to deal with Callotec first," he said.

Callotec was just as he had appeared when last Yulan saw him. Subdued, now, with none of his bluster to create the illusion of authority. Someone who did not know his name would not have guessed him to be a man of such consequence, Yulan suspected. Yet the loathing and contempt that Yulan felt welling up inside him, chasing away all that earlier elation, said he must be of consequence, somehow.

He stood in the centre of the village, with the six men who had been beside him to the very last. All of them had been stripped of sword and shield and helmet. They stood in grim silence, facing twelve of the Free. Archers, lancers, Hamdan and Yulan and Akrana all stood in a single line, staring at Callotec. Drann was not there, Yulan noticed. He looked around, and saw the contract-holder standing some way further back, his hand absently resting on the parchment case at his belt that had begun all this.

"I suppose I should be honoured, to have so many of the Free gathered here on my account," the last of the Hommetic line said sneeringly.

"Honour has nothing to do with it," Yulan said.

"No? Well, perhaps you are correct." Callotec shrugged. "We always had different ideas about the meaning of honour, you and I. Do you think you've finally won, Captain of the Free?"

"No," said Yulan. "But I think you've finally lost."

He regarded the six Armsmen who stood alongside Callotec. One or two of them looked afraid.

"You men can go," Yulan said. "We don't need you."

They hesitated. Doubt was in their eyes.

"Go!" Hamdan shouted, brandishing his arms, and they were off like hares.

Because Yulan knew the archer as well as he did any man in the world, he could hear the fury in that cry and knew its target. The guilt and hatred that had brought the Free to this moment were not Yulan's alone. They never had been.

"Get back here!" Callotec howled after the disappearing warriors, but no one was listening to him. Not any more.

The six men scattered over the battlefield, scavenging horses, riding off. None of them looked back. Callotec glared after them in barely suppressed rage. His shoulders shook, just a little. There was a tear at the corner of his eye, Yulan noticed. He could not tell whether it was born of anger, or fear, or disbelief. Eventually, the Dog-Lord turned back and faced his captors. He folded his arms across his chest.

"I do not fear you," he said.

Yulan did not believe that. He looked at the beaten man and found it ever harder, with each passing heartbeat, to summon up that loathing he had once thought limitless, eternal. Callotec was spent, and could hurt no one now.

"Do you regret what you've done?" Yulan asked him quietly.

Callotec frowned at him.

"Regret?"

"Never mind. Tie his hands. We'll take him back to Creel."

"No!' cried Callotec as soon as Hamdan took a step forward to do as he was bid. "I will not go back to Armadell-on-Lake. If I do, they will make a spectacle, or gaming piece, of me and one day they will torture me to death. Perhaps cut me up into parts, as they did my cousin, and spike each of those parts above some city gate. No!"

"We have a contract," Yulan said wearily. He was terribly tired of this man now. This small man who had for too long cast such a shadow over Yulan's life, over the village in which he now stood. "You go to Creel of Mondoon. I do not know or care what he will do with you, beyond the fact that you are most likely right: it will not be gentle, in the end."

"Do you not care? You lie!' spat Callotec. "You always cared too much, didn't you, brown-skin? That's why you're here now, because you never did learn that what's done cannot be undone, and you never could bear the thought of the tide bringing me back ... "

Hamdan's sword was in his hand. He rushed forward, raising the blade and reaching with it for Callotec's neck. The Dog-Lord would have died then, and none was more surprised than Yulan that it was he who prevented it. He caught Hamdan's arm and held it. There was a passing instant of struggle between the archer's ire and Yulan's certainty, as Callotec shrank away from the two of them. Then Hamdan yielded.

"There's none shares the instinct more than me," Yulan said quietly to his friend, "but when it comes to it, I find I'd not have the last deed of the Free, under their last contract, be the petty vengeance of killing a beaten man who has no means of defending himself."

Hamdan settled his sword back into its sheath. He averted his eyes from Callotec, regarding the dry dust beneath his feet.

"Let his blood lie on the hands of others, if that is what they want," Yulan breathed. "I think I'll walk away from here a little taller, knowing that at the last, we chose to keep our hands unmarred. We have done what we came to do. Let that be enough."

"As you wish," Hamdan said, almost tenderly, and he turned and walked away.

36

And Still They Came

If the Bereaved was unsettling rather than frightful to be close to, it seemed to Drann that the Clamour was nothing less than appalling. Its wagon had been laboriously brought down into the village, but the great Permanence could not yet be returned to its cage, since Hestin still fought for the control without which there could be no safety for any of them.

Her cloak, the beacon of her strength and token of the surety with which she held the beast, was brown. The edges of its leaves were curling. It teetered upon the verge of disintegration. The old woman who was not old knelt before the Clamour, out on the path through the fields. Yulan knelt beside her, murmuring to her. Drann stood a short distance behind her.

Close enough to feel the Clamour's heat. Hear its heavy, grinding breathing. Close enough to understand for the first time just how massive it was. It was hunched down, yet still huge. Its head was turned slightly to one side, so that he could see some part of its face. Mucus hung in strands from flat, open nostrils. Saliva trailed from a lipless mouth studded with black, broken teeth.

Its skin was nowhere smooth. It was strewn with humps and hollows. Studded with great boil-like pustules as if the fury within seeped out and corrupted its hide.

"He sinks," Drann heard Hestin say faintly. "Sleeps. Small."

Yulan straightened and stretched his back.

"Come away," he told Drann, and led him back towards the village. "She'll walk it in when she can. We all need rest now. It's been hard to come by of late."

"Why does she call it 'he' all the time?" Drann asked as they walked along the track. As he had asked before, and had had no answer.

"Because her father made it," Yulan said simply. "He died making it. She thinks it her last connection to him. She thinks herself bound to protect the world against it."

"But it's not him."

"No. He's dead. It's the Aestival. That's all. That's more than enough."

Drann did sleep, eventually. In a bed in one of the cottages, which the villagers told him he could have. They had wanted to send to bring their families back out of hiding, but Yulan had forbidden it.

"Not until we're gone," he had said. "Tomorrow we'll be away, and you can have this place back. Tonight, there are Permanences here, and they're neither of them safe."

That was what he had said. But Drann caught the scent of other cares, other intents. Callotec was here, bound and secured in one of the houses, and the men of Towers' Shadow knew it.

They wanted the man's life, and for reasons Drann did not fully understand, Yulan thought it better that their captive should live. He had somehow persuaded those few villagers still here of the wisdom in mercy, but surely could not be certain of his ability to sway four or five times as many.

So – whatever the reasons – there remained a multitude of empty houses, empty beds. Drann lay in the one he had been given, and closed his eyes and saw, endlessly, the face of the man he had impaled.

Thick eyebrows, with flecks of grey. He had been about the same age as Drann's father, whose spear had been in his belly. Moles beside his mouth. A faint scar running up one side of his nose. Brown eyes. Drann could not have recalled the eye colour of any but a handful of the people he had met in his life. Yet he would never forget that this man had brown eyes.

Had he not been utterly exhausted, tired in a deadening way unlike anything he had felt before, these visions would have kept him from sleep all through the night. His weariness overcame even that, and at last sent him into a dreamless sleep.

He was woken by light streaming in through a window, for he had not thought to close any shutters. He could tell by the quality and strength of that light that dawn was long gone. Swinging his legs round and over the edge of the bed, he found himself to be more renewed, more refreshed than he had felt in a long time. He yawned and stretched. Outside the window, he could hear chickens clucking and pecking. That sound put a smile on his face with its simple familiarity.

Outside, Hamdan was grooming the horses, which were neatly lined up. Some were already saddled. Further down the track stood the Clamour's wagon. Drann was surprised, and slightly alarmed, to see that the Permanence was still not caged. It sat there by the wagon, Hestin next to it. Her cloak had recovered some of its green hue, though. She had mastered the beast.

"What's happening?" Drann asked Hamdan, stretching again.

"Yulan'll be telling us that once he's decided." Hamdan nodded to one of the nearby houses. "Him and Akrana are talking it out now. They'll dig up an idea or two, no doubt."

"Back to Creel?" suggested Drann.

Hamdan snorted, combing away vigorously at a bay horse's hide.

"Oh, no. You really think life's so easy? No, there's the small matter of finding out where we stand with the School. Finding out whether we're still in a war, and how we might win it."

That dulled Drann's humour somewhat. He wandered across to the well and splashed water on his face. Lebid and another of the archers were there, filling water skins.

"Lazy-a-bed," Lebid taunted Drann good-naturedly.

"I'd be lazy-a-bed every day for the rest of my life if I could," Drann said.

"Boy's a sage," Lebid smiled.

There was a tiny splinter of guilt under Drann's conscience, in truth. He was the last by a long way to rise. Everyone seemed ready to leave at a moment's notice, save him.

He made his way back to his bed, and began to roll up and bind the blankets. One of the villagers, the youngest of those who had fought alongside him, appeared in the doorway. Drann looked up and nodded to him. The youth returned the gesture but said nothing. Satisfied with the state of his bedding, Drann straightened. His belt was digging into his side, so he loosened it and rebuckled it.

"Who're they?" the youth at the door asked.

"Who're who?" Drann said without looking round. He could not get the case holding Creel's contract to close properly. It had taken a blow of some sort during the fighting, and the damage left it loose. He found that more annoying than was reasonable.

"Them up there," the youth said.

Drann glanced at him, just a little irritated. More with the case than the villager. Who was pointing up at the ridge beyond the Old Threetower Road, over which Drann had ridden into Towers' Shadow. Upon which the Clamour had appeared to save them. Drann went to lean out of the doorway and look up there. He frowned.

There were perhaps twenty or thirty riders on the skyline, strung out in a long line. Then more. More and more figures appearing, extending that line further along the ridge's crest. Thickening it as they filled in gaps. Drann stood up.

"Who d'you think they are?" asked the youth again, all curiosity.

Curiosity was not what Drann felt. He felt sick. A hundred, he thought. And still they came. He stumbled out into the road, almost tripping as he went. Two hundred. With a blue hint to many of their tunics. Still coming. He spun about and ran for the cottage where Yulan and Akrana were in discussion.

He was almost knocked down by Yulan himself, bursting out through the doorway with Kerig cradled in his arms.

"The School . . ." Drann stammered, pointing.

Yulan ignored him.

"Run!' he cried. "Ride, those who can. All of you to the Kingshouse! Take nothing but what you hold. Run!"

37

Fools

The Kingshouse had not been made to house many men. In its dilapidated state, its capacities were still further reduced. All but the most irretrievably rotten of the floorboards had been torn up and carried away. The rooms, just two to each floor, were damp and cobwebbed. There were holes in the walls.

Rudran, drifting in and out of consciousness, Kerig and Hestin were stowed away on the uppermost of the three floors. Kasuman slumbered alone below that, with Akrana watching over him from the parapet outside. And on that parapet, laid out on the flagstones at her feet, was Callotec. Bound and gagged. Yulan had told her – softly, with no one else to hear – to kill the man at the last, if the day was lost.

He felt diminished by that command. It had taken no small will to save Callotec from Hamdan's wrath, and the even more just wrath of the people of Towers' Shadow; yet he had not hesitated to set constraints, and limits, upon that salvation. He could not countenance the possibility of Callotec outliving the

Free, or worse yet somehow escaping captivity entirely through ruse or treachery or guile. The man must go to Creel, or die. Yulan could conceive of no other outcome. He had led people to their deaths – some already met, some most likely soon to come – and Callotec was somewhere at the root of that. The cause of it. And the sense-summoning answer to it. Wasn't he?

At the foot of the keep, the Clamour waited. Yulan very much feared that he might need it. Already, it was restless, shifting and snuffling in its leadenly titanic way. That did not bode well.

The Bereaved was hidden away in a corner of the tiny, crude stable – nothing more than a sloping roof held up by wooden struts, in truth – crammed in amongst the few horses the Free had managed to get to the Kingshouse. More had slipped their grasp in the confusion and haste.

Yulan had known when he sent everyone rushing to this tiny fortress that the Clamour's wagon would not pass through the narrow gate in its encircling wall. They had carried the Clamour up here in its cage, Hestin driving the bull faster and harder over that short distance than ever she had before, and then abandoned cage, wagon and bull alike outside the wall. They were there still, the bull despondently cropping the grass.

And beyond it, down at the foot of the hill, was the doom that had come to claim the Free. Yulan, standing on the walkway behind the Kingshouse's ring wall, had stopped counting them once he got beyond two hundred, and saw many more still arriving. It would gain him nothing to learn the full extent of what opposed him.

Sullen made no attempt to conceal himself. He rode back

and forth behind the spreading lines of his Clade warriors as they arrayed themselves in a long arc around the hillock. No blue tunic, no badges for him, the corsair boy grown to be commander of the School's army. He still wore those same dull and ragged clothes, those same braids and beads in a half-head of hair, that he had when pretending to be one of the Free. If Yulan had to guess, he would say that Sullen pretended still. He was no more one of the Clade than he had been of the Free. He was, as he had probably always been from the moment of his birth, unlike other people, unwedded to their cares and concerns. A lone beast, stalking through the forest of humanity; imitating those around him with all the skills of a finely honed predator, but never truly belonging. Perhaps the School would come to see that too, after all of this was done.

Sullen did not, at least, appear to have brought many Clevers with him. There were two or three unmartial-looking figures down there, setting a camp slightly separate from the rest. Small, and hunched and cloaked. Other than that, it was swords and bows and spears and axes, all around and everywhere.

Yulan lifted his eye to the vertiginous towers that stood in mute observance of the scene. High up and far away, but still dominant. Still speaking of greater works than the rude and low struggle to be played out beneath them. Carrion birds were spilling down from the tops of those towers. Gliding on wide wings down and down, along the face of the escarpment, and settling in the fields around Towers' Shadow. Come at last to feast on yesterday's work, while those in and around the Kingshouse prepared another banquet for the morrow.

He had thought he would feel despair, standing here and looking out upon the ruin of all his hopes. Yet he did not. Towers' Shadow stood, and would stay standing, for Sullen cared not one whit for that place or its people. The host arrayed before the walls overmatched the Free, but still they had the Clamour, and Akrana. There was hope still to be found, if the search was diligent enough.

Drann came along the wooden walkway and joined him. Together, they looked out upon the gathering of the Clade.

"You have to send them away," Drann said at length, and then added when Yulan looked questioningly at him: "The villagers. You've ten men in here with no cause to die for. They don't belong."

"I see," Yulan said.

Drann faced him with stern certainty. No trace of doubt, or admiration, or awe. Not a flicker of yearning to belong in those eyes, Yulan thought. Good.

"It's not their fight," Drann insisted. "It's not about saving their village any more, not about saving everyone from the Orphans. That's done. This is the Free and the School."

"That it is," Yulan agreed. "You think I should parley, then."

"I do."

"I had Hamdan send a message arrow out a few minutes ago," Yulan smiled. "The Free don't need others to die for us. We do that for ourselves, when it's needed."

Yulan came out from the gate of the Kingshouse on to the bare hillside. Perhaps the rashest act of his entire life, as both Hamdan and Akrana had explained to him at great and angry length. He did not disagree, but nor did it concern him. He felt liberated from thoughts of consequence, and what he might gain from this risk felt more than sufficient justification for it. Lives were precious, after all. They were worth fighting for, and sometimes perhaps you could fight for them by talking.

And there was, too, the conviction within him that Sullen would not try to kill him now. Not when so many others he no doubt wanted dead remained behind the walls of the Kingshouse, and when Sullen had an army to do the killing of them for him. He watched the man, the traitor, striding up the slope towards him. Coming to parley, as Yulan had suspected he would if given the chance. Out of arrogance, self-importance, curiosity. In search of the pleasure he would derive from baiting a cornered quarry.

"Close enough," Yulan said, when Sullen was twenty or so paces below him.

Sullen came to a halt and spread his empty hands.

"Here I am, Captain," he said. "Is someone going to put an arrow in me now?"

"No one's going to try to kill you," Yulan said.

He could have closed the gap in little more time than it took to think it. There his foresight failed him, for he could not see clearly what would happen. He knew Sullen could match him, perhaps better him, once blades were drawn.

And if he attempted it, even if he succeeded in it, Yulan would know that he had not truly tried to avert what would come after. Every death – the Free, the villagers – would be one more regret for him to remember and carry through what remained of his life, however brief that might be. He had enough of those already. For the same reason, he had refused

Hamdan's pleas to be allowed to skewer Sullen's throat with an arrow from the wall. So he would attempt something still more difficult than killing Sullen. Bargaining with him.

"I saw a flock of birds unlike any I've seen before as we rode up here," said Sullen calmly. "A long way off, but I saw it pass through the roof of a forest. I heard trees falling, I think. Would that be Wren's doing, perhaps? Her legacy to the world?"

Yulan said nothing to that. Sullen was undeterred.

"Her gone. Kerig a ruin, I imagine. You've spent your Clevers freely this time, Yulan. Only got that white-haired witch I bled back at White Steading still to call on. Is that right?"

"The Clamour, if you leave me without choice."

"Yes, of course."

Not a flicker of concern at the invocation of that terrible Permanence, Yulan noted. No chinks in Sullen's dour armour.

"I will yield the Bereaved to you, to the School, if you stand aside," Yulan said.

"Certainly. Bring it out and you can be on your way. That is all the Mistress of the School seeks. The Bereaved."

Yulan stared at him. Sullen did not look away. The intensity of Yulan's gaze could find no purchase on those dead eyes. It spilled from their impermeable sheen.

"Usually I know when a man is lying to me," Yulan sighed. "Not you. I never could tell with certainty, no matter how I suspected it. I think it's because there's no part of you, not the faintest memory, that knows or cares what honesty is. Nothing to stir when you lie, and betray you."

"You might be right."

"I know you're lying this time, though. Whatever that poor

fool of a Mistress imagines, your desires have never really trod-den the same path as the School's. It would break your dead heart to see us walk away from this, wouldn't it? And in any case, whatever Wren did to bring Kerig out from your grasp, I don't suppose the School is likely to forgive or forget that, are they?"

"Think what you will," Sullen said with indifference.

"I've eleven men of the village in there. I want to send them away. They're of no interest to you."

Sullen's eyes narrowed just a touch. The workings of that rep-tile mind.

"I don't find anyone interesting, Yulan. Not even you. But yes, you can march your levies out if it pleases some notion of mercy you hold dear. It'll speed along the end to all this, so I could hardly object."

"Why do you need that ending so badly? What is it that's eating you inside out, that won't let you turn aside?"

"I don't need anything. I want it. You, the Free, are the one and only time I've failed in an undertaking. You're the only ones to have slipped through my fingers. I've greatly enjoyed my service in the Clade. The School, after all, gives me licence to indulge my pleasures."

"And makes you feel important, no doubt," Yulan grunted.

"But they shrink from the final step against you. Even after I killed Merkent, they couldn't see that it no longer mattered what Crex thought, what the law dictated. They or you must pass from the world. I waited a long time for the circumstances to arise that might bring about what was necessary. I do under-stand these things, you see. Kill or be killed. I understand that.

"I've understood it since that day at White Steading. Since I put a blade in Merkent's belly. Because I know you, Yulan, and I know your lackeys. I understood that some day, somehow, you would come for me. You, or Akrana, or that little archer friend of yours; one of you would find me and kill me. Whatever it meant for the Free, however much wrath it brought down on you, you would eventually find a way. That's what you like to tell yourselves, isn't it? The Free will find a way."

"True," Yulan acknowledged.

"Now you see' – Sullen gestured behind him without looking round – "I have brought all these fine men to kill you first, because I have no wish to die. Not yet. I'm not finished with the world."

"You've no ambition but to spread hurt and havoc and harm. You can mime reason and life, but they're not in you. The world has no use for a blight such as you, Sullen."

"No? We'll see, won't we? We'll see whose nature is the stronger."

"I would have bested you then, on that bridge, if you hadn't thrown yourself into the river. I had already bested you. I'll do it again."

Yulan did not imagine that goading this soulless shell before him would serve any great purpose. Nor did it seem likely to do any harm.

"Recollections can differ. I'm still here, after all, and Merkent's still dead. I feel unbested. Certainly today, because the truth is a simple one here, isn't it? You waited too long, Yulan. If you had come for me first, then perhaps you might have had the better of it. But you didn't. I'm the first to make the lunge, and so here we are, with most of the Free scattered and hiding, the last of it penned up in this absurd little turret of a castle, waiting to die.

"And I've had a great deal of time to prepare for this day. For the Free. I have given it much thought. Do you know what I concluded?"

Yulan shook his head. He had what he wanted, if the villagers could come out of this alive. Further sparring would win him no more ground.

"I think I can beat you," Sullen said. "I can't be sure, of course. We know, men like you and me, that in such a game there cannot be certainty. But I think I can. I think I know how."

And that did set loose a flutter of doubt in Yulan's breast. It felt incautious, ill judged. Neither of which were traits he would hang upon Sullen's shoulders. It might be a lie, of course. But there was something about it that had a more subtle, more grey scent. And one fragment of truth it most certainly contained: Sullen would have been anticipating this day, preparing himself for it, for years.

If he could not instil doubt, but only acquire it himself, Yulan knew there was no purpose in further delay.

"I'll send the villagers out," he said, and turned on his heel. He walked up towards the gate. His back tense and exposed. Readying itself for injury. Sullen had only words to fling, though.

"Do it quickly, would you? Don't play me for a fool, or I might take against you."

Yulan sought Drann out as the villagers gathered beside the postern gate at the rear of the Kingshouse.

"I told Sullen there were eleven villagers," he said. "This isn't your fight, any more than it's theirs. The only ones out there who might recognise you are Sullen himself and the men with him when Kerig was taken. Sullen's on the other side of our little hill, and he'll have his trusted men at his side. So it's past time for you to take your leave of the Free."

The young man did not look offended, as Yulan had feared he might, so much as puzzled.

"If I'd stopped Sullen when he came for Kerig, if I'd brought Wren back from the drowning pool, maybe none of this'd be happening. Maybe it is my fight."

"Two answers to that," Yulan said, shaking his head. "First, ifs are—"

"Hares. I know."

Yulan frowned. "Hares?"

"Ifs are hares, Akrana told me once."

That did sound very much like the sort of thing Akrana would say, Yulan acknowledged. She had turned the horrifying wound of her lost childhood into a scar, ever present but not crippling, by ruthlessly narrowing her vision. No looking back, or ahead. Watching only her own feet on the path. No wondering what might have been, or what might yet be, because she could not bear to trust either of those things.

"I was going to say they're chains. There's more than enough other folk willing to set chains upon you, one way or another. No need to add to them with ones you forge yourself out of things that didn't happen. Right or wrong, done is done.

Sometimes you can try to mend it, and you can certainly regret it, but you can never undo it, so don't waste time imagining it undone.

"Second, you know as well as I do, there's not a thing you could have done to stop all this. These people – Sullen, Kerig, Wren – they're not so easily turned from their chosen paths. Not by the likes of you. Not even the likes of me."

"Even so," Drann stubbornly persisted. "You saved my life yesterday. It might be you saved everybody's life, from here to Armadell, when you took the Bereaved away from Callotec. And they're going to kill you anyway, aren't they? Sullen and the rest. Even if you gave them the Bereaved, they would kill you."

"They would try," Yulan nodded.

"I'll stay. I can make it my fight. I can choose that, can't I?"

"All are allowed to choose to be fools," Yulan smiled. "I think we spend half of our lives that way, don't you? I've a better idea, though. You can do me one last service, one that matters."

Drann raised his eyebrows questioningly.

"Walk out of that gate, with the villagers. Keep your face down if you can, but if anyone asks, you're an exile from the north who's made a home here. Get one or two of the others to agree your tale, and it will be fine. And once you're out there, find some safe place not too far away and wait to see what happens. Watch the last day of the Free, because one way or the other, that's what it will be. The end of us, by our choice or by Sullen's.

"And when it's all done, go to Creel of Mondoon and tell him everything that's happened, from the day we rode out of his camp. He's the only one of the Council worth anything. And he'll pay you well for the story, if I know him at all. After that, go back to your home, and as you go, you can tell anyone and everyone the tale of the last day of the Free, because it'll be a tale worth the telling and we'll want it told. Whatever happens, we'll want it told."

Yulan had thought that Sullen would come as soon as the villagers were away. He did not. His ranks did not move from their posts at the foot of the hill. That was puzzling. But then Sullen was not entirely like other men. There was nothing to do but wait. Yulan did it atop the keep, sitting with his back to the uppermost battlements. He could hear, rising up from below, the faint and indistinct sound of Callotec snarling abuse at Akrana, through the dirty cloth that gagged him. That made Yulan bitter, and prey to bleak thoughts, so he shut it out.

He had found a stick inside and, for no reason he could precisely explain, taken to cutting away at it with his knife. Trying to whittle it into some more pleasing or purposeful shape. It was a thing he had often done, and done well, when he was a child.

Hamdan was sitting beside him, watching his clumsy efforts to recover that childhood talent.

"Do we die today, you think?" the archer asked.

Yulan considered for a moment, turned the thin piece of wood in his hand. His working of it really was rough, compared to what he had been able to do when he was young. It was a pity, to have lost the knack of that.

"Maybe," he said eventually. "Sullen certainly thinks it likely."

Hamdan nodded. Scratched at his beard.

"Where will you go, after this is all done? When the Free's done with?"

"You know the answer to that," Yulan said.

"Hestin? The Clamour?"

Yulan nodded.

"You think that's what she'd want?" asked Hamdan.

Yulan let the wood fall. He returned his knife to its sheath along his calf. He was not going to be relearning the craft today, so it could wait for another time. Another place.

"Don't know. It's what I'll do, though, for as long as it needs doing. It was me who kept her alive and let her try to tame it. Me who persuaded Merkent that the Free could accommodate it, and her. Use them."

"Huh," Hamdan grunted. "That was a miserable bloody hunt, wasn't it? Going to be the Free's greatest failing, if Hestin hadn't shown up. Done our work for us."

"A good many of us would have died," agreed Yulan. "More than already had done. It took ... what? Six of us? And we could never have stopped it. Not without her. We owe her a debt for that. I owe her a debt. Seems only right it should be me who walks alongside her to the end."

"That's a road you can't know where it's going."

"But it'll come to an end sometime, somewhere. I always had a notion that when she was failing, when it was slipping out from under her bonds, I'd buy a ship and strand it on an island far out to sea. Silly idea. As if that would do any good."

"And then? After your voyaging was done?"

Yulan could not help but smile sadly at that. The unthinking humour of life and the world had earned that much from him, after all.

"Then, if I still lived, I was going to find a way to kill

Callotec and Sullen. Since they and I find ourselves gathered upon this little hill far from anywhere, I can't help but feel the world, or life, is trying to convey some message to me."

"One less thing to worry about," Hamdan said. "That's the message. Anyway, I'll go with you. With Hestin and the Clamour. Two's better than one, trying to keep her, and the world, safe."

"I know. I always knew that, Hamdan."

Yulan heard feet pounding on the stairs inside the keep. He guessed their meaning and lifted himself up, twisting to peer over the top of the battlements. The Clade were advancing. He hurried to the top of the stairwell and clambered down, shouting. He went down through the Kingshouse, floor by floor, and out into the yard. Shouting all the way.

"One last day to be the Free. Every one of you think on that, because there's nowhere to go, nowhere to be but here, on these walls, at this gate. You're to be the last of the Free and it's for you to choose what they say of us in days to come! How we lived or died, how we fought in the last hour of the last of the companies!"

38

The Kingshouse

Callotec had been cautious, calculating, when he came at them in Towers' Shadow. Sullen, Yulan understood at once, was not. They all came, on all sides, at once.

Behind the front ranks of spearmen and swordsmen marched rows of archers. They halted, some fifty paces short of the wall, while the rest marched on. Yulan, descended to stand at the ring wall just beside the modest gate, ducked down as the first sheet of arrows leapt into the air. He was slightly surprised to find Akrana crouching there beside him.

"Don't you need to be watching over Kasuman and Callotec?" he asked.

"Callotec's bound hand and foot, tight enough to squeeze them off, and stilled by a sharp tap to the head. Kasuman will not wake for an hour or two, even without my attentions. I think that is long enough for me to find more useful employment elsewhere."

"It is," Yulan said.

One way or the other, he doubted this would last even a small part of an hour.

"You've done well, these last few days, Akrana," he said to her as arrows began to rattle against the walls of the keep, and to drop down into the narrow yard around it. "You might do yet better today, don't you think? There's only two things inside these walls that might unlock this cage Sullen's put us in: the Clamour, and you."

Then suddenly a chunk of stone was blown out from the very wall behind which Yulan was sheltering. It fell painfully on to his back. He glimpsed the blur of the arrow that had torn the stone loose flashing over his head and striking the keep in a cloud of mortar and chips. Punching through that wall and beyond it.

"Clevered arrows," muttered Akrana.

Yulan glanced round in alarm. In time to see one of the Free's archers, venturing to rise above the keep's parapet and loose an arrow of his own, struck in the centre of the chest. A hole was torn straight through him, big enough to pass a fist from front to back. He was thrown backwards heels over head. The arrow that had killed him went feathers-deep into a stone block behind him, splitting it.

Akrana and Yulan rose together as the first of the Clade men topped the wall beside them, clambering up on the backs and shoulders of his comrades. They had brought no ladders, no ropes to this siege. They would simply swarm the Kingshouse. Flood it.

Akrana fought in silent fury, weaving with her blade a terrible web that swept back and away every hand or arm or body cresting the wall. Yulan stood at her side, and matched her. Bettered her. There was no space for worries about Clevered arrows – any arrows – only the constant, unrelenting need to thrust and stab, and hold that tiny stretch of meagre wall. It was everything to him. He heard the arrows, though. He was aware of the occasional thump and boom as they smashed stone from stone.

"Get the Bereaved into the keep," he shouted to Akrana.

He glanced after her as she leaped down into the yard, and saw Clade swordsmen spilling over the top of the ring wall. Setting feet on the low walkway and looking around for someone to kill. He ran at them. Swept them away in veils of blood.

He felt a hard blow, then lancing pain in the back of his left shoulder. Spun about, but there was no one there. He fumbled clumsily over his shoulder with his right hand and felt an arrow standing there, deep in his flesh. The vision flashed through his mind of what a Clevered arrow would have done, tearing away his whole shoulder and arm and sending them tumbling like butchered meat. It distracted him for a dangerous moment, and he saw the hammer coming towards his face too late to do anything but jump off the walkway, out of its path.

He landed on his back, snapping the arrow, and he could not help but cry out at the pain. The warrior who had tried to kill him bared his teeth and leapt down, hammer raised, straight at him. Yulan rolled and rose and lashed his sword round in a flat arc as he turned away. It hit his assailant on the side of the head and sent him down, dead weight.

He took a moment to look around. The Clade were spilling over the outer wall now. There were bodies everywhere, but even the Free could not stem this tide coming at them from every direction at once. Not when they were so few. So wearied.

"Into the keep!' he cried. "As high as you can go."

They rushed from every side to the keep's entrance. The door that must once have been there had been stripped away, so they could not prevent pursuit. Only outrun it, for a moment or two. Yulan turned in the doorway. Akrana brushed past him, bearing the Bereaved like a sleeping child in her arms. He saw one of Rudran's lancers coming, reached for him, but the man was cut down from behind.

Yulan darted backwards into the gloom of the tiny keep. He glimpsed the Clamour, hulking there in the shadows. Raking its fingers over the cobbles. Shifting its weight from one haunch to the other. Akrana went up the steps before him. His shoulder was throbbing, as if the arrowhead buried there was beating like an angry heart.

"Let it loose, Hestin!' he cried as he climbed.

A Clevered arrow smashed through the wall an arm's length from his face, spraying sharp stone fragments across his cheek Drawing blood, he thought. The Clade's warriors were boiling into the keep behind them.

"Let it loose, Hestin!' he cried again. "We've nothing else left! Let it loose!"

And she did.

Yulan fell on to his face on the boards of the floor above. He felt someone – Hamdan? Akrana? – probing at the arrowhead in his shoulder with hard, stiff fingers. He hissed out his pain.

"Leave it there," he heard Akrana saying. "Do more harm to pull it out."

The Clamour's howl rose, and shook the keep. Yulan felt the floorboards trembling against his cheek. The wailing ran through his head and scoured all thought from his mind. Mixed in with it there was screaming, the crash of stones torn loose. The tumult passed out into the yard.

Yulan got to his feet and ventured to a narrow window, to look out upon the carnage. Sullen's scores of warriors were pouring back out over the walls. They had thrown open the gates that they might escape that way. The Clamour came after them, tore them down, broke bodies. It was too wild, too huge, for the gateway to contain, so it burst it asunder, shattered the wooden posts that were as thick as a man's thigh, brushed rock from the walls with its shoulders. It surged out on to the hill.

"Will she get it back?" he heard Hamdan wondering.

"I don't know," he said. He had a suspicion, though. Not a happy one. It might have been better to have died, if the Free's last legacy was to be the Clamour, unbound.

A thud behind them made them turn. Rudran had come stumbling, hobbling down from the keep's upper floor. He had fallen as he descended, almost landing on Kasuman's prostrate, somnolent form.

"I can fight," the lancer rasped at Yulan, seeing the protestation in his captain's face. "You don't think you need me?"

"Maybe," Yulan said. "We'll see soon enough."

He turned back to the view from the window. The slopes of the hillock were a mass of fleeing blue-clad figures. Flowing down as if blown before a plunging wind. The Clamour was faster. It raged amongst them, left a trail of trampled and crushed and dismembered bodies in its wake. A bloody slick down the flank of the hill.

A horn sounded out, cutting through even the Clamour's incessant ululation. Yulan looked for its source. Sullen stood there, a hundred paces from the Clamour, blowing that horn with all his might. Not fleeing. Nor were the dozen archers kneeling in a line before him, their bows drawn, held flat, aiming at the Clamour.

"What's this?" Akrana asked, coming to the window and leaning past him.

The Clamour turned towards the sound of the horn. Sullen let it fall from his lips. The Clamour began to bound across the hillside towards him, towards the archers. Its fists made a deep thunder in the earth, gouging loam. Sullen held aloft a long spear, with a stone blade like a wide leaf.

"Oh, fool," breathed Yulan, suddenly understanding. Seeing what Sullen had done, and meant to do. And not knowing whether it was possible or not.

The archers loosed their arrows. Twelve shafts flashed across the rapidly diminishing distance to the Clamour. Staggered it and flung it about as they tore flesh from it, plunged so deep into its body that they disappeared. Flicked a ragged ear away. Turned a hand to bloody mist on the air.

"Can they kill it with Clevered arrows?" Akrana wondered aloud.

"Not with the arrows alone," said Yulan dully.

Sullen pushed through the line of archers as they set fresh shafts to their strings. The Clamour reeled. Recovered itself. Came on as fast and fierce as ever, on the stump of a hand. Moments. It would be on them in moments.

Twelve more arrows flew. The archers fled as soon as they were loosed. Sullen ran too, but not in flight. He rushed towards the Clamour, following those arrows in, spear levelled.

Sprays of blood and skin surrounded the Permanence as the second volley battered home. Arrows passed right through it. A crimson cloud of cruel injury enveloped the beast. And Sullen threw himself through that cloud, driving the long spear deep into its flesh.

The Clamour reared and flailed. Sullen was tossed into the air. The spear broke in his hands and he tumbled away, clutching only the stub of it. The rest of it remained planted in the Permanence. It bellowed as it never had before. Yulan covered his ears, ignoring the pain in his shoulder as he did so. It was far less than the pain inflicted by that desperate, immense cry.

"He bent the Weaponsmith to his will," Yulan shouted amidst the terrible cacophony, not knowing whether anyone would hear him. "Probably killed him in the making of that spear."

He saw the Clamour sinking down on to the ground, losing its form. Softening, like wax put to the flame. It writhed and flailed at the ground with loose limbs, tearing great furrows in the turf. It died, if a Permanence could die. It grew still. Silent. A mound of corrupted flesh, slumped into shapelessness.

Sullen got stiffly to his feet. Swayed slightly. Held the broken shaft of the killing spear above his head, and brandished it in the direction of the keep. Behind him, below him, his warriors were gathering themselves at the bottom of the hill. Setting themselves once again into ordered ranks. Beginning to climb.

Upstairs, high in the keep, Yulan could hear Hestin crying out.

39

Came The Winter

Yulan turned heavily away from the window. Saw how pitifully few of his people remained to him, crowded into the part-floored room in the heart of the Kingshouse's keep. Lebid was gone. Dead somewhere at the wall or on the keep. All but one of Rudran's men.

Kerig came staggering, feeble and shrunken, down the stairs.

"What's happening?" he asked faintly.

The Clever's cheeks were sunken and grey. His skin still a tapestry of fresh scars and yellowing bruises.

"Get back upstairs," Yulan said. "See if you can quiet Hestin. Help her."

Hamdan was standing in the aperture that led out on to the narrow parapet. He sent one arrow after another skimming away. His face was expressionless. His movements curt and precise. He reached back to his quiver, and his hand found nothing there. His shoulders sagged for a moment, then he backed away from the light.

"Out of arrows," he said quietly. "Perhaps we can hope they are too. Out of the nasty kind, at least."

Yulan could hear them coming in through the gate. Running feet, eager cries. He picked up his shield from where he had rested it against the wall. The weight of it put a painful pull into his injured shoulder, but he was far beyond caring about such things now.

"Where's the Bereaved?" he asked

"Already up top," Hamdan told him. "I've got one of my boys watching over it."

"Yulan!' came the cry from down below, beneath their feet. Sullen. "Did you see what I did, Yulan?" the Clade's commander called up.

Yulan had never heard such life in the man's voice. Such fierce vigour. Such pride.

"Everyone to the top," he muttered, and they began to move to the stair.

All save Akrana. She was making for the doorway that led out on to the exposed parapet. She hefted her sword with intent.

"Callotec's moment has come," she said to Yulan, but he shook his head.

"That's mine to do."

Clevered arrows came bursting up through the floor, erupting in clouds of dust and splinters, crashing through the ceiling. Flying the height of the keep, tearing out its innards. Rudran howled as one hissed through him, in through his groin, blowing out bone and gristle from his shoulder. He toppled backwards and fell through the floor, crashing down on to the archers below.

"Up! Up!' shouted Yulan.

They went, but he did not. He turned at the foot of that last narrow flight of stairs. Two men were within his reach, if he but chose to extend his blade. Both of them he would gladly see dead, and gladly let loose his own life for the winning of that prize. Only one of them might, by dying, offer any faint glimmer of hope for the rest of the Free, though.

"I'm ready for you now, Sullen," he shouted.

The arrows stopped coming. There were whispers down below. Groans of the injured, the dying from above. Yulan did not want to know who it was, how many. He did not need to know.

It was not Sullen that came charging up the stair but his warriors, pouring up one after another. And Yulan killed them as they came. With sword and shield he hacked and battered at every movement, every flash of blue. He gorged himself on them, and none of it sated him.

Until at last a spear tip found his calf and pierced the muscle there. He went down on one knee. Caught an axe on his shield as it swept down upon him.

He was pulled violently backwards, thrown on to his side.

"Get out of the way," Akrana said.

He stared at her. She had no blade, no shield.

"What are you doing?" he cried.

"I will not lose what family I have left," she said distantly. "Get them out of the keep. It will not survive."

And then came the winter. Searing cold blasting down through the keep. Crackling frost racing across the walls, spreading veins of ice through every crevice and cranny. Crystals of ice springing into being across the skin of her face. A white storm of shards and blinding snow that went before Akrana as she descended into the mass of Clade men below.

Yulan shielded his eyes against the wintry gale. His breath burned in his lungs, as if ice was crackling in there too. The air was like splintered glass. He could feel it rasping away skin from his face. Snow and ice churned all around him, all but blinded him.

Through the storm he glimpsed Hamdan struggling down from above, barely supporting Hestin above him, Kerig below. Yulan limped to them, and took as much of Kerig's weight as he could. He shook his shield from his arm and let it fall. He tried to sheathe his sword, but his arm was clumsy, his feet unsteady. The blade too he dropped to the trembling floor.

They were shaken back and forth by the tempest. Not just by that, Yulan realised. The keep was breaking apart. Ice was tearing through its bones, heaving them one from another. The floor beneath his feet was slick with a skin of ice, buckling and cracking as the boards beneath broke. Stone blocks were wrenched out from the walls by great gelid columns thrusting up from below.

"Is there anyone else?" Yulan shouted.

"I don't think so," the archer said. "I don't know."

"We'll have to jump," cried Yulan. "This is coming down."

They struggled out on to the parapet, and the sky howled at them. There was nothing but white fury swirling about them, flinging lances of ice and rock-hard hail. Even as they stepped out from the meagre shelter of the keep's walls, even as Yulan moved towards Callotec to drag the man up, stonework ruptured and groaned and great slabs of stone went sliding away into the storm. Half the terrace upon which they stood tore itself free and slipped into nothingness, carrying Callotec's prostrate form with it.

Yulan cursed, and backed away from the ragged, crumbling edge. He looked down over the battlements. He could see nothing, not even the ground. He cast his shield aside, vaulted over and plunged down into the winter maelstrom. He landed hard, on a frozen corpse that shattered beneath him. It did not hurt his wounded leg, because he could feel nothing there. No sensation, in leg or arm or hand. Hamdan lowered first Hestin and then Kerig down to him, all fumbling numbly.

"What about the Bereaved?" Hamdan shouted, invisible in the ice blizzard. "Kasuman?"

"Leave them," cried Yulan. He could feel his flesh dying. He could feel frost trying to grow across his skin. His whole body was shaking violently, so that he was not even certain how far he could walk. A great net of ice had enveloped the outside of the keep. He could see the huge building blocks of its outer skin crumbling to dust as the ice strove to drag it down into the earth.

"Leave them," he shouted again. "There's no time. We'll find them after, if there's anything to find."

Hamdan dropped to the ground, and even as he did so, the keep began to collapse. The storm and the ice tore it apart and dragged it down.

They fled, the four of them, out over the crumbling ring wall, as the Kingshouse died behind them, subsiding in a long, low grinding roar. Even that was quickly drowned out by the raging of the winter Akrana had shaped. There was no grass, only sheets of snow and frost over which they slid and slithered. Rushing down and away from the unleashed Hibernal entelech.

An unleashing that was surely beyond Akrana to turn back, Yulan thought dimly. Wren and Kerig had always wondered if she might not be stronger even than them, for all her reluctance to employ that strength. But this must be too much. It must be going to claim her.

The ice scored bloody tracks across Yulan's hands. The wind tumbled him and rolled him, and spat him out at last on flat ground, where the winter did not seem to quite reach. The rest of them came stumbling, or crawling, out from the tempest. Fell to the ground beside him.

Hamdan, Kerig, Hestin. All that was left. All that had come safe out of the long storm. And Drann, perhaps. Somewhere out beyond the storm's reach, perhaps.

Yulan and Hamdan searched across the frozen landscape. It broke and cracked under their feet. Faces stared out at them from beneath sheens of frost and ice. Dead faces. Scores of bodies, twisted and contorted and broken. Impaled upon icy shafts. Heaps of rubble where walls and keep had been, thrown down by pillars of ice thrust up from out of the ground.

The flanks of the hill were white and blue. Nothing remained of grass or soil. The winter that had come had sunk deep into the ground. Made that hill and all who stood upon it entirely its own. Yulan hobbled, holding his injured arm close in at his side. He fell, and groaned, and rose. Fell again. He kept on, shivering.

He found Sullen just outside what had been the gate into the Kingshouse. His skin was white, and ruptured. The ice had come from within him, lancing out through mouth and eyes and chest. He stared down at that corpse for a little while, and thought distantly, without great feeling, that he would not be unpleased to find one more body yet amidst this chaos: Callotec.

A drop fell from the tip of an icicle that had thrust out from Sullen's neck. A single drop. It was melting. Hope surged in Yulan, and all thought of the Dog-Lord fled from his mind. This was not a Permanence.

"She's still here somewhere," he shouted. "Akrana's still alive."

It was him who found her too, lying on her own at the very edge of the wintry havoc she had wrought, down at the foot of the slope. Her hair was purest white. Her cheeks, her fingers were black and frostbitten. Whatever stern beauty she had possessed had been taken, replaced by a deathly, gaunt visage. Her limbs had lost their strength. But she breathed. Tiny, faint flutters of air.

She was light in his arms as Yulan cradled her, pressed her head gently against his chest. He held her like that for a long time.

"Well done," he whispered.

He stayed there with her until he heard Hamdan shouting from atop the hill.

"I can't find Kasuman, or the Bereaved."

40

In Embrace

Drann stood amidst the great frozen mound of rubble that had been the Kingshouse. There was no way to search beneath it, or to move any of the huge stones. All were locked in ice.

He still shook, just to be amongst this desolation. It breathed its cold over him, even though the sun now shone clearly above. Some sensation was coming back to his fingers, slowly. That was no boon, for he had torn and bruised them, clawing futilely with Hamdan at the rubble.

He had seen it, from the edge of Towers' Shadow. He should have retreated further, perhaps, but the horror of the Kingshouse held him in its grip and he could not turn away, could not back away. He watched the waves of Clade warriors overwhelm it, so quickly he thought all of the Free must be dead in that one engulfing surge.

Then the Clamour had come, and he had fallen to his knees and covered his ears. Seen its destruction only through narrowed, wincing eyes. And seen the Kingshouse overrun again.

Last had come the winter, and it had swept down the slopes of the hill and shrouded it all in seething, spitting white storm. Even from where he stood by the village, he had felt its crushing cold on his face. He had watched it, dumbstruck, and known it must be the Hibernal. Akrana. She must have been passing as Wren had done, he thought. Vanishing into the other place from which all these powers came, leaving behind her a tempest of ice that would never cease.

But it did cease, and a silence more deep than any he had known fell across the place. The mists and frost clouds cleared and the Kingshouse was gone. The hill was turned to winter.

He climbed up there, and found Hestin and Kerig, both feeble, both curled in upon themselves. He half carried, half dragged them one after another as far as he could from the frozen wreckage of the Kingshouse, then went back there, to the heart of it all, and found Hamdan scrabbling amidst the immovable rubble.

Drann wanted to embrace the archer, so astonishing did it seem that he should still be alive, but Hamdan was obsessively searching. He seemed almost desperate, so Drann joined him and helped him. Still they found nothing.

"I can't find Kasuman, or the Bereaved," Hamdan shouted down to Yulan.

The Captain of the Free was lower down the slope, holding Akrana in his arms. Alive, which amazed Drann. What she had done here, the Clever, seemed a match for Wren's workings, yet she had survived.

"I care only for the Bereaved," Yulan called up from far below. "We need it, if it's here to be found."

Drann worked his way around the edge of the ruin. Again and again he almost slipped and fell on the treacherous ground. Bit by bit a melt was setting in, but that only made the footing more dangerous, as it laid a thin skin of water over the ice.

He came to the eastern flank of the hill, where he could look towards the Old Threetower Road, running away into the valley that would lead it, eventually, to Curmen and beyond. He narrowed his eyes. Down there, at the edge of the river that flowed near the road, he thought he could see something out of place. He stared, and squinted.

Someone kneeling, or sitting, at the riverside. It came to him whole and clear, like the simple opening of a door upon memory. A story he had been told by Old Emmin, all the stories he had heard of the Bereaved. Its tears.

"They're there, by the river!' he cried, and went skidding and flailing down the hillside.

His feet went from under him. He threw himself down over the ice and snow. He did not know if anyone else had even heard him.

"They're there, by the river!' Drann cried out.

Yulan looked. He saw, out beyond the iced fringes of the hill, on the grass beside the river, Kasuman kneeling at the side of the Bereaved.

Drann was coming wildly, recklessly down the ice slopes. Too far to go and not enough time, Yulan thought. He laid Akrana down and rose unsteadily to his feet. His injured calf was cramping from the cold and his immobility. The arrow-brought wound in his shoulder throbbed and burned like a hot coal buried in his flesh. He limped heavily towards Kasuman.

The Bereaved had its hands stretched down into the gurgling river. The Clever was speaking to it, his lips at its very ear. He was pressing his hand to the pale, inhuman creature's shoulder. The Permanence was a frail, hunched white shape. Kasuman was white too. Frosted with Akrana's magics. Working some terrible magic of his own.

"Let my man be."

The cracking, crumbling voice brought Yulan to a halt. He turned.

Callotec was shambling towards him. Not the Callotec who had been, though; the Callotec Akrana and the Hibernal had made. Half his face was a black and red welt of dead flesh, killed by winter. One eye was ruined; the other gleamed with madness. His left hand was gone, broken off at the frozen wrist. His clothes hung ragged about him, studded with crystals of ice. In his remaining hand he bore a short sword, blued by the cold.

Yulan blinked. He was terribly weakened. Terribly tired. Above all, he was tired.

"No more, Callotec," he murmured, even as he bent stiffly to free his knife from its sheath at his boot.

"No more?" the monstrous figure rasped. "Not your choice to make, Massatan. The Bereaved is set loose, and that means a great deal more. I'll dance on a thousand, thousand graves yet."

"You know," said Yulan as he shuffled clumsily sideways, "you took away my right, or my desire, to call myself a Massatan a long time ago. After that, I was only of the Free."

Callotec came on, half-dead mouth twisted in mad glee.

"Now the Free are no more," Yulan continued, "so perhaps

I can choose differently this time. Perhaps I can be just Yulan the Massatan again. And he thinks it was a mistake not to kill you when he had the chance."

The Dog-Lord lunged, cold air hissing out between his teeth. Yulan was so slow and hampered by pain that the sword cut across his forearm even as he tried to spring from its path. He had nothing left. His body remembered all of its martial and murderous gifts, but lacked the strength and nimbleness to use them. He slashed wildly at Callotec's head as he struggled to regain his balance, and opened a gash in the Dog-Lord's scalp.

Callotec was no less damaged, no less diminished than was Yulan, but he had some deranged fury driving him and came flailing and stabbing on like a tree thrashing in the wind. Yulan backed up, barely keeping his footing. He could all but feel his injured leg shedding the last of its strength. Beyond Callotec, he glimpsed the paired forms of Kasuman and the Bereaved, still there at the waterside.

"Enough," he said quietly.

He stepped in to meet Callotec. There was no artifice, no intent to it. They blundered together. Yulan felt his body gathering another wound to itself, as the sword nicked his flank, but it was a small thing compared to the burdens he already carried. He wrapped his arms about Callotec's midriff and twisted with the last dregs of his vigour. They fell to the ground together.

Yulan lay atop the Dog-Lord. That sword was beating at his back. Cutting him perhaps; he could not be sure. Not killing him though, not yet. That was all that mattered. He forced his own knife upward and set its point beneath Callotec's chin.

"There's a village over there called Towers' Shadow," he whispered. "That's why. Remember that."

And he drove the knife upward as hard as he could.

The Dog-Lord spat blood over Yulan's breast as he died, but Yulan paid that no heed. Shaking his head to try and recover some clarity, some balance, he lurched to his feet.

Drann was running down, stumbling and tumbling as he slithered from ice on to slick, cold grass. Neither of them was going to reach Kasuman in time to make much difference, Yulan thought dully. He staggered that way in any case, for there was nothing else to do.

Then, through the haze of weakness and weariness, he realised that one of the corpses close by was a Clade archer. Both of the man's legs were ice from the knees down. His mouth and eyes were open and crusted with frost. His bow lay just beyond one outstretched hand. Yulan bent, groaning at the pain that awoke, and picked it up. He took an arrow from the quiver on the corpse's back.

It was difficult to balance on only one good foot. The arrowhead nested in his own shoulder carved away at him from within as he drew the bowstring back. It was a big bow. Powerful. His arm trembled as hammer blows of pain beat in his shoulder.

"Wait!' he heard Hamdan shouting from somewhere behind him. "I'm almost there."

"Did you ever meet a Massatan who couldn't use a bow?" Yulan muttered under his breath in irritation.

Then he pressed his lips together, breathed out and let the arrow fly. He staggered sideways and fell as soon as it was gone,

but watched it all the way. Saw it skim flat and fast in front of
Drann, hiss to the river and smack into the side of Kasuman's
head.

The Clever straightened and reached up, brushing the shaft
of the arrow with his fingers. Then he sank slowly down and fell
beside the Bereaved.

Yulan gave a slightly surprised grunt and let the bow fall
from his hand. Hamdan came and stood over him. Kerig was
leaning on the archer's shoulder. The Clever was more intent
and more clear-eyed than Yulan had seen him since he came
back to them from Sullen's cell.

"Let me see it," Kerig croaked. "The Bereaved."

Hamdan extended a hand and Yulan clasped it. He gasped as
he came to his feet.

"Were you aiming for his head?" Hamdan asked quietly as
the three of them struggled along.

"What do you think?" Yulan said.

"I think nobody ever aims for the head."

Drann had reached the Permanence before them. They saw
him cautiously approach, and lean to look at the Bereaved. He
edged around it and stared into its face.

"It's too late!' he shouted. "The black tears."

"What?" Hamdan murmured.

"Too late," Kerig whispered.

Black tears were indeed spilling from those unearthly eyes.
Trailing slowly down its face, over its shoulders. Kerig pushed
away from Hamdan as they drew near, and went unsteadily to
kneel beside the Permanence, much as Kasuman had done. He
looked into its eyes.

"Get away," he said faintly.

He reached down and carefully lifted the Bereaved's hands from the river. He rested them in its lap, and took hold of its shoulders.

"What's happening?" asked Yulan.

Kerig gently turned the Bereaved to face him. Still it wept.

"Get away," he hissed. "I can't stop this. But I might shape it, drain it. It'll kill you if you stay."

Drann took a few hesitant steps away. Kerig embraced the Bereaved. He took it in his arms. He pressed his cheek to its cheek.

"What about you?" Yulan asked.

"It doesn't matter."

As Kerig spoke the words, his skin began to split and rupture. Strands of his hair slipped from his scalp, fell like spider's web to the grass. He shook.

"Please go," he murmured thickly.

He was weeping, water tears to match those black ones of the Bereaved. His fingers thickened and bled pus. His frame began to shrink in on itself.

The sight of Kerig dying with the Bereaved by the river struck Yulan dumb. It felt like it was breaking his heart, something that his frame no longer had the strength to withstand. Hamdan pulled him backwards. From the place where Kerig and the Permanence knelt, a sickly black stain was spreading through the earth. The grass curled and died. The soil darkened. It flowed not into the river, but through Kerig, from him into the ground and away up the long slope towards the hills to the north.

Kerig's flesh was melting away from him, taking his clothes with it. His face loosened, sagged about his skull.

Drann turned away. He went quickly, and Hamdan pulled Yulan after him. Of them all, only Yulan watched it to its end. As the three of them retreated, towards the ice and snow fields that Akrana had made, he looked back and he watched.

And only when he at last said, "It's over," did Drann and Hamdan turn to look.

They too saw the great scar of deepest black etched into the hillside. And at the point from which it flowed, kneeling by the bubbling, pure river, the two skeletons, one tiny, one larger, locked in embrace. Holding one another. The bones were blackened as if they had been burned, pitted and eroded, but they supported one another.

41

Free

They parted in Towers' Shadow.

Yulan's leg and shoulder were salved and bound. The villagers were glad to do it, but there was no hiding the way they looked at him and the others who had come alive out of such havoc. Who had left so many bodies in their wake that the pyres were taller than a man. Who had destroyed a Kingshouse, and laid a great black stain into the hillside just a little way down the valley.

"No one can touch it, or go near it," Yulan said earnestly to Metta. "Never."

She nodded sagely at that.

"And if anyone asks you how it came to be," he went on, "tell them that some men came through this way with a small child, pale as bone, and it was the child that made that mark. And when it was done, they carried it off again, eastward. Towards Armadell. Can you tell people that?"

Again she nodded patiently.

"Who are you?" she asked him.

"Just Yulan," he told her.

"That's all?"

"That's all."

Akrana was awake, yet not entirely so. Her eyes were glazed, her breath shallow. She was coming back to herself slowly, Yulan thought, but coming back to a damaged, brittled body. She had lost fingers. She had lost years, and the vigour that went with them. She had been terribly reduced. But she lived, and for that Yulan was profoundly grateful. It felt like finding one small pearl amongst the wreckage of a venture. One pearl that he could hold on to, and hold up to the light, and know that not everything went to ruin. Not entirely.

If Hestin was coming back to herself at all, it was a painful, hurtful process. She wept, sometimes. She sat on a chair, like a wizened old lady, while Yulan was having his shoulder bandaged, and her frail shoulders shook, her tears fell.

And through withered lips, she whispered again and again one word: "Free?"

Yulan did not know how to answer that. "Yes, you are," he could have said, but he did not know whether that was the answer she wanted. He could not tell from her intonation what she meant. So all he ever said to her, whispering it as he had so often whispered over the years, was: "It's over, Hestin. I'll take you home. I'll take you home soon."

"You saw the last day of the Free, as I said you would."

"I did," Drann said.

He stood with Yulan and Hamdan on the road, by the tree where Lebid had gulled Callotec's lancers, where the Clamour had done great slaughter.

"I don't know what I should think of it, or what story I should tell," the youth who had been Creel's contract-holder said.

"Tell them that the Free died, but they did it well, and bravely," Yulan told him. "Tell them that they won and lost. Tell them that there was no glory to it, except for when there was. Whatever you like. It's only a story."

"But what did happen?"

"The Free ended," Yulan said. "That's all. Not as it should have done, or as it deserved to, perhaps. But it ended. That's all that matters."

"Where will you go?" asked Drann.

"Away," Yulan said. "To find other endings. They're all the same, at the last. Give him the head, Hamdan."

Drann made a vaguely disgusted face as Hamdan pressed a heavy, twice-wrapped sack into his hands.

"Creel will want to see it," Hamdan said. Not as much mirth in his voice as there had once been. Yulan was not surprised at that. Perhaps it would return, but not soon, he thought. It would have a long way to travel to outdistance what they had seen and done here.

"Do I have to carry this thing?" Drann asked.

"It's the Free's last contract," Yulan said. "We did as we were asked in that, at least. But no, you don't have to go back to Creel. There're coins waiting for that head, that contract, mind. Think on it as you walk, perhaps. Whatever you do, don't take too long. Go back to your home soon as you can."

"Things might go bad, without the Bereaved," Drann said. Not a question, but a thought without an answer.

"They might. Or it might be a long, long time before anyone believes it's truly gone. If we never speak of it again, if the people here don't ... who knows?" Yulan shrugged. "Perhaps Creel can persuade the world it resides still in the palace by the lake. He's no fool, that one."

"You sure you don't want a horse?" Hamdan asked.

Drann smiled and shook his head. He took Yulan's hand in his own. Hamdan set an arm about Drann's shoulders. And with that they parted, and Drann walked away from Towers' Shadow.

They watched him for a while, the two Massatan warriors who had been of the Free, but were no more. They did not speak. Drann looked back only once, and when he did, they raised their arms in salute to him. That done, the two of them walked slowly back into Towers' Shadow, and where they had been there was only the tree, and the road and the river, with three horned towers soaring above it all.

The birds that were not birds flew. They set their course not by the stars, nor the moon or sun. They paid no heed to winds that might seek to steer them, for they carried their own wind beneath their wings. They went as they would, without constraint of season or storm. Nothing stayed them, nothing coerced them.

They flew across hill and valley, along the course of shining rivers, over sand and heat-blown jungle. Out across expansive seas. They went without purpose save the fulfilment of their nature, which was grief and anger and endless movement, and the raw, hot substance of which the world and all its sentiments were formed.

They flew without ceasing, unto the wreck and ruin at the end of the world.

Acknowledgements

These things – books, I mean – would never make it out into the world without a whole lot of people making a contribution of one sort or another. With that in mind, I'm very happy to acknowledge the assistance I've had from:

The team at Orbit, my publishers, all of whom not only seem to know what they're doing, but do it with good humour and enthusiasm. Particular thanks are due to Tim Holman and Anna Gregson, for keeping this show on the road.

Tina, my agent.

Friends and family, whose encouragement and positivity is kind of indispensable if you're going to make a habit out of writing books. In particular, my parents. The whole Nature vs Nurture thing remains a mystery, but as they were responsible for both, I'm fairly sure none of this would have happened without them.

Fleur and Daniel, who make it all possible in more ways than one.

And three other people. Name-checking influences is a slippery slope, but it'd be churlish not to recognise that these folks had at least a little something to do with the book you're about to read: Akira Kurosawa, John Sturges and Sam Peckinpah, who between them (with a lot of help from others, of course) gave the world *Seven Samurai*, *The Magnificent Seven* and *The Wild Bunch*. I make no comparison whatsoever between my work and theirs (I'm not crazy!), and the influences have become more deeply buried as the writing has gone on, but there's no denying I was thinking about those films when I started this particular journey.

extras

orbit

meet the author

Self

BRIAN RUCKLEY was born and brought up in Scotland. After studying at Edinburgh and Stirling Universities, he worked for a series of organizations dealing with environmental, nature conservation and youth development issues. He lives in Edinburgh. Find out more about Brian Ruckley at www.brianruckley.com.

introducing

**If you enjoyed
THE FREE
look out for**

WINTERBIRTH

Book One of the Godless World Trilogy

by Brian Ruckley

*An uneasy truce exists between the thanes of the True Bloods.
Now, as another winter approaches, the armies of the
Black Road march south, from their exile beyond
the Vale of Stones.*

*For some, war will bring a swift and violent death.
Others will not hear the clash of swords or see the corpses
strewn over the fields. Instead, they will see an opportunity
to advance their own ambitions.*

*But soon, all will fall under the shadow that is descending.
For while the storm of battle rages, one man is following
a path that will awaken a terrible power in him—and his
legacy will be written in blood.*

Preface

They say the world has fallen far from its former state.

In the beginning there was but one race. It failed the Gods who made it and, though it wounded their hearts to do so, they destroyed it. In its place they fashioned five which they put in the world to inhabit it, and these were the races of the Second Age: Whreinin and Saolin, Huanin and Kyrinin, and Anain.

The sky turned a thousand thousand times and beneath the gaze of the Gods their children prospered. Cities, empires, rose and fell. But at last the Huanin and Kyrinin wearied of the cruelties of the wolfenkind, the Whreinin. Despite the will of the Gods they made war upon that race, and they destroyed it utterly and it passed out of time and history. For this deed are the Huanin and Kyrinin named the Tainted Races. And upon that deed were the hopes of the Gods broken, for they saw that what they had made was flawed beyond mending, marred by an unyielding vein of discord and hubris. The Gods took council upon the highest peaks of the Tan Dihrin, where the rotating firmament grinds sparks from the mountain tops, and they chose to look no longer upon the failure of their dreams and to suffer no longer the rebellions of their children. They left the world, departing to places beyond the thoughts or imaginings of any save their own kind, and with them went much that was best in the peoples they abandoned.

This is how the Second Age ended and the Third began. It is how this came to be a Godless World. That is what they say.

Prologue

I The Third Age: Year 942

The solitude of the wild goats that made their home on the rock faces above the Vale of Stones was seldom interrupted. The Vale might be the only pass through the high Tan Dihrin, but it was a route that led nowhere: the bleak and icy shores of the north were home only to savage tribes. There was nothing there to draw traders or conquerors up from the lands of the Kilkry Bloods to the south.

When a sudden river of humanity began to flow up and over the Vale of Stones, it therefore sent unease darting through the herds of goats on their precipitous territories overhead. Bucks stamped their feet; does called for their kids. Soon, the cliffs were deserted and only the mute rock was left to witness the extraordinary scenes below, as ten thousand people marched into a cold exile.

The great column was led by a hundred or more mounted warriors. Many bore wounds, still fresh from the lost battle on the fields by Kan Avor; all bore, in their red-rimmed eyes and wan skin, the marks of exhaustion. Behind them came the multitude: women, children and men, though fewest of the last. Thousands of widows had been made that year.

It was a punishing exodus. Their way was paved with hard rock and sharp stones that cut feet and turned ankles. There could be no pause. Any who fell were seized by those who came behind, hauled upright with shouts of encouragement, as if noise alone could put strength back into their legs. If they could not rise, they were left. There were already dozens of buzzards and ravens drifting lazily above the column. Some had followed it all the way up the Glas valley from the south; others were residents of the mountains, drawn from their lofty perches by the promise of carrion.

A few of those fleeing through the Stone Vale had been wealthy—merchants and landowners from Kan Avor or Glasbridge. What little of their wealth they had managed to salvage in the panic of flight was now slipping through their fingers. Mules were stumbling and falling beneath overladen panniers, defeated by the desperate whips of their handlers or the weight of their loads; the wheels and axles of carts were splintering amidst the rocks, cargoes spilling to the ground. Servants cajoled or threatened into carrying their masters' goods were casting them aside, exhaustion overcoming their fear. Fortunes that had taken lifetimes to accumulate lay scattered and ignored along the length of the Vale, like flakes of skin scoured off the crowd's body by the rock walls of the pass.

Avann oc Gyre, Thane of the Gyre Blood and self-proclaimed protector of the creed of the Black Road, rode amongst the common folk. His Shield, the men sworn to guard him day and night, had long since abandoned their efforts to keep the people from straying too close to their lord. The Thane himself ignored the masses jostling all about him. His head hung low and he made no effort to guide his horse. It followed where the flow carried it.

There was a crust of blood upon the Thane's cheek. He had been in the thick of the fighting outside Kan Avor, his beloved city, and survived only because his own Shield had disregarded his commands and dragged him from the field. The wound on his cheek was little more than a scratch, though. Hidden beneath his robes, and beneath blood-heavy bandaging, other injuries were eating away at his strength. The lance of a Kilkry horseman had pierced the Thane through from front to back, breaking as it did so and leaving splinters of wood along the tunnel it drove through his flesh. He had a fine company of healers, and if there had been time to set his tent, to rest and tend to his wounds, they might even have been able to save his life. Avann had forbidden such a delay, and refused to leave his horse for a litter.

What was left of the Thane's armies came behind. Two years ago the warriors of Gyre had been one of the finest bodies of fighting men in all the lands of the Kilkry Bloods, but the unremitting carnage since then had consumed their strength as surely as a fire loosed upon a drought-struck forest. In the end virtually every able-bodied man—and many of the women—of the Black Road had taken to the field at Kan Avor, drawn not just from Gyre but from every Blood: still they had been outnumbered by more than three to one. Now barely fifteen hundred men remained, a battered rearguard for the flight of the Black Road into the north.

The man who rode up to join his Thane was as bruised and weary as all the rest. His helm was dented, the ring mail on his chest stained with blood, his round shield notched and half split where an axe had found a lucky angle. Still, this man bore himself well and his eyes retained a glint of vigor. He nudged his horse through the crowds and leaned close to Avann.

"Lord," he said softly, "it is Tegric."

Avann stirred, but did not raise his head or open his eyes.

"My scouts have come up, lord," the warrior continued. "The enemy draw near. Kilkry horsemen are no more than an hour or two adrift of us. Behind them, spearmen of Haig-Kilkry. They will bring us to bay before we are clear of the Vale."

The Thane of Gyre spat bloodily.

"Whatever awaits us was decided long ago," he murmured. His voice was thin and weak. "We cannot fear what is written in the Last God's book."

One of the Thane's shieldmen joined them, and fixed Tegric with a disapproving glare.

"Leave the Thane be," he said. "He must conserve his strength."

That at last raised Avann's head. He winced as he opened his eyes.

"My death will come when it must. Until then, I am Thane, not some sick old woman to be wrapped warm and fed broth. Tegric treats me as a Thane still; how much more should my own Shield?"

The shieldman nodded in acceptance of the reprimand, but stayed in close attendance.

"Let me wait here, lord," said Tegric softly. "Give me just a hundred men. We will hold the Vale until our people are clear."

The Thane regarded Tegric. "We may need every man in the north. The tribes will not welcome our arrival."

"There will be no arrival if our enemies come upon us here in the Vale. Let me stand here and I will promise you half a day, perhaps more. The cliffs narrow up ahead, and there is an old rockfall. I can hold the way against riders; spill enough of their blood that they will wait for their main force to come up before attempting the passage twice."

"And then you will be a hundred against what, five thousand? Six?" Avann grunted.

"At least," smiled Tegric.

An old man fell in the crowds that surrounded them. He cried out as a stone opened his knee. A grey-haired woman—perhaps his wife—hurried to help him to his feet, murmuring "Get up, get up." A score of people, including the Thane and Tegric, flowed past before she managed to raise him. She wept silently as the man hobbled onward.

"Many people have already died in defense of our creed," Avann oc Gyre said, lowering his head once more and closing his eyes. He seemed to shrink as he hunched forward in his saddle. "If you give us half a day—if it has been so written in the Last God's book—you and your hundred will be remembered. When the lands that have been taken from us are ours again, you will be named first and noblest amongst the dead. And when this bitter world is unmade and we have returned into the love of the Gods I will look for you, to give you the honor that will be your due."

Tegric nodded. "I will see you once again in the reborn world, my Thane."

He turned his horse and nudged it back against the current of humanity.

Tegric rested against a great boulder. He had removed his tunic, and was methodically stitching up a split seam. His mail shirt was neatly spread upon a rock, his shield and scabbarded sword lying beside it, his helm resting at his feet. These were all that remained to him, everything he had need of. He had given his horse to a lame woman who had been struggling along in the wake of the main column. His small pouch of coins had gone to a child, a boy mute from shock or injury.

Above, buzzards were calling as they circled lower, descending toward the corpses that Tegric knew lay just out of sight. His presence, and that of his hundred men, might deter the scavengers for a while longer, but he did not begrudge them a meal. Those who once dwelled in those bodies had no further need of them: when the Gods returned—as they would once all peoples of the world had learned the humility of the Black Road—they would have new bodies, in a new world.

From where he sat, Tegric could see down a long, sloping sweep of the Stone Vale. Every so often he glanced up from his stitching to cast his eyes back the way they had come. Far off in that direction lay Grive, where he had lived most of his life: a place of soft green fields, well-fed cattle, as different from this punishing Vale of Stones as any place could be. The memory of it summoned up no particular emotion in him. The rest of his family had not seen the truth of the creed as he had. When Avann oc Gyre, their Thane, had declared for the Black Road they had fled from Grive, disappearing out of Tegric's life. In every Blood, even Kilkry itself, the blossoming of the Black Road had sundered countless families, broken ties and bonds that had held firm for generations. To Tegric's mind it was a cause for neither regret nor surprise. A truth as profound as that of the Black Road could not help but have consequences.

introducing

If you enjoyed
THE FREE
look out for

PROMISE OF BLOOD

Book One of the Powder Mage Trilogy

by Brian McClellan

It's a bloody business overthrowing a king...

Field Marshal Tamas's coup against his king sent corrupt aristocrats to the guillotine and brought bread to the starving. But it also provoked war with the Nine Nations, internal attacks by royalist fanatics, and the greedy to scramble for money and power by Tamas's supposed allies: the Church, workers unions, and mercenary forces.

It's up to a few...

Stretched to his limit, Tamas is relying heavily on his few remaining powder mages, including the embittered Taniel, a brilliant marksman who also happens to be his estranged son, and Adamat, a retired police inspector whose loyalty is being tested by blackmail.

But when gods are involved...

*Now, as attacks batter them from within and without,
the credulous are whispering about omens of death and
destruction. Just old peasant legends about the gods waking to
walk the earth. No modern educated man believes that
sort of thing. But they should...*

Chapter One

Adamat wore his coat tight, top buttons fastened against a wet
night air that seemed to want to drown him. He tugged at his
sleeves, trying to coax more length, and picked at the front of the
jacket where it was too close by far around the waist. It'd been half
a decade since he'd even seen this jacket, but when summons came
from the king at this hour, there was no time to get his good one
from the tailor. Yet this summer coat provided no defense against
the chill snaking through the carriage window.

The morning was not far off but dawn would have a hard time
scattering the fog. Adamat could feel it. It was humid even for early
spring in Adopest, and chillier than Novi's frozen toes. The soothsayers in Noman's Alley said it was a bad omen. Yet who listened
to soothsayers these days? Adamat reasoned it would give him a
cold and wondered why he had been summoned out on a pit-made
night like this.

The carriage approached the front gate of Skyline and moved on
without a stop. Adamat clutched at his pantlegs and peered out the
window. The guards were not at their posts. Odder still, as they
continued along the wide path amid the fountains, there were no
lights. Skyline had so many lanterns, it could be seen all the way
from the city even on the cloudiest night. Tonight the gardens were
dark.

Adamat was fine with this. Manhouch used enough of their taxes for his personal amusement. Adamat stared out into the gardens at the black maws where the hedge mazes began and imagined shapes flitting back and forth in the lawn. What was... ah, just a sculpture. Adamat sat back, took a deep breath. He could hear his heart beating, thumping, frightened, his stomach tightening. Perhaps they *should* light the garden lanterns...

A little part of him, the part that had once been a police inspector, prowling nights such as these for the thieves and pickpockets in dark alleys, laughed out from inside. *Still your heart, old man*, he said to himself. *You were once the eyes staring back from the darkness.*

The carriage jerked to a stop. Adamat waited for the coachman to open the door. He might have waited all night. The driver rapped on the roof. "You're here," a gruff voice said.

Rude.

Adamat stepped from the coach, just having time to snatch his hat and cane before the driver flicked the reins and was off, clattering into the night. Adamat uttered a quiet curse after the man and turned around, looking up at Skyline.

The nobility called Skyline Palace "the Jewel of Adro." It rested on a high hill east of Adopest so that the sun rose above it every morning. One particularly bold newspaper had compared it to a starving pauper wearing a diamond ring. It was an apt comparison in these lean times. A king's pride doesn't fill the people's bellies.

He was at the main entrance. By day, it was a grand avenue of marbled walks and fountains, all leading to a pair of giant, silver-plated doors, themselves dwarfed by the sheer façade of the biggest single building in Adro. Adamat listened for the soft footfalls of patrolling Hielmen. It was said the king's personal guard were everywhere in these gardens, watching every secluded corner, muskets always loaded, bayonets fixed, their gray-and-white sashes somber among the green-and-gold splendor. But there were no footfalls, nor were the fountains running. He'd heard once that the fountains only stopped for the death of the king. Surely he'd not have been summoned here if Manhouch were dead. He smoothed the front of his jacket. Here, next to the building, a few of the lanterns were lit.

A figure emerged from the darkness. Adamat tightened his grip on his cane, ready to draw the hidden sword inside at a moment's notice.

It was a man in uniform, but little could be discerned in such ill light. He held a rifle or a musket, trained loosely on Adamat, and wore a flat-topped forage cap with a stiff visor. Only one thing could be certain... he was not a Hielman. Their tall, plumed hats were easy to recognize, and they never went without them.

"You're alone?" a voice asked.

"Yes," Adamat said. He held up both hands and turned around.

"All right. Come on."

The soldier edged forward and yanked on one of the mighty silver doors. It rolled outward slowly, ponderously, despite the man putting his weight into it. Adamat moved closer and examined the soldier's jacket. It was dark blue with silver braiding. Adran military. In theory, the military reported to the king. In practice, one man held their leash: Field Marshal Tamas.

"Step back, friend," the soldier said. There was a note of impatience in his voice, some unseen stress—but that could have been the weight of the door. Adamat did as he was told, only coming forward again to slip through the entrance when the soldier gestured.

"Go ahead," the soldier directed. "Take a right at the diadem and head through the Diamond Hall. Keep walking until you find yourself in the Answering Room." The door inched shut behind him and closed with a muffled thump.

Adamat was alone in the palace vestibule. Adran military, he mused. Why would a soldier be here, on the grounds, without any sign of the Hielmen? The most frightening answer sprang to mind first. A power struggle. Had the military been called in to deal with a rebellion? There were a number of powerful factions within Adro: the Wings of Adom mercenaries, the royal cabal, the Mountainwatch, and the great noble families. Any one of them could have been giving Manhouch trouble. None of it made sense, though. If there had been a power struggle, the palace grounds would be a battlefield, or destroyed outright by the royal cabal.

Adamat passed the diadem—a giant facsimile of the Adran crown—and noted it was in as bad taste as rumor had it. He entered the Diamond Hall, where the walls and floor were of scarlet, accented in gold leaf, and thousands of tiny gems, which gave the room its name, glittered from the ceiling in the light of a single lit candelabra. The tiny flames of the candelabra flickered as if in the wind, and the room was cold.

Adamat's sense of unease deepened as he neared the far end of the gallery. Not a sign of life, and the only sound came from his own echoing footfalls on the marble floor. A window had been shattered, explaining the chill. The result of one of the king's famous temper tantrums? Or something else? He could hear his heart beating in his ears. There. Behind a curtain, a pair of boots? Adamat passed his hand before his eyes. A trick of the light. He stepped over to reassure himself and pulled back the curtain.

A body lay in the shadows. Adamat bent over it, touched the skin. It was warm, but the man was most certainly dead. He wore gray pants with a white stripe down the side and a matching jacket. A tall hat with a white plume lay on the floor some ways away. A Hielman. The shadows played on a young, clean-shaven face, peaceful except for a single hole in the side of his skull and the dark, wet stain on the floor.

He'd been right. A struggle of some kind. Had the Hielmen rebelled, and the military been brought in to deal with them? Again, it didn't make any sense. The Hielmen were fanatically loyal to the king, and any matters within Skyline Palace would have been dealt with by the royal cabal.

Adamat cursed silently. Every question compounded itself. He suspected he'd find some answers soon enough.

Adamat left the body behind the curtain. He lifted his cane and twisted, bared a few inches of steel, and approached a tall doorway flanked by two hooded, scepter-wielding sculptures. He paused between the ancient statues and took a deep breath, letting his eyes wander over a set of arcane script scrawled into the portal. He entered.

The Answering Room made the Hall of Diamonds look small. A pair of staircases, one to either side of him and each as wide across as three coaches, led to a high gallery that ran the length of the room on both sides. Few outside the king and his cabal of Privileged sorcerers ever entered this room.

In the center of the room was a single chair, on a dais a hand-breadth off the floor, facing a collection of knee pillows, where the cabal acknowledged their liege. The room was well lit, though from no discernible source of light.

A man sat on the stairs to Adamat's right. He was older than Adamat, just into his sixtieth year with silver hair and a neatly trimmed mustache that still retained a hint of black. He had a strong but not overly large jaw and his cheekbones were well defined. His skin was darkened by the sun, and there were deep lines at the corners of his mouth and eyes. He wore a dark-blue soldier's uniform with a silver representation of a powder keg pinned above the heart and nine gold service stripes sewn on the right breast, one for every five years in the Adran military. His uniform lacked an officer's epaulettes, but the weary experience in the man's brown eyes left no question that he'd led armies on the battlefield. There was a single pistol, hammer cocked, on the stair next to him. He leaned on a sheathed small sword and watched as a stream of blood slowly trickled down each step, a dark line on the yellow-and-white marble.

"Field Marshal Tamas," Adamat said. He sheathed his cane sword and twisted until it clicked shut.

The man looked up. "I don't believe we've ever met."

"We have," Adamat said. "Fourteen years ago. A charity ball thrown by Lord Aumen."

"I have a terrible time with faces," the field marshal said. "I apologize."

Adamat couldn't take his eyes off the rivulet of blood. "Sir. I was summoned here. I wasn't told by whom, or for what reason."

"Yes," Tamas said. "I summoned you. On the recommendation of one of my Marked. Cenka. He said you served together on the police force in the twelfth district."

Adamat pictured Cenka in his mind. He was a short man with an unruly beard and a penchant for wines and fine food. He'd seen him last seven years ago. "I didn't know he was a powder mage."

"We try to find anyone with an affinity for it as soon as possible," Tamas said, "but Cenka was a late bloomer. In any case"—he waved a hand—"we've come upon a problem."

Adamat blinked. "You...want my help?"

The field marshal raised an eyebrow. "Is that such an unusual request? You were once a fine police investigator, a good servant of Adro, and Cenka tells me that you have a perfect memory."

"Still, sir."

"Eh?"

"I'm still an investigator. Not with the police, sir, but I still take jobs."

"Excellent. Then it's not so odd for me to seek your services?"

"Well, no," Adamat said, "but sir, this is Skyline Palace. There's a dead Hielman in the Diamond Hall and..." He pointed at the stream of blood on the stairs. "Where's the king?"

Tamas tilted his head to the side. "He's locked himself in the chapel."

"You've staged a coup," Adamat said. He caught a glimpse of movement with the corner of his eye, saw a soldier appear at the top of the stairs. The man was a Deliv, a dark-skinned northerner. He wore the same uniform as Tamas, with eight golden stripes on the right breast. The left breast of his uniform displayed a silver powder keg, the sign of a Marked. Another powder mage.

"We have a lot of bodies to move," the Deliv said.

Tamas gave his subordinate a glance. "I know, Sabon."

"Who's this?" Sabon asked.

"The inspector that Cenka requested."

"I don't like him being here," Sabon said. "It could compromise everything."

"Cenka trusted him."

"You've staged a coup," Adamat said again with certainty.

"I'll help with the bodies in a moment," Tamas said. "I'm old, I need some rest now and then." The Deliv gave a sharp nod and disappeared.

"Sir!" Adamat said. "What have you done?" He tightened his grip on his cane sword.

Tamas pursed his lips. "Some say the Adran royal cabal had the most powerful Privileged sorcerers in all the Nine Nations, second only to Kez," he said quietly. "Yet I've just slaughtered every one of them. Do you think I'd have trouble with an old inspector and his cane sword?"

Adamat loosened his grip. He felt ill. "I suppose not."

"Cenka led me to believe that you were pragmatic. If that is the case, I would like to employ your services. If not, I'll kill you now and look for a solution elsewhere."

"You've staged a coup," Adamat said again.

Tamas sighed. "Must we keep coming back to that? Is it so shocking? Tell me, can you think of any fewer than a dozen factions within Adro with reason to dethrone the king?"

"I didn't think any of them had the skill," Adamat said. "Or the daring." His eyes returned to the blood on the stairs, before his mind traveled to his wife and children, asleep in their beds. He looked at the field marshal. His hair was tousled; there were drops of blood on his jacket—a lot, now that he thought to look. Tamas might as well have been sprayed with it. There were dark circles under his eyes and a weariness that spoke of more than just age.

"I will not agree to a job blindly," Adamat said. "Tell me what you want."

"We killed them in their sleep," Tamas said without preamble. "There's no easy way to kill a Privileged, but that's the best. A mistake was made and we had a fight on our hands." Tamas looked pained for a moment, and Adamat suspected that the fight had not gone as well as Tamas would have liked. "We prevailed. Yet upon the lips of the dying was one phrase."

Adamat waited.

"'You can't break Kresimir's Promise,'" Tamas said. "That's what the dying sorcerers said to me. Does it mean anything to you?"

Adamat smoothed the front of his coat and sought to recall old memories. "No. 'Kresimir's Promise'... 'Break'... 'Broken'... Wait—'Kresimir's Broken Promise.'" He looked up. "It was the name of a street gang. Twenty... twenty-two years ago. Cenka couldn't remember that?"

Tamas continued. "Cenka thought it sounded familiar. He was certain you'd remember it."

"I don't forget things," Adamat said. "Kresimir's Broken Promise was a street gang with forty-three members. They were all young, some of them no more than children, the oldest not yet twenty. We were trying to round up some of the leaders to put a stop to a string of thefts. They were an odd lot—they broke into churches and robbed priests."

"What happened to them?"

Adamat couldn't help but look at the blood on the stairs. "One day they disappeared, every one of them—including our informants. We found the whole lot a few days later, forty-three bodies jammed into a drain culvert like pickled pigs' feet. They'd been massacred by powerful sorceries, with excessive brutality. The marks of the king's royal cabal. The investigation ended there." Adamat suppressed a shiver. He'd not once seen a thing like that, not before or since. He'd witnessed executions and riots and murder scenes that filled him with less dread.

The Deliv soldier appeared again at the top of the stairs. "We need you," he said to Tamas.

"Find out why these mages would utter those words with their final breath," Tamas said. "It may be connected to your street gang. Maybe not. Either way, find me an answer. I don't like the riddles of the dead."